THE GIRLS IN BLUE

Miranda Beddoes is forced to take refuge with her grandparents down on the Dorset coast. With both her parents doing their duty for king and country, Miranda longs to do the same. She joins the WAAF, working hard to help win the war. Despite her determination to dedicate herself to her work, Miranda falls for charismatic fighter pilot Gil Maddern – a man known for his passion for flying. As the battle rages in the skies above them and she learns that Gil's plane has been hit, it is only the friendship of her fellow girls in blue that keeps Miranda going as she waits for news...

THE GIRLS IN BLUE

THE GIRLS IN BLUE

by

Lily Baxter

Magna Large Print Books
Long Preston, North Yorkshire,
BD23 4ND, England.

British Library Cataloguing in Publication Data.

Baxter, Lily
The girls in blue.

A catalogue record of this book is
available from the British Library

ISBN   978-0-7505-3673-8

First published in Great Britain in 2012 by Arrow Books

A catalogue record for this book is available from the British Library

Published in Large Print 2013 by arrangement with
Arrow, one of the publishers in the Random House Group Ltd.

Magna Large Print is an imprint of Library Magna Books Ltd.

Printed and bound in Great Britain by
T.J. (International) Ltd., Cornwall, PL28 8RW

For Janet and John

Chapter One

East London, Summer 1940

The air raid siren wailed its terrifying warning, shattering the peace of what had been a glorious summer day in the leafy east London suburb. Miranda had been making her way home from secretarial college and had just reached the spot on the common where a lone tree, reputedly killed by a lightning strike years ago, pointed its stark branches at the cloudless sky. She came to a sudden halt, wondering if this was yet another false alarm, but the drone of an approaching aircraft engine made her look up. Shielding her eyes from the sunlight she spotted a single plane, flying low and seeming to skim the rooftops in the street where she lived. At first she thought it must be an RAF plane returning to one of the nearby airfields, but then a reverberating boom made the ground shake beneath her feet and clouds of dust and smoke billowed into the air. The thunderous noise went on and on, ricocheting off the tall elms and oaks that separated the rows of detached houses from the common land, and having done its worst the enemy aircraft soared upwards and away to the east.

Miranda watched it with a feeling of unreality. This must be a nightmare: at any moment now she would wake up and find her mother shaking her and telling her to get up or she would be late and miss her bus to college. But gradually the ground stopped moving and the sound of falling masonry ceased, leaving the world around her deathly quiet. Even the birds had stopped singing. Then the breathless silence was broken and she could hear people shouting and screaming for help. She broke into a run, teetering on her high heels as she raced across the tussocky grass to the footpath that led through the thicket of hawthorn bushes to Linden Avenue and home.

Nothing could have prepared her for the sight that met her eyes as she emerged from the cool shade into the heat and choking brick dust. Several houses had been completely demolished by the German bombs and those left standing were badly damaged. Her hand flew to her mouth, stifling a cry of horror as she realised that her home had not been spared. Moving like a sleepwalker, she threaded her way through the crowds of shocked neighbours who had emerged from their Anderson shelters to inspect the damage. The all clear rang out, but it was hardly a joyous sound.

'Don't go in there, love.' Mr Walker, one of the local ARP wardens, grabbed her by the arm as she was about to open the garden gate. 'The roof's gone and the whole lot might come down at any minute.'

Miranda stared at him dazedly. 'But it's where I live.'

He patted her on the shoulder. 'Not now, it ain't, ducks.' He frowned. 'Was anyone at home?'

'No. My father is in the army and Maman works in London.'

'So she does,' he said with a knowing smile. 'The missis told me about her. French lady, ain't she? Works as a secretary in the War Office.'

'That's right, and I must go indoors and telephone her. I need to tell her what's happened. It's too awful for words.'

Sucking in air through clenched teeth, he shook his head. 'My orders are clear, miss. I have to direct you to an emergency shelter where the ladies of the WVS will look after you. A nice hot cuppa will make you feel better. You've had a nasty shock.' He took her by the shoulders and spun her round to face a middle-aged woman wearing a WVS uniform and badge. 'Will you take this young person to the shelter, Mrs Jenkins?' He lowered his voice. 'I daresay it's a case of shock.'

Mrs Jenkins put her arm around Miranda, smiling gently. 'There, there, my dear. Come with me and we'll look after you.'

Miranda broke away from her, frowning. 'Thank you, but I'm not in shock. I'm hopping mad with the wretch who dropped his bombs on our house, and I want to go inside and telephone my mother. She must be told.'

'Of course she must, dear. But there are procedures to follow. You can phone from the church hall, which is where we've set up our emergency shelter.' Mrs Jenkins beamed at her, but there was a steely glint in her myopic blue eyes and a determined set to her jaw.

Realising that it was useless to protest, Miranda allowed herself to be led like a child to the church hall where another woman gave her a mug of hot, sweet tea and a digestive biscuit. There were

13

several of her neighbours already seated at small tables drinking tea, smoking cigarettes and talking in hushed voices. Colonel Bullwinkle marched in with his bulldog on its lead. 'I will not tie Buller up outside, madam,' he said in a loud voice. 'I didn't fight in the Great War to be told I can't bring my dog into the church hall by an officious busybody.'

'But, Colonel, animals are not allowed in here. If we break the rule for one we would have to do the same for everybody.'

'Pish-tush, woman. Buller is as well behaved as any properly brought up child, and probably more so. We've just escaped death by inches thanks to that Jerry swine, and I want a cup of tea and a bowl of water for my dog. Surely that's not too much to ask?'

The woman sent a pleading look to Mrs Jenkins, who left Miranda's side and hurried over to placate the irate gentleman. Miranda had known Colonel Bullwinkle since she was a small girl, and she knew who would win this particular battle and it would not be the ladies of the WVS. She took the opportunity to slip out through the side entrance and made her way home. Mr Walker was fully occupied marshalling the Fowler family with their seven unruly children from their house which, although untouched, was next door to Dr Herriot's house, which had been razed to the ground. Luckily the doctor and his wife were away on holiday. Miranda knew this for a fact as she had been given the back door key so that she could get into the house and water Mrs Herriot's collection of indoor plants. There would, she thought sadly, be

14

no need to do that now.

She opened the gate and ran down the path, pausing to glance up at the chimney stack which stood alone in the gaping hole where the roof had once been. She let herself into the house and closed the door behind her. Apart from the thick layer of dust and rubble which covered everything, the ground floor appeared to have escaped the worst of the blast. She picked up the telephone receiver and was amazed to find that it was still connected to the exchange. She dialled the number and asked to be put through to her mother's office. She had been calm until now and feeling slightly detached from everything that was going on around her, but the sound of her mother's melodious voice with the charming lilt of a French accent that she had never quite lost, brought tears to her eyes. 'Maman, I don't know how to tell you this, but our house has been bombed and it's in ruins. You must come home right away.'

'Oh, mon Dieu! Where are you now, Miranda?'

'I'm at home, but we haven't got a roof and everything is in a terrible mess. I don't know what to do.'

'You must get out of there. It doesn't sound safe.'

'But all our things are here, Maman.'

'I'm coming home. I'll be there as soon as possible. Go to one of the neighbours and wait for me there. The colonel will take you in, I'm sure.'

'His house is nothing but a pile of rubble, and the Herriots' too.'

'Merde.'

A bubble of hysterical laughter rose in Miranda's throat. Her mother always lapsed into French whenever her emotions got the better of her, but she rarely swore. 'It's all right, Maman. I'll go to Miss Sharkey's house. I'm sure she could do with the company.'

'I'll be with you as quickly as possible. Please leave the house immediately, Miranda.'

'Yes. Don't worry.' Miranda replaced the receiver but instead of following her mother's instructions she made her way upstairs, taking each step slowly and carefully. She had no intention of bringing the rest of the house down around her ears but she was not going to leave without salvaging at least a change of clothing.

She reached the landing without mishap, but it was strange to look up at what had once been the ceiling and see nothing but blue sky with a few puffy white clouds scudding overhead. She went to her bedroom and gasped in horror at the sight of the plaster, tiles and fragments of brick that covered her bed and littered the floor, but to her surprise and delight the wardrobe placed against the chimney breast had survived intact. She lifted two suitcases from the top and brushed the dust off with her gloved hand, sighing with relief to see that they were dented but not seriously damaged. She opened the wardrobe door and began ripping garments off their hangers. She tossed them into the cases, throwing shoes on top of dresses, handbags and hats. Her underwear was in the deep drawer at the base of the old-fashioned Edwardian piece of furniture and she gathered up an armful of slips, bras and panties. Even as she worked small pieces of tile and rubble had begun to slide off a small section of the roof attached to the chimney stack. Fearing the worst, she slammed the lids on the cases and headed for the stairs, but she hesitated, wondering if she dared risk going into her mother's room to see if there was anything she could save. She could hear ominous cracking sounds coming from the brickwork but she was determined to salvage something for her mother. Dropping her cases on the carpet she crossed the landing to her parents' room, but a rafter had fallen across the doorway and part of the outer wall had collapsed onto the bed. She felt the floor beginning to shake and she reached in to grab a photo of her father from the chest nearest the door. Tucking it into her pocket she managed to reach the top of the stairs just as a deep-throated rumble preceded the crash of several chimney pots tumbling into the room she had just vacated. She hurried downstairs, hefting her heavy cases, and just made it out of the house before the chimney stack toppled into what had been her bedroom with a thunderous clatter of bricks and cement.

She put the cases down and turned slowly to stare at the wreckage of the detached suburban villa that had been her home since she started kindergarten. Before that she had only vague memories of living in married quarters abroad, but this was where she had spent her formative years and it felt as though part of her life had been destroyed by a single act of violence. She lifted her hand to dash a smut from the tip of her nose and saw that her white gloves were blackened and torn. Maman had always insisted that young ladies wore gloves when they went out, and now hers were ruined. It was such a little thing compared to the loss of their home, but it seemed like the end of the world. Tears flowed down her cheeks and she slumped down on one of the suitcases, burying her face in her hands.

Someone tapped her on the shoulder and Miranda looked up to see Miss Sharkey's anxious face. 'Your mother rang me, dear. She wants you to come to my house and wait for her.'

Miranda stared at her blankly. 'It's all gone, Miss Sharkey. Everything we had is gone.'

Miss Sharkey helped her to her feet. 'Not everything, Miranda. You are still alive and well and your mother is on her way home. When it comes down to it, my dear, things are just material objects that can be replaced. With people it's a different matter altogether.'

Miranda sniffed and wiped her hand across her eyes. 'I suppose you're right.'

'I am. Now come with me and we'll put the kettle on and have a nice cup of tea.'

'Thank you, Miss Sharkey.' Miranda had to stifle the desire to laugh hysterically. Why did people think that a cup of tea would put everything right? She picked up her cases and followed Miss Sharkey to her house three doors along the road.

'Thank you. A cup of tea would be lovely.' Jeanne Beddoes smiled and waited until their neighbour had left the sitting room. 'Even after all these years I can't quite get used to the English and their love of tea.' She sat down on the sofa next to Miranda and patted her hand. 'Are you all right, chérie?'

'I am now, Maman. I'm afraid I let myself down a bit earlier and cried like a baby.'

'You are still my baby, chérie. Even if you are nineteen and almost a woman, you will always be my little girl.'

Something in her mother's tone made Miranda suddenly alert. 'There's something you're not telling me. What is it?'

Jeanne reached for her handbag and took out a silver case. She opened it and selected a cigarette. 'Your father gave me this for my twenty-first birthday,' she said with a wistful look in her dark eyes. 'You were just a baby then, not quite a year old.'

'Maman, if there's something you have to tell me, please do it before Miss Sharkey comes back with yet another tray of tea.'

Jeanne fished in her bag for a lighter and lit her cigarette. 'It had to be today,' she mused softly. 'The wretched German had to drop his bomb on our house at a time when I had something important to tell you.'

'Just say it, Maman. Don't keep me in suspense.'

Jeanne stared down at the smouldering tip of her cigarette, avoiding her daughter's gaze. 'I have to go away, chérie. Because I am French I've been selected for a training course. It's top secret so I can't tell you any more.'

'But you're just a secretary. Surely you can't need more training to do your job.'

'This will be more than just being a secretary, Miranda. My boss is heavily involved in starting up a top secret organisation, and I'm going to be one of the first operatives. That's all I can tell you.'

Miranda stared at her in amazement. 'They want you because you speak French?'

'That's right.'

'You're going to be a spy?'

Jeanne laid her finger on her lips. 'You must never tell anyone, and you mustn't discuss it with your grandparents. You never know who might be listening.'

'What are you saying, Maman?'

'After you rang me today and told me about the house I telephoned Grandpa Beddoes.' Jeanne rose to her feet, and taking a last drag on her cigarette, tossed it out of the open window onto a crazy paving path. She turned slowly to face her daughter. 'My course starts tomorrow, and now that the house is gone I'm afraid you'll have to go and stay with your grandparents in Dorset.'

'Leave London? But it's still term time. I haven't taken my shorthand exam yet and I've been working so hard, even though I hate it.'

'I'm sorry, Miranda. Thanks to the Luftwaffe we have no choice. At least I know you'll be safe and well looked after with Granny and Grandpa. It's what your papa would want.' Her voice broke and her eyes were suddenly bright with tears. 'I am doing this for him and for you, chérie. I don't want to leave you but we must all do what we can to end this terrible war, and bring our loved ones home.'

Miranda rose to her feet. 'I tried to get into your room, Maman. I wanted to salvage something for you but this was all I could save.' She put her hand in her pocket and took out the photograph of her father. 'He looks so handsome in his uniform.'

Jeanne's lips trembled and she clutched the frame, her eyes bright with unshed tears. 'My brave girl. Thank you for this, but I can't take it with me.' She kissed the photo and handed it back to Miranda. 'Keep it safe for me, chérie. One day we will all be together again, but not yet.'

'Oh, Maman.' Miranda wrapped her arms around her mother. 'I don't know what I'll do without you.'

'You will do superbly well, ma chère.'

They held each other, their tears mingling, but they moved apart as Miss Sharkey barged into the room carrying a tea tray.

Jeanne looked round, painting a smile on her face. 'How kind of you, Edith. I'm sorry to put you to so much trouble.'

Miss Sharkey beamed at her as she put the tray on a table near the window. 'You are more than welcome, Jeanne. And if you would both like to stay tonight I'll air the beds in the spare rooms. I so seldom have visitors that it will be quite a treat to have company.' She glanced at the wall above the cluttered chiffonier, where the faded image of a young man gazed solemnly from a gilded frame, his peaked cap clutched in his hands and a swagger stick tucked beneath his arm. 'Things would have been so different if Lionel had not been killed at Passchendaele. And now we are at war again. It's so sad.' She sat down and began pouring tea into dainty bone china cups. 'What

21

will you do now?'

Jeanne shot a warning glance at Miranda. 'Well, I have to go on a training course, and Miranda will be going to spend the summer with her grandparents in Dorset.'

Miranda said nothing. She adored her grandparents but the last thing she wanted was to leave London and spend the rest of the war in the country. If Maman could do something brave for the war effort, perhaps she could too. One thing was certain: she would not be content to laze around on the beach all day. There must be something she could do for King and country.

As she stepped off the train Miranda realised that the war had spread its deadly tentacles even further than she had imagined. Despite the fact that her mother had been convinced that Weymouth was a much safer haven than London, the neat row of guest houses abutting the station were sandbagged and their windows taped as a precaution against flying glass. Childhood memories of long hot summers, golden sands, waves gently lapping on the shore, Punch and Judy shows and ice cream stands were receding rapidly as her fellow passengers rushed past her heading for the barrier with their tickets clutched in their hands, and their gas mask cases hitched over their shoulders.

The train had been packed with men and women in uniform and the smell of cigarette smoke clung to Miranda's clothes and hair. She had been reading a copy of *The Times* that someone had left on the seat when they got off the train in Bournemouth, and suddenly the war in Europe seemed too close for comfort. The news that German troops had moved through France to occupy the Channel Islands, and that their army was just a hop, skip and a jump away from England, had made the threat of invasion frighteningly real.

She glanced up and down the platform but there was no porter to help her with her heavy suitcases, and when she finally reached the station concourse it was crowded with white-faced women trying to cope with tired, fractious children. For a wild moment Miranda thought that the Germans must have landed on the local beaches and the town was being evacuated, but from snatches of overheard conversation she realised that these were some of the evacuees from the Channel Islands. The reality of what war could do to people had become even more apparent, and she realised how lucky she was to be going to her grandparents' home where she was assured of a warm welcome.

She made her way outside but there was no sign of her grandfather's car, and there were no taxis waiting on the rank. She put her cases on the ground, wondering if Granny and Grandpa had forgotten that she was due to arrive today. Maybe they had mistaken the time of her arrival, which was a distinct possibility as Granny was notoriously absentminded, and they might turn up at any moment full of apologies. She decided to wait for a while before going in search of a telephone box. She pulled her straw hat down a little further over her eyes to shield them from the bright sunlight and made an effort to be patient.

The crowds dispersed and still there was no sign of the ancient Bentley that Grandpa George loved almost as much as his wife. Granny had never bothered to take driving lessons and, even if she had been so inclined, Miranda doubted if Grandpa would have allowed her to get behind the wheel of his precious car. She waited a while longer but she was beginning to fret. If Uncle Jack had been at home he would have come for her in his black and yellow roadster, Chloe, but he had broken with family army tradition and joined the RAF. She had not given it much thought until now, but the house would seem terribly dull without him, and Jack would not have left her standing here alone and abandoned like a lost parcel. With their home in ruins and her parents off fighting the war in their different ways, Miranda realised that she was just as much a refugee as the unfortunate Channel Islanders.

She wiped her eyes, overwhelmed by a sudden and unexpected wave of homesickness. She sniffed and opened her handbag searching for her hanky, but with a sigh of resignation she realised that hers were buried in the ruins of number twenty-seven Linden Avenue. This was ridiculous; she would be twenty at Christmas. She was legally old enough to be married, even if she was still considered to be a minor in law, and yet here she was snivelling like a baby.

'What's up with you, ducks?'

A cheerful voice at her side made Miranda look round. She found herself face to face with a skinny

24

girl roughly the same age as herself. 'Nothing. I've got something in my eye.'

The girl pulled a grubby hanky from her skirt pocket and offered it to her. 'Hurts, don't it?'

Not wanting to appear ungrateful, Miranda accepted it and dabbed at her cheeks. 'Thanks.' She glanced at the girl's shabby clothes and battered cardboard suitcase. 'Is anyone meeting you?'

'I dunno. They was supposed to, but it looks like I've been forgotten too.' She slapped Miranda on the shoulder. 'I'm Rita Platt from Stepney. What's your moniker, love?'

'Miranda Beddoes. I'm from London too, but I'm spending the summer here with my grandparents.'

'I'm going to live with some old fogey I hardly know and all because of bloody Hitler.' Rita's grey eyes filled with tears and her bottom lip quivered. 'It was just Mum and me until she got sick. A ruptured appendix they said it was, but I blame the munitions factory. I reckon they poisoned her with their chemicals. Anyway, she was a goner and me nan's doolally. They packed her off to Barley Lane loony bin, so that left me on me tod.'

'Oh dear, how terrible. I'm so sorry.' Miranda shuffled her feet, not knowing quite what to say. 'Haven't you got any other relations you could go to?'

Rita threw back her head and laughed but it was not a merry sound. 'I got no one, ducks. That is, except this old biddy what me mum used to char for before she moved from London to this bleeding dump. I wanted to stay in our flat and keep on with me job in the chippie, but the

25

landlord chucked me out. Said I was a minor and too young to rent on me own.'

'So do you know where you're going?'

'Someone was supposed to meet me. Maybe the old girl changed her mind and don't want the bother.'

'Perhaps she's been held up. My grandfather was going to pick me up and he's not here yet.'

Rita pulled a face. 'Well, I ain't going to stand around here all day like a lemon. I'll go and find a copper. They'll have to take me in a squad car to the old besom's house, unless of course she's gone and snuffed it. That would be just my blooming luck.'

Miranda forgot that she had been feeling sorry for herself. She had met someone in a far worse plight. She laid her hand on Rita's thin shoulder. 'Why don't you come home with me? Grandpa is a JP. He's a magistrate,' she added, seeing Rita's blank expression. 'He'll know what to do. He might even know the lady who's going to take you in. He knows just about everyone in this town.'

'It don't look like that would take much doing,' Rita said, glancing round with a cynical grin. 'Seagulls and sand, that's all you got here. I'm going back to London as soon as I've got enough money saved up.'

'Really?' Miranda stared at her in amazement. 'But you can't be much older than me. How will you manage on your own?'

'I'm nineteen, and I left school four years ago. I got fed up with them trying to cram me head with useless rubbish. I'm going to get a job as a pin-up girl with me photo plastered all over magazines. That's what I want to do.'

Miranda gave her a speculative glance. Rita was quite pretty in an obvious sort of way, but she had a figure like an ironing board. 'I think we ought to start walking,' she said, changing the subject. 'It's only two or three miles.'

'What? I can't walk that far. Not with this heavy bag, I can't.'

Miranda had not given any thought to the heaviness of her luggage and she decided that Rita had a point. Looking round in desperation, she spotted a familiar face. As a boy, Tommy Toop had occasionally run errands for her grandmother, although more often than not he had ended up in the magistrates' court in front of her grandfather. He must be at least twenty now, but he still looked like a callow youth with a head that seemed too big for his body and ears that stuck out at right angles. He had always fascinated her, mainly due to the fact that she had been forbidden to have anything to do with him. The Toops were a notorious family of troublemakers. The father was a drunkard and he and his two eldest sons spent more time in prison than out of it. Poor Mrs Toop, a downtrodden little mouse of a woman, had worn her fingers to the bone working as a char by day and washing glasses in a local pub at night. Tommy, no doubt, was a chip off the old block, but he seemed to be in possession of a rickety-looking handcart and was touting for business. Time was moving on and Miranda was convinced that her grandparents had forgotten that she was arriving today; the choice was simple. She waved her hand. 'Tommy. Tommy Toop, over here.'

Chapter Two

Halfway along the beach road, one of the oddly assorted pram wheels spun off its axle and rolled into the water-filled dyke that drained the salt marsh. Miranda could feel blisters forming painfully on both heels, and her head was beginning to ache. The sun beat down from a cloudless sky and she took off her straw hat, wiping the sweat from her forehead. 'I didn't think that contraption would take the weight of three suitcases,' she said, ramming her hat on with an exasperated sigh.

'What d'you expect for blooming tuppence?' Glaring at her, Tommy slumped down on the grass verge.

'Get up, you lazy devil,' Rita said, nudging him with the toe of her sandal. 'Fix the wheel on and let's get going. I'm getting freckles on me nose and that's no good for me career.'

Tommy shrugged his shoulders. 'Can't fix it. Got no tools.' He was pale beneath his tan and he looked as though a puff of wind would blow him over.

Miranda was beginning to feel sorry for him. She frowned at Rita, shaking her head. 'Nagging won't help.' She turned to Tommy, leaning down to pat him on the shoulder. 'Come on, Tommy. We're more than halfway there. You can't give up now.'

'I'm getting burnt to a crisp,' Rita said crossly. 'I can see me nose getting redder by the second.'

Miranda took off her straw hat and thrust it into Rita's hands. 'Here, wear this and stop grumbling. You're not helping.' She shaded her eyes, squinting into the distance as the road stretched before them in a line as straight as a pencil sketch in a child's drawing book. With the salt marsh and reed beds on their left and the sea on the other side of the beach wall, they were caught in a no man's land of heat and dust. The fresh briny smell of the sea was tainted by the stench of rotting vegetation and warm mud emanating from the marsh. It was all achingly familiar to Miranda, but it was a shock to see the defences constructed from barbed wire and scaffolding that made it impossible to climb over the wall or to walk along it and enjoy the view of the bay. The only sounds she could hear were the mournful cries of the seagulls circling overhead, and the waves sucking gently at the pebbles on the shore.

'You've broken me cart,' Tommy said, struggling to his feet. 'I should have charged you sixpence for giving me so much trouble.'

'Oh, shut up, you miserable sod.' Rita glanced up and down the deserted road, screwing her face up as if she had been sucking a lemon. 'Ain't there no buses in this godforsaken hole? Nothing's gone past since we started out on this trek to nowhere.'

'Petrol's rationed,' Miranda said sternly. 'You should know that, Rita.'

'Oh, sorry, miss. I weren't listening in class. We can't afford cars where I come from.'

Miranda decided that she was fighting a losing battle with both of her companions. 'I'm going to Elzevir Shipway's cottage. Maybe he'll give us a lift on his cart.'

'Who's he?' Rita cocked her head on one side like an inquisitive robin. 'That's a daft name if ever I heard one.'

'No need to bother him,' Tommy said, springing to his feet. 'I'll fix the wheel.' He scrambled down the bank into the ditch where he waded knee-deep in foul-smelling water, splashing around until he found what he was looking for. He clambered out, grumbling all the time as he attempted to fix the wheel on by hammering it with a small rock.

'You'll not do it that way.' Rita pushed him aside, aiming a kick at the wheel.

'Here, don't do that,' Tommy protested.

'It worked, didn't it?' Rita stood back, smirking. The wheel, as if to prove her point, stayed on.

'It won't hold,' Tommy said, flinging the rock back into the muddy water.

Miranda decided it was time to take charge. She was beginning to feel like a schoolmistress dealing with a couple of squabbling infants. 'You don't know until you try,' she said firmly. 'Anyway, you can't abandon us here, Tommy. I've paid you to take the luggage to Highcliffe House and that's that.'

He grabbed the handle and gave it a heave, but after pushing the cart for a few yards the wheel wobbled and fell off again. The suitcases slid onto the ground and Rita uttered a roar of displeasure as the rusty locks gave away and her case burst open, spilling its contents onto the road. 'Bloody hell,' she exclaimed, scrabbling about and gathering up her belongings. 'Give us a hand, you twerp.'

Tommy's face flushed a deeper shade of red and he glowered at her. 'Shut up.'

He looked so much like an angry pixie that Miranda had to stifle the urge to laugh. She felt a bubble of hysteria rising in her throat but she controlled it with difficulty. She was hot, thirsty and could quite happily have walked off and left the two of them to fight it out, but she could not leave her cases blocking the road and they were too heavy to carry very far. 'It's no good. I shall just have to ask Elzevir for help.' She pointed to a cottage which stood alone on the edge of the marsh: a ramshackle one-storey building with tall chimney pots, one at each end, sticking up like rabbit's ears from the corrugated-iron roof. Elzevir Shipway, whose official job was to operate the sluice gates twice daily in order to drain the water from the marsh, supplemented his meagre wage by selling logs and doing odd jobs. He lived with his spinster sister, Annie, who had been the daily help at Highcliffe House for as long as Miranda could remember.

'You can count me out,' Tommy said crossly. 'I don't want nothing to do with old Elzevir. Evil-Eye, that's what everyone calls him.' Grabbing the handle of his cart he turned it around and started off towards the town, balancing it precariously on three wheels.

Rita stuffed the last sock back into her case, closed the lid and sat on it. 'What's up with him?'

'He's scared of Elzevir, because years ago he

31

and some of the other local boys used to throw stones at his windows and call him names. I could hear Elzevir yelling at them from my grandparents' garden and he'd box their ears if he caught any of them. He's a big chap and I wouldn't want to get on the wrong side of him. Anyway, his muscle is what we need now so I'll go and see if he's in. You wait here.'

'Can't do much else,' Rita said gloomily. 'The bloody locks are busted.'

Miranda frowned. 'Er, you might want to watch your language when you meet my grandparents. They're a bit old-fashioned, if you know what I mean.'

'Stuck up, you mean.' Rita pulled a face. 'Don't worry, Miranda, mate. I can act like a lady when I want to.'

Miranda had no answer to that and she set off for the cottage. What should have been a ten-minute drive with her grandfather had turned into a tiresome trek, and when she knocked on the door and received no answer she was beginning to feel quite desperate. She went back to where Rita was still sitting on her suitcase. 'He's out,' she said, shaking her head. 'We'll just have to walk. It's only about half a mile from here.'

Rita gave her a pitying glance. 'So how do you suggest I carry this thing? It won't shut and I got nothing to tie round it. We'll have to wait for a bus.'

'I don't even know if they run buses on this route these days. We'll just have to leave our luggage here and get someone to pick it up later.'

'What?' Rita's voice rose to an agitated squeak.

32

'Some bugger will come along and pinch everything. This is all I got left in the world.'

'I'm sure they won't,' Miranda said, making an effort to sound calm. 'If we pile them up on the grass verge we can get my grandfather to collect them.'

'I ain't budging. You might be trusting but I ain't. I'm sitting here until someone comes to my rescue.'

Miranda opened her mouth to tell her that she might be waiting for a very long time when, as if by some miracle, she heard the sound of a car engine coming from the direction of the town. She leapt into the middle of the road, waving her arms frantically at the speeding vehicle. The car came to a halt with a screech of brakes and the smell of burning rubber. A young man in RAF uniform leapt out of the driver's seat, his face ashen. 'What the hell d'you think you're doing? You might have been killed, dancing about in the middle of the road like an idiot.'

Rita jumped to her feet. 'Steady on, guv. You was driving like a bat out of hell anyway.'

He looked from one to the other and suddenly his grim expression melted into a smile. 'Fair comment, I suppose.' He fixed his gaze on Miranda and was serious again. 'Are you all right? You aren't going to pass out on me, are you?'

Miranda shook her head. She was feeling slightly sick and a bit dizzy, but she was not going to admit it or that she had acted in a reckless manner. 'I'm fine, thank you. But we need help.'

He glanced down at the damaged case and at Miranda's slightly battered but expensive leather luggage. He nodded his head. 'I can see that. Where are you two ladies going?'

Miranda pointed to the hill at the far end of the road. 'Highcliffe House. It's not very far, but we can't manage the cases.'

'That's Major Beddoes' house, isn't it?' he said, frowning.

'Yes. He's my grandfather.' Miranda sensed a change in his attitude, but she knew that her grandfather was extremely outspoken and quite often offended people. She met his gaze with a determined lift of her chin and held out her hand. 'Miranda Beddoes. How do you do?'

'Raif Carstairs. How do you do?' He seemed to relent and shook hands with an attempt at a smile. 'I can give you a lift if you don't mind a bit of a squash.'

'My mum told me never to get into a car with a strange man,' Rita said with a flirtatious grin.

He clicked his heels together and saluted. 'Flight Lieutenant Raif Carstairs. How do you do?'

Rita's face split into a wide smile as she grabbed his hand, pumping it up and down. 'Rita Platt. Pleased to meet you. Ta for the offer, mister.' Without waiting for a second invitation she climbed into the passenger seat. 'Hop in, Miranda, mate. There's room for two little 'uns like us.'

Miranda hesitated. 'But there isn't any space for the luggage.'

'We'll leave them in Shipway's garden,' Raif said decisively. 'They'll be safe there. No one would dare steal anything from him.' He moved the cases one at a time to the safety of the tiny front garden surrounded by a rather dilapidated picket fence.

'That Evil-Eye bloke sounds like a right 'un.' Rita patted the seat beside her. 'Come on, Miranda. What are you waiting for? Let Prince Charming see to the cases. We're travelling in style.'

Miranda hesitated, torn between the desire to get to her grandparents' home as quickly as possible and the indignity of squashing in beside Rita. Flight Lieutenant Carstairs must think they were a couple of silly young girls. It was humiliating to say the least, and she dared not think what Grandpa George would say when he found out how she had risked life and limb to flag down the speeding motorcar.

'He's a bit of all right,' Rita said, craning her neck to get a better view of Raif. 'D'you think he'll ask me for a date?'

Miranda felt the blood rush to her cheeks. She could not help admiring the lean athletic and rather dashing figure that Raif Carstairs presented in his smart blue uniform. He was quite good-looking, although she would not have described him as handsome, but he was charming and he obviously knew it. She squeezed in beside Rita. 'He wouldn't look twice at you, Rita Platt.'

'Wanna bet?' Rita said in a phoney American accent.

'Move over, please.' Miranda nudged her gently in the ribs. 'The door handle is cutting into me.'

'With pleasure. It gives me an excuse to cuddle up to the glamour-boy.'

Miranda said nothing. She sat very still during the drive, suffering torments of embarrassment as she tried to ignore Rita's flirtatious behaviour. Luckily it was a very short journey. Raif dropped them at the gate and drove off with a cheery wave.

Rita met Miranda's frown with a carefree chuckle. 'Your face will stick like that if the wind changes.' She paused, clutching the gatepost with an agonised expression. 'Oh, hell. I need the lav. I'll wet me pants if I don't go soon.'

Wishing she had never taken pity on Rita Platt, Miranda opened the garden gate. She pointed to the outbuildings at the back of the house. 'The gardener's lavatory is the one with the blue door. Wait there when you're done and I'll come and find you.'

Rita took off down the crumbling red-brick path as if the devil were on her heels and Miranda followed at a slower pace, but as she emerged from the shade of the overhanging laburnum and the tamarisk she spotted her grandmother on her hands and knees weeding a flowerbed. She broke into a run. 'Granny. Here I am.'

Maggie Beddoes clambered to her feet, struggling to disentangle her skirt from the clutching thorns of a rose bush. 'Miranda, my dear girl. We weren't expecting you until tomorrow.'

'Maman told Grandpa that I'd be arriving on the eleven forty-five train today. Friday the twenty-first.'

'No, dear. Surely not. Tomorrow is the twenty-first, isn't it?' Maggie stared at her in dismay. 'Oh, bother. I must have looked at the calendar with the wrong spectacles, or maybe I forgot to change the month. I do that quite often.' She

36

dropped the trowel she had been clutching in her hand and wrapped Miranda in a hug.

Laughing, Miranda drew away as the secateurs in her grandmother's apron pocket threatened to impale her on their open blades. 'It doesn't matter. I'm here now, but there's a small matter of my luggage. Tommy Toop's cart lost a wheel and I had to leave my cases in the Shipways' front garden.'

'You poor girl. I am so sorry. What must you have thought when there was no one to meet you at the station? And you must be exhausted having walked all that way in this heat.'

'A really nice RAF officer gave us a lift.'

'Gave you a lift? You accepted a ride in a car with a strange man? Oh, my God. This is all my fault.'

'No, honestly, he introduced himself very politely. He said his name is Raif Carstairs.'

Maggie's eyebrows snapped together in a frown. 'You should have telephoned and we would have come for you. Never accept a lift from strangers.'

Miranda stared at her grandmother in surprise. She was normally easy-going but now she seemed really upset. 'He was quite respectable, Granny.'

'Even so, he might have been a spy, or a fifth columnist, besides which we don't have anything to do with that family.' Maggie wiped her hands on her apron, leaving streaks of dirt on the coarse material. 'As to Tommy, the wretched fellow will end up in jail one day, just like his father. Or else he'll make his fortune and buy us all out. Anyway, it's his mother I feel sorry for. Poor woman, she does try to keep the family on the straight and narrow.' She took Miranda by the hand. 'Come indoors and have some of my homemade lemonade. I've been baking cakes too.'

Miranda smiled. She remembered only too well her grandmother's culinary efforts. They were unforgettable and not for a good reason. Granny was a truly dreadful cook, but no one liked to tell her so, and Miranda had been schooled in the art of the polite lie from a very early age. 'That would be lovely, Granny. But what about the luggage?'

'Don't worry, darling. I'll get Annie to fetch it. She's as strong as an ox, just like her brother, but thank goodness her language isn't as colourful.' She snatched up her trowel and proceeded to drag Miranda through the tangle of rose bushes and encroaching brambles, slashing away with the implement like an explorer cutting her way through the jungle with a machete.

Highcliffe came into view as they emerged from the dense thicket and Miranda felt a tug of pure love for the eccentric example of Victorian Gothic architecture. With its ornate ironwork veranda, square bay windows, and a tower with a conical roof placed above a widow's walk, the house always looked as if it were on the point of hurling itself over the cliff in an attempt to escape from its own ugliness. It was, she knew, an optical illusion. Although part of the land had crumbled into the sea during a terrible winter storm not long after the building was erected in the late 1800s, there remained enough expanse of cliff top to ensure its survival for at least another hundred years, or so her grandfather had told her in reassuring tones. When she was a small child she had had nightmares when the walls in her bedroom suddenly disappeared and she found herself flying over the waves on her brass bedstead. Luckily she always woke up before it landed in the water.

Maggie released her hand to hurry on ahead, but she came to a halt with a cry of fright when she reached the outbuildings as Rita leapt out of the gardener's toilet with a wild scream. She was white and trembling but her eyes flashed angrily. She stalked up to Maggie wagging her finger. 'What sort of place is this, missis? You got rats the size of tigers in your lav.'

Maggie bridled and drew herself up to her full five feet four inches. 'Gypsy,' she said, pointing at Rita. 'George.' Her voice rose to a shriek. 'Gypsies. They're after our hens again. Come quickly.'

'No, Granny,' Miranda said calmly. 'Rita isn't a gypsy and she hasn't come to steal your hens, or anything else for that matter.'

'She looks like a gypsy. I've lost several of my best laying hens to the vagabonds who camp near here.' Maggie glared suspiciously at Rita. 'Who is she and what is she doing here?'

Rita fisted her hands at her sides. 'Here, missis. You watch what you're saying. I ain't no didicoi. I'm an evacuee from London and I've come to a madhouse overrun with sewer rats.' She uttered a loud shriek as a large grey cat shot past her.

Miranda bent down to scoop it up in her arms. 'Is this your rat, Rita?'

'I dunno. It might be,' Rita said sulkily. 'All I saw was two big eyes shining in the darkness and it was furry.'

'This is Dickens and he looks nothing like a rat.' Maggie took the cat from Miranda and smoothed his ruffled fur. 'He's a pedigree British Blue and you must have terrified the poor creature.' She put him down on the ground and he stalked off with an offended twitch of his tail.

'No harm done,' Miranda said, breathing a sigh of relief. 'I'm sure he'll get over his fright.'

'No harm!' Rita looked from one to the other in disbelief. 'I almost died in there. You lot are barmy. I wish I'd stayed in London and risked being blown to bits.'

'So you're an evacuee.' Maggie looked her up and down and her expression softened. 'I'm sorry, my dear girl, but why are you here? Are you sure you've got the right address?'

'I brought Rita here, Granny,' Miranda said hastily. 'She was supposed to be staying with a lady in Weymouth who knew her late mother, but there was no one to meet her at the station. Just like me.'

'Well you'd better come inside, Rita. We'll telephone the person in question and find out what's gone wrong.' Maggie tucked a wisp of silver hair behind her ear with an exasperated sigh. 'It's all been very badly organised, but it is wartime and everything is different now, except of course for those wretched gypsies. I've a good mind to get a guard dog to watch over my hens. Come to think of it I'd better go and see that they're all right. Miranda, I leave you to take care of your friend.' She disappeared round the side of the house.

'Come along, let's go indoors,' Miranda said

with an apologetic smile. 'I could do with freshening up and I expect you could too.'

'Is your gran always like this? I mean she seems a bit...' Rita hesitated, biting her lip, 'you know what I mean.'

'She's a dear when you get to know her but she's had a thing about gypsies ever since she lost some of her hens. Grandpa said he thought it was a fox that had taken them, but there were gypsies camped not far away, and they always seem to get the blame for anything that goes wrong.'

'Just because I look like this don't mean I'm a criminal,' Rita said, pouting. 'It's okay for you lot with your big houses and posh cars, but some of us live in the real world. My mum worked her fingers to the bone to bring me up proper.'

'What about your father?'

'Never knew him. He disappeared from the scene the moment Mum told him she was up the spout. Her family chucked her out and never spoke to her again. Me nan came round eventually but then she was barmy.'

'That must have been ghastly for her.' Miranda led the way out of the yard, taking Rita along a narrow path lined with sweet-smelling shrubs. Bees droned happily as they collected pollen from the flowers and hedge sparrows popped in and out of the leaves like tiny automatons. Nothing seemed to have changed in this timeless spot and Miranda was finding it hard to believe that war had touched this peaceful haven filled with happy childhood memories. It was cool in the shade but the heat hit her as she stepped onto a crazy-paving path at the back of the house. A wide expanse of lawn sloped gently to the cliff top with a breathtaking view of the bay. The sea was a calm turquoise deepening to purple at the horizon, but the sight of barbed wire and tank traps on the beach below was a stark reminder of the fear of invasion and the conflict raging across the Channel.

'Get a move on,' Rita said impatiently. 'You might have come home but I've still got to sort out where I'm going to put me head down tonight.'

'Don't worry. I'm sure it will be all right.' Miranda hesitated in the doorway. Rita's story had touched her more deeply than she could have imagined. 'Your mother must have had a terrible time. How on earth did she manage?'

'A spinster aunt took her in, and she looked after me while Mum went out to work. Then Auntie Doreen died and we was on our own. Now it's just me.'

Miranda's throat constricted and she swallowed hard. Rita's life must have been incredibly tough, and now she was all alone in the world. She turned away, unable to think of anything to say that would not sound shallow or patronising. 'Come inside, Rita. Let's get cleaned up.'

'I'm going to be a pin-up girl,' Rita said, following close on her heels. 'I'll show them all what Rita Platt can do.'

'I'm sure you will.' Miranda entered the drawing room which in contrast to the searing heat outside was deliciously cool. The scent from vases filled with roses, sweet peas and syringa mingled with the pungent aroma of lavender and beeswax floor polish. 'Watch out for sliding mats,' she said, stepping carefully on a faded Persian rug. 'Annie polishes the floor until it's like glass. I've seen people go skating across the boards and ending up flat on their backs.'

Rita glanced round at the eclectic mix of furniture, well-worn chintz-covered sofas, Regency chairs, inlaid Indian tables and bookcases spilling over with assorted and obviously well-thumbed editions. The walls were hung with oil paintings and watercolours, and every available surface crammed with framed family photographs and a variety of ornaments; Japanese ivories and fat Buddhas with jolly faces jostled for position between Dresden shepherdesses and startling examples of native African art. 'Looks like a bloody museum,' Rita murmured.

'The family travelled a lot. My grandfather was an army doctor and they lived in India for a while, and in Kenya. Anyway, we'd better get a move on. I don't know about you but I'm getting hungry.'

'I could eat a bloody horse,' Rita said with feeling. She met Miranda's look of disapproval with a casual shrug. 'Sorry. I'll try not to swear in front of the old folks.'

'Even at my age I'd get a rocket if I used words like that.' Miranda opened the inner door and led the way through a maze of passages to the front of the house and the main hall. She blinked as her eyes grew accustomed to the dimness. The only natural light filtered through a stained-glass window on the bend of the staircase, creating a kaleidoscope of patterns on the encaustic-tiled floor. She had always accepted the slightly biz-arre nature of Highciffe without question, having spent virtually every school holiday in the old house, but seeing it through someone else's eyes made her realise that it was unusual to say the least. She ushered Rita into the cloakroom. 'There aren't any cats in here – or rats,' she said, grinning. 'Let's get cleaned up and then we'll eat.' She could only hope that Annie had done most of the cooking. It would be too embarras-sing if they were faced with one of Granny's special dishes like tripe and onions or liver fried until it was the consistency of leather and tasted of iron filings.

As she ushered Rita into the kitchen they were almost blown backwards by a waft of hot air and the smell of burning. Swathed in a floral pinafore Annie Shipway, a raw-boned woman of above average height, was up to her elbows in hot water at the sink, washing net curtains. The smell of Sunlight soap, ammonia and burnt bacon fat was overpowering. Maggie burst through the back door and came to a stop in the middle of the room, gazing helplessly at the saucepan on the range which was belching smoke. 'You've let the ham boil dry, you stupid woman,' she said angrily. 'That was our meat ration for a week. Now we'll have to eat fish every day and you know that the major isn't partial to seafood.'

Annie glanced over her shoulder. 'Well take the pan off the hob then. Can't you see I'm busy? I can't do everything round here. You said wash the nets, not watch the pot.'

'You're just being difficult. Those nets needed a good wash.' Maggie moved warily towards the stove and wrapped her apron round the handle. Lifting the pan and holding it at arm's length she hurried out into the yard leaving a trail of smoke in her wake. She returned moments later with a resigned smile. 'Oh well. That's that. At least the hens are laying well. I checked on them and all present and correct. Besides which we should have plenty of potatoes if your grandfather hasn't used them all up in his silly experiments.'

Miranda exchanged puzzled glances with Rita, but before she had a chance to question her grandmother as to the nature of the experiments, Maggie had gone off on another tack. 'Annie dear, would you be kind enough to fetch the girls' cases? They had to leave them in your garden when that Toop boy left them to fend for themselves.'

'I've only got one pair of hands, Mrs B. I'll go as soon as I've hung out the washing, which I'm about to do now, unless you'd like me to sweep the chimbley first or climb up on the roof and replace a few tiles.'

'No, my dear. That will be all for now,' Maggie said calmly. 'I'll get the girls something to eat and drink and then we'll see about finding where Rita is to be billeted. I'm sure the major will know the woman who is going to take her in. He knows almost everyone in town.'

'Everyone who's committed a crime.' Annie tossed the nets into a wicker laundry basket. 'I'll go and see if Elzevir is home. Even I can't carry three suitcases at once. You might treat me like a

45

workhorse, Mrs B, but I'll thank you to remember that I'm a woman just like you.'

'Oh, get on with you. Do as you please, Annie. You always do.' Apparently unruffled by her domestic's uncompromising attitude, Maggie shooed her out of the kitchen.

Mumbling beneath her breath, Annie took the laundry outside, leaving a wet snail-trail behind her as water leaked through the loosely woven wicker.

'She's getting worse,' Miranda said severely. 'You oughtn't to let her speak to you like that, Granny.'

Maggie laughed and shrugged her shoulders. 'Oh, she's all right. I don't take any notice of Annie Shipway. We've been together for what seems like a lifetime. She was all sweetness and light today. You should see her when she's in a bad mood. Anyway, forget about her and I'll make you a sandwich or something. You must be starving.' She went to the pantry and Miranda could hear things being moved about in an apparently random manner.

'Mad as a blooming hatter,' Rita muttered beneath her breath.

Miranda raised a warning finger to her lips. 'Shh. She'll hear you.'

Carrying a large china jug and a plate of cakes, Maggie backed out of the cupboard and laid her finds on the table. 'My special homemade lemonade and the rock cakes I baked this morning,' she said proudly. 'Miranda, dear. Find some tumblers, will you? I can never remember where Annie keeps them. In fact, I'll swear she changes the contents of the cupboards just to confuse me and to underline the fact that this is her domain and not mine.'

Miranda knew exactly where to find the glasses. They had been on the same shelf for as long as she could remember, but she realised that this was a mere detail as far as her grandmother was concerned. Granny's mind was always somewhere else when it came to domestic matters. She poured the lemonade and gave a glass to Rita before sipping hers. It was delicious, but it was common knowledge in the family that the only effort Maggie put into her homemade potion was to pour hot water onto Eiffel Tower lemonade crystals and mix. It did not take a culinary genius but the end result was refreshing and delicious. The rock cakes were another matter.

'Do have one,' Maggie said, offering the plate to Rita. 'Don't be shy.'

Rita took one. 'Ta,' she said, eyeing it doubtfully.

Miranda could not let the side down and she bit into hers, giving Rita an encouraging smile as she chewed and swallowed the sawdust-dry offering.

'I can't say that cooking is my forte,' Maggie said modestly. 'But everyone loves my rock cakes, although it's difficult with rationing, but we manage somehow. Unfortunately the ham joint was the last of poor Percy. I don't think I can face keeping a pig again; it's too traumatic when one has to send the poor thing to the abattoir. I grew to love that grumpy old fellow.'

Rita choked and reached for the lemonade.

'Won't you have one, Granny?' Miranda proffered the plate, knowing that her grandmother would refuse, but unable to resist the temptation to tease her just a little.

'No, dear. I'm not at all hungry.' Maggie cocked her head on one side, listening to the sound of heavy footsteps outside the back door. 'That will be your grandfather, Miranda. Now whatever you do, don't mention Dunkirk.'

'Why not?'

'He's only just recovering, darling. Like a mad fool he forgot that he's no longer a young man and insisted on accompanying Colonel Winterton in his motor cruiser when he risked life and limb to save those poor souls stranded on the beaches. I begged him not to go but he wouldn't listen to me.'

'Cor blimey.' Rita's eyes widened. 'You don't say so.'

'I do say so, Rita. They were foolhardy but extremely brave, and they saved the lives of sixteen men. Sadly the colonel suffered a heart attack soon after they got back to England and he died. It was a sad end to a courageous venture, so please don't say anything. Your grandfather doesn't like to talk about it.'

Miranda nodded vigorously. She had never thought of her grandfather in the light of being anything other than a slightly eccentric but lovable old man. Now suddenly she was seeing him as something of a hero. 'I wouldn't have mentioned it anyway, but I'm glad you told me.' She looked round and smiled as her grandfather strode into the kitchen. He stopped suddenly, staring from

48

one to the other with a bemused expression on his leonine features.

'Miranda? You weren't due until tomorrow.' He crossed the floor and gave her a hug.

'I'm afraid we got it wrong, George,' Maggie said with a rueful smile. 'Apparently we mistook the date and the poor girl was left waiting at the station with no one to meet her.'

'I could have sworn it was tomorrow. Never mind, you're here now and I see you've brought a friend with you.' He released Miranda and turned to Rita, holding out his hand. 'And you are?'

Rita glanced anxiously at Miranda. 'I really ought to be going now.'

'He won't bite,' Miranda whispered. 'Shake hands. It's the done thing.' She turned to her grandfather. 'This is Rita Platt, Grandpa. She came from London on the same train as me, but there wasn't anyone to meet her either.'

'How do you do, Rita?'

Somewhat reluctantly, Rita shook his hand. 'How do, mister?'

'We have to get in touch with the woman who's to take her in,' Maggie said firmly. 'Who is she, dear? I forgot to ask her name.'

'Mrs Proffitt. Hilda Proffitt of Belle View Road. Me mum used to char for her when the old girl lived in London. It was all arranged.'

'Proffitt,' Maggie said, frowning. 'Hilda Proffitt ran the flower club.'

'Ran?' George raised his bushy eyebrows so that they merged with his mop of wild grey hair. 'Do you mean that the poor lady is dead?'

Chapter Three

A sharp intake of breath from Rita made them all turn to look at her. She shook her head. 'That settles it. I'm off to London on the first train.'

'There's no need to panic, my dear,' Maggie said firmly. 'The last I heard she was in hospital after having had a stroke.' She smiled at Rita who was staring at her open-mouthed. 'However, she might be feeling better by now, so come with me and we'll make a few phone calls. You mustn't worry. We'll soon sort this out.' She put her arm around Rita's shoulders. 'George, look after Miranda. Perhaps she'd like to help you in your laboratory until Annie has time to make us something for lunch.'

'I'm going to need more potatoes, Maggie,' he said plaintively. 'I can't find any in the outhouse, and I'm hungry. What time is lunch?' He sniffed the air. 'What's that awful smell?'

'Burnt ham, dear. I'm afraid the last piece of Percy was cremated.' Maggie held up her hands. 'Not my fault, I assure you. Anyway, I sent Annie to get the girls' luggage, but she shouldn't be long. She'll rustle something up when she gets back. In the meantime a rock cake will tide you over. I made them this morning.' Maggie ushered Rita out of the room without giving him a chance to protest.

He took a cake and stuffed it in his pocket. 'I do

miss poor old Percy. He came in very handy on baking day. It's fortunate that Annie is a good cook or we would all be thin as laths and Percy would have expired from apoplexy.'

'Oh, Grandpa,' Miranda said, chuckling. 'That's very wicked. You know that Granny tries her hardest.'

'Yes, it's very trying for all of us. I'd been looking forward to a nice piece of boiled ham.'

'At least the hens are laying well, and Annie makes a lovely omelette. I'd offer to help but cooking isn't my strong point.'

He grinned. 'You take after your grandmother in that.'

'I know, but I haven't had much chance to practise. Maman does all the cooking at home, or rather she did.' Miranda struggled against an overwhelming surge of emotion. She had tried not to think about the dangerous path that her mother had chosen to follow, but it was proving hard to keep up the pretence that all was well and that this was just another summer holiday by the sea. She took a deep breath. 'Will you show me what you're doing in the laboratory?'

'Of course I will, and I must get Elzevir to pick up a fresh supply of potatoes from the farm. At least they aren't on ration, not yet anyway.' He made for the doorway. 'I wonder if the hens will eat cake.'

Miranda followed him out into the yard and round to the stable block, which now served the dual purpose of garage and workshop, or laboratory as her grandfather preferred to call it. He opened the double doors and went inside, beckoning Miranda to follow him.

She hesitated in the doorway, taking in her surroundings with a degree of curiosity. This was all new. The last time she had been in this part of the stables it had been the disused tack room, but now it seemed to have been adapted for a completely different purpose. She watched with interest as her grandfather took his place at a bench littered with flasks, retorts, glass and rubber tubing and a couple of Bunsen burners. There was a pervading odour of gas mixed with an unfamiliar smell of something akin to alcohol or methylated spirits, she could not decide which. The floor was ankle deep in screwed up pieces of paper, potato peelings and pencil shavings. She walked the length of the workbench, trailing her fingers in the film of dust and wondering how he managed to work in such conditions. The area was lit by a single bare bulb and a little natural light, which had to struggle through windows caked with grime and festooned with a net curtain of cobwebs.

While her grandfather busied himself with what looked like a large chemistry set, Miranda explored the part of the coach house that was now used to garage the ageing Bentley. Parked next to it and hidden beneath dust sheets was her Uncle Jack's yellow and black roadster, Chloe. She lifted the covers and ran her fingers over the glossy surface of the bonnet. Poor Chloe, she thought, how undignified for the old girl to be laid up like an invalid while Uncle Jack was away fighting for his country. It seemed a shame to see his pride and joy mothballed and suffering from neglect.

Miranda closed her eyes as she recalled the heady days before Jack had joined the RAF. He had given up his much hated job in the City and had come home, spending the summer in an alcoholic haze after partying until dawn while he waited for a place in pilot training school. She was only too well aware that her father disapproved of his younger brother's playboy lifestyle, and although her mother admitted a soft spot for Jack, she made no secret of the fact that she thought it high time he settled down and behaved like a responsible adult.

Miranda had never forgotten a conversation she had overheard as a child. Her mother had been taking tea with a friend and they had been chatting while Miranda was supposed to be doing her homework. 'Jack was an afterthought,' Jeanne had said in hushed tones, which had made Miranda prick up her ears. 'Ronnie says that Jack has always been an embarrassment,' her mother had continued in a disapproving tone. 'He was a menopausal surprise and his sister Eileen's nose was put out of joint when he arrived on the scene. After all, the poor child had been the centre of attention for twelve years and then suddenly she has a baby brother to steal the limelight. No wonder she married the first man who proposed to her. I think living with that boring civil servant in Nairobi was preferable to returning to England and playing second fiddle to Jack. In fact I'm certain that Ronnie only went to Sandhurst in order to get away from his mad family.'

Her friend had jerked her head in Miranda's direction. 'Little pitchers have big ears, Jeanne.'

Miranda had attempted to melt into the background but her mother had turned on her, frowning. 'Don't you dare repeat a word of this when you visit your grandparents in the summer. Anyway, shouldn't you be doing your homework, or something?'

Miranda sighed. She adored her mother, but as a child she had sometimes felt she was in the way, especially when her father came home on leave. She had often felt excluded by her parents' need to re-establish their relationship. If she had had a brother or sister things might have been different: she would have had an ally in the household, someone to play with or even to squabble with when she was younger. As an adolescent she had found herself relegated to the position of being seen but not heard. She was the token well-behaved, neatly dressed, perfectly mannered daughter, who sat silently in the back seat of the car during family outings which almost inevitably turned into romantic dates for the reunited lovers. Left to her own devices, Miranda had learned to be patient and wait for her presence to be remembered or even noticed.

With Uncle Jack it was different. He had always treated her like a chum, but then Jack had a reputation as a ladies' man. He had been engaged more times than Miranda could remember, and had had his heart broken each time a relationship ended, or so he said, but he seemed to bounce back quickly enough. When he was not chasing some bit of fluff, as he called his lady friends, or suffering from a dreadful hangover, he had occasionally taken Miranda out for a spin in Chloe. It had been exhilarating to speed through the quiet Dorset lanes with the wind taking her breath away and whipping her hair into a tangled mass. Jack always drove much too fast, accelerating when he came to a humpback bridge and making Chloe fly through the air, coming down with a bump that made Miranda laugh and protest that they had left her stomach behind. She smiled to herself as she polished the nearside headlamp with a corner of the dust sheet. Those days before the war had been filled with innocent fun but it now seemed like a childhood dream.

It would be lovely, she thought, if Jack had leave while she was at Highcliffe. Perhaps he knew Raif Carstairs; maybe they were good friends. He might even invite him to the house and then she could thank him properly for coming to their rescue. Granny would realise then that Raif was a thoroughly respectable person and not one of her fifth columnists who, according to her, were even worse than gypsies.

A clatter of metal on concrete from the far end of the room brought her down to earth, and she looked round to see her grandfather bending down to retrieve the fallen object. She knew by the intense look of concentration on his face that he had forgotten her presence and she replaced the dust sheet. 'Bye bye, Chloe,' she whispered. 'See you soon, old girl.'

She went to see if she could help her grandfather to find whatever it was he had dropped.

'You still here, Miranda?' he said, smiling vaguely. 'I thought you'd gone out to make sure that the sea was still there.'

'Grandpa, you've made the same terrible joke every time I've come for a visit since I was six or seven.'

'Have I? Well, I expect I have. Old people are inclined to repeat themselves, and I forget that you're a young lady now and not a little girl.' He gave a grunt of satisfaction as he spotted the paring knife down by his feet and he bent over to pick it up. He selected a large potato from the sack propped up at his side and began peeling it.

'What are you doing with all these potatoes? I thought we were going to have them for dinner tonight.'

'This is an experiment, my dear. If it works, and I don't see why it shouldn't, the final result is going to keep us warm in the winter.'

Mystified, Miranda shook her head. 'I don't understand.'

'I'm working on a method of turning potatoes into ethyl alcohol, and then hopefully into benzene. If I can convert the coke boiler to use benzene instead of solid fuel, we'll be able to keep the central heating going during the cold weather and be patriotic at the same time.'

'You're so clever, Grandpa.'

He shook his head. 'I didn't invent the process, my dear, and if it were for consumption it would be totally illegal. In fact, I am skating on thin ice as far as the law is concerned, but if I can find a way to manufacture large quantities of the stuff it would help the war effort. As it is I don't want anyone to find out or they might get the wrong idea. Do you understand?'

'I think so.'

'And there's always the possibility that this may not work. I'm a doctor and a soldier by profession, not an engineer or a chemist. But if I do succeed, then I'll pass my findings on to the Ministry. Until then it must remain a closely guarded secret. Now, if you want to help me in my project you can tell Annie that I want her brother to bring me fresh supplies.'

'Supplies of what, Grandpa?'

He tapped the side of his nose, winking. 'Potatoes. Elzevir will know what I mean.' He paused, cocking his head on one side. 'If I'm not mistaken those dulcet tones are Annie's and she's calling you. Go now and tell her that I'm starving to death and would be most obliged if she could knock up an omelette or a sandwich. Anything other than rock cakes.'

Miranda reached up and kissed his whiskery cheeks. 'I love you, Grandpa.'

He blinked and a dull flush suffused his face. 'And I love you, precious. Now off you go and don't let Annie boss you around too much.'

Almost as the words left his mouth the outer door was wrenched open and Annie stamped into the building. 'I've been calling you, miss. Have you got cloth ears or something?'

'Sorry, I didn't hear you,' Miranda said truthfully. 'What is it?'

'You'd better come quick. You too, sir. She's off on one of her wild schemes again. It'll be worse than her plans for growing watercress in the bathtub.'

'I really don't think this is a good idea, Maggie.'

57

George ran his hand through his mop of unruly grey hair, leaving it standing on end so that he looked even more like Miranda's idea of a mad professor. If her grandfather was puzzled, then so was she. Why her grandmother had taken it into her head to ask Rita to stay with them at Highcliffe was baffling everyone, including Annie whose bottom lip was sticking out so far she could have balanced a half-crown on it. Rita had her head down and was apparently studying her feet. Miranda stared from one bemused face to the other not daring to say a word. Granny might be easy-going but she would not appreciate her decision being challenged by anyone. Miranda could only hope that this would be one of the rare occasions when Grandpa put his foot down, but her heart sank as she saw his expression change subtly even though he was smiling. Granny was used to getting her own way and woe betide anyone who dared to challenge her authority. A quick glance at her grandmother's set jaw and the determined tilt of her chin was enough to convince Miranda that this battle of wills had already been won.

'George, darling, it's just a temporary arrangement. I've told Rita that she can stay with us until Mrs Proffitt gets out of hospital. It seems the least we can do for the poor child.'

This last remark brought Rita's head up with a jerk. 'Don't talk about me as if I wasn't here, and I ain't a kid; I can look after meself. If the old girl's still in hospital after a stroke the chances are she's not going to get well enough to take me in. So if you'll run me to the station, guv, I'll get the next train back to London.'

'But where would you go?' Miranda could keep silent no longer. It was obvious that Rita was close to tears despite her attempt at bravado. 'You told me that you didn't have anybody else.'

'I'll get a job in a munitions factory, or maybe I'll go to the film studios at Ealing and see if I can find work there. I could be one of them starlets you read about in *Picturegoer* and *Picture Show*. I love them magazines, don't you?'

Maggie gave her a pitying look. 'But you're little more than a child, Rita. You need someone to look after you.' She nudged her husband in the ribs. 'Say something, George. You know that Rita's a minor; she shouldn't have to fend for herself. I can't see what objections you could possibly have to her staying here on a temporary basis.'

'We need to talk about this, Maggie.' He drew her aside.

Miranda waited anxiously for their decision. She had not warmed to Rita from the start and nothing she had said or done had changed that first impression, but a small voice in her head was telling her not to be so mean. She was seeing her with new and slightly more sympathetic eyes. When they met this morning she had thought her rather common and a bit annoying, but looking at her now, with her skinny arms clasped tightly around her equally scrawny frame, Miranda felt a sudden surge of sympathy. Not only was Rita's cotton dress faded and grubby, it was at least a size too large, suggesting that it was second-hand. Her cardigan was in holes where her bony elbows had worn through the wool, and her shoes were scuffed and down at heel. All that she owned was packed in that battered cardboard suitcase and, even worse, Rita was all alone in the world.

'What do you think, Miranda? Wouldn't you like to have someone of your own age to keep you company? We both feel that you should have a say in this.'

Miranda came back to the present with a jolt to find her grandmother waiting eagerly for her response. She knew what was expected of her. 'Yes, Granny.' She turned to Rita with an attempt at a smile. 'Please stay with us until Mrs Proffitt is well enough to leave hospital.'

'I'm sure it will work out very well for all concerned.' Maggie turned to Rita with an encouraging smile. 'It's entirely up to you, my dear. But I want you to know that you will be most welcome to stay here for as long as you like. We've plenty of room and it will be absolutely no trouble. What do you say?'

Rita shrugged her shoulders. 'I don't mind if I do, but what about him?' She jerked her head in George's direction. 'He's the guvner. Don't he get the last word?'

'If I do it will be the first time ever,' he said drily. 'And I see that I'm outnumbered. You're welcome to stay with us, Rita.' He moved towards the doorway. 'And now please may we have some lunch, Maggie? I don't know about these girls but I am absolutely starving.'

'Thank God someone's had the nerve to mention it,' Rita said with a heartfelt sigh. 'I'm so hungry I could eat a bloody horse, hooves and all.'

There was a stunned silence, but Maggie was the first to recover. 'Sandwiches will be the order of the day, Annie. I'm sure there must be some cheese in the larder.' She took Rita by the hand. 'Come with me, dear. I think we need to have a little talk before we go any further.' She glanced over her shoulder as they were about to leave the room. 'We'll join you in a minute. Rita and I have some things to sort out first.'

'I wouldn't like to be in her shoes,' Annie muttered as they left the room. 'But that young lady needs putting in her place. She's got too much to say for herself for my liking.'

'I'll be in my workshop.' George headed for the back door. 'Call me when lunch is ready.'

'I'll go and start unpacking.' Miranda was about to follow her grandmother and Rita from the kitchen but Annie caught her by the sleeve. 'No you don't, young lady. You can stay here and help me make the sandwiches. You've got all afternoon and evening to sort your things out.'

'I suppose so, but she's getting off lightly.'

Annie pulled a face. 'When you've suffered the rough edge of your granny's tongue as I'm sure young Rita's doing at this minute, then you'll be able to decide who's come off best. Now get along with you and less of the lip. I've been with this family too long to put up with any nonsense from spoilt little girls.'

'I'm not a little girl and I'm not spoilt.'

'I didn't mean you. I was thinking of Miss Eileen; she was the apple of your grandad's eye, even after Master Jack was born. She only had to ask and she could have had the top brick off the chimbley.'

'I only met Aunt Eileen once. She came home on leave with her husband and their two children.'

'I'd rather forget that visit. They were the two worst behaved little brats I've ever had the misfortune to meet. Anyway, we'd better stop gassing or you'll be eating lunch at teatime.' Taking a loaf from the bread bin she began slicing it. 'The cheese is in the larder and there's a jar of pickles on the shelf. By the way I'll need your ration book and Rita's too. I hope she doesn't eat too much. We're all out of horsemeat.' She made a gruff gurgling sound, laughing at her own joke. 'Cheer up, Miranda. It might never happen.'

'What?'

'Whatever it is that's made you look like you lost a shilling and found sixpence.' Annie's lined face creased into a caricature of a grin. 'Don't worry; your granny will knock Miss Rita into shape. She won't stand for any nonsense. Now spread the butter very thinly. There's a week's ration there, unless I can do another deal with Farmer Drake.'

Miranda paused with the knife clutched in her hand. 'What sort of deal?'

'Never you mind.' Annie tapped the side of her nose. 'Times are hard and going to get a lot harder before this war's over. We're going back to the old ways of bartering for things, but that's between you and me and the gatepost.'

Rita was unusually silent but appeared to be unchastened after her heart to heart with Maggie.

She limited her conversation to please and thank you during lunch and Miranda hoped that she was not going to sulk for the rest of the day. It was going to be hard enough to find common ground between them, and almost impossible if Rita would not meet her halfway.

The lack of verbal communication seemed to have affected everyone seated around the table and the silence was getting on Miranda's nerves. She swallowed a mouthful of sandwich. 'There were crowds of people at the railway station today,' she said, making an attempt at conversation. 'I overheard someone saying that they were evacuees from the Channel Islands.'

Maggie looked up, her eyes alight with interest. 'I heard that on the wireless this morning. Poor souls, it must be heartbreaking to be in such a terrible situation.'

'The authorities are doing all they can to help.' George selected another sandwich and put it on his plate. 'The WVS are doing a great job, but it's a logistical nightmare.'

'There seemed to be hundreds of them at the station,' Miranda said with a catch in her voice. 'They were mostly mothers with very young children.'

Maggie frowned thoughtfully. 'Is there anything we can do, George?'

'I think it's all in hand, my dear. Best leave it to those who are experienced in these matters.' He rose from the table. 'I'll be in the workshop if anyone needs me.'

'Yes, dear,' Maggie said meekly. She waited until the door closed behind him before rising to

63

her feet. 'Your grandfather is still coming to terms with the terrible things he saw at Dunkirk and the loss of his old friend, Miranda, and we must take care not to upset him. However, that mustn't stop us doing our Christian duty. We've got important work to do.'

'But, Granny, we haven't unpacked yet and you haven't said which bedroom Rita is to have.'

'Don't worry about me,' Rita said through a mouthful of bread and cheese. 'I can sleep in the dog kennel if I have to.'

'That won't be necessary. We can sort the sleeping arrangements out later. We're going into town.' Maggie snatched her handbag from a chair by the door. 'Get a move on, Miranda; you too, Rita. There are people who need our help.'

It seemed that they were doomed to walk the whole length of the beach road and even further. By the time they reached the town Miranda was hot and breathless and wishing she could throw the wretched gas mask into the sea. Rita had trudged along silent, but patently out of sorts. She had barely said one word since they left the house and then it was only to complain that she had a stone in her shoe.

The Esplanade was crowded with people and every sort of conveyance from buses to horse-drawn carts and pony traps. Maggie strode purposefully towards the ferry terminal but as they reached the Alexandra Gardens she came to a halt. The grounds around the theatre were overflowing with evacuees and the officials who were attempting to help them.

'Wait here,' Maggie said firmly. She crossed the road to speak to a group of women who seemed to be in charge.

If anything, Miranda thought with a feeling of sympathy, the volunteers looked even more tired and frustrated than the people they were helping. She waited patiently while her grandmother and the officials embarked on a seemingly endless conversation, but she was beginning to feel light-headed with fatigue. It had been a long day and an emotionally exhausting one.

'This is nuts,' Rita said, shifting from foot to foot. 'I dunno what she thinks we can do here.'

Miranda shielded her eyes from the sunlight. 'I think we're about to find out. She's coming back and it looks as though she's got a boatload of women and kids following her.'

'Oh my God.' Rita clapped her hand over her mouth. 'You and me are going to be sleeping in the outside lav at this rate.'

Maggie came striding towards them leading her flock. She paused for a moment as she caught sight of Tommy Toop, who had apparently fixed his cart and was touting for business. 'Tommy Toop, come here this minute.'

He approached her warily. 'What's up, missis?'

'Help the ladies to put their cases in your cart.'

He shook his head. 'I can't take that lot.'

Maggie bit her lip. Behind her the children were crying and some of the women were demanding to know what was going on. 'No,' she said at length. 'You're right. Miranda, take Rita and see if you can find someone with any kind of conveyance which will take these poor people

65

and their belongings to Highcliffe. Never mind the expense. This is an emergency.' She turned to the women with an encouraging smile. 'Don't worry, ladies. We're just finding suitable transport. Please be patient for a little while longer.' She jerked her head in the direction of the harbourside. 'Go on, girls. Chop-chop. You too, Tommy.'

'What on earth are we supposed to do?' Rita demanded as soon as they were out of earshot. 'There's no chance of finding a taxi in this dump.'

'Hang on,' Tommy said crossly. 'Just because you come from London don't mean you can be rude about our town. There's a war on, you know.'

Rita thrust her face close to his. 'Of course I know it, you moron. I wouldn't be seen dead in a backwater like this if it wasn't for the bloody war.'

Miranda could see another conflict looming and she decided to take charge of the situation. 'You two go along the harbour and I'll walk along St Mary Street. Maybe we can find a carter or someone with a van who's willing to take them to Highcliffe.' She hurried off before either of them could argue.

The atmosphere in the streets seemed to be charged with urgency, as if the war had suddenly arrived on their doorstep and shattered the peace of the seaside town. Miranda quickened her pace, dodging through the crowds and cutting down one of the narrow side streets as she headed for the town centre, but as she rounded the corner she cannoned into someone laden with cardboard boxes. Everything flew up in the air and Miranda stumbled off the edge of the kerb, falling to her knees in the gutter.

'Hell and damnation. Look where you're going.'

'I'm sorry.' Brushing the hair back from her face, Miranda squinted up at the tall figure of a man silhouetted against the sunshine.

Chapter Four

Miranda scrambled to her feet and found herself looking into the irate face of Raif Carstairs. 'Oh, it's you.'

He stared at her for a second and his angry expression melted into a grin. 'I thought I'd deposited you and your friend safely on the other side of town. You are a traffic hazard, Miss Beddoes.'

'I said I'm sorry, and anyway you weren't looking where you were going either.' She bent down to help him retrieve the boxes, most of which had remained intact, except for one which had burst open spilling its contents onto the pavement.

'Shoes,' he said, picking up a pair of high-heeled court shoes and replacing them in their box. 'Not mine I assure you. My mother buys everything by the dozen or half dozen. No half measures. I was collecting them for her. She's convinced that clothes and footwear will be rationed before long, hence the panic to buy out almost the entire stock.'

She piled the last box on top of the ones he was

already holding. 'Sorry again. I hope they're not damaged.'

'No harm done, but why the hurry? You came round that corner as if the devil himself was on your heels.'

'I've got to find transport for some evacuees. My grandmother has decided to take them in. She's like that.'

'I see. I'm afraid I've only got my two-seater or I'd offer to help.'

'Yes, of course.' Miranda backed away, hoping that he had not noticed that she was blushing furiously. Of all the people in the town she had to bump into it was the person who already thought of her as a silly young girl, and the fact that he was a dashing RAF pilot made it even worse. Her one aim now was to put as much distance between them as humanly possible. 'Got to go, sorry.'

'Stop apologising. Anyway, you'll never find any form of transport on a day like this, but I might be able to help.'

'You can?'

'I have a pal who owns a removal firm. If we're lucky he might have a van in the garage. We can but ask.'

'Thanks, but you needn't put yourself out for me.'

'I'm not. This is for the war effort. We've all got to do our bit, even collecting shoes for women who have enough pairs in their wardrobe to last a lifetime. Follow me, Miranda.' He strode off along the street clutching the shoe boxes in his arms. 'Hurry up,' he called over his shoulder.

'I've only got a twenty-four-hour pass, and so far today I've done nothing but run errands for my mother. Anyway, we'd better get there before they close or your grandmother's guests will have to walk to Highcliffe.'

Miranda hurried after him, but she could not help wondering if she was doing the right thing. Granny's reaction at the mention of Raif's name and her overt disapproval of someone she professed not to know was quite baffling. She realised with a start that she had almost lost sight of him in the crowd, and she had to run to catch up. Perhaps if her grandmother were to meet Raif she might change her mind, as it was his family she seemed to dislike and not him personally. Anyway, he seemed determined to help and she had the feeling that once he had made up his mind to something it would be very hard to persuade him otherwise.

She followed him to the inner harbour where he had parked his car. He tossed the shoe boxes into the boot, locked it and strode off without waiting to check that she was following. In fact her patience was being stretched to the limit and she was rapidly growing resentful of his cavalier treatment. She was planning to tell him so if she ever caught up with him, but then he stopped suddenly and ushered her into a yard filled with commercial vans. 'Wait here.' He went to the office and disappeared inside, emerging moments later and brandishing a set of keys. 'The only vehicle free is an open truck, but it's better than nothing.' He crossed the yard to where an ageing and slightly dilapidated lorry was parked, and opened the cab door. 'Hop in. You can ride shot-gun.'

She eyed the truck doubtfully, wondering whether it would be suitable, but as there did not seem to be any alterative she walked across the yard with as much dignity as she could muster and climbed into the passenger seat. 'This is very good of you, Flight Lieutenant Carstairs.'

He gave her a quizzical look as he leapt into the driver's seat. 'That's very formal, Miss Beddoes. How did you know my rank?'

'You introduced yourself to us this morning, and I know what two stripes on your cuff means. I'm not a child, Lieutenant.'

He was suddenly serious. 'I can see that, Miranda. You're a very enterprising young lady.'

'Now you're being patronising. Have you got any sisters?'

'Yes, as a matter of fact I have a younger sister.'

'Really? What's her name?'

'Isabel, but we always call her Izzie.' He started the engine. 'And before you ask, she's nineteen, several years my junior.'

'I'm not that nosey, Flight Lieutenant.'

He checked the rear view mirror and began to reverse out into the street. 'Where do we pick up our passengers?'

There was no mockery in his smile and in spite of everything she felt herself warming to him for the second time that day. She relaxed into the worn leather seat. 'Alexandra Gardens. I left them standing on the pavement with their babies and toddlers. Tommy Toop and Rita went off to see if they could get help too.'

'Let's go then. Operation Nippers about to commence.'

Forgetting her irritation, Miranda smiled. Perhaps she had misjudged him, she thought, giving him a sideways glance as he concentrated on the road ahead. He was not handsome like Jack, who had the archetypal good looks of a film star, but Raif Carstairs had a strong profile, a determined chin and a twinkle in his dark eyes. He had taken off his peaked cap, revealing a high forehead and wavy brown hair. He seemed to sense that she was staring at him and he took his eyes off the road long enough to give her an encouraging grin. 'Don't worry. We'll get them there, although I have a nasty feeling this contraption is being held together with string and rubber bands.' He swore softly beneath his breath as he crashed the gears. 'Sorry. I forgot I had a lady in the cab. I'm not used to driving a truck, but let's hope it doesn't conk out before we get you home.'

'You'll have plenty of people to get out and push.' Miranda leaned out of the window as they pulled out on to the Esplanade. 'There they are.'

He indicated and drew the cumbersome vehicle to a halt at the kerbside. Miranda jumped down to the pavement. 'This is the best we could do, Granny.'

Maggie did not look too impressed. 'Is it safe? And who is that man?' She squinted short-sightedly at Raif as he climbed out of the driver's seat, pausing for a moment to put on his cap.

'It's Flight Lieutenant Carstairs, Granny. He gave Rita and me a lift when the wheel came off Tommy's cart.'

Maggie's lips tightened into a thin line of disapproval. 'So that's the fellow.'

'How do you do, Mrs Beddoes?' Raif tipped his cap, but his smile faded as he met her ice-cool gaze.

'How do you do?' She turned to Miranda, lowering her voice. 'That contraption doesn't look roadworthy.'

'It's probably the last vehicle in town, Granny. I think you ought to thank Mr Carstairs for putting himself out like this.' Flushing with embarrassment, Miranda shot a sideway glance at Raif but if he had heard he did not seem unduly put out by her grandmother's ungrateful reaction.

'I'm glad to be able to help in an emergency,' he said smoothly. 'But I think we'd best get the women and children on board as quickly as possible, don't you?'

Maggie answered with an almost imperceptible nod of her head. 'I suppose so.'

He moved swiftly to the rear and opened the tailgate. 'I'm afraid this isn't exactly the height of luxury, but we should be able to get everyone in.'

Maggie peered into the truck. 'Whoever used it last didn't bother to clean up after them.' She beckoned to Tommy who was leaning against the railings with Rita at his side. 'Make yourself useful. There's a pile of sacks in the far corner. Climb up and spread them on the floor so that the ladies have something to sit on.'

Tommy scowled at her. 'I ain't here for me health, missis. What's in it for me?'

'Nothing, but you might get a better character reference when you next come up before Major

Beddoes if you do as I ask.'

He sidled across the pavement and climbed into the truck. When he had finished Miranda was quick to observe that Raif slipped him a florin for his pains and Tommy sauntered off to get his cart.

With Raif's help they managed to get the women and children settled, with Miranda and Rita the last to clamber onto the truck. Maggie sat in the cab with Raif and they set off for Highcliffe with everyone clinging on for dear life.

Halfway along the beach road Rita decided that the older children would benefit from a singsong and after a lot of encouragement she had them carolling 'Ten Green Bottles' at the tops of their voices. Miranda had never experienced anything like it and was frankly embarrassed by such loud behaviour in public. She was uncomfortably aware that they were receiving some strange looks from people walking or cycling home from work. By the time Raif pulled up outside Highcliffe they had started on 'Run Rabbit Run' and somewhat self-consciously Miranda had joined in, but the sight of a telegram boy in his navy-blue uniform sent a chill running down her spine and she held her hand up for silence. Not for nothing were these youngsters known as messengers of death. She jumped down from the truck and stood, frozen to the spot, staring at the fresh-faced boy who clutched a yellow envelope in his hand.

'Telegram for Mr and Mrs Beddoes.'

Miranda closed her eyes, praying silently. *Don't let it be my father. Please God, don't let it be him.*

There was complete silence as Maggie opened the envelope and stared at the telegram. Even the babies had stopped crying and their mothers were staring at her with anxious faces. Then, to Miranda's amazement, her grandmother threw back her head and laughed. A murmur of consternation rippled round the women. 'It's shock,' one of them whispered. 'I was like that when our cat got run over.'

Her companion nudged her in the ribs. 'Shh.'

'Granny, what is it?' Miranda's lips were so dry she could barely frame the words.

'I'll kill that son of mine,' Maggie said, wiping her eyes on a lace-edged hanky. She took a deep breath, tucking the crumpled telegram into her pocket with a rueful smile. 'I'm so sorry, everyone. I must apologise for the drama caused by my thoughtless son Jack. I'll have more than a few words to say to him when he gets here.'

Miranda found herself clutching Rita's hand so tightly that her knuckles stood out beneath her skin. She let go with a murmur of apology.

'It's not bad news then, Mrs Beddoes,' Raif said politely.

'On the contrary. My errant son says he's got leave and he's on his way home. If the Luftwaffe don't kill him I very well might.'

'You don't mean that, Granny.' Miranda glanced anxiously at Raif, hoping that he did not think that the entire Beddoes family was mad.

'No, of course I don't, but I just aged about twenty years. Then that's my younger son all over. Thoughtless, feckless and utterly charming, just like...' She broke off, frowning. 'Never mind.'

The telegram boy cleared his throat in an attempt to attract her attention. 'Any reply, lady?'

Maggie opened her handbag and took out her purse, handing him a coin. 'What I have to say to my son would set the paper on fire. No reply, thank you.' She turned to Raif. 'Thank you for your help. I'm sure the ladies are very grateful to you, but now I expect you want to get the truck back to its owner.'

If her cool tone came as a surprise after his efforts to help, Raif did not betray his inner feelings. He smiled. 'It was my pleasure.' He turned to the women who were attempting to control their overtired and over-excited children. 'Goodbye, ladies. I hope you find comfortable billets and that you can return to your homes in the not too distant future.' He climbed into the cab and drove off.

With mixed feelings, Miranda watched the vehicle lumber down the hill on its journey back to town. Fate had thrown her quite literally into Raif Carstairs' path twice that day, but now he was gone and it seemed unlikely that they would meet again. She should have been happy that the message in the telegram was good, but she felt deflated and even a little depressed. She came back to earth as Rita nudged her with a bony elbow. 'Wake up, sunshine. I think we're supposed to be helping.'

There was a sudden burst of conversation as her grandmother marshalled the women and children through the garden gate. Miranda was about to follow them but her legs felt like jelly and she was certain that they would give way beneath her if she attempted to take a single step.

'What's up with you?' Rita demanded.

'Nothing. I'm fine.'

'You're as white as a sheet.'

'I thought the telegram was telling them that my dad had been killed in action.' Miranda choked on a sob.

'Yeah, well, it happens. I never knew mine so I wouldn't know if he was alive or dead. Anyway, yours is okay so stop snivelling and do something useful. If we don't get in quick we'll find ourselves dossing down with dozens of snotty kids.'

Rita's abrasive manner was all that was needed to goad Miranda into action. 'You're right. I don't mind sharing my room with you at a push.'

'Ta, your majesty. That's very gracious, I'm sure.' Rita tempered her words with a cheeky wink and a grin. She linked her hand through Miranda's arm. 'I'm glad it wasn't your dad, and I can't wait to meet Jack. He sounds like a bit of all right.'

'Rita, you wouldn't! He's twenty-seven if he's a day.'

'I like older men. They're much more fun than boys my age and they've got more money. Has Jack got a girlfriend?'

'Lots. You'll have to join the queue and I don't fancy your chances.'

'We'll see about that. In fact, I'm beginning to think I'll like it here after all. Let's hope Mrs Proffitt doesn't get better too quickly.'

Miranda had no answer to this. 'We'd best go indoors and see what we can do to help.'

The moment they set foot in the house Miranda and Rita were sent to help Annie find enough clean linen to make up beds while Maggie allocated rooms, sorted out squabbling children and soothed anxious mothers with promises of tea and cakes. Miranda had overhead the last remark and smiled to herself, wondering if the ladies knew what they had let themselves in for.

'You'll have to share your room with Rita,' Maggie said as they passed her on the stairs. 'I'd have let the women use Jack's room, but as he's turning up like the proverbial bad penny they'll have to double up in the guest rooms.'

Annie stuck her head over the banisters. 'How many are we talking about, Mrs B? There seem to be dozens of kids running loose. Can't their mothers keep them under control?'

'They've just lost everything,' Maggie said severely. 'The least we can do is to help them rest and get themselves straight before they go on their way. But in answer to your question, there are seven mothers and eighteen children, although six of them are babes in arms. We can take drawers out of the tallboys to use as makeshift cots and I think there are some camp beds stored in the attic. We'll need to bring them down and all the bedding you can find.' She continued downstairs without waiting for anyone to question her.

Annie shook her head. 'Madness. That's what it is. You heard what your granny said, Miranda. You and Rita can fetch the camp beds and put them in the spare rooms and I'll see to the bedding. I don't trust you two in my linen cupboard, you'd muddle everything up.'

'Come on, Rita.' Miranda took the remainder of the stairs two at a time. She paused on the landing waiting for her to catch up.

'How many rooms in this gaff?' Rita demanded, staring around wide-eyed and obviously impressed. 'It's like a blooming hotel.'

'There are six bedrooms and a boxroom on this floor and then up the next flight is my Uncle Jack's room, that's my favourite because it leads out to the widow's walk. There are some smaller attic rooms, but they haven't been used for years.'

Rita followed her along the landing and up the second flight of stairs. 'What's a widow's walk when it's at home?'

'It's just a balcony really, overlooking the sea. This house was built in Victorian times by a sea captain. His wife used to watch for his ship coming home from the widow's walk.'

Rita frowned. 'But if she was a widow her old man would be dead.'

'I suppose a lot of the seafarers didn't return, and I don't think it's a proper widow's walk. As far as I know they're more American than English, so I think it's probably just a story that somebody made up to explain why they put a balcony at the top of this crazy old house.'

'Let's go and have a look,' Rita said as they reached the second floor. 'I want to see this widow's walk.'

'We haven't got time. Maybe later.'

'Spoilsport.'

Miranda spun round, glaring at her. 'Look,

78

Rita. I'm not mad about this either but if you're going to stay here you'll have to fit in and do what my grandparents say. It's their house and they've taken you in.'

'You too, don't forget.'

'I'm family.'

'Thanks for reminding me that I haven't got one.'

Miranda met her angry gaze and was instantly ashamed of her hasty words. 'Sorry. I didn't mean it to come out like that.'

'You'll be going back to your cosy home at the end of the summer holidays, but I'll be stuck here with the old lady I've never met, if she ever gets out of hospital.'

'I won't as it happens. Our house was bombed and I'm going to have to stay here for the duration, but I know I'm lucky and I'm sorry if I spoke out of turn.' Miranda held out her hand. 'Come on, Rita. Let's go and find these camp beds. I don't like going in the rooms where the maids used to sleep, it's spooky.'

'You mean the house is haunted?'

'Not that I know of, but I don't like the feel of them. I'd hate to have been a servant in those days.'

'It would have been better than starving in the gutter, mate.' Rita strode on ahead to the next door, which had been left ajar, but as she pushed it open a furry mass leapt out at her and she fell backwards with a cry of fright.

'It's all right,' Miranda said, chuckling as she bent down to stroke the irate cat. 'It's only Dickens. He must have come up here to escape from the kids.'

'The bloody thing almost gave me a heart attack.' Rita fanned herself with her hand, glaring at the cat who was now purring loudly and arching his back with pleasure as Miranda fussed over him.

'Poor old boy. Did that nasty girl frighten you?'

'Oh, for God's sake stop drooling over the animal and let's get this over.' Rita hesitated in the doorway, peering into the room. 'If you're a ghost get out of me way. I'm coming in.' She marched through the doorway. 'There's nothing in here but a lot of old junk and spiders' webs.'

Eventually, after a lot of running up and down stairs carrying the ancient wood and canvas camp beds, they turned drawers into makeshift cots for the babies and the spare rooms became dormitories for the mothers and children. Miranda was relieved to find that her grandmother had not allocated her old room to anyone else, even though she would have to share it with Rita.

It was now late afternoon and the sunlight streamed through the large bay window that overlooked the back garden and the wide sweep of the bay. Rita flung herself down on one of the twin beds and closed her eyes. 'I could kip for a week,' she said, yawning. 'Wake me up in time for tea.'

Miranda would have liked to unpack her cases and hang her clothes in the bird's-eye walnut wardrobe, but she had barely begun when Annie poked her head round the door and informed them that their services were needed in the kitchen. It was a command rather than a request and Miranda knew better than to argue. She followed Annie downstairs with Rita trailing behind them.

The air in the kitchen was blue with cigarette smoke and filled with steam from the kettle singing away on the hob. Maggie had already made one pot of tea and was in the process of making another. She left this to Annie and instructed Miranda to give the children milk or lemonade, and Rita was left to dole out the remainder of the rock cakes and given a packet of Rich Tea biscuits to hand round.

Miranda was pleased to see that the women seemed to be in better spirits and beginning to talk things over between themselves. She felt genuinely sorry for them and it was obvious that they were all deeply distressed by their recent experiences, but the older children seemed to think the whole thing was a game, and fortified by food and drink they began to explore. Annie was struggling to cope with the air of a martyr about to be burnt at the stake, but Maggie appeared to be in her element. Miranda could only guess that the years her grandmother had spent as an army wife both in India and East Africa must have prepared her to rise to such an occasion, which she was doing magnificently.

'Miranda.' Maggie took her aside. 'We have to think about feeding these people. I want you to go to the coach house and liberate the sack of potatoes that Elzevir delivered to your grandfather earlier this afternoon.'

'But he needs them for his experiments.'

81

'Feeding hungry mouths is more important.' Maggie pressed a large iron key into her hand. 'Go now while he's taking his constitutional along the cliff top, and you'd best take Rita with you. A hundredweight of potatoes is too much for one girl to carry.'

Miranda unlocked the door but Rita was first inside the coach house, exclaiming in wonder. 'I thought places like this was just in the flicks. What with haunted attics and this old ruin, you could make horror films here. Before Mum got sick we used to go to the pictures once a week. I loved *The Raven* with Boris Karloff, and then there was *Sweeny Todd: the Demon Barber of Fleet Street* with Tod Slaughter. I can't get enough of creepy movies.'

'It's just an old coach house, only now it's used as a garage and Grandpa's workshop. You've got an over-active imagination, Rita.' Miranda headed for the place where her grandfather kept the sack of potatoes, but when she realised that she was on her own she had to retrace her steps. She caught Rita peering beneath Chloe's dust sheet.

'Blooming hell! It's a posh motor. Don't tell me that your grandad drives this.'

'He doesn't and don't touch. This is Chloe and she belongs to my Uncle Jack. Now leave her alone and help me with the sack. I can't lift it by myself.'

Rita replaced the covers with a sigh. 'I'd give me eye teeth for a ride in that thing. I wonder what else you got hidden in the Gothic mansion.'

'Shut up,' Miranda said, losing her patience.

'For the last time, Rita, are you going to help me or not?'

Later that evening, when the evacuees had been fed on mashed potato and fried eggs, and the mothers had taken their children up to their respective rooms, the house was suddenly quiet. Miranda had left Rita unpacking her suitcase with strict instructions not to move her things. Sharing the room that had been hers for as long as she could remember was not something she would have agreed to had it not been forced upon her, but she kept telling herself that she must be kind to Rita, who had lost everything. She must not be mean and selfish. She did not want to end up like Auntie Eileen who had houseboys to wait on her hand and foot, and according to Annie expected the same treatment whenever she deigned to visit her parents.

Miranda made her way downstairs, moving as quietly as possible so that she would not disturb anyone. Clutched in her hand was the photograph of her father in its dented silver frame, the only personal item she had managed to salvage from her parents' room before the chimney stack collapsed. She tiptoed to the drawing room and placed it on the mantelpiece next to a photo of her grandfather in his army uniform. The startling likeness of father and son brought a lump to her throat and she stood for a moment, gazing at the smiling images of the two most important men in her life. 'Goodnight, Dad,' she whispered, closing her eyes and screwing up her face as she had done as a child when she said her prayers at bedtime. 'Please God keep my dad safe from harm, and Maman too, wherever she is now.'

The atmosphere in the room had become oppressive and she needed some fresh air. It was almost ten o'clock and the long summer evening was drawing to an end as she slipped out through the French windows onto the veranda. Deep shadows were engulfing the shrubbery, disguising the fact that there was an abundance of bindweed and brambles attempting to strangle the mockorange and Weigela. Night-scented stocks filled the warm air with their sweetness, adding to the perfume of the tea roses in the flowerbed below the iron railings. Through the open windows of the small sitting room that was her grandmother's retreat, Miranda could hear the strains of music emanating from the wireless. She could only guess that Granny had taken refuge there, and was probably snoozing in the saggy old chair that she refused to throw out, even though the upholstery had worn through on the arms and the springs beneath the cushions had long ago given up the ghost.

Grandpa was probably in his study where he retired every evening using the excuse that he had official papers to read before morning, although Miranda knew that he went there to smoke his pipe and enjoy a little peace and quiet. Granny disapproved of smoking, which demonstrated how far she was prepared to go in order to make the evacuees feel at home. No one in the family would normally have been allowed to smoke in the house, even Jack.

Miranda stood at the top of the flight of steps

leading down to the garden and breathed deeply. The sweet scents of summer, mingling with the salty smell of the seaweed washed up on the beach, brought back happy memories of family holidays spent at Highcliffe. She felt her throat constrict as she remembered her father teaching her to swim in the warm shallows close to the beach, and her mother sunbathing on the sand with a straw hat shading her face. She recalled outings to the Swannery to see the newly hatched baby swans and cream teas in the surrounding villages. They had gone shrimping at Ferrybridge and taken long walks along the coastal path on hot summer afternoons, ending with a cream tea in a quaint tearoom. It all seemed like a dream now, far removed from the reality of barbed wire and concrete and the constant fear of air raids. A shelter had been dug into the lawn at the far side of the garden and with its spiky covering of turf it looked like a giant hedgehog slumbering in the lengthening shadows. She sighed, wondering if life would ever be the same again.

'Hey there.'

Startled, she stifled an involuntary cry as a man emerged from the shrubbery.

Chapter Five

'Sorry, darling. Did I make you jump?'

'Uncle Jack – you brute.' She sank down on one of the steamer chairs, clutching her hand to her racing heart. 'You scared me half to death.'

He took the steps two at a time and dropped his valise on the decking. 'I didn't know you'd be here, poppet.'

'You're in for it,' she said, smiling and shaking her head. 'I thought Granny was going to have a heart attack when she saw the telegram boy.'

'I know. I'd had a few sherbets when I sent it and I realised too late that it was a damned silly thing to do, but it was gone midnight and I knew everyone would be tucked up in bed, and that I wouldn't have time today.'

'Why couldn't you contact Granny this morning? What have you been up to?'

He perched on the veranda railing, tossing his uniform cap onto the rattan table. Taking a cigarette case from his pocket he flipped it open and offered it to her. 'Have you acquired the habit yet?'

She shook her head. 'No, I haven't. Anyway, please be serious for a moment and tell me what's going on.'

He lit a cigarette and inhaled deeply, exhaling with a satisfied sigh. 'I needed that. Had to travel all the way in a non-smoking compartment; what

86

we men do for love.'

She rose to her feet, her patience stretched to the limit. 'Uncle Jack, if you don't stop talking in riddles I'll push you into the rose bed.'

'For heaven's sake, stop calling me Uncle Jack; it makes me feel as if I'm forty and over the hill.'

'Okay, I will, but only if you start from the beginning. Why are you here at all and who's your latest popsy?'

He stared at her in mock horror. 'Who taught you such vulgar slang, Miranda?'

'You did, Jack.'

'Fair enough. Well, as it's you I'll tell all, but it's a secret. I don't want the family to find out. Not yet, anyway.'

'My goodness. You must be serious about this one.'

'So young and yet so cynical.' He drew on his cigarette and blew a perfect smoke ring. 'She's the prettiest little thing you ever saw. Not that I'd expect you to appreciate that, but this one is different. She's a lady.'

'No! Well, that's a turn up for the books. You usually go for the peroxide blonde bimbos.'

'You've grown up, Miranda Beddoes. Where's that cute little girl with pigtails and freckles who used to think I was the sparrow's chirp?'

'I still do, but as you say I'm an adult now, and there's a war on. Everyone will have to grow up, including you.'

His smile faded and he flicked the dog-end into the flowerbed. 'I'm under orders to join my squadron tomorrow afternoon, and as far as I can see we're going to be operational straight away.'

'I don't like the sound of that.'

He leaned over to pat her on the shoulder. 'Nor me, darling. But we've got to sort this thing out soon and I'm going to do my bit.'

'And your new girlfriend? Where does she fit in?'

'She's beautiful and she's got brains.' He held up his hands. 'I know, not my type at all, but I can't help that. I met her at a party last night and I'm well and truly smitten.'

'You only met her last night?' Miranda stared at him in disbelief. 'That's quick, even for you, Jack.'

'Love at first sight, poppet. A coup de foudre as the Froggies call it.'

'And does she feel the same about you?'

'I very much hope so.'

'And are you going to see her again?'

'I'm seeing her tomorrow, but I don't want anyone to find out. Not yet, anyway. You won't tell on me, Miranda?'

'Tell what?' Maggie burst through the open French windows like an avenging angel, but the illusion was somewhat marred by the fact that she was wearing her dressing gown and slippers. 'What have you done this time, you libertine?' Despite her angry words she was smiling. 'You'd better have a good reason for scaring me half to death, you bad boy.'

Jack leapt to his feet and enveloped her in a hug. 'I'm sorry, Mother. I couldn't phone because it was very late at night and...'

'And you were drunk,' Maggie said, holding him at arm's length. 'Why doesn't that surprise me, Jack? Aren't you ever going to turn into a respectable man like your father?'

He looped his arm around her shoulders. 'I'm a reformed character, dearest. But before I collapse with hunger, could you rustle up something for me to eat? I'm absolutely starving.'

'Come to the kitchen and I'll see if there's anything left. The gannets are going to eat us out of house and home.'

'Gannets? What are you talking about, Mother?'

'Evacuees,' Miranda said before her grandmother had a chance to explain. 'Granny is being a war hero, I mean heroine, and she's taken in refugees from the Channel Islands. The house is bursting at the seams with mothers and their kids. I'm even having to share with Rita.'

Jack looked from one to the other, shaking his head. 'Who the hell is Rita? What's going on, Mother?'

Maggie took him by the arm. 'I'll explain everything.'

'I can scramble eggs.' Miranda was about to follow them but her grandmother barred her way.

'It's bedtime for you, young lady.'

'But Granny...'

'Rita will be lonely on her first night away from home and you've had a busy day. You can see Jack in the morning but now it's up the wooden hill to Bedfordshire.'

Next morning Miranda was up early and after a cat's lick of a wash she put on a clean frock, brushed her hair and slipped her feet into her sandals before going downstairs. She had planned to make an early morning cup of tea for Jack in the hope of finding out exactly what was going on in his complicated love life, but as she opened the kitchen door she was engulfed by a wave of noise and cigarette smoke and the aroma of hot fat sizzling in a frying pan.

Standing by the kitchen range, wearing one of Annie's floral pinafores, Jack tossed a pancake and slid it onto a plate held by one of the older evacuee children. 'Form an orderly queue, if you please,' he said cheerfully.

The children obediently fell into line clutching their plates like small Oliver Twists. Jack poured a ladleful of batter into the pan. 'Miranda, you're just in time for a pancake, but you'll have to get to the end of the queue. There's no favouritism here.'

She shook her head. 'No, thanks. I'm not very hungry.'

'He's a dab hand at cooking,' one of the women said, smiling. 'You don't know what you're missing, dear.'

'I'll be with you in a minute,' Jack said, raising his voice to make himself heard over the babble of conversation and the eager chatter of the children. 'I expect the ladies could do with some more tea, though. Would you be an angel and make a fresh brew?'

'Yes, sir.' Miranda gave him a mock salute and picked up the big brown teapot. She had filled it several times before Jack finished cooking. He took off his apron with a flourish. 'I'm afraid the cookhouse is closed for the time being, ladies.' He smiled and bowed as the mothers gave him a round of applause. 'Thank you for that, and now I'm sure I can leave you to clear up the terrible mess I've made.' He gave them his most charming smile. 'I am but a mere male and can't compete when it comes to making order out of chaos.' He ushered Miranda hastily from the room without giving them the chance to object.

Outside in the sunny back yard he lit a cigarette. 'Thank God I'm only expected to fly an aeroplane. I take my hat off to cooks and chefs slaving away over a hot stove all day.'

'Just what are you playing at?' Miranda studied his handsome face, wondering what it was about her uncle that made women fall over themselves to please him. It was not just his undeniable good looks or inborn charm; there must be something else. He could treat women badly and yet they always seemed to forgive him. It was a mystery.

Jack took a last drag on his cigarette and tossed it onto the concrete, grinding it to pieces beneath the toe of his shiny black shoe. 'Come on, Miranda. Let's go for a spin in Chloe.'

'Lovely. But where to?'

He strode off, calling over his shoulder. 'That's for me to know and you to find out.'

It was cool in the country lanes where the ancient beeches, oaks and horse chestnuts leaned over to interlace their branches forming a tunnel of green shade. They had travelled several miles in companionable silence but when Jack slowed Chloe down, changing gear as they approached the entrance to what appeared to be a country estate, Miranda's curiosity got the better of her.

'Where are we going?'

He signalled left and drove through the open gateway. Miranda had often passed the intricate wrought-iron gates on her way to Dorchester, but until today she had not given a second thought to what lay behind them. She twisted round in her seat. 'Who lives here?'

'She does,' he said with a beatific smile. 'The love of my life lives here. This is my idea of heaven.'

'So why the secrecy?'

'It's a long story and even I don't know the whole of it.' He pulled up in front of the main entrance and switched off the engine. 'Wait here for a moment. I'm not sure what sort of reception I'll get.' He climbed out without giving her a chance to interrogate him further and he bounded up the front steps to the impressive Georgian portico.

Miranda sat in the car, hardly able to contain her curiosity. The house was set like a jewel in a vast expanse of private parkland, and it seemed like another world as yet untouched by war. It was like stepping back in time with a mystery thrown in for good measure. The suspense was almost too much to bear, but luckily she did not have long to wait before the door was opened by a middle-aged woman wearing a white pinafore. She did not look grand enough to be the lady of the manor and the house was certainly large enough to warrant staff to run it, even in wartime. Perhaps it was a secret military establishment and Jack had been recruited to work as a spy. Miranda was mulling this over when Jack turned and beckoned to her. She needed no further encouragement to leap out of the car and join him at the top of the steps.

'Mrs Beasley, this is my niece, Miranda. She's very keen to meet Isabel.' He gave Miranda's hand a gentle squeeze and she realised this was her cue.

'Yes, that's right,' she said with an emphatic nod.

'You'd better come in, sir.' Mrs Beasley stood aside, ushering them into the spacious entrance hall.

Miranda gazed about her and was both impressed and overawed by the classic simplicity of the marble-tiled floor and the high ceiling supported by Corinthian columns. A cantilevered staircase swept upwards to a galleried first floor and the scent of roses and lilies filled the air. It was a bit like a film set but Miranda was quick to note the homely touch of a dog's lead draped over a hall chair and a riding hat set askew on the alabaster bust of a long dead poet.

Mrs Beasley closed the front door. 'If you'd like to wait in the morning room I'll tell her you're here.' She led the way to a large sunny room at the back of the house.

'What's going on?' Miranda demanded as soon as they were alone. 'I don't understand it, Jack. If you've only got a few hours with your girlfriend, why have you dragged me along to play gooseberry?'

He met her puzzled gaze with a rueful grin. 'Sorry, kid. I shouldn't have left you in the dark, but it's a bit delicate.'

'Oh, for goodness' sake, Jack, spit it out. You like this girl and she likes you. What's the problem?'

'An old family feud, that's the problem. The Carstairs and the Beddoes don't get along. I don't know the full story but it goes back years, and I was afraid that if her family got wind of our relationship they would try to put a stop to it.'

'Carstairs?' Suddenly it was beginning to make sense. 'Has she got a brother called Raif?'

Jack's eyes widened. 'D'you know him?'

'Not really, but he gave Rita and me a lift home when there was no one to meet us at the station. Then when Granny sent me to find transport for the evacuees I happened to bump into him and he offered to help.'

'I can't imagine him going out of his way to help the Beddoes family.'

'I don't know about that. Anyway, he borrowed a truck and drove us all home. I thought that Granny was a bit cool towards him and I couldn't understand why.'

'Well, now you know, and that's why I brought you here today. I thought it would look better from the Carstairs' point of view if I had you to chaperone their daughter.'

She linked her hand through his arm. 'You really have got it bad, haven't you?'

'I was smitten the moment I saw her. You'll see why when you meet her. She's an absolute angel.'

'So you said before. I can't wait to meet this paragon.'

'Shh. Someone's coming.' Jack pulled free from her to straighten his tie as the door opened and a pretty, fair-haired girl hurried into the room.

'Jack. I didn't think you'd come.' She stopped, gazing at Miranda with a puzzled half-smile. 'Hello.'

Sensing Isabel's confusion on seeing her new boyfriend with another girl, and realising that her normally urbane uncle was suddenly at a loss for words, Miranda stepped forward holding out her hand. 'I'm Jack's niece, Miranda. How do you do?'

'How do you do, Miranda? I'm so happy to meet a member of Jack's family. I daresay he's told you that our parents don't exactly see eye to eye.'

'You look lovely, darling,' Jack said, brushing her cheek with a kiss. 'I couldn't wait to see you again.'

She blushed prettily. 'Don't, Jack. You'll embarrass Miranda.'

'Is your brother at home?' The words spilled from Miranda's lips before she could stop herself. 'I mean, he did us a big favour yesterday. I just wanted to say thank you.'

'Did he?' Isabel eyed her curiously. 'I didn't realise that Raif knew Jack's family.'

'Is he at home?' Jack glanced round the room as if he expected Raif to pop up from behind a chair. 'Did you tell him about me, Izzie?'

She shook her head. 'No, I didn't get a chance. He was called back to the aerodrome at Warmwell last night even though he had a twenty-four-hour pass. I think his leave has been cancelled, that's why I'm surprised to see you here today, Jack. I thought you would have gone by now.'

'Actually that's a huge coincidence. I'm to

report at Warmwell late this afternoon.'

'So you'll be in my brother's squadron?'

'It looks like it. Anyway, I've got until after lunch, so I thought perhaps we could all go for a spin in Chloe, and have a bite to eat at a country pub, unless you've got anything else planned.'

'Not a thing and that sounds like heaven, but is it all right with you, Miranda? I mean it seems a bit unfair for me to butt in when you've only seen your uncle for such a brief time.' Isabel's smile transformed her face from pretty to almost beautiful. If it had not been for a slightly crooked tilt of her lips and a mischievous dimple in her right cheek her features would have had the perfect symmetry so beloved of the Renaissance sculptors. Miranda could see why her uncle had been utterly captivated by Isabel Beddoes. Not only was she lovely to look at but she was nice as well, and that in Miranda's experience was a rare quality. The girls she had known at school who were considered to be the best lookers were often conceited and sometimes bitchy. 'I don't mind if you don't, Isabel.'

'That's wonderful, and please call me Izzie. I feel as though I've done something naughty if people call me Isabel.'

'Perhaps I should ask your parents first,' Jack said anxiously. 'I'm prepared to tell your father that I've disowned my family if that would make him view me more favourably.'

'Daddy is still in London,' Isabel said with a giggle. 'He only comes down at weekends and not even then if he's operating on Saturday morning.'

'He's a brain surgeon,' Jack said proudly. 'A top

96

class brain surgeon, and Izzie's mother is an actress.'

Miranda was doubly impressed. 'Is she famous?'

'She's quite well known in the theatrical world,' Isabel said modestly. 'She's in *Rebecca* at the Queen's Theatre at the moment, although it does worry me that they're both in London. If Hitler decides to bomb the capital I hate to think what will happen.'

'That's what the RAF is for, darling. We'll stop the Luftwaffe before they have a chance to drop their bombs on London.' Jack glanced at the Edwardian lantern clock on the mantelpiece. 'I think perhaps we'd best get going. Time is the enemy today.'

'I'll just tell Mrs Beasley not to expect me back until later,' Isabel said, moving towards the doorway. 'If you'd like to wait for me in the car, I won't be a moment.'

'Isn't she wonderful?' Jack murmured as the door closed on her. 'She's the best thing that ever happened to me, Miranda.'

'Yes. She's absolutely lovely.'

'Promise me that you'll keep an eye on her while I'm away.'

'How can I do that if our families are at loggerheads? What's wrong with them?'

'I don't know, sweetheart. It's something that happened before I was born, but it mustn't be allowed to blight my relationship with the most perfect girl I've ever met.'

'The silly old feud didn't seem to bother Raif. He was a perfect gentleman.'

'It looks as if I might have been posted to his

squadron, so I'm going to do my best to sort this thing out once and for all. Anyway, let's enjoy today. Come along, Miranda, we mustn't keep Izzie waiting.'

Sitting in the dicky seat and being third party to a couple who were just starting out on what was obviously going to be a passionate love affair was not Miranda's idea of a great day out. If she had been less fond of Jack she might have asked to be dropped off at home after the first half hour, but she suffered in silence and made an effort to play her part, although she really could not imagine that her presence made the slightest bit of difference. Chaperonage must have gone out with the high button boot, but if it helped smooth the path of true love, she was willing to do anything that would make her uncle happy.

They had lunch in a pub on the outskirts of the town but Miranda was the only one who seemed to have much of an appetite, and having trailed after the lovers in Thorncombe Woods following the Roman road as far as Black Heath, she was both footsore and weary. Eventually, after tactfully turning away while they kissed for the final time, Miranda led the way back to the car and tried to look as if being a chaperone was her ultimate choice for whiling away a Saturday afternoon. In the end their outing was curtailed by the fact that there was not enough petrol in the tank to take them very far, and Jack had to report to the air station before five o'clock.

Miranda climbed into the passenger seat and waited while Jack and Izzie said a fond goodbye.

Their emotional parting on the steps of Thornleigh Court would have had the whole audience sobbing into their hankies had it been on stage, and Miranda had a lump in her throat even though she was relieved that her part in their clandestine meeting was now over. She tried valiantly to cheer Jack up as he drove home, but he seemed determined to act like a star-crossed lover and she sat in silence for the rest of the way.

Jack brought Chloe to an abrupt halt outside the coach house. 'Oh, God, no,' he muttered, as his mother emerged from the house and came striding towards them with her skirts billowing and hairpins flying in all directions. If the day had been less than wonderful for Miranda she could see that it was about to get worse. She realised that she had been gone for hours without having told anyone where she was going. The look on her grandmother's face as she approached the car said it all. Jack leapt out of the driver's seat to stand before his mother like a small boy caught stealing jam tarts from the larder.

'Where the hell have you been, Jack?' Maggie slammed the car door so violently that flakes of rust showered onto the concrete. 'Your father and I have been out of our minds with worry. How could you be so thoughtless?'

He wrapped his arms around her rigid body. 'I'm so sorry, Mother. I took Miranda for a last spin before Chloe is mothballed for the rest of the war, and I completely forgot the time.'

Miranda clutched her hands tightly in front of her. 'I'm sorry, too, Granny. We had lunch in a pub and went for a walk in Thorncombe Woods.

We didn't stop to think.'

'No, you didn't. You're just as thoughtless and selfish as your uncle. You might have met with a fatal accident or been strafed by German planes and left mortally wounded in a field for all we knew.'

George appeared in the coach house door, looking puzzled. 'What's all the fuss about, Maggie?'

She threw up her hands. 'It's these two. They've bowled up as if they've had a lovely day out.'

He smiled vaguely. 'Well, I hope they have enjoyed themselves. For heaven's sake, the boy has only had a few hours home leave. God knows what he'll be facing when he reports for duty.'

'Trust you to be on his side. I've been left to cope with a houseful of evacuees on my own. Nobody pays any attention to my feelings.'

'As I recall you took them in, Maggie. It was your idea and had nothing to do with Jack or Miranda. Highcliffe isn't a refugee camp, my dear. Perhaps you should have thought of that before you offered largesse to the masses.'

'I took pity on a handful of unfortunate women and their children. I did my duty, and anyway they'll be gone from here on Monday. The Red Cross have made the necessary arrangements.' Maggie drew herself up to her full height. 'But I'd expect more support from my family and a little common courtesy from my degenerate son.'

'Come along now, Mother dear. You know what I'm like. I do things without thinking, and I'm desperately sorry if I've upset you.' Jack shot an appealing glance at his father. 'I think a tot of your so-called embrocation might be called for at this juncture.'

'I've never called it that,' George said, frowning. 'And it's definitely not for consumption and it certainly isn't for topical application to the human body.'

'But it's very efficacious in times of stress, Father. Ask Elzevir and Farmer Drake.'

Maggie's fierce expression faded into a guilty look that might have been comical at any other time. She nudged her son in the ribs. 'That's supposed to be a secret,' she muttered beneath her breath.

'No one knows about my experiments outside the family.' George gave her a searching look. 'Do they, Maggie?'

'Of course not, dear. Go back to your laboratory. I'll call you when dinner is ready.' She turned to Jack, scowling ominously. 'You've put your foot in it now, my boy. What a trial you are.' She marched back to the house.

He turned to Miranda with a weary smile. 'She'll get over it. I'm her blue-eyed boy, after all. Come and talk to me while I pack my things. I'll have to be off soon.'

'Perhaps we'd better go round to the French windows and creep in through the drawing room,' Miranda said tactfully. 'We're not too popular at the moment.'

'Good plan.' Jack fell into step beside her. 'I'm sorry I've upset the old folks but it was worth it to spend the day with Izzie. I'm absolutely crazy about her.'

'No! I would never have guessed.'

'You wait until you fall head over heels for some

young chap, you'll know how it feels then.' He stopped suddenly as they emerged from the shadow of the outbuildings onto the wide sweep of lawn at the back of the house. 'This is what it's all about, Miranda,' he said, encompassing the view of the cliffs and sea with Portland rising from the mist with a wave of his hands. 'This is what we're fighting for, and now I've got a real reason to come through it all.'

'You will be careful, won't you, Jack? You won't go all heroic and stupid on me?'

'Careful is my middle name, sweetheart. It's going to take more than the Luftwaffe to bring Jack Beddoes down.' He turned to her, his expression suddenly serious. 'You will keep in touch with Izzie, won't you, Miranda? And if the worst should happen to me, I hope you'd continue to be her friend.'

She had never seen him in such a serious frame of mind and she struggled to find the right words of comfort. She nodded and reached out to hold his hand. 'Of course I would, but you mustn't think like that.'

He was about to say something but the French windows burst open and a rush of small children tumbled out onto the veranda and sped down the steps to the lawn. Rita followed them more slowly. She struck a pose. 'The little sods have busted one of your gran's china thingummytites. Got any glue?'

Chapter Six

He had gone. Jack had left with his mother's forgiveness and his father's blessing, and only Miranda knew that he had a bottle of raw spirit packed in his overnight bag. Elzevir had given him a lift on his cart and Miranda suspected that another bottle of the euphemistically entitled embrocation might have changed hands by way of payment. She could only hope that her grandfather never discovered the illicit use of his attempt to solve the fuel shortages.

The evacuees had been fed and the younger ones were being made ready for bed. Miranda could hear sounds of merriment and a lot of splashing emanating from the bathroom as she made her way upstairs seeking the solitude of her own room. She had put up with Rita grumbling all the time they were helping Annie with the supper things, and she had narrowly escaped a lecture from her grandmother thanks to one of the young mothers who was convinced that her baby was mortally ill, although luckily it turned out to be nothing worse than colic and nappy rash.

Unused to living with a large family, Miranda had wanted nothing other than to curl up with a book, but the older children were still in the garden, rampaging through the shrubbery as they searched for a lost ball. Their shrieks and shouts were no doubt music to their mothers' ears, but Miranda pulled down the sash, closing her window with a decisive bang. She had spent ages gluing the head and an arm back on one of the Dresden shepherdesses and she could only hope and pray that nothing else got broken. She was about to sit on the window seat and open her book when Rita burst into the room.

'Do us a favour, ducks? Lend me something half decent to wear.'

'Why? Where are you going?'

'To town, of course. It's Saturday night and I ain't staying here with all those kids rushing around and screeching their heads off.'

'But you don't know anybody in Weymouth. Where will you go?'

'I dunno, but there must be a dance hall of some sort, or maybe I'll go to the flicks. I don't suppose you've got any cash on you? I'm a bit short as it happens.'

'Have you asked my grandmother if you can go out? I don't think she'd approve of you going off on your own.'

'She can't stop me.'

'She feels responsible for you, Rita.'

'Very kind of her, I'm sure, but she's got no say in what I do. If I can look after meself in London, I'm sure I can cope in this one-horse town. Come on, Miranda, don't be stuffy. I'm going anyway, but all my duds are creased like rags and I'm flat broke.'

Miranda could see that Rita was going to do what she wanted no matter what anyone said. She opened the wardrobe and rifled through her clothes, selecting a crêpe de Chine dress with a delicate floral pattern on a white background. 'Will this do?'

Rita's eyes sparkled as she took it from her, holding it up against her slender frame. 'I might have to pad the bust out with a couple of socks, but it'll do fine. I don't suppose you've got a nice pair of shoes that would go with it?'

She was about to say no, but she realised that Rita's eagle eye had spotted the white high-heeled strappy sandals that her mother had bought for a friend's wedding and had only worn once before passing them on. 'They're almost new,' Miranda said hastily. 'I haven't had a chance to wear them yet.'

Rita bent down to snatch them from the shelf. 'Don't worry, love. I'll break them in for you. Are you sure you won't come with me?'

'No, thanks. I've upset the family enough today.' Relenting, Miranda reached for her handbag and took out her purse. 'How much do you need?'

'Ten bob should do it.'

'Ten shillings. That's half of what I've got.'

Rita took the note and stuffed it in her purse. 'I'll pay you back, ducks. If I'm going to be stuck here for a while I'll need money, and there must be plenty of work locally. Although if this bloody war goes on much longer we'll probably end up in the army; not that I'd mind being with all those soldiers. It might be quite fun.' She undid the buttons on her frock and let it fall to the ground.

Miranda tried not to stare but she could not help noticing that Rita's bra was obviously homemade and she was wearing navy-blue school knickers. 'I don't want to be rude, but those will show through.'

'I know,' Rita said, pulling a face. 'Awful, ain't they? But these are all I've got.'

Miranda opened a drawer at the base of the wardrobe and fished out some of her own undies. She tossed them onto the bed. 'Help yourself.'

'Are you serious?' Rita picked up a Kestos bra and a pair of white silk panties. 'These must have cost a fortune.'

'My mother paid for them. She buys all my clothes for me.'

'Lucky you.'

'You can have them, Rita. I don't want them back.' Miranda averted her gaze as Rita stripped off her underwear.

'I'll still need them socks,' she said, sticking out her chest. 'You've got bigger boobies than me.'

Miranda retired to the window seat and picked up her book. 'Granny locks the doors at ten. If you're going to be later than that you'd better warn her.'

'And have her tell me I've got to stay in and be a good little girl? Not bloody likely. I'll get in somehow even if I have to pick the lock.'

'You wouldn't?'

'Of course not, silly. Just because I come from the East End don't mean that I was born with a jemmy in me hand.' She chortled with laughter. 'You should see your face, Miss Prim and Proper. Don't worry, love. I'm a good girl, most of the time.' Rita slipped on the dress and shoes, primping in the mirror. 'I don't suppose you've got a bag

106

to go with this, have you, Manda, old girl?'

Raif was just about to kiss her when Miranda woke up. It had seemed so real that she could hardly believe that she had been dreaming. She opened her eyes, staring into the darkness, and her heart was thudding against her ribs. There it was again, the clatter of something hitting the windowpanes. It did not sound like rain and it was the middle of summer, too warm for hailstones. She sat up and slid her legs over the edge of the bed, cocking her head on one side and listening. Perhaps it was her imagination, but then it happened again and she was on her feet, padding over to the window to draw the blackout curtains. It was not quite a full moon but the garden, cliff top and sea were bathed in silvery light making the shadows seem even darker and deeper. Another miniature fusillade hit the windowpane level with her head and she threw up the sash.

'Oy. It's me.' Rita was standing on the path below, waving her arms above her head. 'Let me in.'

Miranda leaned out, holding her finger to her lips. 'Shh. You'll wake the whole house.'

'Open the bloody door.'

'I'm coming.' Pulling down the sash, Miranda left the curtains drawn so that she could find her way out of the room without tripping over Rita's camp bed. She tiptoed downstairs hoping that no one could hear the occasional creak of a floorboard as she crept through the dark hall and entered the drawing room. She barked her shin on an occasional table, stifling a cry of pain, but it was pitch dark and she had to feel her way towards the French windows. She turned the key in the lock and opened the door. 'Rita,' she said in a stage whisper. 'Where are you?'

Rita sprang from the shadows. 'You took your time.'

'It's two in the morning,' Miranda said, peering at her watch in a shaft of moonlight. 'Where have you been?'

'Mind your own beeswax.' Rita made a tipsy grab for the door handle. 'I brought someone home with me. He needs a bed for the night.' She glanced over her shoulder. 'Come in, you twerp. She won't bite.'

'Who's out there?' Miranda demanded anxiously. 'You can't just bring anyone into the house.'

'It's not just anyone.' Rita pushed her out of the way. 'Come in, Tommy. It's okay. Miranda says you can doss down on the sofa.'

Tommy Toop sidled through the door, dragging off his pork-pie hat. 'Is that all right with you, miss?'

'What's he doing here?' Miranda closed the door quickly, just in case Rita had any more waifs and strays waiting outside.

'He was being a gent and he walked me home,' Rita said with a drunken grin. 'We ain't half had a good time tonight. Or is it tomorrow? I lost track.'

Tommy stood by the door clutching his battered trilby in both hands. 'I should be going now.'

'Yes, I think you should.' Miranda was suddenly

overcome with embarrassment as she realised that she was stark naked beneath her thin cotton nightgown. 'It was good of you to bring Rita home, but I don't think my grandparents would be too pleased to find that you'd slept here, Tommy.'

'I'll be off then.' He opened the door and stepped outside, pausing only to ram his hat on his head before sauntering down the steps.

Miranda locked the door. 'You'd better go to bed and sleep it off, but for goodness' sake be quiet about it. God only knows what my grandparents would say if they found you in this state.'

'Hoorah for Rita Platt. That's what they'd say. It's good to see the girl enjoying herself.' She staggered and would have tripped over a footstool if Miranda had not supported her.

'You're completely sozzled,' Miranda said crossly. 'What were you drinking?'

'I dunno.' Rita leaned against her, giggling helplessly. 'There were some lovely chaps at the dance. They bought me drinks.'

'You don't say. Come on, Rita, let's get you upstairs.'

'They offered me a job.'

'That's nice. Can you walk if I help you?'

Rita took a step and stumbled onto the sofa. 'I'll just sleep here, if you don't mind. They want me to work with them, Manda. I'm going to be very rich...' She closed her eyes with a sigh and fell instantly asleep.

Miranda covered her with the Spanish shawl that her grandmother had insisted on draping over the baby grand piano ever since she had seen something similar in *Woman's Journal*. 'You're an idiot,' she said softly. 'And you were lucky that Tommy brought you home. I can see you're going to be trouble, Rita Platt.'

Rita was very unwell next day. Miranda had left her and gone back to bed but had awakened early and had somehow managed to get her troublesome new friend up the stairs to their room before anyone saw her. She dosed Rita with Andrews Liver Salts, explaining her malaise away by telling her grandmother that it was a simple bilious attack, and luckily for Rita Maggie was too busy attending to the needs of her house guests to worry about such a minor ailment.

There was a buzz of nervous anticipation in the air as the mothers repacked their cases and prepared to leave next day for their final destinations. Maggie spent most of the morning on the telephone confirming details of travel, and holding court in her small sitting room as the women trailed in one by one to find out where they were going to be billeted. Luckily it was fine and the children spent the morning rushing around the garden as if it were some great pleasure park designed specifically for their entertainment.

George shut himself away in his workshop and Annie remained in the kitchen, grumbling about the amount of extra work and complaining that she only had one pair of hands. Miranda listened patiently and did her best to help by peeling the vegetables she had dug from the garden, podding peas and preparing a basketful of runner beans for Sunday lunch. There was no roast meat to go with the Yorkshire puddings but Annie had been reading a Ministry of Food leaflet and was trying out a recipe for barley mince, which seemed to consist mainly of pearl barley, onion, water and beef extract.

Realising that Miranda was watching closely, Annie stopped stirring for a moment. 'Your face will get stuck like that if the wind changes,' she said crossly.

'Sorry, but it doesn't look very much like meat.'

'I'm not a magician. I'm doing my best with what's left in the larder. To think we used to give what was left of the Sunday roast to the dog.'

'But we haven't got a dog.'

'Not now, but your granny had a beagle once. She called him Houdini with good reason; the little wretch was always running off.'

Miranda bent down to stroke Dickens, who had wandered in from the garden. 'This old chap is the only pet I ever remember being here.'

'It was a long time ago, before your Uncle Jack was born. Your grandfather bought the dog to keep your granny company while he was abroad.'

'I thought she always went with him.'

'Not so much when the children were young. Your dad went to boarding school but Miss Eileen kicked up such a fuss when she thought she was going to be sent away that your granny gave in to her, as she always did, and Eileen went to a private prep school in the town. She was a handful, I can tell you.' Annie dipped a spoon in the simmering mixture and tasted it, pulling a face. 'Like I said before, I'm not a magician. Have you finished shelling those peas?'

Miranda held out the brimming colander. 'Yes, I have. So what happened to Houdini? Granny's never mentioned him.'

'He escaped once too often. The little blighter got run over.'

'Oh, no.' Miranda felt her throat constrict at the thought of an animal in pain. 'Was he badly hurt?'

'Broke one of his back legs. Mr Carstairs was just as upset as your granny.'

'Carstairs?' Miranda's heart did a funny little flip inside her chest. 'Was he any relation to the man who helped us out the other day?'

'Probably, I don't really know.' Annie took the pan off the heat and tipped its contents into a pie dish. 'I don't think that's going to look anything like meatloaf.'

Miranda tried another tack. 'What happened then?'

'If they're hungry they'll eat it.' Annie wiped her hands on her apron. 'What are you on about, Miranda?'

'Mr Carstairs. You said he was terribly upset about the poor dog. Was that the start of the family feud?'

'Questions all the time. Haven't you got any vegetables left to peel?'

'I've finished them all, but I'll wash up for you if you tell me what you know about Mr Carstairs.'

'It was a very long time ago.'

'Yes, but do you know why there's a rift between the families? It can't be just because Mr Carstairs injured Granny's dog, although that's bad enough, but it was an accident after all.'

'Stop pestering me. Ask your granny if you want answers.' Annie flounced out of the kitchen leaving Miranda to wash the pots and pans with questions still buzzing around in her head.

Rita finally surfaced later in the day, looking pale and peaky but insisting that she was quite well now, and ravenous. Annie had gone home as it was her afternoon off, and it was left to Miranda to find her something to eat.

Rita settled down at the kitchen table and tucked into a plateful of bread, two pickled onions and a chunk of farmhouse cheese. 'I'm starving,' she said, helping herself to a liberal amount of margarine. 'At least this stuff isn't on ration. Tastes like cart grease but it's better than nothing.'

Miranda pulled out a bentwood chair and sat down opposite her. 'What were you babbling about last night before you passed out?'

Rita chewed and swallowed. 'I dunno. Can't remember.'

'You said you'd been offered a job.'

'Did I? Well, yes, in a manner of speaking. I was chatting to these blokes in the pub before we went to the dance hall, and they said there was a vacancy for a salesgirl in the place where they worked. They said I'd be an asset to any business and I should apply first thing tomorrow morning.'

'So where is this shop?'

'I can't remember, but you'll probably know it, Morris and something else beginning with M.'

'Morris and Mawson. It's the only department store in town.'

'That'll be it. If I could work in the perfumery

and make-up department I'd be halfway to being a pin-up girl.'

'I don't see how.'

Rita stabbed a pickled onion with her fork. 'Because I could learn to make meself up like a film star.' She took a bite and gulped it down with a faraway look in her eyes. 'I could afford to get me hair bleached by a proper hairdresser so that I didn't look like a cheap peroxide blonde, and then I'd be ready to go back to London and begin my career. Can't you see, Manda? It's a start in the right direction.'

Despite Rita's obvious flights of fancy, Miranda could see that she had a point, and the thought of being able to earn money straight away instead of doing her final exams at college and end up working in a boring office was tempting. She had never wanted to be a secretary anyway, but then she had not given much thought to career prospects. What she really wanted was to do something worthwhile, just like Maman, but her French was not good enough and anyway she was probably too young to be considered for the SOE. She had been toying with the idea of joining one of the forces, but she knew that her grandparents would never give their permission and it would be impossible unless conscription for women became compulsory. She eyed Rita thoughtfully as the idea of getting a job began to germinate in her mind. 'I might even go with you,' she said casually. 'I know where that shop is. I'll show you.'

'Okay. Suit yourself.' Rita lifted the lid of the cheese dish and found it empty. 'Is there any more? I hope they never ration it because I love

114

the stuff. My mum used to say I was part girl, part mouse.' Her eyes clouded over and her lips trembled. 'She was a bit of a wag, was my mum.'

Miranda rose hastily from the table. 'I expect everything nice will be rationed soon, but I'm sure there's more cheese in the larder. Wait there. I'll go and have a look.'

'We could always pinch a bottle of that rot-gut your grandad makes and trade it at the farmhouse,' Rita said with a touch of her old spirit. 'I'm not daft, Manda. I know what's going on here. Good for Grandad George, that's what I say.'

Miranda snatched a piece of cheddar from the marble slab and hurried back to the table. 'Keep your voice down. It's top secret and he's trying to make fuel for the boiler. It's not for consumption and he'd be horrified if he knew people were drinking it.'

'Tell that to the marines, Manda.' Rita winked and cut another slice. 'But mum's the word.'

It was time for the evacuees to go on their way. Maggie was surrounded by grateful mothers wanting to express their thanks for the brief respite in their journeys to various parts of the country, while Annie handed out packs of sandwiches to the older children.

Miranda stood by with a baby in each arm, giving them back to their respective mothers as they finished saying their goodbyes. Rita was rounding up the older children and shepherding them into the coach, while the driver stowed the cases in the luggage space, and eventually everyone had boarded and taken their seats. The last sight of their visitors was the children in the back seat pressing their faces against the window and waving madly.

'I can't say I'm sorry to see the back of those kids. Count me out next time you get all public spirited, Mrs B.' Annie stomped back towards the house.

'She's got a bit too much to say for herself,' Rita said, frowning. 'My mum would have slapped me around the legs with a wet dishcloth if I'd been cheeky to her.'

'Your mother was obviously a woman of good sense.' Maggie was about to follow Annie, but she paused in the gateway. 'What are you two girls going to do today? Perhaps it would be a good idea for you to visit Mrs Proffitt in hospital, Rita.'

'Maybe later, but I've got – ouch!' She glared at Miranda who had nudged her in the ribs. 'What was that for?'

'Sorry. I slipped.' Miranda seized her by the elbow. 'We're going into town, Granny. Can we get you anything at the shops?'

Maggie shook her head. 'We're out of tea and sugar and most of the essentials. I'll have to ring my order through to the grocer.' She met Miranda's questioning look with a vague smile. 'You don't have to remind me that we've used up our rations on those poor women and their children, but this is the country. We barter things like garden produce and eggs. That reminds me I must go and check the hen coop. If those gypsies have been at it again I'll have the law on them.' She hurried off in the direction of the chicken run.

'What was that for?' Rita demanded, rubbing

116

her side.

'How were you going to explain the fact that you've got a job interview without admitting that you went into town and got paralytic?'

'I never give it a thought.'

'Well, if you do anything like that again don't expect me to cover for you.'

Rita's lips curved into a persuasive smile. 'Come on, Manda. You don't mean that. We're mates, aren't we?' She slapped her on the back. 'And mates help each other out, so I don't suppose you could lend me something a bit tidy to wear, could you? I got to look the part.'

Miranda was tempted to refuse. 'I just spent almost half an hour trying to wash the beer stains out of my white dress. It's probably ruined and that was your fault.'

'It was cider, not beer.'

'It doesn't matter now. What time is your interview?'

'When I get there, ducks.' Rita grabbed her by the hand. 'Now about that outfit...'

An hour later, after a short bus ride into town on the rattle-trap bus, popularly known as the toast rack, they arrived at Morris and Mawson's emporium. Rita was neatly attired in a white cotton blouse and navy-blue skirt, although she had insisted on wearing the strappy sandals which, Miranda thought privately, did not entirely go with the outfit. She herself had chosen to wear a pink gingham dress with a white collar and cuffs and the white gloves which her mother insisted were a must at all times. She had offered to lend a pair to Rita who had declared that she would not be seen dead wearing gloves unless the temperature was subzero, and the same applied to hats. Miranda had pointed out that a straw hat was not only neat, but prevented sunburn. Rita's answer was to snatch up her purse and rush out of the door. It had proved to be a futile gesture as she had apparently squandered the borrowed ten shillings during her night out and Miranda had had to pay for both of them on the bus.

Unabashed, Rita peered into the shop window where mannequins were displayed in casual poses showing off beachwear. Colourful striped towels were laid out on sheets of yellow paper representing sand and an open picnic basket had been placed beside a deckchair. 'Pathetic,' Rita said, curling her lip. 'Look at that background. Some twerp thinks that sloshing blue paint on a bit of cardboard looks like the sea. They should take a trip to Oxford Street and see how the big stores do things.'

Miranda glanced nervously over her shoulder in case anyone from the store might be hovering outside. 'I wouldn't let them hear you say things like that when you go for your interview.'

'I'm not that daft.' Rita braced her shoulders. 'Here goes.' She opened the glass door. 'Aren't you coming in?'

Miranda had been about to walk on but she hesitated. 'I was going to do some window shopping.'

'I thought you might like to see where I'll be working.'

'Do you want me to come in with you?'

'I don't care either way.'

Miranda was quick to catch the note of uncertainty in Rita's voice and she relented. 'I might just come in and browse.' She stood aside as a large overdressed woman pushed the double doors open and sailed out with her male companion trailing behind her, half hidden by a pile of bandboxes.

'Seems like someone's got plenty of cash,' Rita said loudly.

Miranda shoved her unceremoniously through the doors before they could swing shut. 'Keep your voice down,' she whispered. 'This is a small town compared to London, and everybody knows everybody.'

Rita flicked her hair back with a toss of her head. 'I don't care. Anyway, I've got to go and find those blokes. That's if I can remember what they look like.'

'You said you'd got an interview.'

'I have, in a way. It was more a suggestion than an actual offer.' She paused in between the perfume counter and the toiletries. 'There's one of 'em. Cooee! Bertie, it's me, Rio Rita.'

There was a sudden hush as shoppers and counter assistants alike turned their heads to stare at her. Miranda wished the floor would open up and swallow her. 'What are you doing?' she hissed.

'There's me pal, Bertie,' Rita said, waving furiously. She teetered through the crowded aisles between the counters to throw her arms around his neck.

He slipped free from her clutches, flushing to the roots of his hair. 'Excuse me, miss,' he said loudly. 'My name is Albert, miss. May I be of assistance?'

'Oh, c'mon, ducks. You remember me, don't you?'

He straightened his tie. 'Are you looking for something in particular, miss?'

'You and that other bloke – can't remember his name – you told me there was a job vacancy in the store. Or was you just chatting me up?'

Miranda could see the manager stalking towards them in his swallowtail coat and starched Gladstone collar. She tapped Rita on the shoulder. 'Perhaps there's been a slight misunderstanding.'

'Shut up, Manda. This is between laughing boy here and me.'

'Really, miss,' Albert said, lowering his voice. 'I think your friend is right. You are labouring under a misapprehension.'

'Whatever that is when it's at home, it ain't what I'm labouring under, mate. You said there was a job going and I'm here for an audition – I mean interview.'

By this time a small crowd of onlookers had gathered around them and Miranda was wishing that she had walked away and left Rita to her own devices, but the manager was upon them and his dark eyebrows had knotted together in an ominous frown. 'What is the problem, Mr Scott?'

Chapter Seven

Albert gulped and swallowed, his flush deepening. 'Nothing, Mr Wallace. It's just a case of mistaken identity. This young person seems to think that we've met, but I can assure you that it's quite untrue.'

Rita's eyes flashed. 'You're a...'

'You're probably right, Mr Scott,' Miranda said, giving her a warning look. 'That's what you were going to say, wasn't it, Rita?'

Mr Wallace fixed Rita with a cold stare that would have silenced an ordinary mortal. 'I suggest we continue this conversation in my office, Miss er...'

'Platt,' Rita said, squaring her shoulders. 'Miss Rita Platt from London, and I don't like being called a liar, mister.'

Albert shifted from one foot to the other, glaring at Rita. 'I never did, Mr Wallace.'

'I'll deal with you later, Mr Scott. There are customers waiting to be served. Ladies, if you would care to follow me, we will sort this matter out in private.' Motioning them to follow him, Mr Wallace strode off towards the back of the premises.

'You're a lying bastard, Bertie,' Rita muttered as she walked past him.

'She's upset,' Miranda said hastily. 'She didn't mean it.'

He ran his finger round the inside of his collar. 'I could lose my job if that young lady doesn't keep her mouth shut.'

There was nothing she could say to this. She had little sympathy for a man who had plied a young girl with drink and empty promises, and she was thankful that Tommy Toop had been around to prevent Rita from committing a serious error of judgement. She left him to deal with the queue of curious customers and hurried after Rita, catching her up as Mr Wallace ushered her into the office. He closed the door and went to sit behind his desk. 'Please take a seat, ladies. Perhaps we can discuss this without resorting to raising our voices?' He addressed this remark to Rita who had slumped down on the nearest chair.

'Your mate promised me a job,' she said, pouting. 'I was taken in.'

'How and when did this occur, Miss Platt? I need to know the details.'

Miranda pulled up a chair and sat down beside Rita. 'Do we need to go into all this, Mr Wallace? I'm sure my friend would accept an apology from Mr Scott, since it was obviously a simple misunderstanding.'

'I can speak for meself, ta very much, Manda,' Rita said, frowning.

Miranda chose to ignore her, concentrating her efforts on Mr Wallace. 'Is there a job vacancy or not? That's the question, and if there is Miss Platt would like to apply for it.'

'I'm not sure I want the blooming job now,' Rita said sulkily. 'And I wasn't lying.'

'And I'm not sure that you are exactly the person we are looking for, Miss Platt.' Mr Wallace leaned his elbows on the desk, steepling his fingers. 'But you, Miss – I'm afraid I didn't catch your name?'

'Me?' Miranda stared at him in surprise. 'My name is Miranda Beddoes, but I don't see...'

A slow smile spread across his florid features. 'Are you related to Major Beddoes, by any chance?'

'I'm his granddaughter and Miss Platt is our guest at Highciffe. She's a very respectable young lady.'

He raised an eyebrow. 'I'm sure she is, but what I was about to say is that you are exactly the sort of person we would like to join our happy Morris and Mawson family. This is an old established business, Miss Beddoes; founded in 1887 and has served the community ever since. Quality and service is our motto.'

Rita rose to her feet. 'Are you offering her a job and not me?'

'I think you've answered your own question, young lady. We at Morris and Mawson are very particular about the type of person we employ, and I'm afraid your...' he paused for a moment as if weighing his words, 'your rather forthright manner might offend some of our valued clientele.'

'You mean I'm too common to work in a shop?' Rita leaned over the desk, gripping the edge as if she would like to tip it over and unseat him. 'Is that what you're saying, moosh?'

'Don't you take that tone with me.' He rose to his feet. 'I'm going to have to ask you to leave the

123

premises, Miss Platt. Or do I have to call the floor walker and have you removed?'

'Him and whose army?' Rita demanded angrily. 'Anyway, I'm going. I wouldn't stay in this dump a moment longer, and you've lost my custom, mate. So much for your blooming motto.'

Miranda stood up. 'I think we'd better go, Rita.'

Rita marched past her to open the door, but she paused, seemingly determined to have the last word. 'Oh, and your man, Scott. He's not above trying to get off with girls by getting them drunk and making promises he can't keep. If he's the sort of bloke you employ it ain't safe for a nice girl to work here.' She stalked out of the office with her head held high.

Miranda made to follow her but Mr Wallace called her back. 'Miss Beddoes, may I have a word in private?'

She turned to face him. 'Yes?'

'This has all been a terrible misunderstanding. I hope you won't breathe a word of it to your grandfather.'

For a moment she almost felt sorry for him. 'I think it's best forgotten.'

'And will you think about my offer of a job, Miss Beddoes? You are just the sort of person we're looking for.'

Miranda thought quickly, considering her options. She had not finished the secretarial course and without qualifications she would be unlikely to get a job in an office. At least working in the department store would give her some financial independence, until the time came for her to join up. With both parents wholly absorbed in the war

124

she was determined to do her bit when the oppor-
tunity arose. 'I will take you up on that, Mr
Wallace,' she said slowly. 'But only if you give Miss
Platt a job too.'

Before he had a chance to speak, Rita poked her
head round the door. 'Are you coming, Manda?'

'I'll be with you in a moment.' She waited until
Rita was out of earshot. 'Miss Platt really does
need a job. Her mother died recently; she's lost
her home and she has no other family. She's very
bright and keen to get on, and I'm sure there
must be something she could do in a big and
successful store like Morris and Mawson.'

'I suppose I might find something for her to do
in packing. If your grandparents have taken her
in that is a recommendation in itself. Major
Beddoes is an important man in this town.'

'Then can I take it that she's got a job?'

'You drive a hard bargain, Miss Beddoes.' He
opened a drawer in his desk and took out a
printed form. 'Get her to fill this in and return it
to me. I'll start her in the packing department
and see how she gets on, but I'll be keeping an
eye on Miss Platt. You can tell her that from me.'

'Packing?' Rita stared at Miranda in disbelief.
'That old stuffed shirt has offered me a job in
packing?'

It had started to rain and they were sheltering
in the shop doorway. 'Don't go off at the deep
end. It's a job and you'll earn some money. You
need work if you're going to save up enough to go
back to London.'

Rita's bottom lip trembled. 'But I wanted to be

125

a lady working in the perfume and cosmetics department.'

'And you might yet. If you do well and try not to fly off the handle every five minutes, you could get promoted. You need to show them just what Rita Platt can do, and forget about Scott. He's a pig, but you won't be working with him. Unless, of course, you're afraid you can't cope.'

'Me? Afraid? Don't talk soft. I can handle men like him. I'll have to when I'm a pin-up girl. They'll be begging for signed photos and taking me out on dates to expensive restaurants. I'll be a star.'

'Of course you will. Now let's get the bus home before we get soaked to the skin, and you can tell Granny the good news.'

The air raid siren screamed its warning signal just as Miranda, Rita and the rest of the staff walked through the shop doors. There was a moment of stunned silence followed by mild panic.

'Is it a practice run, Mr Wallace?' One of the older women clutched her hands to her heart as if she were about to collapse in a faint.

'I don't know. Everybody go downstairs to the basement. Mr Scott, make sure that everyone in your department leaves the shop floor.' Mr Wallace rushed into his office and came out again with a tin hat on his head and a whistle in his hand. He blew a sharp blast as the terrified staff rushed towards the staircase. 'Single file. Don't rush. That's an order.'

'Give a chap a tin hat and a whistle and he thinks he's Hitler,' Rita whispered, giggling.

'Hush, he'll hear you.' Miranda gave her a warning look, but she doubted if Mr Wallace could have heard Rita's comment above the agitated chatter of the women and the deeper voices of the men, who were all trying to appear cool and calm, even though some of them had pushed to the front.

'Whatever happened to women and children first?' Rita demanded in a loud voice.

'I'll look after you, love.' A middle-aged man with dark hair greased back from his forehead and a thin pencil moustache like those favoured by Hollywood heart-throbs attempted to put his arm around her shoulders, but Rita slapped his hand away.

'Give over, you silly bugger.'

'Have you forgotten me already, Rio Rita? I'm Joe.'

'Hurry along,' Mr Wallace said with another sharp blast on his whistle. 'No talking. Get under cover.'

'It's a practice. I know it is.' A thin girl with suspiciously blonde hair pushed past Joe in an attempt to get to the stairs first. 'Get out of my way.'

'It's a false alarm, Liz. Don't blow a fuse, darling.'

'Pig,' she said, making a grab for the handrail. 'You might think you're God's gift to women, but you're not.'

'This is a wonderful start to a new job,' Miranda whispered, receiving a wink and a smile in response from Rita as they were swept downstairs to the basement.

When they were all assembled Mr Wallace carried out an impromptu roll call. Minutes later the all clear sounded and everyone trooped back upstairs to take their positions as the doors were opened and the first customers began to trickle in.

Miranda and Rita spent the first ten minutes in Mr Wallace's office receiving their instructions. He sent Rita downstairs to the packing department, and she slouched off with her shoulders hunched in a mute gesture of rebellion against what she considered to be a menial position.

'Now then, Miss Beddoes,' he said smoothly. 'I have great hopes for you and so I'm starting you off in the haberdashery department under the aegis of Mrs Dowsett, who is one of our longest serving and most respected employees. She will explain your duties.'

'Thank you, Mr Wallace.'

He moved towards the doorway. 'Follow me.' He led her through the store, and having introduced her to the buxom lady behind the counter, he sauntered off to speak to a group of customers.

Mrs Dowsett seemed less than delighted to have Miranda assigned to her counter. She looked her up and down as if trying to find something in her attire to criticise. 'I know your grandmother.'

Miranda was instantly wary. 'I believe she's quite well known.'

'Notorious, I should say.' Mrs Dowsett sniffed and continued to tidy the ribbon drawer. 'You may finish this for me. When you've done that come to me and I'll find you something else to do.'

'Just a moment.' Miranda caught her by the sleeve of her black dress. 'I'm sorry, Mrs Dowsett, but you can't make remarks like that and just walk away.'

'And who are you to question me? You are on dangerous ground, Miss Beddoes. I'll allow such a piece of insolence to pass this once, and only because you are new here, but if I have cause to reprimand you for anything further you will find yourself in Mr Wallace's office.'

'But...' Miranda bit her lip. She could see that this was not the time to press the matter further, but she was burning with indignation and even more determined to get to the bottom of such a defamatory remark. She set to and tidied the rolls of ribbon, and did all the mundane tasks allotted to her without comment. At lunchtime she met Rita outside the building and they walked to the seafront where they sat on a pile of sandbags and ate their meat paste sandwiches.

'I'm down in the bloody basement,' Rita said, swallowing a mouthful of food. 'I'm working with that idiot Joe Hoskins, who thinks he's the reincarnation of Rudolph bloody Valentino, and a young boy who's a bit simple.'

Miranda took a sip from her bottle of Granny's lemonade. 'It's a job, Rita. I hate mine too but until something better turns up, it looks as if we'll have to put up with it.'

'It makes me even more determined to get back to London as soon as I've saved up enough. I'm not hanging about in this place and getting me bum pinched by Joe Hoskins whenever he passes me in the corridor.'

'He didn't!'

'He damned well did, and he got a slap around the chops for his pains.'

Miranda almost choked on her sandwich. 'Good for you.'

'I'm not going to be messed about with.'

Miranda glanced at the clock on the Esplanade. 'Good Lord, look at the time. We'd best get back to work.'

'Back to slavery, you mean.' Rita scrambled to her feet.

Miranda stowed the bottle in her handbag and stood up. 'At least you don't have to work for an old cow like Mrs Dowsett. She's said some nasty things about Granny and I want to know why.'

'She's probably just jealous. I'd ignore her if I was you.' Rita linked her hand through the crook of Miranda's arm. 'C'mon. Back to the coalface.'

Halfway through the afternoon, Miranda was standing by while Mrs Dowsett demonstrated yet again how to measure material and cut to the required length. The customer waited patiently and Miranda tried to look interested, but she found her attention wandering. Mrs Dowsett seemed to have a sixth sense for such things and she paused. 'Are you observing this, Miss Beddoes?'

The customer tut-tutted beneath her breath but it was still audible enough, and Mrs Dowsett smiled apologetically. 'I am so sorry, madam. Training new girls is always a tedious process. Pay attention, please, Miss Beddoes.' She cut the cloth, snapping the blades of the scissors with a flourish. 'There, you see – a perfectly straight line with no wastage. Now you may fold and wrap Madam's purchase.'

'Yes, Mrs Dowsett.' Outwardly meek but inwardly fuming, Miranda made a neat package and was about to give it to the customer when Mrs Dowsett snatched it from her.

She examined it closely. 'It will do, but it's a bit slipshod, Miss Beddoes. Do better next time.' She passed it across the counter. 'Young girls these days have to be taught everything. One cannot get the staff.'

'Beddoes?' The customer peered into Miranda's face. 'Are you related to Maggie Beddoes by any chance?'

Ignoring the warning look from Mrs Dowsett, Miranda smiled and nodded. 'She's my grandmother.'

'I know her well. We're both members of the Women's Institute. Tell her that Doris Appleby sends her regards.'

'Yes, I will.'

'Well, goodbye, dear,' Mrs Appleby said, dropping the parcel into her basket. 'Good luck with your new job.' She acknowledged Mrs Dowsett with a brief nod of her head and walked off.

'Don't ever do that again,' Mrs Dowsett hissed.

'What have I done wrong now?'

'And don't take that tone with me, young lady. You are a junior here and you do not enter into personal conversations with customers.'

'I'm sorry, but she spoke to me. All I said was...'

'Miranda, is that really you?' Isabel Carstairs edged her way through the crowded shop floor to approach the counter. 'You didn't tell me that

131

you worked here.'

'It's my first day.' Miranda shot a sideways glance at Mrs Dowsett who was now positively seething.

'What did I just tell you, Miss Beddoes? This is not a cocktail party, although I hear there are plenty of those at Highcliffe.'

Isabel stiffened. 'I beg your pardon, but I was speaking to my friend. I'm a customer and I don't think Mr Mawson would be too happy to hear that one of his senior staff had been discourteous.'

Mrs Dowsett's haughty expression faded into one of total chagrin. 'I beg your pardon, madam. No offence intended.'

'None taken,' Isabel said, smiling. 'Now, if I may have a word with your assistant perhaps you would like to attend to that lady who is waving a pair of gloves in order to attract your attention.'

Mrs Dowsett moved off, every inch of her considerable frame bristling with indignation.

'Izzie, that was very naughty of you,' Miranda whispered. 'I'll be for it when you've gone.'

'I don't think she'd dare. Anyway, what are you doing here? I wouldn't have thought this was your sort of thing, Miranda.'

'It's not, but I'm going to be staying in Weymouth for longer than I thought, and I have to do something. I was offered the job and I wanted to earn some money.'

'Well, I admire your spirit.' Isabel glanced over her shoulder as Mrs Dowsett finished serving the customer. 'We can't talk here. What about lunch tomorrow?'

'We only get half an hour.'

'How about dinner? To tell the truth, I'm so bored I could scream. I'll pick you up at seven, if that's all right with you. I'm sure Mrs Beasley can make us something delicious, despite rationing.'

'Thanks. That sounds lovely.'

'I'll look forward to it. Bye, Miranda.' Isabel leaned across the counter. 'Don't let the old tabby bully you.' She strolled off towards the lingerie department.

Miranda waited for the inevitable dressing down, but Mrs Dowsett seemed to have her temper under control. However, she managed to exert her authority by sending Miranda down to the basement to tidy up the stockroom. In the narrow corridor at the bottom of the stairs she narrowly missed a collision with Rita, who was laden with parcels and small packages tied up with string. 'Where are you going?' Rita demanded. 'Is there another air raid practice?'

'No. I've been sent to tidy up the stockroom. Where are you going with those?'

'There's a van waiting in the delivery bay, apparently. You'll never guess who's driving for them.'

'Who is it?'

'The docket says T. Toop. At a guess I'd say that was our friend Tommy.'

'Let's hope he isn't taking them in his handcart,' Miranda said, chuckling.

'Maybe they've got one of them bicycles with a big basket on the front.' Rita pulled a face. 'I'd give anything to see him pedalling along with his bony arms and legs stuck out at angles and a fag hanging out of the corner of his mouth.'

'Miss Platt? That had better not be your dulcet tones I can hear out there.' A sudden loud voice emanating from the packing room caused them both to jump.

Miranda's smile faded. 'Who's that?' she whispered.

'It's Joe the bum pincher. He thinks he owns me body and soul, but he's got another think coming. Anyway, got to go. See you at six.' Rita moved on slowly, balancing her load with considerable skill.

Miranda made her way to the stockroom and unlocked the door. She was beginning to feel as though she had been working here forever. Time seemed to move at a slower pace in Morris and Mawson's empire, and there was still another hour before closing time. She switched on the light and gazed in dismay at the litter of empty boxes, cardboard cartons and general disorder. It would take hours of hard graft to bring order from chaos, but at least it was quiet and peaceful down here, and she did not have the dragon Dowsett breathing down her neck. She set to work with a will.

Next morning Mrs Dowsett sent Miranda straight to the stockroom, barely giving her time to take off her hat and gloves. It was becoming obvious to Miranda that the tyrant of the haberdashery department considered that banishment to the basement was the best way to discipline a new recruit to the workforce, especially one who had the effrontery to be higher up the social scale than she was. Miranda decided to make the best of things,

134

and she set about her task methodically. Albert Scott came down to check on her progress in the middle of the morning and was suitably impressed. She could only hope that he would put Mrs Dowsett firmly in her place the next time she ran to him telling tales.

Rita popped her head round the door several times during the course of the day, and they ate their packed lunch on the seafront, but by closing time Miranda was feeling like a mole. She was hot, dusty and longing for a bath. If she were to be honest she did not feel up to an evening at Thornleigh Court with Izzie Carstairs. She liked her well enough, but she had the feeling that Izzie's sudden wish to have her as a friend was based on her desire to learn everything about Jack, and perhaps to overcome the animus that existed between their families. She was anticipating a rather dull evening being questioned as to Jack's likes and dislikes, how many girlfriends he had had and every detail that she could bring to mind about her uncle's past life. It was not as if she had anything in common with Izzie, who was rich, beautiful and probably quite spoilt.

Even after wallowing in a hot bath and washing the dust from her blonde hair, Miranda still had some misgivings about the evening ahead. She had not had the nerve to tell her grandmother where she was going, but had said simply that she had been invited to have supper with one of the girls from work. Rita had teased her mercilessly but she had agreed to keep up the fiction. They had even invented a person called Sandra Barker, who was a beauty consultant for Elizabeth Arden.

Rita had warmed to the story and had given Sandra a family history that would have done credit to Susan Coolidge, including a near fatal accident during childhood resulting in her losing the power of her legs and her subsequent miraculous recovery. Sandra had a boyfriend who was in the merchant navy and her parents were conveniently out of the country, her father being something in the colonial service, which made it impossible for Maggie to corroborate or refute the story. Rita herself had a date with Tommy Toop and they kept that a secret too.

Miranda had a nasty feeling that they were spinning a spider's web of lies around themselves which might make life even more complicated as time went by. She had almost decided to ring Thornleigh Court and make an excuse for not going, but as she went to pick up the telephone receiver she glanced out of the window and saw a car drawing up outside. Her heart sank and a sudden sense of foreboding seized her as she spotted Izzie about to open the garden gate.

Chapter Eight

Terrified that her grandmother might suddenly appear on the scene and see the daughter of her old enemy walking down the garden path, Miranda put the telephone back on the elephant table, snatched up her bag and gas mask case and hurried out of the house.

'I'm sorry I'm a bit late,' Izzie said, smiling a greeting as Miranda ran to meet her. 'I got held up, but I'm here now. Climb in, Miranda. I'll try not to terrify you with my driving. I haven't passed my test yet and I gather they've been shelved for the duration.'

'I can't drive,' Miranda said, settling into the passenger seat of the MG Midget.

'It's easy. I could give you lessons, if you like. Poor Bessie is getting on in years but she's still a game old girl.'

'You've got a car called Bessie?'

Izzie started the engine and put it into gear. 'So what? Jack's car is called Chloe.'

'Yes, of course.'

'Have you heard from him since he joined his new squadron?'

Miranda took her cue. 'No. Have you?'

'Practically every day.' Isabel reached the end of the road, signalled and executed a right turn. She changed gear. 'He rings me when he's off duty, and when I don't hear from him I go into a flat spin.' She smiled. 'Isn't that silly?'

'Not really. You're in love. It's supposed to be like that.'

'Yes, I am. I still can't quite believe it. Everything happened so suddenly. One minute I was just Izzie Carstairs, fancy free and not even thinking about having a relationship with anyone, especially at this frightful time, and then I met Jack and wham! That was it. I think it was the same for him too.'

'I know it was. He told me so.'

Isabel swerved to avoid a pothole. 'Did he? Did

137

he really?'

'Of course he did. I don't know why you need me to tell you that. I'm sure Jack is quite capable of convincing you that you're the love of his life.'

Isabel took a bend a little too fast and Miranda had to hold on to her seat. 'Sorry, I didn't mean to do that. But do you really think I am the one? I mean, I've been told that Jack has quite a reputation with the ladies. Not that I'm surprised, of course. I expect they chase him because he's so handsome and adorable, but I don't want to be just another notch on his belt, so to speak. You do understand, don't you?'

Miranda's suspicions were confirmed by every word that spilled from Isabel's pretty lips. She was here to confirm the fact that her uncle was sincere and not just having one of his flings, but if she were to be entirely honest, Miranda was not certain. How could she know exactly what was going on in Jack's mind? She could only hope that he would not wake up one morning and realise that it was all a huge mistake, and that he had become bored with Isabel in the same way he had tired of all his other girlfriends. She kept her gaze fixed on the green hedgerows and the open countryside flashing past them as Isabel put her foot down and accelerated.

'Have you ever been in love, Miranda?'

The question came so suddenly and unexpectedly that for a moment Miranda was at a loss for words. She thought carefully before she answered. 'I don't know. I've had a couple of boyfriends but I don't think I was in love with them. I've met men that I fancied, but I'm not sure if

138

that's the same thing.'

Isabel let out a long sigh. 'Oh, you'll know, Miranda. When it's the real thing you'll know it.' She slowed down a little as they came to the familiar tunnel of trees that Miranda remembered from her last car ride with Jack, and the beginning of the stone wall that surrounded the Carstairs' estate. 'We're almost there. I do hope you like trout, Miranda. They were caught this morning and Mrs Beasley makes this gorgeous sauce with butter, lemon juice and toasted almonds. I hate to think how we'll have them when we can't get any of those things. I've already used my month's petrol ration, so I suppose I'll have to get my trusty old bike out and ride that when I want to go anywhere.'

Miranda was about to say that if doing without luxuries was all that was worrying her she was lucky, but Isabel had pulled up outside the house. She switched off the engine and climbed out. 'Come on, Miranda. Let's go in and have a sherry before dinner.'

There was nothing she could do other than to put a brave face on it and Miranda followed her into the house. They were met by the ecstatic barking of a springer spaniel and a bouncy Jack Russell. 'Down, boys,' Isabel said, laughing. 'They get so excited when they hear the car.'

Miranda hesitated as the dogs rushed past her to the front door. 'It sounds as though you've got visitors, Izzie.'

Isabel stopped and turned to her, frowning. 'I wonder who it can be? I wasn't expecting anyone. It was meant to be just us girls.'

Miranda knew who it was even before the front door opened. Raif entered the house and was almost bowled over by two excited dogs. Laughing, he dropped his case on the floor and bent down to make a fuss of them.

'Raif. What are you doing here?' Isabel stared pointedly at his suitcase. 'Have they kicked you out of the air force?'

'No, silly.' He looked up and his smile faded when he saw Miranda. 'Oh, hello. I didn't expect to find you here.'

Isabel bridled angrily. 'What sort of greeting is that? Don't tell me that you're going to be sniffy about the Carstairs family as well. It's too ridiculous for words.'

'I'm sorry,' he said apologetically. 'You're a nice girl, Miranda, and the ill-feeling between our families has nothing to do with you. I was just surprised to see you here.'

'That's okay.' Miranda bent down to pat the spaniel in an attempt to cover her embarrassment.

'Why have you come home, anyway?' Isabel demanded. 'I thought you were supposed to stay close to the aerodrome.'

'I brought my washing for Mrs Beasley to do as there isn't a laundry in the village, and I'd like a few words in private, Izzie.'

'As you can see I'm entertaining a guest. It'll simply have to wait.' Isabel beckoned to Miranda. 'Let's have that sherry and leave old Mr Grumpy to sweet talk Mrs Beasley into washing his smalls. She always did spoil him rotten.'

Miranda could sense the tension between brother and sister and she wished now that she

140

had followed her instinct and made an excuse to stay at home. Her pulses had begun to race the moment Raif walked through the door but his cold manner had sent chills running down her spine. She was beginning to wonder what had attracted her to him in the first place and the last thing she wanted was to be caught up in a family row. 'Er, perhaps I should go,' she said, edging towards the door. 'I don't mind walking.'

'Don't be ridiculous,' Raif said, frowning. 'It's a good five miles to Highcliffe and it looks like rain.' He met her agitated gaze and his expression softened. 'There's no need for you to stay and witness our stupid squabbles. Why don't you go through to the drawing room? What I have to say to my sister won't take long.'

Isabel caught Miranda by the arm. 'Stay here. I'm sure it's something and nothing. Say what you have to say, Raif, and be quick about it.'

Miranda stared at her in amazement. Her first impression of Isabel might have been influenced by Jack's description of her as sweet and angelic, but this kitten obviously had claws, and Isabel was clearly ready for a fight. 'This is between the two of you,' she said, pulling away. 'I'd rather not get involved.'

Raif held up his hand. 'No, on second thoughts perhaps you'd better stay. This does concern your family and maybe you should hear it first hand.'

'Get on with it, Raif.' Isabel folded her arms across her chest.

'All right then, it's quite simple, Izzie. I don't want you to have anything to do with Jack Beddoes.'

'Is that all? For heaven's sake, Raif. Tell me something new.'

'Jack Beddoes is a seducer of silly young girls like you. He's had more conquests than Casanova. It's well known in the mess. In fact they're taking bets on who will be next and how many notches he'll have on his bedpost before Christmas.'

The colour faded from Isabel's cheeks and her eyes widened in shock. 'That's a beastly thing to say.'

He crossed the floor to take both her hands in his. 'Izzie, don't think I'm enjoying this, because I'm not. But I won't stand by and see my sister taken in by a man who seems to have made a career of ruining women's lives.'

She pushed him away. 'Are you sure you're not getting Jack muddled up with Father? He's the original ladykiller, and he's the reason why you've never trusted yourself to have a meaning-ful relationship with a woman. I think you're just jealous of Jack and you don't want me to be happy.'

He was silent for a moment, and then he shook his head. 'All I want to do is to protect you from a man who'll break your heart.'

Miranda had had enough. She moved to Isabel's side. 'Leave her alone, you bully. And it's not true what they're saying about my uncle. Jack is a good person and he truly loves Isabel. You shouldn't listen to gossip.'

'Naturally you'd stand up for him, Miranda. You're too young to know what goes on in the real world.'

His tone was offhand and she was rapidly revising her good opinion of Raif Carstairs. 'I'm almost twenty,' she said icily. 'I don't know what your family has against mine, but it seems to me that you're using some sort of ancient feud to make your sister's life miserable.'

'Go away, Raif,' Isabel said, linking arms with Miranda. 'You've said your piece and it doesn't make the slightest bit of difference. I love Jack and nothing you can say will change that. Come along, Miranda. I think we need two very large sherries and a bottle of wine with dinner.'

The meal was delicious but Miranda had lost her appetite; she managed to swallow a few mouthfuls of asparagus soup and she toyed with the trout almondine, but her throat felt as though it was about to close and she would choke if she attempted to eat another morsel. She was tempted by the delicious summer pudding made with fruit from the walled garden, so Mrs Beasley proudly said when it was served, but Miranda only nibbled enough to be polite. Isabel on the other hand ate heartily. She licked the last of the fruit juices from her spoon, glancing ruefully at her empty plate. 'I really would love another slice, but that would be greedy.' She consulted her watch. 'I wonder if Raif's eaten. I'm beginning to feel guilty about dining so well when he's probably had something ghastly in the mess.' She drained her wine glass and reached for the bottle. 'More wine, Miranda?'

'No, thanks. I've had more than enough. My head's spinning.'

Isabel refilled her own glass. 'Daddy says that a

woman should be able to hold her drink.' She giggled, spilling a drop of white wine on the table-cloth. 'But then he should know; he's a notorious womaniser. It's so unfair of Raif to put Jack in the same category. I daresay Daddy's philandering is the real reason why our families are at logger-heads.'

Miranda almost dropped her spoon. 'What do you mean?'

'Oh, I don't know. Don't take any notice of me, I'm a bit squiffy.'

'But you must have had some reason for saying such a thing.'

'I was just adding two and two and making five.' Isabel raised her glass. 'Here's to improved relationships between the Carstairs and the Beddoes clans. Maybe all it needs is for Jack and me to get together and everything will be fine.' She put her glass down carefully and stood up, swaying slightly. 'I think I'd better drive you home now, Miranda.'

'No, really. I can walk.' Miranda rose to her feet. It was painfully obvious that Isabel was in no condition to get behind the wheel. 'After such a lovely meal the exercise will be good for me. Thank you for inviting me here tonight.'

'It was a disaster,' Isabel said with a tipsy chuckle. 'My dear brother saw to that. C'mon. I'm quite okay to drive. It'll sober me up.' She staggered from the room, leaving Miranda with no alternative but to follow her to the entrance hall.

Isabel wandered over to the console table and began rifling through the contents of her handbag. 'Where did I put my car key? I'm sure I didn't leave it in the ignition.'

'Is this what you're looking for?' Raif strolled into the hall, brandishing a set of keys.

Isabel held out her hand. 'Did you take them from my bag?'

'You're not fit to drive, Izzie. I'll take Miranda home.'

'Thank you, but I'd rather walk.' Miranda made for the front door, but Raif barred her way.

'I'm going past Highcliffe. It's no trouble.'

'No, you're not. It's completely the opposite direction to the aerodrome.'

'Stop arguing. I'll take her.' Isabel made a grab for the keys but Raif held them out of reach.

'Go to bed, Izzie, you're potted.' He turned to Miranda with an attempt at a smile. 'It's no trouble, and it's getting late. Your grandparents wouldn't want you walking home in the dark.'

'It's still quite light.'

'It won't be by the time you've trudged five miles along narrow country lanes. Stop arguing and get in the car. Please,' he added when she failed to move. 'I'm late as it is, and giving you lifts is becoming a habit.'

'How could a girl refuse such a charming invitation,' Isabel said, curling her lip. 'It's a pity you didn't inherit some of Daddy's winning ways, Raif. It's little wonder that I fell for Jack. At least he's a gentleman.'

'Go to bed and sleep it off, Izzie.' Raif turned his back on her and went to the front door. He opened it and was about to step outside but he hesitated, glancing over his shoulder. 'Please accept a lift, Miranda. I might not be my sister's

145

idea of a perfect escort, but I won't leave a young girl to walk home alone.'

'I hate you, Raif,' Isabel said, shaking her fist at him. 'G'bye, Miranda. We must do this again some time soon.' She teetered off towards the staircase.

Miranda knew when she was beaten and she followed Raif out of the house, pausing to take a deep breath of the cool evening air. Tall shadows stalked across the neatly cut lawns and the rich fruitcake smell of dew-soaked earth and leaf mould mingled with the heady perfume of night-scented stocks and honeysuckle. The old house in its lovely setting should have been a haven of peace and contentment, but an atmosphere of melancholy seemed to linger over it in a suffo-cating cloud.

Raif held the car door open. 'I'm sorry about tonight. You didn't see us at our best.'

For a brief moment Miranda thought about making a grand gesture and telling him to go to hell, but she really did not relish the long walk home. It had been a long and exhausting day and she got into the car without saying a word, but she was still seething with anger at the way Raif had spoken about her uncle. She waited until he had taken his seat behind the wheel. 'What you said about Jack was unfair and unforgiveable. No wonder Izzie got drunk. I think I would too if I had a brother like you.'

He started the engine, staring straight ahead. 'I'm sorry you feel that way.'

There was nothing left to say. Miranda sat in stony silence during the drive to Highcliffe, thanking him politely but coolly when he dropped her off at the door. She stood for a moment in the gathering gloom, listening to the gentle swish of the waves on the shore and the accompanying rattle of the pebbles as they moved with the incoming tide. She was still furious with Raif, but she could not find it in her heart to hate him. Just being in his company did strange things to her sense of equilibrium. Why, she wondered, did life have to be so complicated? Whatever had gone wrong in the past could not simply have been due to the fact that Max Carstairs had accidentally run over Granny's dog, however upsetting that must have been at the time. There must be something else, and whatever it was cast a long shadow, just like the beech trees that surrounded the grounds of Thornleigh Court. She went indoors, and having let her grandmother know that she was home, she made her way upstairs to her room.

It was blissfully quiet and peaceful now that Rita had moved into one of the spare bedrooms recently vacated by the evacuees. Miranda took a long time preparing for bed, but she found it hard to put the quarrelling Carstairs family out of her mind. It would be for the best, she decided, to have as little to do with them as possible. Jack might be better off with someone less rich and beautiful than Isabel. Maybe he would fall for Rita when she blossomed into a pin-up girl. Miranda was smiling as she finally drifted off to sleep.

In the days and weeks that followed it seemed to

Miranda that Rita had become an integral part of the Beddoes household. They ate their meals together and caught the same bus to work every morning, returning on the same route in the evening. Rita borrowed her clothes, helped herself to Miranda's makeup, and was constantly begging for a loan to get her through until payday. She had repaid her original debt when she received her first week's wages, but she had spent the remainder on stockings and a Tangee lipstick. It had become obvious to Miranda that despite having her pay packet on Friday, Rita would always be broke again by Monday. As time went by Miranda felt that she had suddenly acquired a sister, and a rather bothersome one, but without her life at Highcliffe would have been incredibly dull.

The weeks stretched into months and they slipped into a routine, except that Rita seemed to attract trouble, especially at work. She had a habit of speaking her mind and challenging authority, and this did not go down well with Mr Wallace or Joe Hoskins, who had at long last met his match. His wandering hands and suggestive remarks had apparently gone unchallenged for years as most of the females who worked in the shop were too scared to make a fuss. Rita was not. She had slapped his face on her first day but that had not deterred him, and after putting up with constant harassment she made an official complaint. Joe was let off with a mild reproof.

'That bloke gets away with murder,' she grumbled as she took her seat next to Miranda on the bus that evening. 'If any of us girls does anything wrong we get our pay docked or the sack. He gets a slap on the wrist and told not to be a naughty boy, but I bet they're in the pub now laughing about it and thinking they've won.' She opened her purse and handed the money to the conductor. 'The usual, please, love,' she said, winking at him.

Miranda paid for her ticket, waiting until the conductor had moved along before nudging Rita. 'Do you have to flirt with everything in trousers?'

'He's old enough to be me dad. Anyway, all the best ones have joined up.'

'There's always Tommy.'

'He's no Clark Gable, but he treats me to the flicks and buys me sweets and the occasional drink, so although he's no angel I'll string along with him, as the song says; or something like that.'

'You're heartless, Rita,' Miranda said, chuckling.

'Not me, I'm all heart.'

Miranda stood up to ring the bell. 'I doubt if Joe Hoskins thinks that. You've hurt his male pride. He thinks he's the original ladykiller.' Even as the words left her lips she realised that she had repeated Isabel's description of her father, and the memories of the fateful evening at Thornleigh Court came flooding back. She had not heard anything from Isabel since then, but after what Raif had said about Jack she had not really expected her to maintain contact. As to Raif, she had almost given up hope of ever seeing him again – but not quite.

'Stop daydreaming and move along,' Rita said, giving her a push towards the exit.

'Sorry.' Miranda staggered along the aisle between the seats as the vehicle lurched to a halt at the bottom of the road leading up to High-cliffe.

'Penny for 'em,' Rita said as they walked up the hill towards the house. 'You was miles away. I know you was dreaming about Bertie. You really fancy him, don't you?'

'Of course I do,' Miranda said, taking the easy way out. She could hardly explain her feelings for Raif to anyone when she did not understand them herself. She hated him for his attitude towards her family, but he had a habit of creeping into her thoughts when she least expected it. She quickened her pace. 'I hope Annie has left something for supper. I can't face another plateful of Granny's bubble and squeak.'

'It's all bubble and no squeak if you ask me,' Rita said, quickening her pace in order to keep up. 'I'd sell me soul for a proper fry-up with bacon, sausages and a couple of slices of black pudding. Mum used to do that on special occasions and we'd have fried bread with loads of tomato ketchup.'

'You can't get it now,' Miranda said, pausing by the garden gate. 'I haven't seen any in the shops for ages.'

'Bloody war. You ought to tell your grandad to start making tomato sauce instead of that rot-gut. Tommy keeps on at me to half-inch a bottle, but I says not on your life, Tommy, mate. Gran-dad George has been good to me and I ain't no tea leaf.'

'You haven't told anyone else about Grandpa's

invention, have you, Rita?'

'What d'you take me for? I may be a bit common, – but I'm not an idiot.'

Miranda breathed a sigh of relief and she smiled. 'You're not common, Rita. I'd say you were colourful.'

'You wait until I'm the cover girl on one of them glossy magazines. I'll be colourful then, all right.'

Miranda started down the path towards the house. 'I wonder whose car that is parked outside? There can't be many people who've got enough petrol coupons to make social calls.'

Rita edged past her. 'Looks like she's wearing a WVS uniform. It's probably something your gran's doing for the war effort. She's quite a girl is our Maggie.'

'I'm sure she'd be flattered to hear you say so, but I'm curious.'

'There's only one way to find out.' Rita hurried on as fast as she could on the high-heeled sandals that Miranda had given up hope of ever wearing again.

The visitor was just saying her goodbyes when they reached the front steps. She acknowledged them with a nod and a smile as she climbed into her car.

Miranda took the steps two at a time. 'Who was that, Granny? I didn't recognise her.'

'Come inside, both of you,' Maggie ushered them into the house. 'I'm afraid I've got some rather bad news for you, Rita.'

'What's up, Mrs B?'

'That was Adele Linklater, who does voluntary

151

work at the hospital. We've known each other for years, which is why she came in person.'

Miranda had only registered the words 'bad news'.

'Has something happened to Mummy?'

Maggie shook her head. 'No, dear. As I said, it concerns Rita.'

'Spit it out, Mrs B. It can't be that bad because I got nothing left to lose.'

'That's so sad.' Miranda gave her a hug. 'You've got us, Rita.

'Of course she has.' Maggie took a deep breath. 'There's no easy way to say this so I'll be blunt. I'm afraid that Mrs Proffitt passed away last night after suffering a second stroke.'

Rita shrugged her shoulders. 'So the old girl's gone. I'm sorry.'

'I'm sorry too, my dear. I realise you didn't know her, but you were pinning your hopes on staying with her for the duration.'

'Not me, Mrs B. It's sad that she died, but like you said, I never met her and I wasn't too keen on staying with a complete stranger in the first place.' Rita made a move towards the staircase.

'Are you all right?' Maggie asked anxiously. 'Perhaps I should have broken it more gently.'

'I'm fine, ta, Mrs B. I'm going upstairs to pack.'

'Why?' Miranda followed her to the foot of the stairs. 'Where would you go?'

Rita sniffed and swallowed hard. 'I'll do what I always intended to do, ducks. Go back to London and get a room somewhere and start me career as a pin-up girl. Only, I'm a bit skint at the moment.' She lowered her voice. 'You couldn't lend me a fiver, could you? I'll pay you back out of me first wage packet when I'm a starlet.'

Miranda opened her mouth to argue but Maggie shook her head. 'You won't lend her a penny, Miranda. And Rita, you can stop being silly. You've got a home here for as long as you need it. I won't hear of you going back to London until you're at least twenty-one and legally able to take care of yourself.' She made a move towards the kitchen. 'Who's for bubble and squeak? We'll eat first and then we'll sit round the wireless and listen to the BBC news.'

The news never seemed to be good. London had been bombed ruthlessly and now the Luftwaffe had attacked Coventry and cities in the north. Christmas was coming and Miranda had no idea where her mother and father were. She tried not to think about the dangers they must be facing daily, but sometimes it all became too much and she needed time to be alone with her thoughts.

After the news ended, she took refuge in Jack's room at the top of the house. She opened the window and stepped out onto the widow's walk. There was a halo round the moon and the sea gleamed like liquid silver. Smoke from chimneys hung in a misty veil over the town and it was bitterly cold. She thought about the men at sea risking their lives daily in the convoys bringing vital supplies and the Navy which was there to protect them. There had been several air raids that week, but she could never forget that men like Jack and Raif were also in desperate danger as they took on the enemy in their fighter planes.

She felt small and insignificant under the dark canopy of star-studded sky, and her life seemed trivial and of little use. Sorting ribbons, buttons and packets of pins would not help to win the war; there must be something she could do other than measuring out dress lengths of material under the disapproving gaze of Mrs Dowsett.

Suddenly it all became clear. She went downstairs to find her grandmother and Rita who were in the kitchen making cocoa. 'Granny, I've made up my mind. I'm going to join the WAAF.'

'You'll do no such thing,' Maggie said vehemently. 'Miranda, this is utter nonsense.'

Rita clapped her hands. 'Good for you, Manda. I think it's a blooming good idea. I might even join up with you.'

Maggie gave her a deprecating look. 'I can't stop you doing such a foolish thing, Rita, but I can put a stop to Miranda's wild scheme as she's under age and in my care.'

'If my mother can risk her life for her country then so can I,' Miranda said firmly. 'You're not my legal guardian, Granny, and much as I love you, I'm going to do this.'

Maggie's face blanched and her lips trembled. 'But what would your parents say if I allowed you to rush off and enlist?'

'They can't expect me to sit the war out here. Anyway, if it goes on much longer they'll probably conscript young women as well as the boys and men.'

Rita nodded in agreement. 'That's right, Manda. We'll be there first with all those blokes. We'll have our pick.'

'You might,' Maggie said firmly. 'But Miranda most certainly will not. Just wait until your grandfather hears about this mad scheme. He'll hit the roof.'

Chapter Nine

RAF Fighter Command, Henlow Priory, January 1942

After an eight-hour shift in the ops room working as a plotter, Miranda needed something to calm her nerves. It had been a particularly busy eight hours with little time to stop even for a cup of tea as the information flowed in from the filter room. She could not begin to imagine how the girls doing that particular job had stood up to such pressure. It was highly specialised work as they had to correlate information received from the radar stations regarding imminent enemy raids and pass it on to the operations room. Being at the sharp end had sounded exciting and glamorous when Miranda was undergoing her basic training, but now she was glad that she had not been picked for the filter room.

Her breath curled around her in the frosty night air as she lit a cigarette, taking a puff which made her cough and she pulled a face. Smoking was something that almost all the other girls did with apparent enjoyment, but somehow she had not managed to acquire the habit. All it did for

155

her was give her a sore throat and left a nasty smell clinging to her hair and clothes, but Rita could puff away with the best of them. She could even blow smoke rings, which had been her party piece when they did their initial training together. Miranda sighed. She would never have thought it possible but she actually missed Rita. They had hoped to share the same posting, but the powers that be apparently had other ideas and Rita was now somewhere in rural Dorset, and probably having the time of her life. She might not be pursuing a glittering career on the covers of magazines, but Miranda was certain that she would be the most popular pin-up at the aerodrome.

After another tentative drag on the cigarette she decided that it was time to give up, and she ground the butt beneath the heel of her serviceable black lace-up shoe. She shivered and walked on towards the WAAF quarters situated in a Nissen hut on the far side of the main building, but she had to steel herself to cross the wide sweep of gravel outside the façade of Henlow Priory. The officers, male and female, were billeted there, but it was a creepy ancient pile dating back to the eleventh century, and the rumour that it was haunted had encouraged the telling of ghoulish ghost stories after lights out. Even now Miranda could feel the hairs on the back of her neck standing on end. She knew that the tales of unhappy spirits roaming the house and grounds were likely to be based on folklore, but on a crystal clear night, with the priory silhouetted against a black velvet sky by a bomber's moon, it was possible to believe almost anything.

Being stationed in the depths of the country-side was a far cry from growing up in suburban London or living in a bustling seaside town. Now the only sound she could hear was the crunch of her leather soles on the frozen gravel, and the occasional eerie hoot of a hunting barn owl. She quickened her pace, telling herself that an over-active imagination was playing havoc with her senses, and as she drew nearer to the hut she heard the welcome sounds of everyday life.

Audrey was belting out a Vera Lynn song, but her tinny soprano was at odds with the loud swing music being played on the portable gramophone owned by the irrepressible Janice Goodman, who lived for Saturday night dances in the local village hall. It was in the hot, sweaty atmosphere where the only refreshments were tea and digestive bis-cuits that the girls had the opportunity to mix with the air and ground crews from the aero-drome a few miles east of the priory. There were a few local men as well, but they were either exempt because of age, unfit for active service or in reserved occupations.

Even as she reached the door Miranda knew that the fug from the cast-iron stove, mingled with the scent of Lifebuoy soap, cigarette smoke and nail polish remover would hit her like a slap in the face. She knocked, tapping out the code they used to confound Flight Sergeant Frances Fosdyke, whose habitual pout and proptotic grey eyes had earned her the nickname of Fishface. Her habit of descending upon them unannounced in order to catch someone flouting the rules had incurred the dislike of all the girls. The punishments were severe, and unless someone had a penchant for cleaning latrines and the ablutions block they soon realised that it was best not to get on the wrong side of the sergeant. With this in mind, Miranda knocked a little harder as she was beginning to lose all feeling in her fingers and toes. She stamped her feet while she waited for someone to unlock the door. Eventually, during a lull as the record came to an end and Audrey stopped singing, the door opened and Miranda hurried inside. As she had anticipated, the air was thick with cigarette smoke, which rose to form a nimbus cloud below the curved ceiling. Janice and her friend Valerie were practising their version of the jitterbug to the strains of a Glenn Miller record, while others sat about chatting and keeping their hands busy with knitting or darning their laddered stockings.

Gloria, the girl who had let Miranda in, adjusted the blackout curtain over the door. 'Don't want old Fishface catching us breaking the rules,' she said, taking the cigarette from her lips and exhaling smoke through her nostrils. 'That woman can arm-wrestle the blokes and win. Got any fags, love? This is my last one.'

Miranda rummaged in her handbag and produced a packet of Woodbines. There was only one missing and it was no sacrifice to give them to Gloria who had a twenty a day habit. 'Here, you have them, Glo. I'm trying to give up.' She handed them to her with a smile.

Gloria slapped her on the back. 'You're a pal. I'll do the same for you one day.'

'Forget it. You're doing me a favour.' Miranda dropped her handbag and gas mask case on her bed, which was nearest the door. She had been the last to arrive at Henlow and it seemed that no one else had wanted to sleep in the draughty spot furthest away from the stove. Not that it mattered very much as she was generally so exhausted at the end of her shift that she could have slept on a bed of nails.

She took off her peaked cap and stowed it on the top shelf of the wooden locker beside her bed, followed by her navy-blue serge overcoat. She glanced anxiously at the clock, realising that in a few short minutes Corporal Draper would emerge from her room at the far end of the hut to carry out her routine inspection. June Draper was almost as unpopular as Fishface, but it would be a serious mistake to underestimate her power to make their lives a misery, should she feel so inclined. June's fiancé was supposed to have jilted her at the altar, and at the start Miranda had made allowances for her, but as time passed she began to think that the chap had shown a streak of good sense. Any man who married June would be doomed to live permanently in the doghouse.

Miranda perched on the edge of her bed and peeled off her thick grey lisle stockings. She would have loved to step into a nice hot bath, even if there were only five inches of water in the tub, but a lukewarm shower was all that she had to look forward to, and that only if she was first in the queue at the washhouse next morning. She glanced round to make sure that no one was watching before she stripped to her brassiere and the hideous standard issue knickers, commonly known as blackouts. She knew that it was ridiculous to be self-conscious, but she had still not quite come to terms with the lack of privacy, or the ghastly underwear which would make the most gorgeous bathing beauty look a complete fright. She wondered how Rita was coping with such privations, and smiled to herself, thinking that Rita would have found a way round the regulations by now. She sighed.

'What's the matter, ducks?' Audrey said, peering at her through a haze of cigarette smoke. 'Have you got something that the rest of us girls don't have?'

Startled, Miranda slipped her dressing gown around her shoulders. 'Sorry?'

'Don't worry, love. You'll get used to us common lot sooner or later.' Audrey sauntered off to sit on her own bed.

Miranda bit her lip. She never quite knew how to take Audrey's jocular comments, but she had learned from experience that to allow her to have the last word was fatal. 'What was that you were singing earlier? I could hear you from outside the hut.'

'Are you trying to tell me that I got a voice like a foghorn?'

'Yeah, she was,' Gloria said, stubbing out her cigarette in a metal ashtray. 'But she was being kind. I wouldn't call it singing; it's worse than the air raid siren.'

The girls squatting on the next bed playing a hand of cards burst out laughing. One of them, a redhead by the name of Angela, turned to Miranda with a sympathetic smile as Audrey flounced off, the towelling turban on her head wobbling like a vanilla blancmange. 'Don't take any notice of her, old thing. She's a touch sensitive and having been forced to endure her whole repertoire one can see why.'

'I didn't mean anything by it,' Miranda said anxiously. 'I wouldn't be so unkind.'

'Of course you wouldn't, darling. I'd ignore her little tantrums if I were you.' Angela winked and turned her attention back to her hand of cards.

'Turn that bloody gramophone down,' Audrey shouted, making a move towards it with a threatening gesture.

Janice glared at her, pausing in the middle of a complicated dance step. 'Shut up, Trotter. It's better than the noise that comes out of your big fat gob.'

'If you don't turn it down I'll vaccinate you with the bloody gramophone needle.'

'Keep it down, ladies,' Gloria said in a low voice, jerking her head in the direction of the corporal's closed door. 'She'll have your guts for garters if you start a fight, Trotter.'

Miranda could see that things were going to turn nasty as Janice clawed her fingers and Valerie squared up to Audrey. The situation was beginning to look dangerous, but Gloria reached out a long thin arm and tweaked the towel off Audrey's head. 'Calm down, love. They're just having you on.' She turned to Janice and Valerie with a frown. 'And you two, leave the poor cow alone.'

'Leave it out, Glo,' Janice said, shrugging her shoulders. 'We were just having a bit of fun. She's

161

so easy to wind up.'

Audrey tossed her damp hair back from her face. 'I was top of the bill in the summer concert party at Southend.'

'Pity they didn't throw you off the end of the pier,' Janice said, grinning.

Gloria caught hold of Audrey just as she was about to launch herself at her tormentor, but everyone froze as the door to the corporal's room opened.

Keeping a wary eye on June Draper, Miranda could not help noticing that she was looking decidedly peaky, and her eyes were suspiciously red-ringed as though she had been crying. Miranda felt almost sorry for her. Keeping control of a group of young women from widely varying backgrounds thrown together by the exigencies of war could not be an easy task.

June wagged her finger at Janice. 'I might have guessed it was you, Aircraftwoman Goodman.'

Miranda hoped that for once Janice would keep her mouth shut, as the feisty Brummy had almost spent more time in jankers than she had in the plotting room, but there must have been something in June's expression that had registered with everyone, even Janice, who cast her eyes down. 'Sorry, Corporal.'

June glanced round the room and no one moved a muscle. 'I should put all three of you on a charge,' she said in clipped tones, 'but as this is my last night in hut five, I'm going to let you off.'

Gloria, who Miranda had often noticed was rarely lost for words, cleared her throat. 'Where are you going, Corp?'

162

'I'm being posted nearer home,' June said with a break in her voice. 'My dad died this morning and I've got a few days' compassionate leave before I report for duty.'

A ripple of sympathy ran round the room and Miranda knew that had it been anyone else there would have been a rush to hug and comfort June, but they were all too well disciplined to let their emotions get the better of them. There was an awkward silence and Miranda realised that no one knew quite what to say. She stepped forward. 'I'm sure we're all very sorry, Corporal.'

June's cheeks flamed and she bit her lip. 'Thanks,' she said gruffly. 'As you were.' She retreated into her room, pausing for a moment in the doorway. 'We'll skip inspection tonight, and keep it down, girls. I've got a splitting headache.' She went inside and closed the door.

Gloria was the first to speak. 'You heard the corp. I'm going to turn in and I suggest you lot do the same. Lights out in fifteen minutes, and no smoking in bed. If anyone does I'll personally tip a jug of water over them.'

After the quick trip to the ablutions block and the latrines, the girls scurried back to hut five and settled down for the night. Desultory snatches of conversation soon petered out as they drifted off to sleep, but Miranda lay on her hard mattress staring into the darkness. She had been away from home for what seemed a lifetime but she could not help worrying about all those she had left behind. She thought of her father and mother doing their bit for the war effort, and prayed that they were safe. She had received brief letters from her grandmother informing her that Jack was alive and well at the time of writing, but of course there was no mention of Raif or Isabel, and although their last meeting had been marred by his scathing comments about Jack, time had softened the memories and made her think that perhaps she had been too hard on both him and his sister. They were all victims of this beastly war, which seemed to be going on forever. Nowhere in the country was safe these days. German bombers had attacked the naval base at Portland and the torpedo works on the edge of the fleet as well as residential areas. Where, she wondered, would it all end? She closed her eyes, willing herself to sleep.

June's replacement arrived next day but Miranda was on an early shift and did not meet her until she came off duty. She could tell immediately that she was not going to like Corporal Diana Fox, and the feeling seemed to be shared by the other girls. June, who had never been popular, had suddenly achieved the status of a saint and everyone was reminiscing about the good times they had shared. Personally, Miranda could not think of any, but when Corporal Fox told her that she had failed kit inspection and detailed her off to clean the ablutions, Miranda began to think they had misjudged June Draper.

It was Saturday, and as she had been on late duty the previous day Miranda was free to spend the evening as she pleased. After emptying the chemical toilets in the latrine block and mopping the floors with disinfectant she was tired and

164

feeling out of sorts. She would not have minded the punishment had she done something to deserve it, but Corporal Fox had picked on her for no reason – it was so unfair. Miranda flopped down on her bed and kicked off her shoes.

Janice looked up from the magazine she had been reading. 'I don't reckon much to that new corp,' she whispered. 'That wasn't right what old Foxy did to you. Are you okay?'

Miranda nodded. 'I'm fine. Just a bit fed up to tell the truth.'

'Val and me are going to the village hop this evening. D'you want to come too?'

'I – well, that's very kind of you, but...'

'No buts, love. You're coming and that's final. You need a bit of cheering up, and I think a few of the lads from the aerodrome might be coming along tonight. We might meet some of the boys we've known only by their call signs. I think they owe us a trot round the dance floor and a drink or two.'

'I don't know, Janice,' Miranda said doubtfully. 'It's jolly nice of you, but I'm not sure I'm in the mood.'

'"In the Mood" – I love that tune,' Janice said dreamily. 'I'd like to meet Glenn Miller and tell him how much I enjoy his music.'

'You go with Val and have a lovely time, Jan. I think I'll spend the evening in the priory library, curled up with a good book.'

Janice threw her magazine on the floor and leapt from her bed. She dragged Miranda to her feet. 'No you don't, miss. You're coming with us if Val and me have to carry you there. Now get your glad

165

rags on and let Val do something with your hair.' She tossed her slipper at her friend, who was staring into her compact mirror and plucking her eyebrows. 'Hey, Val. Can you give this woman a proper hairdo? She can't go dancing with it scraped back in a bun.' She tweaked a couple of hairpins from Miranda's hair and loosened it with her fingers. 'You've got lovely blonde hair. It's all right looking prim and proper in the ops room but we're going to have a good time tonight.'

Despite her protests, Miranda's hair had been washed and persuaded into a shining pageboy style with the aid of curling tongs heated on the top of the stove. She would have been quite happy to put on a cotton blouse and skirt and go as she was, but the girls had other ideas. Val went through Miranda's locker like someone possessed, tossing the garments on her bed with exclamations of dismay. 'You can't wear this. That one would make you look like a schoolgirl, and this one would suit my gran.' She threw up her hands in despair. 'Have you got anything, Janice? The kid can't go to a dance looking like flaming Judy Garland in *The Wizard of Oz*.'

'No, really,' Miranda said, deciding that this had gone far enough. 'Please don't bother. I'll wear this.' She snatched up the white crêpe de Chine with the floral print that Rita still coveted. 'With my lovely new hairstyle this will be fine.'

Janice angled her head. 'I suppose so, but you need some mascara.' She delved in her handbag. 'Here, use my Rimmel one and a touch of lipstick. It's fine being a natural blonde, but you're

166

a bit pale.'

'Thanks, but it wouldn't be fair. I know make-up is hard to come by these days.' Miranda rarely used anything apart from a dash of lipstick, but Rita's letters had read like a wish list – *Things I would like for my birthday* – followed by a catalogue of virtually unobtainable cosmetics.

Janice thrust them into her hand. 'Nah! Share and share alike, ducks. Isn't that right, Val?'

Valerie nodded vigorously. 'Stop yapping and get on with it, Miranda. We've got to get ourselves glammed-up and that takes time.'

Walking a mile in high heels along a narrow country lane in total darkness was not something that Miranda would have chosen as the start of a night out, but Janice and Val tottered along, singing at the tops of their voices. The thin reedy beam of their torches gave just enough light for them to avoid the worst of the potholes, but the ground was already coated with ice and very slippery. In the end there was nothing for it but to link arms and hope that nothing was coming, as it was almost impossible to see oncoming vehicles now that headlamps had to be masked, shedding just a sliver of light onto the road surface. Miranda was worried that by singing so loudly they might drown out the sound of an approaching car engine, but she did not want to spoil their mood.

They were cold and breathless when they finally arrived at the hall, but inside it was warm, smoky and very noisy as the pitch of voices rose in competition with the music on the gramophone, which was turned up to full volume. The dance floor was crowded with couples wrapped in each other's arms moving very little as there was quite a crush. Miranda could see that being an expert in the foxtrot or the quickstep mattered very little when there was barely any space to perform, not that it seemed to be affecting the dancers' enjoyment. Janice and Val had already shed their outer garments and hung them on a row of wall pegs, and Miranda followed suit. She was beginning to regret her decision to forgo an evening huddled in a leather wing-back chair in the library. The smell of musty books and the draughts whistling though the casement windows seemed like a haven of peace and quiet compared to the hubbub in the church hall.

'Cooee,' Janice called, waving her hand to a young man in civvies who was leaning nonchalantly against the tea bar. His face creased into a broad grin and he started towards them, weaving in and out through the gyrating couples. 'That's Cyril,' Janice said coyly. 'He's ever such a good dancer, and before you ask, he works for the gas board so he didn't get called up.'

'He looks nice,' Miranda murmured as Cyril drew closer. 'You kept him quiet, didn't you?'

'He's just a dance partner,' Janice said airily. 'I never said it was serious.' She moved towards Cyril with her arms outstretched. 'Hello, darling. How've you been?'

Valerie patted her long dark hair into place. 'Do I look all right? I'd go to the ladies' but I don't want to miss anything.'

Miranda glanced round the hall. There seemed to be plenty of girls without partners and not very many unattached men. 'Is it always like this?'

'Sometimes, but the boys from the aerodrome should be here soon, that's if they haven't been scrambled. I forgot to ask Gloria how things were going when I saw her briefly in the mess.'

Miranda edged out of the way as a couple more girls breezed in on a gust of ice-cold air.

'Let's have a cuppa, I'm parched, and we won't look so desperate if we're doing something.' Valerie headed for the tea bar, manned by two formid-able-looking matrons wearing floral pinafores and felt hats. 'Two teas, love.'

The woman who served her picked up the large teapot. 'Haven't we forgotten something?'

Valerie grinned. 'Milk and sugar?'

'Very funny, young lady, but I meant the little word that's most important.'

'Please.'

'That's better, but there's no sugar. There is a war on, you know.' The woman filled two cups. 'That'll be tuppence, please,' she said, putting the emphasis on the last word.

Valerie raised an eyebrow. 'Daylight robbery.'

Miranda took her purse from her bag and ex-tracted two pennies. 'Thank you,' she said, plac-ing them in the woman's hand. 'I'm sure it's a lovely cup of tea.'

'At least someone round here has manners.' With a scornful glance in Valerie's direction the woman moved on to serve someone else.

Valerie took a mouthful of tea and pulled a face. 'Stewed. I knew it would be. They must make it

169

an hour before the doors open.' She moved away to sit on one of the wooden chairs set out along the wall. 'Sit down, love. You're making the place look untidy.'

Miranda took the seat beside her and sipped the lukewarm brew. Val was right, the tea had a metallic taste and was quite bitter, but it was better than nothing and she drank slowly, still wishing that she had stuck to her original plan. If she had followed her own inclinations she could have been ensconced in the oak-panelled library now, reading a book that would take her mind off the wretched war. Instead of which, she was now an official wallflower and it was not a comfortable feeling. She felt even more out of place as she cast a sideways glance at the girls who were waiting patiently for someone to claim them for the next dance. Without exception, they were done up to the nines, their faces powdered and rouged, their eyelashes bristling with mascara and their lips painted scarlet. Miranda could not help wondering how they managed to get hold of makeup when it was so scarce in the shops, but she felt suddenly underdressed and dowdy. She decided to wait until Valerie had a partner and then slip away unnoticed.

Someone had changed the record and Janice and Cyril were now jiving quite expertly to Benny Goodman and his orchestra's rendition of 'Sing, Sing, Sing (With a Swing)' and the other couples were attempting it with varying degrees of success.

Valerie put her cup and saucer under her chair. 'Hurry up and put in an appearance, chaps,' she murmured, folding her arms and tapping her feet. 'I don't want to sit here all evening like a lemon.'

Almost before the words had left her mouth the doors opened and a group of RAF officers entered to warning cries of 'Remember the blackout and keep that door shut' from the ladies behind the counter.

Valerie rose to her feet, catching Miranda by the hand. 'Get up,' she hissed. 'I know that chap who came in first. I danced with him a couple of weeks ago. He's hot stuff.'

Miranda had no option other than to stand up and she craned her neck to get a better look. As always she found herself comparing Val's hot stuff to Raif, who seemed to have set a standard in her head by which to measure the attractiveness of men. 'Who is he?'

'That's Gilbert Maddern. Isn't he just super?'

Miranda was unimpressed. 'He looks okay.'

'Are you blind? He's absolutely gorgeous and all the girls in hut five would just die for a date with Mad Dog. That's his call sign and it suits him.'

'Well, what are you waiting for? Go and ask him for a dance.'

Valerie shook her head. 'I couldn't do that. I don't think even Gloria would go up to a bloke and ask him to dance.' She stiffened, clutching Miranda's arm. 'Oh my God! He's coming this way. He must have spotted me.'

'Now's your chance then,' Miranda said, giving her a gentle push in his direction.

Valerie opened her mouth to speak but he did

not seem to notice her as he approached Miranda with a disarming smile. He held out his hand. 'Gil Maddern. How do you do?'

She was too surprised to do anything other than respond politely. She shook his hand. 'Miranda Beddoes. How do you do?'

'Now that we've introduced ourselves, would you care to dance, Miss Beddoes?'

She could feel Val breathing down her neck and she hesitated. 'I – I mean we were just having a cup of tea,' she said, casting an imploring look in Val's direction.

'Don't mind me,' Val said, curving her lips, into the semblance of a smile.

'That's all right then,' Gil said, taking Miranda by the hand. 'Shall we?'

'He's a heartbreaker,' Val whispered in Miranda's ear. 'He's had more girlfriends than I've had hot dinners.'

Miranda was quick to hear the note of jealousy in Val's tone. She could quite believe that Gil Maddern might be a practised flirt, but his smile was infectious and there was a wicked twinkle in his hazel eyes and a lopsided quirk to his lips as though he was about to grin. He was also clasping her hand in a firm grasp that would have made it quite a struggle to pull free. She could feel Valerie's eyes boring into her but she could hardly refuse his request without offering a good excuse – and she had none. 'Yes, thank you.' He was still holding her hand as he led her onto the dance floor, where the pace had slowed considerably as the couples moved slowly to Glenn Miller's 'Basin Street Blues'.

'I haven't seen you here before,' Gil said, taking her in his arms. 'Are you one of the girls from Henlow Priory?'

'Yes. How did you know that?'

'You're obviously not from the village.'

'How can you tell?'

'Perhaps I'm psychic.'

He smiled again and she could see why some of the girls were bowled over by him, but his charm was a bit too studied for her liking. 'And perhaps you like to chat up new girls so that you can boast about your conquests.' She could tell by his start-led expression that he had not been expecting this reaction.

'That's not true. I'm actually very shy when it comes to women.'

'Now that is a downright fib,' she said, laughing.

He whirled her round as the record came to an end. 'At least I've made you laugh. You should do it more often.'

'There isn't much to laugh about these days.' She met his amused gaze with a frown. 'I spend eight hours a day, sometimes twelve, moving little blocks around a grid and tracking the flight paths of chaps like you. Sometimes we hear them over the tannoy calling Mayday. It's the most chilling sound you could ever imagine, and even more so when it goes silent. We all hate that.'

He did not release her immediately. 'When I'm up there, kissing the clouds, I'll be glad to know that someone is thinking about me, and caring what happens.'

'Oh, please.' She broke away with an exasperated sigh. 'I bet you say that to all the girls.'

'No. Only the pretty blondes.'

'That is such a corny chat-up line, Flying Officer Maddern.'

'Now I've offended you. I'm sorry, but it was meant to be a compliment.'

'It doesn't matter.' She glanced over her shoulder, looking for Val and Janice, but they were seated at a table chatting to a couple of the young men who had come in with Gil. There was a lull in the music while someone shuffled through a pile of records and the dancers began to leave the floor in search of refreshments.

'How about a truly awful cup of tea or a glass of watered down orange squash?' Gil followed her back to her seat. 'Or a totally tasteless and rather soggy biscuit? People come from far and wide to sample the food here.'

She shot him a sideways glance. 'Are you always like this?'

'Like what, Miss Beddoes?'

'So – so persistent.'

'My Latin master told us that his tutor had had to translate a motto into Latin for an American university: Pep without purpose is piffle. That's always been my motto too.'

'And your purpose is?'

'To get to know you better, Miranda.'

'Now you're shooting a line,' she said defensively. 'I'm not that naïve. I bet you've said things like that to every girl at Henlow Priory.'

His lips twitched. 'Almost all; and it usually works.'

'Sorry, Mad Dog, not this time.' She glanced at the clock on the wall above the tea bar. 'Nine

174

thirty. I'd best be getting back to Henlow.'

His smile faded. 'Are you that eager to escape from my boring company?'

'Not at all, but I have to be up early in the morning. Goodnight, it was nice meeting you.' She walked towards the row of pegs where her garments were now buried beneath a mass of flying jackets. She did not look back, hoping that by now he had got the message that she was not in the mood for a mild flirtation. She had allowed herself to fall for Raif's charms and she was determined not to make the same mistake with Mad Dog Maddern. She was burrowing beneath the coats trying to find hers, when someone relieved her of their weight.

'Allow me. I can't stand by and see you struggle. You could suffocate under that lot.'

Reluctantly, she stood back and allowed Gil to systematically unhook the heavy sheepskin flying jackets. 'Thank you,' she murmured. 'But I could have...'

'Managed on your own; I know.' He turned to her, shaking his head. 'What an independent girl you are, Miranda Beddoes.'

'Yes,' she said nodding slowly. 'I suppose I am, although I'd never given it much thought.'

'Which one?'

She stared at him blankly. 'I'm sorry?'

'Which coat is yours?'

'Oh, yes. I see what you mean.' She pointed to her camel coat and the matching felt beret. 'They're mine.'

'I might have guessed.' He lifted them off the peg. 'Classic, understated and ladylike.'

She took them from him, trying not to snatch. 'In other words, boring.'

'Not at all.' He replaced all but one of the flying jackets and slipped it on. 'Come on then. I'll take you back to Henlow. That's if you don't mind riding pillion on my motorbike.'

Chapter Ten

Ignoring her protests, Gil opened the door. 'Best foot forward – mustn't forget the blackout.'

'Remember the blackout.' The familiar cry of the tea ladies left Miranda with little option other than to hurry outside and close the door. Not that there were any enemy planes droning overhead, nor were there likely to be in these weather conditions, as it had begun to snow. Large feathery flakes swirled from a black velvet sky creating a graceful aerial ballet as they floated down to settle on the frozen ground. The world about them had turned into a monochrome fairyland and Miranda had to smother a cry of pleasure.

'It's beautiful, isn't it?' Gil said as if reading her thoughts. 'But let's get you home while it's still safe to travel.'

'I can walk. You should get back to the aerodrome before the roads become impassable.'

He pulled the collar of his flying jacket up to his chin. 'I wouldn't hear of it. Come on, we're wasting time.' He flicked snow off the saddle and climbed on.

She hesitated for a moment, wishing that she had worn sensible shoes instead of slavishly following fashion. It was painfully obvious that trudging through snow in high heels was asking for trouble, and she hitched up her skirts to sit astride the pillion.

'Hold on,' he said as he kick-started the engine and drove off slowly at first but gathering speed as he negotiated the winding country lanes.

Terrified and yet strangely exhilarated, Miranda slid her arms around his waist and held on, resting her cheek against the soft leather of his jacket. Apart from the occasional sideways slither, the tyres seemed to be coping with the icy surface and she closed her eyes, hoping that he was as good at handling a motorbike as he was at piloting a plane. Even through the thick protective fleece she could feel the tension in his muscles as he struggled to keep the machine on the road. The conditions seemed to be getting worse each minute, and there were moments when she feared they might end up in a ditch, but eventually they drove through the gates of Henlow Priory. Gil pulled up outside the great house. 'Are you okay?'

She nodded. 'Yes, thanks.'

He steadied the bike while she got off, which was a feat in itself as she pulled her skirts even higher exposing an indecent amount of leg, thigh and suspenders. She was very glad that his back was turned and there was no one else to witness her struggles. She straightened up, adjusting her clothing. 'It was very good of you to give me a lift in this awful weather.'

'Actually, I rather like the snow. It makes everything look pure and clean, as if the world had just been invented.' He chuckled, shaking snowflakes from his eyebrows and lashes. 'But there are disadvantages.'

'Well, thank you again.' Miranda was suddenly at a loss. Had she been living at home she would have felt bound to ask him in for a hot drink before setting off on the treacherous ride back to the aerodrome, but that was simply not possible. 'I mustn't keep you.'

'Are you billeted in the house?'

She pointed to hut five. 'I'd have thought you would know where the girls were living.' She could not resist the dig.

'Touché!' He saluted her and revved the engine. 'I'll see you again soon, I hope.'

Her lips were too frozen to allow a smile and she answered with a brief nod. 'Please go now or you'll never make it.'

'Does this mean that you're worried about me, Miranda?'

'Not really. I'm simply freezing to death.'

He leaned over and kissed her briefly on the cheek. 'We'll meet again very soon, and that's a promise.' He drove off and disappeared into the snowstorm.

'I don't think so,' Miranda murmured, turning in the direction of the Nissen hut. 'I'm not in the market to get my heart broken by a glamour-boy whose life is on the line every time he takes to the skies.' As she made her way carefully through the snow she could not help thinking about Raif. She had tried to convince herself that what she felt for him was just a crush, but if that were so then why could she not put him from her mind? He had never shown the slightest interest in her as a woman, and he despised her family. He had done his best to come between Jack and Izzie, and for all she knew he might have succeeded. Why, then, was she constantly comparing every man she met with Raif Carstairs?

She knocked on the hut door and was let in by Audrey, who burst out laughing. 'Bloody hell, mate. Stick a pipe in your mouth and you could pass for a snowman. What have you done with the others?'

Suddenly everything was normal again, or as normal as anything could be in wartime. Miranda gave her eager audience a brief account of the evening, but she was forced to admit that Gilbert Maddern had given her a lift back to camp on his motorbike and this was met with sharp intakes of breath and envious glances.

'You and Mad Dog.' Gloria looked her up and down. 'What on earth does a chap like him see in a goody two-shoes like you, Miranda?'

Everyone laughed and Miranda managed a smile as she tried to rub some life back into her frozen feet. 'I'm not interested in Gil Maddern,' she said firmly. 'You're welcome to him, Gloria.'

'I could eat him for breakfast,' Gloria said, reaching for a packet of Kensitas. 'And lunch and dinner, but I doubt if Mad Dog Maddern would settle for anything less than a section officer.'

'He must have thought you were a challenge, darling.' Angela threw a rolled-up stocking at Gloria. 'If you light up once again, Gloria Jones,

I'm going to personally throttle you, even if I hang for it.'

As if in answer to her problem, the corporal's door opened and Diana Fox took in the scene with a swift glance. 'Lights out, ladies. No smoking, Jones. This isn't the public bar at the Rose and Crown.' She disappeared into her room and closed the door.

'Lucky she didn't do a roll-call or she'd have realised that Jan and Val are missing,' Gloria said, stowing her packet of cigarettes in her handbag. 'I bet the poor sods are walking home in the snow. You're a jammy devil, Miranda. Only you could get a lift home with Mad Dog Maddern and not realise how bloody lucky you are.'

'Shut up, Gloria, do.' Angela tossed her other stocking at her. 'Turn the lights out, Miranda, you're closest to the switch. Goodnight, girls.'

It was pitch-dark in the hut when Miranda awakened suddenly with her heart pounding and her senses alert. She raised herself on her elbow, wondering if there was an air raid although she had not heard the warning siren. There was silence except for the steady breathing of those around her and the occasional creak of a bed, and then she heard it again: the rattle of the door handle followed by the groan of the rusting hinges. She sat bolt upright, ready to raise the alarm as the intruders crept into the hut, but as the last remnants of sleep cleared from her brain she remembered that the door had been left unlocked. She leapt out of bed, seizing the first thing that came to hand which happened to be one of her shoes, and raised it above her head ready to strike.

'What the hell are you doing, you silly bitch?' Miranda lowered her arm, peering into the gloom. 'Janice? Is that you?'

'Who did you think it was? The bloody tooth fairy?' Janice closed the door. 'Put the light on, Val, I can't see where I'm going.'

'Wait. I've got a torch.' Miranda felt around in her locker until her fingers closed on the cold metal outer case. She switched it on and caught them in its beam. 'How did you get back from the dance?'

'One of the local farmers gave us a lift on the milk cart,' Val said through chattering teeth. 'I'm absolutely blooming frozen.'

'And you got off with Mad Dog.' Janice shielded her eyes from the light. 'Stop pointing that damn thing at me.'

'Sorry.' Miranda lowered the torch. 'But I didn't get off with him. He brought me back to camp, that's all.'

'Will you girls shut up? Some of us are trying to sleep.'

'Okay, okay, Angela,' Janice mumbled. 'Keep your hair on.' She shuffled up to Miranda, snatching the torch from her hand. 'I'll give it back in the morning, and then you can tell us exactly how you managed to catch Gil Maddern's eye. We'd all like to know.' She walked off, following the thin trail of light from the torch.

'She's always had a thing for Mad Dog,' Val whispered as she hurried past Miranda. 'Best watch your back for knives, love.'

Miranda climbed into bed and huddled beneath

the rapidly cooling covers. It seemed that everyone had a thing for Gil Maddern except her. She closed her eyes, and it was Raif's face that haunted her dreams.

They had three days without German raids due to adverse weather conditions, but on the fourth day the respite period was over and the operations room was busier than ever. Miranda went about her tasks as usual, but she found herself listening for Mad Dog's call sign and suddenly what had been routine before had become personal. The girls teased her constantly about their relationship, creating imaginary situations where Gil Maddern was there to sweep little Goody Two-Shoes as she had now been dubbed, off her tiny feet. Miranda laughed and treated it all as a joke, but she was beginning to wish that she had never met the camp heart-throb. She realised that there was a touch of jealousy beneath some of the comments she received, although she could not think why as she had vigorously denied any interest on her part in a man who had a reputation for taking risks.

After a fortnight the novelty seemed to have worn off, but she had not been invited to accompany Valerie and Janice to the Saturday night hop. As usual, they were full of it next day, telling everyone about their conquests, although Janice had to admit that she had danced mostly with Cyril, and it was Val who had snared one of the officers as a partner. Miranda did not ask if Gil Maddern had been there, although she assumed that he had, and that he had probably found another popsy to chat up. Not that it mattered to her, nor was it any of her business. Becoming emotionally involved with air crew was a form of torture she could well do without.

She spent the following Saturday night in the priory library, although it was not quite as romantic and peaceful as she had imagined it would be. In fact it was cold, draughty and so spooky that she left early and went to the canteen kitchen to make a cup of cocoa and thaw out her chilled extremities. She went to bed early taking with her a book she had borrowed from the library, although she had to suffer constant interruptions from a new girl called Connie Pearson, who kept up an incessant line of chatter whilst knitting something very ugly in khaki wool.

Next day was the first Sunday off that Miranda had had in two months and she planned to do as little as possible. The snow had melted but it was still bitterly cold and very wet; not the sort of weather for long country walks and without transport sight-seeing was out of the question. There were no buses to town on a Sunday and very few in the week, and she was missing the hustle and bustle of urban streets. In particular she missed the cinema. She had always loved the movies, especially the musicals featuring Fred Astaire and Ginger Rogers. Sitting in a darkened auditorium, watching the silver screen to the sound of rustling cellophane as people dipped into their bags of sweets, was now a fading memory. She made her mind up to spend the day washing her undies and pressing her uniform ready for Monday morning.

She was on her way back from the ablutions carrying a basket of wet clothes, when she heard the roar of a motorcycle engine. At first she thought nothing of it as there were always messengers travelling to and fro between the priory and the aerodrome, but she realised suddenly that it had slowed down almost to a walking pace and was close behind her. She stopped and turned slowly as the rider drew the machine to a halt at her side. He took off his leather helmet and goggles confirming her suspicion that it was Gil Maddern.

'Hello, Miranda.'

'Hello.' She eyed him coolly.

'I thought if you weren't doing anything important, you might like a jaunt into town.'

'It seems a long way to come on the off chance. I might be on duty.'

He glanced at the washing basket. 'Very true, but I telephoned first and checked with your section officer.'

'I don't believe you. She wouldn't divulge something like that over the phone.'

'I had to fib a bit. I said that we were engaged and that I was being posted far away, and this was our last chance to see each other before I left.'

'You're such a liar. How could you make up something like that?'

'Call it quick thinking on my part. That's what keeps us alive in dog fights with the Luftwaffe. You don't get second chances up there, but you and I started off on the wrong foot, Miranda. Will you give me another go? Perhaps we could have a spot of lunch, followed by a sedate walk around the castle ruins, and finish off with afternoon tea in one of those quaint teashops owned by genteel elderly ladies.'

'You think of everything, don't you?'

'Does that mean you'll come?'

She hesitated for a moment, but the wicker basket was heavy and water was dripping onto her shoes. The thought of a day out and some half decent food was too tempting to pass over. She was about to accept but glancing down at her plain grey slacks and thick woollen sweater she realised suddenly that she must look like a complete frump. 'I'll have to change first.'

'You look fine as you are,' he said with a casual shrug. 'Slacks are more suitable for riding pillion than a skirt.'

'You were watching.' She felt her cheeks flame with colour but she looked him in the eyes. 'How did you do that?'

He grinned. 'There's a mirror on the handlebar. Very useful and saves turning one's head.'

She was about to protest when she realised that he was teasing her and she laughed. 'It was dark and it was snowing. There's absolutely no way you could have seen anything.'

'A chap can use his imagination, can't he?'

She shook her head. 'I'll definitely wear slacks. Give me five minutes and I'll be with you.'

It was a good fifteen minutes before she emerged from the hut, still wearing the same slacks but having changed the thick woollen sweater for a cotton blouse and a cashmere cardigan. Stopping for a moment to button her camel coat, she adjusted her beret and climbed onto the pillion.

She knew they would be seen as they left the priory grounds and tongues would start wagging, but somehow she did not care. The lure of a day out was too appealing to resist.

It was cold but the rain had ceased and the drive through the country lanes was uneventful. Gil handled the machine expertly, and after the first couple of miles Miranda began to relax. By the time they reached the town centre she could honestly say that she had enjoyed the experience, although on a couple of occasions when Gil overtook a lumbering horse-drawn farm cart she had had to close her eyes and pray for deliverance. It was midday and they lunched in a mock-Tudor restaurant where the waitresses were motherly middle-aged women who immediately fell for Gil's charms and could not do enough for him. The brown Windsor soup was thick and glutinous but the bread rolls were fresh and still warm from the oven. Miranda noticed with a wry smile that Gil had an extra pat of butter on his plate, and when the main course was served she was certain that his fillet of plaice was at least half as big again as hers. He managed to plough through it together with the huge portion of chips and rewarded the waitress with lavish compliments and his most winning smile.

Miranda waited until their plates were cleared away and the waitress was out of earshot. 'Aren't you ashamed of yourself?' she whispered.

'I was just being polite. It's good to show one's appreciation.'

'You were flirting with that poor woman. You're shameless, Gilbert.'

His eyes danced with merriment. 'Now you sound like my mother. She always calls me Gilbert when she's cross with me.'

It was impossible to keep up the pretence that she was angry and Miranda smiled. 'I bet she spoiled you when you were a child.'

'Not at all; she was very strict.'

'But you were an only child.'

'I don't know what gave you that idea. As a matter of fact I have three older sisters, and I can assure you they didn't spoil me either.'

'Is that how you know so much about women?'

'I learned to respect them, and to appreciate them. My father died when I was six, leaving Mother with four of us to bring up on her own. She took over the business and made a great success of it.'

Intrigued, Miranda leaned her elbows on the table, watching him carefully. This was not the blasé, devil-may-care Mad Dog character he chose to portray. 'What sort of business, Gil?'

'My grandfather was an auctioneer and Father went into the business straight from school. They did well enough but then Father became ill and the firm lost money. It took Mother several years but she built it up again and did even better.'

'She must be quite a woman.'

'She is.'

'And your sisters?'

He paused, looking up to smile at the waitress as she brought them their dessert of apple pie and custard. 'That looks wonderful. Thank you.'

'I hope you enjoy it, sir.' She moved away to serve the couple at the next table.

187

'You were telling me about your sisters.'

'Beth and Mary are both married and Felicity works in the family firm. I'm supposed to be taking over from Mother when she retires, but I know she's not going to give up easily.'

Miranda was intrigued. She was seeing a completely different person from the man she had imagined Gil Maddern to be. 'Do you want to be an auctioneer?'

He pulled a face as he dug his spoon into the pie. 'Perhaps it's not the career I would have chosen, but if I survive this war I suppose I'll settle down and take up the gavel. I owe it to Mother. She worked damned hard to put me through university.'

'Yes, I can see that, but do you think you would be able to give up flying?'

'You understand, don't you? You barely know me and yet you've put your finger on the one thing that would make it almost impossible for me to do my duty by my family. How did you know that, Miranda?'

She shrugged her shoulders, embarrassed by the intensity of his reaction to what had seemed a perfectly natural assumption on her part. 'It's obvious that you love what you're doing, even though it's terribly dangerous and there's a strong chance that one day your luck will run out.' She pushed her plate away. 'I'm sorry, but I really can't manage to finish the pie. It's delicious but I'm full.'

He gave her a long look. 'You're upset, and I can't imagine it's the thought of me buying it that's made you look like that.'

Startled, she raised her eyes to his. 'I – I was

thinking about my Uncle Jack. He's a pilot in Fighter Command.'

'This isn't about him though, is it? I might not be psychic but I've got three sisters. I know when girls are keeping secrets. There's someone else, isn't there?'

'Not really. Well, in a way.' Miranda toyed with her spoon, drawing lines in the custard on her plate. 'It's something and nothing. Just a man I met when my mother sent me to live with my grandparents in Weymouth.'

'Do you feel like telling me about him? I'd like to know. Maybe it would help to talk.'

In spite of everything, Miranda found herself confiding things to Gil that she had never shared with anyone, not even Rita. He listened intently until she had finished speaking.

'I suppose you think it's stupid having a crush on someone who's so antagonistic towards my family,' Miranda said, waiting nervously for his reaction. 'I know how it must seem.'

'Not at all. I think it's perfectly natural and that I've got a serious rival.'

'Now you're teasing me again.' Miranda looked away, wishing that she had kept her thoughts and feelings to herself.

He reached across the table to lay his hand on hers. 'I'm sorry. I didn't mean to sound flippant.'

'You must think I'm awfully silly.'

'No, of course not, and I'm glad you felt able to share that with me.' He raised his hand to beckon to the waitress who had just served the people at the next table. 'May I have the bill, please?'

The cold air outside almost took Miranda's

breath away. The street was quiet and with all the shops closed it was hardly the most exciting place to spend a Sunday afternoon. The wind sent dead leaves dancing across the paving stones and heavy cumulus clouds threatened rain or even sleet.

Gil tucked her hand into the crook of his arm. 'What would you like to do now, Miranda?'

She shivered despite the warmth of his body close to hers. 'It's a bit chilly. Perhaps we ought to be getting back now.'

'Actually, I've a better idea.' He met her curious gaze with a rueful smile. 'I have a confession to make.'

'Really? Okay, now it's your turn.' She fell into step at his side, wondering what was coming next and intrigued in spite of herself. 'Go on.'

'I have a secret passion for Dorothy Lamour, and on the way here I saw that *The Road to Singapore is* playing at the Majestic. If we get a move on we should just make the matinee performance.'

'Well,' Miranda said, pretending to frown. 'I wouldn't want to come between you and Dorothy, and anyway it'll be nice and warm in the cinema. Let's go.'

'Promise you won't get jealous,' Gil said as they quickened their pace. 'I mean, it's deadly serious between me and Dottie. I'm a pushover for exotic women wearing sarongs.'

'Your secret is safe with me.'

It was dark when they came out of the cinema but Miranda hardly noticed the sleet-spiked rain. She had enjoyed an afternoon of pure escapism, and reality had not yet claimed her. 'I really loved that film. Thanks, Gil.'

He slipped his arm around her shoulders as they were jostled by the crowds of cinemagoers pouring out onto the street. 'It looks as if we're too late to find a teashop open.'

'I think I'd better get back to camp anyway. But thanks again. It's been lovely.'

'We must do it again very soon.'

They started off in the direction of the car park, but Miranda was suddenly uneasy. 'Perhaps we'd better leave it for a while.'

'Why? What's the matter?'

'Nothing, really.'

'It doesn't sound like nothing if you don't want to see me again.'

'It's not that, exactly. It's just that, well, girls talk.'

'You shouldn't believe everything you hear.'

'I know, and I don't. But...'

They had reached the car park and he stopped, taking her by the shoulders. 'But what?'

'I've already told you that it's complicated, and anyway I don't want to get involved with a chap who might...' She bit her lip. 'Don't make me say it.'

He let his hands fall to his sides. 'You don't want to fall for someone who might go for a Burton at any given moment.'

'It sounds dreadful when you put it that way.'

'But that's what you were thinking, isn't it?'

'Something like that, I suppose.'

He climbed onto the motorbike. 'I'll take you back to Henlow.'

191

'I'm sorry, Gil. I didn't mean to spoil things. I've had a truly lovely day.' Her voice broke but there was nothing she could do other than get on behind him and hold on as he kick-started the engine. She was not certain if the moisture on her cheeks was due to the rain or her own tears as she rested her head against his back. Somehow it had all gone horribly wrong and she did not know how to make it right again.

The rain had ceased when he dropped her off outside hut five, and the clouds had parted to allow a watery moon to shed its light on the priory and its grounds.

'Goodnight, Gil,' Miranda said warily. 'Thanks again for a super time.'

He slipped his hand into an inside pocket and pulled out a hanky. 'Your mascara's run,' he said, pressing it into her hand. 'Take care of yourself, Miranda.' He revved the engine and drove off before she had a chance to say anything.

She walked slowly towards the hut door, clutching the hanky. She knew that she had done the right thing, but she could not understand why it felt like the worst decision of her life.

Gloria opened the door to let her in. She was frowning ominously. 'Where the hell have you been, Goody Two-Shoes? The section leader wants to see you in her office toot sweet. Looks like you're for the high jump.'

Chapter Eleven

As she sat in the crowded railway compartment, Miranda could still hear the section leader's voice ringing in her ears. She had broken the news to Miranda as gently as was possible, but the knowledge that her father had been killed in action still came as a body blow. Somehow she had never linked danger and death to the fact that he was a professional soldier. Her father had been invincible; a hero who won every battle, but now she had to come to terms with the fact that he had been one of the fatalities of the North African campaign. She could not remember exactly what happened next, except that she had been granted compassionate leave, and now she was on her way to her grandparents' home to comfort and be comforted.

She had telephoned to say that she would be arriving on the midday train, but she was not expecting to be met. She had flung a few things in a small holdall and had resigned herself to brave the chill winds and wait for a bus, but as she left the station she heard someone call her name. She looked round and saw Tommy Toop standing beside a military staff car and to her surprise he was in uniform. She hurried towards him. 'Hello, Tommy. I didn't know you'd joined up.'

He saluted, grinning. 'It weren't voluntary, miss.

I had no choice, but as it happens it ain't so bad. I'm a driver, as you might have guessed.'

'I can see that, but what are you doing here?'

'I've come to meet you.' He opened the car door. 'Hop in.'

She could feel the east wind scything through the streets and sand blasting anyone and anything in its path, and she did not waste time arguing. She waited until he had taken his seat. 'Are you supposed to be doing this?'

'Nope, but your gran sent a message to the camp at Bovington. My colonel's one of your grandad's old pals, apparently. Anyway he was coming here today to inspect a camp near Moonfleet and he said I could pick you up and take you home. Sorry to hear about your dad, by the way.'

'Thank you.' She sat in silence for a moment, struggling to maintain her composure. Dealing with the sympathy of others was almost as hard as coming to terms with the knowledge that she would never see her father again. She took a deep breath. 'So how do you like being in the army?'

'It's okay. In fact I'm having the time of me life.' He shot her a sideways glance and winked. 'There's lots of opportunities for a chap to make a bit on the side. I'm up to all the dodges; legal ones, of course, and I'm even managing to save a bit from me pay. I get three square meals a day, which is more than I ever had living at home, so I can't complain.'

'Lucky you.' Miranda lapsed into silence again until they were halfway along the beach road. 'Have you heard from Rita recently?'

'Yep. She's been transferred to Warmwell which

194

is just down the road from me. We're stepping out regular, only she won't admit it. She's got her eye on one of them glamour-boys at the aerodrome, but she always falls back on good old Tommy.'

Miranda gazed at him in amazement. She could hardly believe how much he had changed since she last saw him. He seemed like a different person now, and she was impressed. 'Good for you, Tommy. Rita needs someone steady in her life, poor girl. But to be honest I never thought it would be you.'

'Nor I, miss. But there you go, that's what war does to folks. You either swim with the tide or you go under. I ain't the type to do that. Unsinkable, that's me.'

'I'm very glad to hear it,' Miranda said and was surprised to realise that she meant it. With his father and brothers constantly in and out of prison, Tommy's future had always been a matter of conjecture, but his devotion to Rita appeared to be genuine and he was obviously determined to better himself.

He dropped her off at the gates of Highcliffe and drove away with a toot-toot on the car's horn, which made her smile. Perhaps he was unsinkable as he said; she hoped so for his sake. She opened the gate, pausing for a moment to take in the view although the world seemed to end at the cliff top, and Portland had disappeared behind a grey veil of fog. A few seagulls mewed mournfully overhead, but otherwise the only sound was that of the waves lapping the shore. The wind had dropped suddenly and the air was eerily still, as if the elements knew that there was sadness and loss hanging in a cloud over the old house. She went down the path and made her way round to the back door.

Annie was in the kitchen, kneading bread dough. She looked up as the door opened and her face cracked into an attempt at a smile. 'It's good to have you home, Miranda.' Her eyes misted with tears but she brushed them away with her sleeve. 'I'll put the kettle on.' Wiping her hands on her apron she went to the stove and put the kettle on the hob. 'She's in her sitting room. It'll do her the world of good to see you.'

Miranda dropped her case in the doorway and rushed over to give Annie a hug. 'I'll go and say hello and then I'd love a cup of tea. I haven't had anything since I left Henlow early this morning.'

Annie moved away, straightening her pinafore. 'I'll make some sandwiches. I'm afraid it'll have to be jam or Marmite.'

'Either, I don't mind.' Miranda watched her as she moved about the kitchen, keeping her hands busy as if clinging on to routine was her lifeline. 'You knew my dad when he was a boy,' she said softly.

'I always had a soft spot for young Ronnie.' Taking a hanky from her pocket, Annie blew her nose.

'I know he was very fond of you,' Miranda said with a break in her voice. 'He always said you made the best jam tarts ever.'

'He was very partial to a jam tart, was Ronnie.' Annie sighed and put her hanky back in her pocket. 'I'll never forget the first time I saw him.

When your gran brought the children back from Kenya your dad was just ten and Miss Eileen was two, going on three. Ronnie spent most of his time with me or going out on his rounds with Elzevir, until he was packed off to boarding school. I had a lot of time for Ronnie.' She bustled into the larder to fetch a jug of milk. 'But thanks for asking. No one else has thought to consider my feelings.'

'I didn't realise that you knew Dad so well. I suppose I just took it for granted that you'd been here forever. It's silly, isn't it?'

Annie screwed her face up in a semblance of a smile. 'I'm just the wallpaper. Always there but no one really notices.'

'I'd say you were more like the glue that sticks this crazy family together, and I'm sorry if I've taken you for granted, Annie. I don't know what we'd do without you, especially Granny; she relies on you so much.'

Annie waved a teaspoon at her. 'Get away with you. You're just like your dad. He could soft-soap his way out of any scrape. Go and say hello to your gran. She's taken it very hard, so don't be surprised by anything she does. It's her way of dealing with the grief.'

Mystified and anxious, Miranda left the room and hurried through the maze of passages that led eventually to her grandmother's inner sanctum. She peered round the door, not exactly knowing what to expect or how she would comfort a bereaved mother when her own feelings were so raw that she felt almost numb. To her surprise she found her grandmother chatting on the telephone as if nothing had happened. She looked up, smiled and motioned Miranda to sit down in the saggy armchair by the window. 'I won't be a moment,' she mouthed. She sat silently for a few seconds, listening intently, and then she nodded. 'Of course. That's fine. We'll look forward to seeing you tomorrow evening at seven.' She paused, concentrating on what the other person was saying. 'Dress? Oh, definitely casual. Ronnie could never stand to see women wearing black. He said it made them look like crows.' She listened again, still nodding. 'Yes, Ivy. It's a celebration of his life: a salute to a brave soldier. Ronnie wouldn't want anyone to feel sad.'

She replaced the receiver on its hook and turned to Miranda, holding her arms out. 'It's so good to see you, darling. Give your poor old granny a hug.'

'I'm so glad to be home, Granny.' Enveloped in her grandmother's arms, Miranda inhaled the familiar scent of Apple Blossom perfume and Nivea Crème, which her grandmother applied liberally to her face every night before retiring to bed. She remembered her father teasing his mother about it during one of their frequent holidays at Highcliffe. Suddenly it all became too much for her and she broke away, fishing in her pocket for a hanky. 'I'm sorry. I promised myself that I wouldn't cry.'

'Darling, you're entitled to shed a few tears for your poor father. Heaven knows I bawled my eyes out when I first heard the news, but I meant what I said just now, Ronnie wouldn't want us to be sad. He was a professional soldier, just like his

198

father, and he knew the score. We'll just have to be brave and be glad that we had him for as long as we did.'

'But what about my mother? Does she know?'

Maggie shook her head. 'Your grandfather has been in touch with the War Office, but the truth is that we simply don't know where Jeanne is at the moment. She will be told, of course, but whatever she's doing is so top secret that we'll just have to wait for her to contact us whenever that may be.' She laid her hand on Miranda's shoulder. 'I am sorry, my dear. It's absolutely ghastly for you to lose one parent and not have the support of the other.'

'I've got you and Grandpa,' Miranda said with a wobbly smile. 'And I just hope and pray that Maman is all right.'

'That's all we can do, darling.'

Miranda blew her nose in the large white handkerchief, and then realised that it was the one that Gil had given her just before they parted. She experienced a sharp stab of conscience, wishing that she had not sent him off thinking that she was a cold-hearted, ungrateful Goody Two-Shoes. Perhaps the name fitted after all. Maybe she should have relaxed a bit and allowed herself to enjoy a mild flirtation, instead of mooning after a man who was not the slightest bit interested in her. 'I'm all right, Granny,' she said, noting her grandmother's worried expression. 'Just a bit of a cold coming on.' She tucked Gil's hanky back into her pocket. 'What were you saying to Aunt Ivy when I interrupted you?'

'Poor Ivy's been bombed out. Did I write and

tell you? No, I probably forgot what with everything that's been going on here. She's staying in a hotel at present, but goodness knows when her house will be habitable again.'

'I'm sorry to hear that, but you were talking about a party, or something?'

'Yes. I've arranged a little soiree for tomorrow evening, Miranda.' Maggie held up her hands. 'Don't look so shocked. It's just a few close friends who knew Ronnie and would like a chance to say goodbye. The most wretched part of all this is not being able to give him a decent burial. It's part of the grieving process that's denied to us, and this way I thought we could do something that my boy would appreciate. Ronnie loved to party, you must remember that.'

Miranda shook her head. 'Not really. They used to go out a lot when he was on leave but I was always left at home with a babysitter when I was younger, and then later on I had friends of my own. I loved him, of course, and I'll miss him terribly, but it's Maman I feel really sorry for. She'll be devastated. I wish I could be with her now and give her a big hug.'

'Yes, of course. It's dreadful not knowing where the poor girl is, but tomorrow evening we are not going to be gloomy. We're going to send Ronnie off in style. He would have loved that.' Maggie turned away to thumb through a well-used address book. 'Now who have I missed out?' She took the receiver off the hook, turning her head to give Miranda an encouraging smile. 'Get Annie to make you some lunch, darling. I won't be long, and then we can have a lovely long chat and you can tell me all about life at Henlow Priory.'

Miranda retired to the kitchen and ate Marmite sandwiches while Annie passed on titbits of gossip, most of which meant very little to anyone who was not a local, but Annie in full flow was virtually unstoppable. Miranda had just finished eating when her grandmother appeared in the doorway, flushed and with a purposeful look on her face. 'Annie, I want you to go into the stables and get two bottles of embrocation. Elzevir has promised to take them to the farm and swop them for some cheese and butter, otherwise there will be no cheese straws for the party tomorrow evening.'

'Are you sure about that, Mrs B? I mean, the Major said no one was to touch the stuff. Not after Elzevir got hauled up before him for being drunk and disorderly last Christmas.'

'George will be at court all day and he's taking the Home Guard practice in the church hall this evening, so what the eye doesn't see the heart doesn't grieve over. Do as I ask, please, and be quick about it.'

'Oh, all right. But on your own head be it.' Annie snatched a key off its hook and stomped outside, grumbling beneath her breath.

'Grandpa would be awfully cross if he knew,' Miranda said warily. 'Don't you think it's a bit of a risk letting Elzevir loose with that stuff?'

'We're having a party. Life is all about risks as I'm sure you're well aware. I've lost one son and might well lose another.' Maggie's eyes reddened and she sniffed loudly, holding up her hand as Miranda made a move towards her. 'No, I don't want sympathy. I have to be strong and so have you. I've telephoned the aerodrome and Jack isn't on duty tomorrow evening. If he can get transport he'll be here, and you'll have a chance to see him and chat about planes and things. It will all be lovely – absolutely lovely.' She hurried from the room, leaving Miranda staring after her and thinking that indeed the whole world had gone stark raving mad.

She saw little of her grandfather that day as he returned from court with only enough time to snatch a quick meal and to change into his Home Guard uniform. She went to the door to see him off. 'You look splendid, Grandpa.'

He leaned over to kiss her cheek. 'Thank you, darling girl. But I'm an old fogey now, not the man I was years ago.'

'You'll never be old, Grandpa.' She raised her hand to touch his lined cheek. 'You are all right about this party thing, aren't you? You don't think it's too soon after...' Her voice trailed off and she did not trust herself to finish the sentence.

'If it helps your grandmother to cope with the grief then it's fine by me. We're all different, Miranda. She doesn't want to let go and yet she knows that she must. It's terrible to lose a child, and this is her way of dealing with it. Now, I must go or I'll be late and that would never do. I'll see you at the bun-fight tomorrow evening.'

She stood on the top step watching him striding towards the ancient Bentley with the vigour of a man half his age, and she felt a surge of love and pride for the grandfather who had given her so much. He had been always ready to lend a sympathetic ear when she was in her teens and rebelling in a quiet way against her strict upbringing. He was patient where Granny was quick-tempered, always flaring up like a firework and then fizzling out when the moment passed and wondering why those around her were upset. Grandpa was solid, dependable and kind. Granny was full of fun but unpredictable as the weather.

The phone rang as she was closing the door and when no one answered it she crossed the hall to pick up the receiver. 'Hello.'

She heard the sound of coins dropping in the box as someone pressed Button A.

'Hello. Who's that?'

She recognised the voice immediately. 'Rita? Where are you?'

'Miranda, is that really you?'

'It most certainly is.'

'I'm in the village phone box and there's a queue. Got to be quick but I'm just ringing to say that me and Tommy will be coming to the party tomorrow. I'm not on duty and Tommy's got a pass too. I'll see you then.'

'I can't wait. It'll be lovely to catch up.'

'There's the bloody pips and I haven't got any more change. Got to go, love...'

They were cut off and Miranda was left with the dialling tone. She replaced the earpiece on the hook. Perhaps the party would not be such a disaster after all.

The guests who lived within walking distance had come on foot and the local doctor and his wife had arrived in a pony and trap. Miranda stood beside her grandmother while she received them, and was almost smothered in Aunt Ivy's capacious bosom as she greeted her with an all-enveloping hug. 'My dear girl, I was so sorry to hear about your father.' Ivy held her at arm's length, gazing at her with moist eyes. 'You poor little thing, and now you're in the forces too; I can hardly believe it. You were still a schoolgirl when I last saw you.'

'Well she's grown up now, Ivy,' Maggie said, motioning her to move on. 'Go and get yourself a drink, my dear, and easy on the gin. Heaven alone knows when we'll be able to get more. Everything is so scarce these days.' She moved forward to greet a distinguished but rather stuffy-looking couple. 'Judge Walters and Mrs Walters, how kind of you to come. I don't think you've met my granddaughter, Miranda. It was her father who gave his life so bravely for his country.'

'How do you do?' Judge Walters acknowledged Miranda with a courtly bow and his wife nodded, smiling vaguely.

'May I take your coats?' Miranda could see that this was going to be a long evening and a dull one at that. She could hardly believe that her father would approve of this event as being a suitable sendoff for a man who had loved to socialise, but Granny appeared to be in her element and was behaving as if nothing untoward had happened. Miranda could not help wondering what would happen to her grandmother when she had to face the fact that she had lost her eldest son and would never see him again. She could only hope that Rita would come soon and save the evening from total disaster. Forcing herself to smile, she saw the judge and his wife through to the drawing room.

She arrived at last, pink-cheeked and windblown. 'Tommy borrowed a motorbike,' she said as she peeled off her gloves and unwound her scarf. 'He can lay his hands on almost anything. It's a gift.'

'I'm sure it must be. Good for him.' Miranda felt a pang of something like regret as she remembered her motorcycle ride with Gil and the awkwardness of their parting. She pushed the thought to the back of her mind. 'Where is he?'

'He's chatting to old Elzevir who was lurking round outside. I think he wanted to be invited to the party.'

The image that this conjured up in Miranda's mind made her chuckle. 'At least his presence would liven things up. I'm beginning to think that this shindig was a really bad idea.'

'I was really sorry to hear about your dad, Miranda.' Rita grabbed her by the hand. 'But cheer up, ducks. I'm here now and we've got loads to talk about. I just wish you was at Warmwell too. We'd have a high old time together.'

'It would be nice to be nearer home, but I don't suppose there's much chance of me getting a transfer. Anyway, come into the warm. You look chilled to the marrow.'

'I'd best wait for Tommy. He's a bit shy when it comes to mixing with the toffs.' She glanced over Miranda's shoulder and her expression changed to one of surprise and pleasure. 'Look who's just walked through the door.'

Miranda turned her head and uttered a cry of pleasure. 'Uncle Jack.' She started towards him but stopped short when she saw Isabel clinging to his arm, looking pale and nervous as Jack introduced her to his mother.

Miranda held her breath as she watched her grandmother's face. Maggie's smile froze. 'Jack, how could you do this to me?'

'Mrs Beddoes, please don't be cross with Jack,' Isabel said in a low voice. 'It was my idea. I wanted desperately to meet you in the hope that we could put an end to the difficult situation that exists between our families.'

Maggie braced her shoulders. 'Jack, I'm afraid I'm going to have to ask you to take this young person home. She is not welcome in my house, and you are a gullible fool.'

She was about to turn away but Jack caught her by the wrist. 'Mother, don't be so bloody rude. I'm not going to stand for this nonsense any longer.'

'How dare you speak to me like that?'

'I dare, mother, because you're being pig-headed and abominably cruel to the woman I love.'

Maggie turned to Miranda with a cry of anguish. 'Go and fetch your grandfather. I won't be treated like this in my own house.'

'I'd better go,' Isabel said urgently, her eyes filling with tears. 'I'm so sorry, Mrs Beddoes. I really don't know what this is all about...' She let go of Jack's arm and was about to retreat down the steps when Miranda leapt forward.

'Don't go, Isabel.' She turned her head to glare at her grandmother. 'Granny, this party or wake or whatever you like to call it was supposed to be in memory of my father. Do you really think he would want this sort of thing to happen? I don't understand why you feel like this about the Carstairs family, but it's not Isabel's fault, or her brother's for that matter.'

'Mind your own business, Miranda. It has nothing to do with you.'

'But it has, Granny. Can't you call a truce for one night at least? My dad's gone and he won't be coming back, but Uncle Jack is alive and well and families should stick together.' Miranda's voice broke on a sob.

Jack put his arm around her shoulders. 'I hope you're satisfied now, Mother. Hasn't Miranda been through enough without you spitting venom at my fiancée?' He nodded his head. 'Yes, that's right. Isabel and I are engaged. I brought her with me tonight so that we could announce it officially to family and friends.'

White-lipped, Maggie drew herself up to her full height. 'I've lost my eldest son. Tonight is about Ronnie, not you.'

'He was my brother and I loved him too, but Isabel is going to be my wife. You'll have to accept that, or lose me too, Mother.'

'We'll talk about this at a more suitable time, but as she's here you'd better bring her in. I've nothing further to say.' Maggie stalked off towards the drawing room.

'I'd better go, Jack,' Isabel whispered. 'It will only spoil the party if I stay.'

His jaw hardened into a stubborn line that Miranda remembered so well. 'No, darling,' he said firmly. 'We'll see this thing through together.' He took Isabel by the hand and led her towards the drawing room.

'Blimey,' Rita said softly. 'That was quite a show. Whatever next?'

Miranda shook her head. 'I can't imagine that Granny will give in easily, but Jack's right. It's ridiculous to bear grudges for such a long time.'

Rita opened the front door. 'Tommy, I know you're there. Come in now. They won't bite.'

He came slowly up the steps and Miranda could not help feeling sorry for him. Tommy might be brash and seemingly full of confidence but she could see that he was feeling uncomfortable and out of his depth. 'It was good of you to come. I know this isn't your sort of thing, Tommy.'

'It's nothing.' He slipped his arm around Rita's waist. 'Come on, love. We'll show 'em.'

Miranda followed them into the drawing room prepared to do her duty, but dreading it all the same. She could only hope that her grandmother would concentrate on her friends and leave Jack and Izzie to enjoy themselves as best they could, although she could feel the atmosphere the moment she walked into the room. She left Rita and Tommy to their own devices while she paid attention to Isabel, who was temporarily abandoned while Jack went to fetch their drinks. She summoned up a smile. 'It was brave of you to come tonight, Izzie.'

'I think I might owe you an apology,' Isabel

said, blushing. 'I know it was a long time ago, but I was a bit tiddley that night. I'm afraid I might have been quite rude to you, although I can't remember a thing. Raif was frightfully cross with me, and I'm sure I deserved it.'

'Can't we forget all that?' Miranda glanced round anxiously, hoping that her grandmother was not within earshot. 'It was ages ago, and it really doesn't matter.'

'Thank you,' Isabel said, smiling. 'I always liked you, Miranda.'

'What does Raif say about you getting engaged to my uncle?'

Isabel's smile faded and she shook her head. 'He doesn't know about it yet, and anyway it's not up to him, but I'm worried about how my parents will react. I haven't told them that Jack and I have been seeing each other.'

'It's the Montagues and the Capulets all over again,' Miranda said with a wry smile.

'Except that I'm not thirteen. I'll be twenty-one in May and then I can do as I please. My family won't have a say in the matter.'

'Good for you.'

'At least the war has made me stand on my own two feet. I've got a job in the torpedo factory. My parents were absolutely horrified, but I didn't really have a lot of choice. I had to sign up for something and I actually quite enjoy what I'm doing.'

'That must have taken a lot of courage, Izzie.'

'Oh, I don't know. Not really. I'm a terrible coward and Jack is so fearless.' Isabel glanced at her fiancé who was making his way towards them with a glass of wine in each hand. 'He's so wonderful and I'm such a lucky girl.'

Miranda was trying to think of something suitable to say when the sound of the air raid siren reverberated around the room bringing conversation to a sudden halt.

'There's room in the shelter for the ladies,' George announced in a loud voice. 'Unfortunately there won't be enough space for everyone, but let's get the ladies to safety and worry about ourselves afterwards. I'll switch off the lights if my wife will open the French windows and lead the way.'

There was a sudden hush when the lights went out, and for a moment no one moved. Miranda grabbed Isabel by the hand and led her towards the blast of cold air whistling in through the open doors. 'Mind the steps.'

'It's so dark,' Isabel said nervously. 'I can't see a thing.'

Rita followed them out onto the veranda. 'I know the way, love,' she said cheerfully. 'Follow me, girls. Rita to the rescue.' She patted Miranda on the shoulder. 'Come on, don't be a hero.'

'You go first. I'll see everyone out.' Miranda glanced up into the sky criss-crossed with searchlights and the tracer fire from the battery of ack-ack guns. Suddenly the lawn was lit like daylight and the women in their high heels and long dresses scampered to the relative safety of the Anderson shelter. Jack appeared at her side. 'Where's Isabel?'

'Don't worry, she's safe. Rita took her to the shelter.'

'You must go too,' Jack said urgently. 'And please don't let Mother bully her, Miranda.'

It was freezing in the shelter and they were crushed together on the wooden benches with their feet in pools of icy water. Shivering in their thin clothes, the women were unusually quiet. Even Rita had nothing to say as they listened to the crump-crump of distant explosions and the constant firing of the ack-ack guns. The silence lay heavily upon them all until Rita started to sing. At first the others stared at her as if she had gone quite mad, and prim little Mrs Walters looked as though she might faint, but Maggie nudged her in the ribs and joined in with the chorus of Run Rabbit, Run in a deep contralto that surprised Miranda almost as much as the fact that Izzie also began to sing. Soon everyone, even Mrs Walters, was singing 'I'll be with you in Apple Blossom Time', followed by 'Say Little Hen', and as the fug from their breath and warm bodies threatened to turn the puddles into steam they heard the all clear and there was an un-dignified scramble to escape from the shelter.

As they made their way back across the lawn Miranda could hear raucous male voices emana-ting from the coach house. She turned to Rita who was walking beside her. 'Oh my God. You know what that means.'

Rita glanced over her shoulder at Maggie, who was helping Mrs Walters negotiate the tussocks of grass. 'I can guess, and I bet Tommy's at the bottom of it.'

'Best get the women into the house before they

realise what's going on.' Miranda sprinted up the steps onto the veranda. She flung the French windows wide open and in the dull glow of the firelight she could see her grandfather, the judge and the doctor sitting around the fire, smoking cigars and drinking brandies. 'Everyone inside quickly,' she said, ushering the women into the room. 'Come in, ladies, and I'll make some nice hot cocoa for anyone who doesn't fancy a stiff brandy.'

'Brandy for me, dear,' Ivy said, pushing past her. 'Gentlemen, who's going to come to the aid of a lady in distress?'

Miranda heard the chairs scrape on the polished floorboards as the gentlemen rose hastily to their feet, and she ushered the rest of the shivering women into the drawing room.

Maggie helped Mrs Walters over the threshold. 'There's a terrible din in the coach house,' she whispered in Miranda's ear. 'Go and see what's happening, and if it's what I think, for God's sake shut them up. If the judge gets wind of what's going on he might leap to the wrong conclusion and your grandfather could end up in prison. Go now, and hurry.'

Chapter Twelve

'What's all that din, Manda?' Rita said breathlessly as she followed Miranda outside.

'That's what I intend to find out.' Miranda came to a halt as she saw Isabel standing at the top of the steps, looking wraith-like in the moonlight.

'I can hear Jack's voice,' Isabel said through chattering teeth. 'I think he must be drunk.'

'And he's not alone by the sound of it,' Rita said, chuckling. 'It must be a hell of a party going on in the coach house.'

Miranda picked up her long skirts and raced down the steps. 'We've got to shut them up before they ruin everything.' She went straight to the coach house, where in the flickering light of a single candle she found Jack perched on a stool by the workbench and Elzevir sitting cross-legged on the floor, while Tommy swayed on his feet conducting an imaginary orchestra. They stopped singing the moment the door opened. Jack raised a half-empty bottle to Isabel. 'Here's to my beautiful fiancée and to the memory of my poor brother. God rest his soul. It's a rotten send-off, but it's the best I can do.' He hiccuped and grinned stupidly. 'Izzie, darling. Come and have a drink.'

She stared at him in dismay. 'Jack. How could you?'

'Leave him alone, miss.' Elzevir struggled to his feet. 'He's a good chap. I won't have anyone say anything against my mate Jack.'

'Elzevir Shipway, that's enough.' Miranda adopted the tone her grandmother might have used. 'You should be ashamed of yourself.' She glared at each of them in turn. 'You should all be thoroughly ashamed of yourselves. You could get my grandfather locked up for having an illicit still on the premises, even if he did intend it for scientific purposes.'

'Hold on, love,' Jack said, focusing on her with apparent difficulty. 'This isn't a still. The old man is making...' he paused, frowning, 'he's making something.' His voice trailed off and he looked suddenly like a small boy. 'Sorry, Izzie. I'm a bit squiffy.'

She rushed forward and snatched the bottle from his hand, throwing it against the wall where it smashed and sent shards of broken glass onto the cement floor. 'You most certainly are. I'm so angry with you, Jack. You've ruined everything and now your mother will hate me even more.'

Rita marched up to Tommy and slapped his face. 'You're an idiot. I don't know why I bother with you, Toop.'

He held his hand to his cheek, gazing at her in astonishment. 'That's not fair, love. We was just having a little drink to keep out the cold.'

Miranda could see that this was getting them nowhere. 'Will you all please shut up,' she said in desperation. 'Elzevir, go home. I'll leave Annie to sort you out in the morning.' She shooed him out of the door and he shambled off into the night muttering beneath his breath. She turned her head to glare angrily at Jack and Tommy. 'You'd better go to the kitchen and stay out of sight. I'll make some black coffee.'

'I'll clear up the broken glass,' Rita said, casting a withering glance at Tommy. 'And you'd better sober up. I'm not riding pillion with you in that state.'

Isabel pushed Jack away as he attempted to put his arms around her. 'That goes for you too, Jack Beddoes. You're an absolute disgrace.' She caught Miranda's sceptical glance and had the grace to blush. 'I mean, anyone can have a bit too much to drink, but you should have had more thought for your mother's feelings.' She walked off without giving him a chance to reply.

'Come on, Jack.' Miranda looped his arm around her shoulders. 'I'm going to stick your head under the pump, because if Granny sees you like this your life won't be worth living.'

Ten minutes later they were in the kitchen with Jack drying his hair on a towel and Tommy seated at the table drinking his second cup of Camp coffee. Miranda had made it as strong as possible and it seemed to be having the desired effect. Tommy had sobered up considerably, although that could have been due to the dressing down Rita had given him when she returned from tidying up the coach house. Isabel was clearly shaken but she had been given the job of making cocoa for the older ladies, who had very nearly been forgotten.

Miranda took the tray of hot drinks into the drawing room, leaving Isabel and Rita to cope with their respective partners. She was met by curious looks but it was Aunt Ivy who spoke first. 'What's happened to the young people, Miranda? Do they find us oldies too boring to associate with?'

Miranda set the tray down on an occasional table. 'Jack and Tommy thought they heard a noise in the hen house and they went to investigate.'

'Gypsies,' Maggie said faintly. 'I knew it. They're just waiting for a chance to steal the rest of my hens.'

George shook his head. 'Nonsense, Maggie. They moved on weeks ago. You can't blame the travellers for everything. It was probably a fox.'

'Yes.' Miranda passed a cup of cocoa to Ivy. 'It was a fox. They saw it slink away but luckily it hadn't got into the hen house.' She moved on to give Mrs Walters her hot drink. 'I'm afraid there isn't any sugar.'

'That's quite all right, my dear. I'm getting used to doing without. We must all do our bit for the war effort.' Mrs Walters took a sip. 'It's quite delicious. Thank you.'

Maggie snatched hers from the tray. 'Where is Jack now? Has he taken that girl home?'

'She's a perfectly nice young lady,' Ivy said with a superior smile. 'You should give her a chance to prove herself.'

'She's a Carstairs.' Maggie slammed her cup and saucer down on the table. 'That speaks for itself.'

Dr Hughes shifted uncomfortably in his chair. 'I think perhaps we ought to be on our way,

Gladys.' He rose from his seat by the fire and his thin wisp of a wife leapt to her feet.

'Thank you for the cocoa, Miranda. It was just what we needed after the air raid.' She leaned over to kiss Maggie's cheek. 'I don't like to be out too late these dark evenings and you never know whether the Germans will strike again. Poor Hattie Langton was bombed out last week, and I'm always afraid that we'll go home and find just a pile of rubble where our house used to be.'

Mrs Walters sent a meaningful look at her husband who was nodding off over his brandy. 'Perhaps we'd best be moving on, Edward. It is getting rather late, but we've had a lovely time, Maggie.' She blushed and dropped her gaze. 'I mean, it was good to be here to remember poor Ronnie. He was a delightful child and a charming man. We'll all miss him terribly.'

Miranda abandoned the tray and left the room. It was blatantly obvious that most of the guests were feeling uncomfortable and eager to leave. She hurried back to the kitchen. 'They're all going,' she said, looking round anxiously. 'Are you sober, Jack?'

He smoothed his dark hair back from his forehead with a rueful grin. 'More or less.'

'I'd like to go home too,' Isabel said stiffly. 'This evening has been a disaster, Jack. I knew I shouldn't have come.'

'And we'd best make tracks.' Rita prodded Tommy in the ribs. 'If you can't drive the blooming bike, then I will. It can't be that difficult.'

He braced his shoulders. 'Stop nagging, woman. I'm fine and I wasn't drunk. I was just a bit merry.'

'That stuff really is lethal,' Jack said, pulling on his uniform jacket. 'My shirt's wet thanks to you, Miranda. I think you enjoyed half drowning me under the pump.'

'Maybe I should have held you under for longer. Anyway, are you sure you're okay to drive? Whose car did you come in anyway? Chloe is still laid up in the stables.'

'I borrowed a staff car,' Jack said casually.

'You borrowed it?'

'He took it without asking.' Isabel sighed heavily. 'I'm afraid he'll be in terrible trouble if he's caught.'

Jack met this with a casual shrug and he rose to his feet. 'I have a perfectly valid pass and I know a back way into the aerodrome. No one will even realise it's missing.'

Miranda exchanged worried glances with Isabel. 'You shouldn't take such risks, Jack.'

'You're talking to a chap who flies a Spitfire day in and day out. I'll be lucky to survive another month.' He moved swiftly to Isabel's side and gave her a hug. 'Just joking, darling.'

'You shouldn't say things like that. It's tempting providence.' Clearly unhappy, Isabel drew away from him. 'Thank you for being so sweet, Miranda. I'll get my things and we'll be off. Please make my apologies to your grandparents.' She left the kitchen and Jack hurried after her.

'That goes for us too.' Rita dragged Tommy towards the door. 'You can go out the back way and get the bike started. I don't want Major Beddoes to smell the drink on you. Serve you right if you go blind boozing on that rot-gut.'

'Have a heart, Rita.' Tommy shuffled out into the yard and she closed the door, turning the key in the lock.

'The poor sod will have a bitch of a headache in the morning.' She gave Miranda's shoulders a squeeze as she walked past. 'Chin up, girl. No one's any the wiser.'

'Thanks, Rita. You're a pal.'

'We're good mates, Manda. Put in for a transfer to Warmwell. I've got good digs in the village. We could share a room and it'd be like old times.'

'I'll think about it, but it's not that easy.'

'I know, but try anyway.' Rita linked arms and led her unprotesting to the hall where Maggie was waving off the last of the guests. 'I'll get my coat,' she whispered. 'You can sort your granny out. She doesn't look too happy.' She darted off, leaving Miranda to face her grandmother.

Maggie turned to her with an exasperated sigh. 'Well, that was an unqualified disaster, and then we had gypsies or that wretched fox as well as the air raid. Are you sure that all my hens are safely locked up?'

'Yes, Granny.'

'Your grandfather's gone to his study, and I'm going to bed. I've left Ivy in the drawing room finishing off a very large brandy. She's going to stay the night and I've put her in Rita's old room. I told her that I've got a splitting headache, so I'll leave you to see that she gets upstairs safely. You know what she's like when she's been drinking.'

'Don't you want to say goodbye to Uncle Jack?'

'I'm not speaking to that reprobate. When he

219

comes to his senses and finds himself a girl from a respectable family, then I might forgive him for debasing the memory of poor Ronnie.' She stalked off towards the staircase before Miranda had a chance to say anything.

Catching sight of Jack loitering outside the cloakroom, she beckoned to him. 'The coast's clear, although I think you should have made it up with Granny. She's very upset.'

'She'll come round in the end. When she realises what a lovely girl Isabel is, she can't fail to like her.'

'You really are smitten this time, aren't you, Jack?'

His serious expression melted into a smile. 'Absolutely and completely. I'm going to marry her and if her parents won't give their permission we'll only have to wait until May and then she can do what she likes.'

Rita approached them, wrapping her scarf around her head and neck. 'Your fiancée is bawling her eyes out in the cloakroom, Jack. I think you'd better go and sort her out.'

'Oh, bloody hell.' He crossed the floor in long strides, pausing to knock on the door before entering.

Rita pulled a face. 'Blimey, he really is head over heels. Can't see the attraction myself, but she must have something.'

'She's very nice really, and she adores Jack.'

'Good luck to them, I say. Anyway, I'm off now. Cheerio and remember what I said about getting transferred. I'm sick of those la-di-dah girls who think they're too posh to get their hands dirty.'

'I promise. Now go, and take care of yourself, Rita.'

'You bet. Same goes for you, ducks. Abyssinia.' Rita opened the door, pausing at the top of the steps to turn to Miranda with a wry smile. 'He's got the damned thing ticking over. Here's hoping we get back in one piece. Bye.' With a wave of her hand she disappeared into the darkness.

Suddenly all was quiet except for the steady ticking of the grandfather clock. Miranda decided to leave Jack to sort out his personal affairs. She made her way to the drawing room where she found Ivy sprawled on the sofa with an empty glass in her hand. She looked up when she heard Miranda enter the room and gave her a bleary smile. 'Is there any brandy left in the bottle, dear? A nightcap would go down very well.'

'Of course.' Miranda took the glass from her and poured a small measure of brandy with a generous splash of soda water. 'Try this. I can add more soda if it's too strong.'

Ivy sipped her drink. 'No, that's perfect.'

'Granny's gone to bed, and I'll be going up soon.'

'That's all right, dear. I'll be going up the little wooden hill to Bedfordshire myself when I've drunk this. It's been a very trying evening, and I'm not surprised that Maggie has a headache.'

'The party was her idea, Aunt Ivy.'

'My dear girl, you can stop using that silly title. It might have been considered polite when you were a child, but you're grown up now and I'm no relation, so you may call me Ivy.'

'That's funny. Jack hates being called uncle.'

221

'It's very ageing.' Ivy sipped her drink, frowning. 'He's right there, but I'm not certain about his choice of soul mate.'

'Isabel is a really nice person, and I think it's high time the Beddoes and Carstairs buried the hatchet, so to speak, and preferably not in each other's heads. Perhaps things will improve when Jack and Izzie are married.'

Ivy gave her a searching look. 'You really don't know the story, do you?'

'I wish someone would enlighten me.'

'Of course, I'm not one to gossip,' Ivy said, lowering her voice, 'but I think Maggie should have told Jack the truth long ago. She'll have to eventually or it's quite possible he'll be marrying his own sister.'

'What rubbish are you spouting now, Ivy?' Jack's voice from the doorway made them both turn with a start. He walked over to the sofa, standing above Ivy with a disbelieving look on his face. 'It's got to be the drink talking.'

She struggled to an upright position. 'It's high time you were told the truth, Jack. Since your mother is too scared to reveal her past, then it's my duty as a friend of the family to...'

'Friend?' Isabel hurried to Jack's side. 'What sort of friend says such terrible things? You ought to be ashamed of yourself.'

Ivy flapped her hand, motioning them to take a seat. 'Sit down, the pair of you. I won't be bullied into silence. Half the town knew that Maggie was having an affair with Max Carstairs while George was serving overseas.'

'I don't believe a word of it,' Jack said angrily.

'You're drunk, Ivy.'

'I may not be entirely sober, but there's nothing wrong with my memory. Someone had to put you straight before you made a terrible mistake and married the girl. Why do you think your mother was so upset?'

Miranda could stand it no longer. She leapt to her feet. 'Stop this at once. You're ruining everything. The ill feeling started when Mr Carstairs accidentally ran over Granny's pet dog. It's wicked of you to even suggest that Jack is related to Izzie.'

Isabel tugged at Jack's arm. 'Take me home, Jack. I won't listen to these awful lies.'

He hesitated, glaring at Ivy. 'You can't prove any of this.'

'I don't have to. Just ask your mother. She might tell you that you were a seven-month baby, but I saw you the day after you were born and you were a bonny boy, unlike any premature baby I've ever seen, and I was a midwife for thirty years.'

Isabel clamped her hand to her mouth. 'I feel sick.' She ran from the room.

'You'd better go after her, Jack,' Miranda said anxiously. 'She's had enough upsets this evening.'

'Best she knows now.' Ivy drained her glass, holding it out hopefully. 'I need a stiff one after all this, Miranda.'

Jack snatched the glass from her hand. 'You've had quite enough, you evil old woman. I think you'd better leave here now, before I really lose my temper.'

Miranda caught him by the sleeve. 'You can't

223

turn her out at this time of night, Jack. Why don't you take Izzie home?'

'I'm not leaving here until this woman admits that it's just spiteful tittle-tattle.'

Ivy rose to her feet, breathing heavily. 'I'm going to bed. My advice to you, Jack, is to speak to Maggie. It's time it all came out in the open, and if your little girlfriend wants to know more detail, then she must ask her father. Max Carstairs was the Casanova of his day, and probably still is.' She sailed out of the room, swaying from side to side.

Jack made to follow her but Miranda tightened her hold on his arm. 'Let her go. You won't get any sense out of her tonight. Izzie's more important right now.'

'What a bloody awful mess. Do you believe her, Miranda?'

'I don't know. It's horrible, but I never really bought that story about poor old Houdini being the cause of the rift between the families. It was just an accident, and the dog survived.'

He shook his head. 'I can't believe that Mother would do something like that. I've always thought that she and Father are a devoted couple.'

'And so they are, but it's just possible Ivy could be telling the truth. Granny was young and lonely and she must have been very attractive in those days.'

'But it's got to be lies. I'm a Beddoes through and through. I even look like the old man.' He stared into the mirror above the mantelpiece, frowning.

'Of course you do.' Miranda hoped she sounded more convincing than she was feeling. It was quite

224

possible for Jack's dark hair and eyes to be a throwback to a distant ancestor, even though the rest of the family were on the auburn side of fair. 'Please go and find Izzie. She must be feeling dreadful. It's been a ghastly evening and the poor girl has had a terrible time.'

'Yes,' he said slowly. 'Yes, I will. We'll get over this, Miranda. Unfortunately I have to be back at the aerodrome tonight, but Mother should have warned me about this, or at least have cut Ivy off her Christmas card list. I can't think why she panders to that woman.'

'Neither do I, but you need to calm down before you talk it over with Granny. If you start shouting at her you'll only make things worse.'

'You're right, of course. I'll take Izzie home and hope that she doesn't finish with me after this debacle.'

'I'm sure she won't. Anyway, I've got to head off for East Anglia tomorrow, so it might be some time before I see you again. Goodbye, Jack, and good luck.'

He bent down and kissed her on the forehead. 'Take care of yourself, Miranda.'

Overcome with exhaustion, she sank down on the sofa. She heard the door close softly and she was alone, but the atmosphere was still charged with emotion. The evening had been a total disaster and she realised sadly that nothing would ever be quite the same again.

It was some time before she could summon up the energy to go upstairs to her room. As she mounted the stairs she could see a sliver of light beneath the door to her grandfather's study and

225

she was tempted to run to him as she had done when she was in trouble as a child, but this problem was bigger than anything she had encountered in the past, and she wondered how much or how little he knew. She could only hope that he had never heard the spiteful gossip. She could not imagine a world where her grandparents were anything but the solid rock to which the family still clung.

It came to her in the early hours of the morning. The one way to discover the truth would be to ask Annie, who had worked at Highcliffe since she left school. She went back to sleep determined to get up early and be downstairs when Annie arrived to begin preparations for breakfast.

She found her next morning collecting eggs from the hen house. Annie glanced up from her task. 'You're up early.'

'I wanted to speak to you in private.'

'If it's about Elzevir I've already given him a good telling off. He won't do anything like that ever again.'

'I'm sure he'll have listened to you, but that's not what I wanted to ask you.'

Annie straightened up, gazing at the eggs in her basket. 'The hens don't lay much this time of year. I'll be glad when spring comes. What was it you wanted to know?'

Miranda took a deep breath. 'There was a bit of a scene last night, not the one where the chaps got drunk, but after that. Ivy had had quite a lot to drink and she told Jack that. .' She hesitated, searching for the right words.

'So it's come out at last.' Annie started back

towards the house. 'I can guess what she said.'

'About Granny and Max Carstairs?'

'She should have told you all long ago. These things have a habit of popping up when you're least expecting them to.'

'Annie, I've got to leave after breakfast. I haven't got much time to find out the whys and wherefores. Tell me, did Granny really have an affair with Mr Carstairs, or is it just spiteful gossip?'

'Of course she did. Who wouldn't in the circumstances? It would have taken a saint to refuse him when he was younger. He was better looking than all those Hollywood film stars and twice as charming. They first met when he studied medicine with your grandfather in London, and he turned up again in Kenya. Then he arrives on the doorstep here: she was lonely and he was single. That's about it.'

Miranda did not know whether to be shocked or amused by Annie's matter-of-fact attitude to an affair that might still wreck the family. 'And was he Jack's father?'

Annie shrugged her shoulders. 'Who knows? I certainly don't, and I doubt if your gran does either. The major came home just in time if you ask me. It would never have worked with Max and your gran. They were too much alike; both of them had a wild streak, but your gran needed someone solid and dependable like the major. I don't see as how it matters now after all these years.'

'Jack brought Isabel Carstairs with him last night. He announced their engagement, and then he overheard Ivy telling me about the affair, and so did Izzie. It's all a terrible mess, Annie. I don't know what to do.'

'Nothing is the answer, my girl. Tell Ivy to keep her mouth shut and leave it to Jack to work things out for himself. That's my advice.'

'Ivy probably won't remember a thing about last night anyway.'

'How about a couple of boiled eggs for breakfast? I'm not wasting them on that troublemaker Ivy Kirk. She's got more skeletons in her cupboard than anyone in the town.' She stomped off towards the house, almost bumping into Maggie as she came flying round the corner.

'Did the gypsies get my hens? Or was it the fox?'

Annie gave her a pitying look. 'Nothing's happened to your precious chickens.' She held the basket under Maggie's nose. 'No gyppos, no foxes. See.'

'Thank goodness for that.' Maggie held her hand out to Miranda. 'Come and have some breakfast, darling. It's such a shame you have to leave today.'

'Coming, Granny.' Miranda went in to breakfast feeling much more hopeful.

Her grandmother's cheerful mood made everything that had happened the night before seem like a bad dream. It had been a shock to realise that Granny and Max had been lovers, but perhaps the rest was just Ivy being spiteful, and hopefully Jack would have managed to convince Izzie that it was small town tittle-tattle. Miranda finished her boiled eggs and soldiers. 'That was lovely, thank you, Annie.'

'I've packed some Marmite sandwiches for you.' Annie cast a sideways glance at Maggie.

'We're out of cheese until Farmer Drake is in a generous mood or needs some embrocation.'

Maggie frowned. 'I'm not stupid. I know what was going on last night. I could hear them as we came out of the air raid shelter.'

'It was something and nothing, Granny,' Miranda said hastily. 'We put a stop to it.'

'And thank God you did. If Judge Walters had caught a whiff of that beastly stuff he'd have had no choice but to report your grandfather to the police. I've told George that it has to stop. He's to dismantle the still and forget about making benzene, or he'll end up in prison.' She paused, listening. 'There's someone at the front door. I can't think who it would be at this time of the morning. Go and see who it is, Miranda. I'm going to take a cup of tea up to your grandfather. If it's gypsies selling pegs or lucky heather, tell them to go away.'

Chapter Thirteen

Miranda opened the front door and stood transfixed, staring at Raif with a mixture of shock and disbelief.

He took off his peaked cap and tucked it under his arm. 'May I come in?'

He did not look angry, but his impassive expression made it impossible to gauge his mood. 'If you've come to make trouble, then I'd rather you didn't.'

'I haven't come to make trouble as you put it, but I would like to speak to your grandparents.'

'No. I'm sorry, but I won't let you upset them. This has nothing to do with you.'

'It has everything to do with me. My sister is in a terrible state, and I want to know why. She won't tell me anything, but I know it has something to do with Jack. She let it slip that they'd been here last night.'

'I think you ought to speak to Izzie again, or have it out with Jack. It's got nothing to do with Granny and Grandpa.' She was about to close the door but he put his foot over the sill.

'I'm not the enemy, Miranda. Believe me, I'm sick and tired of the family feud, but when it affects my sister then I have to act. It's no good asking Jack. He'll just give me a load of bull; he's good at that.'

Miranda could hear her grandmother's footsteps approaching from the direction of the kitchen and she stepped outside, closing the door behind her. 'I'll tell you anything you want to know.' She led him to the shrubbery where they could not be seen from the house. 'What did Izzie say exactly?'

'She was in floods of tears last night when I came home, but she refused to tell me what went on here. I was hoping for some answers.'

'Izzie and Jack are in love. Can't you understand that?'

He met her angry gaze with a steady look. 'I'm not as unfeeling as you think.'

'But you hate Jack.'

He shook his head. 'I don't hate him, but I

don't think he's right for Izzie. Do you?'

'I think they make each other happy. Isn't that enough?'

'There's something you're not telling me, and I'm not leaving until I know exactly what happened last night.'

Miranda shivered, wishing that she had thought to put her greatcoat on over her uniform as sleety rain began to fall from a pewter-coloured sky. 'Come round to the veranda. We can talk there without getting soaked.'

'Lead the way.' He followed her to the relative shelter of the veranda.

She wrapped her arms around her body in an attempt to keep warm. 'I suppose you know that my father died in action,' she said, raising her voice to make herself heard over the crashing of the waves and the wind soughing in the pine trees at the side of the house.

'No. I didn't, and I'm truly sorry.'

'My grandmother took it badly. She decided to hold a sort of wake in his memory. I didn't think it was a particularly good idea, but it wasn't up to me to tell her so.'

'I don't quite understand what this has to do with my sister.'

'Granny must have told Jack about the party and he decided to bring Izzie and announce their engagement.' She could see that this shocked him and she laid her hand on his sleeve. 'Didn't she tell you?'

'No.' His lips twisted into a wry smile. 'Izzie doesn't tell me anything these days.'

'Granny was pretty horrible to her, but Jack

wouldn't let it go, and then there was an air raid, and to cut a long story short, at the end of the evening Izzie overhead something that upset her.'

'Which had to do with Jack?'

'It's just spiteful gossip.'

'Go on, please.'

'It seems that years ago my grandmother and your father had an affair, and it's just possible that Jack is your half-brother. I'm sorry, I can't dress it up.'

He was silent for a moment, staring at the roiling waves crested with white horses, and then he turned his head slowly to meet her anxious gaze. 'Who told you this?'

'That's not important, but first thing this morning I asked Annie if it was true. She's worked for my family for more than forty years, and there's almost nothing that escapes her. Anyway, she admitted that my granny and your dad had a thing going while Grandpa was serving abroad. I'm sorry, Raif.'

He took her in his arms, holding her in a passionless gesture of mutual comfort. 'I am too, Miranda. I was rotten to you, and I apologise unreservedly. We're all victims in this, but it's how we deal with it that really matters.'

'You're not angry?' She drew away, gazing into his eyes.

'I don't know what I feel. If my father and your grandmother had an affair it must have been quite a long time before he met Mother, although that doesn't excuse his behaviour. I always knew that he was a ladies' man, but I didn't think he'd go so far as to seduce the wife of a former colleague.'

'You knew that Grandpa and your father studied medicine at the same hospital?'

'Yes, he made no secret of that. He let us think that George Beddoes had somehow cheated when they both applied for the same job, although he was never specific. I realised that it must have been something pretty serious, but it never occurred to me that my father was the wrongdoer.'

'Izzie must be in a dreadful state.'

'That's putting it mildly, but I suppose she'll get over it in time.'

'That sounds very heartless.'

'I'm just being practical. Izzie hasn't had many boyfriends, and Jack is quite a few years her senior. I can't help hoping that this will finish it; in fact I'm going to have a word with Jack and tell him just that.'

'He's devastated, Raif. He really loves Izzie.'

'Then I'm sorry for him, but if there's the slightest reason to suppose that we're related he's got to end it with my sister.'

'There are blood tests,' Miranda said hopefully. 'They could prove who isn't the father.'

'To do that might destroy two marriages, Miranda. My parents have been together for more than twenty-five years and your grandparents have been married for much longer. Would Jack be prepared to go that far?'

'I don't know.' Miranda looked away. 'I just don't know.'

He dropped his hand to his side. 'Neither do I, and I'm sorry you got involved in all this. I know you're fond of Jack and that you like Izzie. I wish I'd been more understanding from the start.'

233

There was no doubting the sincerity in his voice or the sympathetic expression in his eyes. 'It's all been a bit of a mix-up,' she said softly.

He smiled and the tension between them seemed to evaporate. He held out his hand. 'Friends?'

His warm fingers closed over her cold hand and she felt as though the icicle in her heart had just melted. 'Friends,' she said, smiling shyly. 'It's such an odd way to make up for past misunderstandings.'

'I must go now. I've got to be back at the aerodrome before nine.' He glanced at his watch. 'And I'd better get a move on. Goodbye, Miranda.'

'Goodbye, Raif.' She watched him walk away and she felt a sudden sense of loss, but he had gone and it was unlikely that she would ever see him again. Her senses were numbed by the revelation of what had occurred all those years ago. She could understand a little of what her grandmother must have felt for the dashing Max Carstairs, and the overpowering passion that had led her to risk everything for an affair that would have been doomed from the start. Neither of them could have foreseen or even imagined the repercussions that would echo down the years to affect the lives of their children and grandchildren. Miranda could only imagine how Izzie and Jack must be feeling. She went back into the house preparing herself to act normally as she said her goodbyes.

It took Miranda several weeks to settle down at Henlow Priory. It had been oddly comforting to

234

find that nothing much had changed during her absence, and it was hard to believe that she had only spent a couple of days at home. Time had seemed to stretch into infinity during her brief visit to Highcliffe, but now she was back in the real world and she found that the rigid daily routine helped to ease the pain. When she lay in her bed at night she tried to convince herself that what she had felt for Raif had been puppy love, but she could not forget their last meeting. She could still feel the warmth of his arms around her on that cold, blustery winter's day, and the gentle pressure of his fingers when he had held her hand. She had seen a totally different side to Raif that morning, and she knew that she had not imagined the look of regret in his eyes when they parted, but there was no going back. The rift between the two families went too deep to mend easily.

Each morning she managed to present a cheerful face to the rest of the girls in hut five, and if the mask slipped a little at times it was accepted as being natural for someone who had recently lost their father. She worried constantly about her mother, wondering where she was and what was happening to her in enemy territory. She agonised about Maman's feelings at this time, if she even knew that she had been widowed. It seemed to Miranda that the war had robbed her of both her parents, but she had no alternative but to carry on and live in hope.

She devoted herself to her job, working longer shifts if required and spending her spare time alone in the library or going for long walks in the countryside. Janice and Val tried to persuade her to accompany them to the local hops, but she always managed to find an excuse. They both had regular boyfriends now, and she suspected that they would try to fix her up with a date. Emotionally ragged, Miranda needed time to get over her feelings for Raif, and there was always the chance that Gil might be at the dance. She did not think for a moment that he had been serious about her, but she suspected that his male pride would have taken quite a knock when she did not fall at his feet like his former conquests.

The months passed and she had successfully managed to avoid outings to the dance hall, but when it came to Valerie's twenty-first birthday at the end of October she could not in all conscience refuse to join in the party at the village pub. They set off on foot, but the snows of the previous winter had left the lanes scarred with potholes. The autumn rains had filled them with water, and the gales that ripped the dead leaves off the trees had dried the puddles into pools of thick sticky mud. Every now and then the clouds parted to allow shafts of moonlight to illuminate their way as they walked to the village, and nothing could dampen their spirits. The girls from hut five were in festive mood.

The ceiling of the sixteenth-century pub was stained with nicotine in between the ancient oak beams, and the flagstone floor had been worn away in places by many generations of thirsty customers. A fire crackled cheerfully in the inglenook and the resinous aroma of burning pine logs mingled with the smell of beer and cigarette smoke. When the girls pushed two tables together and began moving chairs, the locals grumbled into their pint pots and shifted closer to the fire.

Miranda bought the first round, and she was just about to pick up the last two glasses of cider and take them to their table when the door opened and a group of airmen breezed in on a gust of cold air. She stood aside as they moved to the bar, giving her appraising glances and grinning. 'Hello, darling. Haven't seen you in here before.'

'I don't think the young lady is interested in you, Trigg.'

Miranda turned at the sound of a familiar voice and saw Gil standing in the doorway.

The young airman saluted and stood to attention. 'Sorry, sir. Didn't know she was your girl.'

Gil returned the salute. 'At ease, Trigg. These young ladies are from Henlow Priory so you boys had best mind your manners.'

'It's all right,' Miranda said hastily. 'He was just being friendly.'

'Ta, miss. That's right, I was.' Trigg shuffled away to join his grinning companions at their table.

'It's good to see you again, Miranda.' Gil's smile faded. 'I heard about your father and I'm sorry.'

'Thank you,' she said, avoiding meeting his gaze.

'I saw Janice and Valerie at the village hall last week. I'd hoped to see you there but they told me you hadn't been out much.'

'They didn't mention it.'

'I asked them not to. I wasn't sure that you

237

would care one way or the other.'

'It's been a long time, Gil. A lot has happened since we last met.'

'My absence wasn't from choice. I would have tried to contact you sooner, but I was seconded to an air station in Lincolnshire for several months. But now I'm back and it's good to see you again, Miranda.'

'And I'm pleased to see you,' she said, realising with a jolt of surprise that she actually meant it.

He glanced over his shoulder at the rowdy party of girls. 'Perhaps you could slip away and have a drink with me?'

'I'd like that, but I'd better take these to the girls before they start complaining.'

'Of course. We'll have a chat later.'

Miranda took the glasses to the table where she received knowing winks from Janice and Val.

'I thought you'd ditched the dishy glamour-boy,' Audrey said, picking up her glass. 'Are you two seeing each other again, Beddoes?'

'Mind your own business, Audrey,' Angela said, frowning. 'And for heaven's sake, darling, don't start singing when you've had a couple of drinks. I'll die of embarrassment if you do.'

'Leave the poor kid alone, Audrey.' Gloria fumbled in her bag and produced a packet of Kensitas. She offered it round but the others shook their heads. 'You're all such goody-goodies,' she said crossly. 'Anyone got a light?'

Immediately a hand shot out holding a lighter and Gloria puffed on her cigarette, exhaling smoke above the head of the young airman who had attempted to flirt with Miranda.

238

'Jim Trigg's the name, darling. What's yours?'

Gloria regarded him through a haze of smoke. 'Does your mother know you're out this late, sunshine?'

He flushed scarlet and moved away to join his friends who were now openly laughing at him. One of them slapped him on the back. 'She's got you there, Jim.'

'Shut up.' Trigg picked up his glass of shandy and downed it in one long gulp.

'Is he old enough to drink?' Gloria called across the room.

'Don't be mean, Glo.' Valerie lifted her glass, looking round at her assembled friends. 'Drink up, girls. The night is young and this is the first time I've been legally able to drink in a pub.'

Miranda sipped her cider but she was acutely conscious of Gil's presence. He was alone at the bar and she murmured an excuse but no one seemed to notice as she rose from the table. She walked up to the bar and perched on a stool beside Gil. 'I feel I ought to apologise for the way I treated you all those months ago. It wasn't very nice, and I'm truly sorry.'

'You did rather give me the cold shoulder.' He laid his hand on hers as it rested on the polished surface of the bar. 'But I should have taken things more slowly. I'm afraid that's me all over.'

'I was a bit mixed up then.'

'And you aren't now?'

'I'm okay.' She met his earnest gaze with a wry smile. 'I'd like us to be friends, Gil.'

'I'm everybody's friend.' He was suddenly serious. 'I mean it, Miranda. I'm not the chap you think I am. I'd really like to get to know you better.'

'I'd like that too.'

'You must have had a rough time since I last saw you.'

His matter-of-fact way of speaking was oddly comforting. Had he been overly sympathetic she knew she would have burst into tears, but the warmth in his hazel eyes spoke volumes. 'My dad was killed in action and my mother's somewhere in France doing something top secret. I haven't seen or heard from her for two years. I don't know if she's alive or dead.' Her breath hitched as she choked back tears.

'That's tough. I'm really sorry.'

'It's nothing to what some people have been going through.'

'But you must be very proud of your mother. She's a brave woman.'

'Yes, she is. I wish I was half as brave as her.'

He squeezed her hand. 'I think you've got the hardest part. It can't be easy to carry on as normal when someone you love is in danger.'

'No, it isn't.' She paused, biting her lip. 'We go through it every day in the plotting room, and most of the time we don't even know the chaps who are risking everything to keep us safe.' She lowered her gaze. 'It's even harder when you do know them.'

'That would be your uncle and the other chap who's a fighter pilot. The one you said you had a crush on.'

She turned her head away. 'I wasn't thinking of them actually.'

'It doesn't matter,' he said gently. 'I'm sorry if I've upset you again.'

'It's all right. I'm fine really.'

'You're a very bad liar, Miranda Beddoes.'

She shot him a sideways glance. 'That's not fair. You don't know me at all.'

'Sometimes you meet someone who is so special you feel you've known them all your life.'

'You do? I mean, you did?'

'When I first saw you at the village dance you were sitting with your hands clasped in your lap and your ankles crossed, like a little girl in Sunday school. You looked up and smiled but there was sadness in your eyes, the same look that I see now. You're no good at keeping secrets, Miranda. You'd be a pretty lousy poker player.'

She felt herself blushing furiously and she could not bring herself to look him in the eye. 'Now I'm embarrassed.'

He tapped her on the arm and when she raised her head she saw that he was balancing a teaspoon on the end of his nose. It was so ridiculous that she burst out laughing. With a slight movement he tossed it in the air and caught it deftly in his hand. He put it down, smiling. 'You look very pretty when you blush. You went bright pink when I first spoke to you and I thought it was quite charming.'

'I never know if you mean what you say, or if you're just flirting with me.'

'I went to that wretched dance hall every week before I was sent to Lincolnshire. I hoped I'd see you there and we could start again. Didn't your friends tell you that?'

She shook her head. 'No. They never men-

241

tioned you.'

'Well, it's true. I always left the minute I realised you weren't going to turn up.'

'I don't know what to say.'

'Say you'll go out with me this Saturday.'

'I can't, Gil. I'm on duty all day.'

'Then swop with one of the other girls. I'm sure you could arrange it if you tried really hard.'

There was no doubting his sincerity and she could not think of a good excuse. 'I'll try.'

He glanced at the clock behind the bar. 'I'm sorry, but I've got to go. I'm not actually supposed to be here. I'm on duty but I managed to wangle a couple of hours off so that I could come tonight.'

Her suspicions were raised. 'Did you know I'd be here?'

'I knew that Val and her chums had arranged to meet here this evening. I didn't think you'd stay away from something as big as a twenty-first birthday beano.'

She was conscious of his nearness as he stood at her side and she knew she was blushing again, but she felt strangely at ease in his company and the moment passed. 'You get ten out of ten for persistence, Mad Dog.'

He retrieved his cap from the corner of the bar. 'I'll pick you up mid-morning on Saturday.'

'I can't make any promises.'

'But you'll try.'

'I will.'

He leaned over and kissed her on the cheek, receiving a cheer of approval from the airmen and a round of applause from the girls. Gil tossed his cap up in the air, caught it in his hand and flipped it onto his head. 'Goodnight, all.' Blowing a kiss to Miranda he strolled out of the pub.

Miranda was conscious that everyone was staring at her and she made her way back to the table. Audrey patted the empty space on the settle beside her. 'Come and sit down. What did he say? Are you going out on another date?'

'I – well, I don't know. He asked me out on Saturday but I'm on duty.'

Gloria leaned across the table. 'Come on, girls, who's got the day off? Someone needs to swop with Goody Two-Shoes here. I'd do it but I'll be stuck in the filter room.'

'Actually, I've got the day off,' Angela said, pushing her empty glass towards Miranda. 'A large gin and a dash of water will clinch the deal, darling.'

Janice slapped her on the back. 'Good for you, posh girl. You're a sport.'

'I'll do your hair,' Val said magnanimously. 'Has anyone seen Veronica Lake in *I Wanted Wings?* Well, she's got this knockout hairdo which would be just the thing for Miranda. I'm dying to get my hands on that mane of yours again, kid. It's a crime against nature to wear it in a bun.'

'How about a victory roll?' Audrey turned her head so that everyone could admire her hairstyle.

Val shook her head. 'Too sophisticated for our little Goody Two-Shoes. She's the ingenue type.'

'I'm sitting here, girls,' Miranda said, torn between laughter and cringing with embarrassment as the airmen at the next table were listening avidly to their conversation. 'Can we change the subject?'

'We're taking you in hand, kid,' Janice said, grinning. 'Not everyone gets a second chance with Mad Dog. Think yourself bloody lucky. I know I would.'

The trouble with looking like Veronica Lake was, Miranda discovered, that the vision in one eye was largely obscured by her hair. Val had used her considerable expertise at finger-waving to create the effect so that Miranda's blonde hair flopped over the left side of her face and hung around her shoulders in a shining pageboy. Angela had insisted on lending her a pink angora sweater with a sweetheart neck and puffed sleeves, but although it was pretty and warm, the fibres tickled Miranda's nose and made her sneeze. She was wearing a pair of navy-blue slacks, despite strong opposition from her self-appointed fashion advisers who kept insisting that a short skirt was far more fetching, even if she did show her knickers when she got on and off Mad Dog's motorbike. Miranda would only go along with them so far and no further. Her experience of riding pillion in the snow had convinced her that slacks were the thing, and she refused to be persuaded otherwise.

'Slacks aren't sexy,' Audrey said, frowning. 'Smart, maybe, but not cute. Men like a bit of leg, and for heaven's sake pull the jumper down a bit. Show your cleavage, Miranda. I'll bet Veronica does. You don't want Mad Dog to think you're a convent girl, do you?'

Miranda glanced at her watch. 'Too late to change anything now. Thanks a lot, girls. I owe you all.' She shrugged on her coat, wrapped a scarf around her neck and jammed her beret on her head. Picking up her handbag and gas mask case, she left the hut before anyone had time to think of any further improvements in her appearance.

She waited on the priory forecourt for half an hour, walking up and down in order to keep warm. The wild wind tugged at her Veronica Lake hairdo, dragging strands from beneath her beret and tangling them in her scarf. She glanced at her watch, wondering whether he had forgotten or had been unavoidably delayed. After an hour she was beginning to think that she had been stood up when she saw Angela running across the gravel from the direction of the ops room. She knew by the expression on her face that something was terribly wrong.

Chapter Fourteen

'But he wasn't even on duty.' Stunned and barely able to believe what she had just been told, Miranda could not accept the fact that Gil was dead.

Val thrust a cup of tea into her hands. 'Angela said the air crew were scrambled and apparently the pilot who was rostered for duty went down with flu, so Gil took his place.'

'He ditched in the sea,' Miranda said hopefully. 'Do we know anything else?'

Janice shook her head. 'No one reported seeing

a parachute. The Hurry was in flames when it hit the water. I'm sorry, love. Rotten luck.'

Miranda put the cup and saucer back on the table. 'I'm sorry, I can't drink it. I feel sick.'

'Thank God my Cyril is a physical wreck,' Janice said, shaking her head. 'At least I know he's safe working for the gas board.'

Gloria lit a cigarette, offering the pack to Miranda. 'Take one, love. It'll calm your nerves.'

'No thanks.' Miranda rose from the chair in the mess where the girls had taken her after Angela had given her the sad news. 'I think I'll get some fresh air.'

'Will you be okay?' Janice asked anxiously. 'D'you want someone to go with you?'

Miranda shook her head. 'No. You've all been very kind, but I think I'd like to be on my own for a bit.'

The rest of the day passed in a haze. Everyone was sympathetic but as Angela pointed out at supper that evening, it was fortunate that Miranda and Gil were not going steady. It was true, of course, but Miranda would have given anything to turn the clock back to their first date. She wished with all her heart that she had given Gil the chance to prove the gossips wrong, but instead she had behaved like a love-struck schoolgirl mooning over a man she barely knew. Gil had been so full of life and that last evening in the pub he had been kind and understanding. She had really thought that they might have something going for them, and now she was finding it hard to believe that he was never coming back. She hoped against hope that there had been a terrible mistake. Details of the dogfight were sketchy and she had to wait until Angela came off duty that evening before she could get more information.

'Is there any chance that he might still be picked up alive, Angela?'

'We heard his Mayday over the tannoy with his call sign, but it was very faint. He'd taken a direct hit, as had Reggie Madigan. We lost two planes in that encounter and no one was able to say if the pilots had bailed out. I'm so sorry, Miranda. It's beastly bad luck.'

'We were just getting to know one another, but it's still a terrible shock. I just wish I'd been nicer to him in the beginning.'

'Darling, hindsight is a wonderful thing. We all say and do things we regret later, but I'm sure he didn't hold it against you. He wouldn't have wanted to see you again if you'd really upset him.'

'No, I suppose you're right.'

'I've been here longer than you, Miranda. I've seen this happen to other girls and some of them were engaged to pilots who bought it. It's all part of the rotten war and there's nothing we can do about it.'

'I feel so guilty, Angela. I believed what the girls said, and I didn't give him a fair chance.'

'But you made it up the other night. We all saw him clowning around and making you laugh. That didn't look like a chap with a broken heart. Try to think of it that way, if you can.'

Miranda did try, but she could not sleep that night for thinking of Gil's last few minutes before his plane crashed. She had heard enough

247

Maydays while working in the plotting room to know the sound of panic and desperation in the pilot's voice. Some of them had survived, but very few were ever picked up alive from the cold waters of the Channel or the North Sea. The numbness she had experienced on hearing of her father's death was replaced by raw-edged pain. Raif was lost to her and now Gil had been taken before they had a chance to really get better acquainted.

Next morning she could hardly drag herself out of bed and she found it almost impossible to concentrate on her work in the plotting room. At lunch time her supervisor told her to take the rest of the day off, and in the middle of the afternoon she received a summons to the section leader's office.

After a brief preamble she perched her glasses on the end of her nose and scanned Miranda's service records. 'I'm granting you a fortnight's compassionate leave, Beddoes.'

'Thank you, ma'am.'

'In cases like this it's common practice to transfer personnel to another station, although I'll be sorry to lose a good plotter.'

'I don't want any special treatment. I'd really prefer to remain here.'

Her stern demeanour softened just a little. 'I'm aware that your mother is working for the SOE, and that you've only recently lost your father. The death of the young pilot following on so soon must have affected you quite badly.'

'It has, but I was only just getting to know him. It's not as if we were engaged or anything. I'd like to keep my job here, ma'am.'

'Very well. As I said, I'd be sorry to lose you, but we can't afford to have someone in the plotting room whose mind isn't fully engaged on the job in hand. Therefore I've arranged a railway pass for tomorrow, and you'll take the compassionate leave. That's an order.'

'Yes, ma'am. Thank you.'

It seemed strange being back at Highcliffe with nothing to do and everyone treating her as if she were an invalid. Annie had been moved to bring her breakfast in bed on the first morning after she arrived home, and Granny had put a vase filled with Michaelmas daisies on her dressing table. It was nice at first to be petted and pampered, but after a couple of days Miranda was beginning to feel restive and even a little bored. Having grown accustomed to the hectic work in the ops room and the crowded atmosphere of hut five, she found the peace and quiet of the old house stultifying. She tried not to think about Gil, but that proved to be impossible. The best she could do was to hope that the end was swift and that he did not suffer.

There was a lull in the local air raids as the Luftwaffe seemed to be concentrating most of their efforts on London, but this was a constant source of worry to Miranda as Jack and Raif were probably in the thick of the aerial battles. She could only pray for their safety, and if her grandparents were worried they kept their fears to themselves. Miranda saw little of them during the day as her grandmother was kept busy with the WVS, and Grandpa combined his duties as magistrate with running his platoon in the Home Guard.

Miranda wandered about the garden when the weather was reasonably fine and dry, feeding the hens, collecting eggs and generally trying to be useful. Driven by curiosity she decided to take a look inside the coach house but found that it was locked and the key was missing. It was obvious from the cobwebs forming lacy curtains on the inside of the windows that no one had been in there for some time, and Miranda suspected that Granny had had a hand in closing down the illicit still, even though it meant she had lost her bartering power with the local farmers. Elzevir, she thought, must be brokenhearted having been deprived of his favourite tipple. Left to her own devices, Miranda retreated to the peace and quiet of the widow's walk, and spent hours sitting outside, wrapped in her grandmother's old fur coat, watching the changing moods of the sea and sky.

At the end of the fourth day she had had enough of her own company and she made up her mind to telephone Izzie, hoping to catch her that evening when she returned from work in the torpedo factory. It seemed mad that all their lives should have been blighted by something that happened all those years ago. She waited until after supper when her grandfather had left for a Home Guard practice and Granny was settled by the wireless in the sitting room attempting to knit balaclava helmets for the army. She could be heard muttering every time she dropped a stitch or misread the pattern, having misplaced her reading glasses.

Miranda picked up the telephone and dialled the number.

'Hello. This is the Carstairs residence.' Mrs Beasley's voice shrilled in Miranda's ear.

'Mrs Beasley, hello. It's Miranda Beddoes. Is it possible to speak to Isabel?'

'Just a moment, Miss Beddoes; I'll see if she's in.' There was a long pause.

'Miranda, is that you?' Isabel's more youthful tones sounded breathless and eager.

'Yes, it is. How are you?'

'I'm okay. What about you? And where are you?'

'I'm at Highcliffe. I've got a few days' leave and I wondered if we could meet somewhere, just to chat. I felt awful after what happened at the party.'

'I can't talk about it now, Miranda.' Isabel dropped her voice to a whisper. 'Daddy is somewhere around and he wouldn't approve at all, but I'd love to see you.'

'It's Saturday tomorrow. Are you working?'

'No, it's my weekend off. I'll have to hang up now, but meet me at the Jubilee clock at midday and we'll talk then. Bye.'

Standing beneath the clock, Miranda had been waiting for what seemed like ages before she saw a familiar figure running towards her. Pink-cheeked and panting, Isabel gave her a hug. 'Sorry I'm late, but the trains never run on time these days.'

'It doesn't matter. You're here now.' Miranda linked arms. 'Let's go somewhere and get a cup

251

of tea and something to eat. I'm starving. There's a café a little further along the Esplanade, let's go there.'

'All right. That sounds like a good plan.'

They walked quickly as the clouds gathered, threatening a shower, and said little until they were seated at a table in the café and the waitress had taken their order.

'How are you, Miranda?' Isabel said, scanning her face anxiously. 'You look a bit peaky.'

Miranda could not bring herself to tell Izzie the real reason for her spell of leave and she made an effort to sound cheerful. 'I'm fine, but more important, how are you? What's happening between you and Jack?'

'We're still seeing each other, but it has to be in secret. I love him, Miranda, and he loves me. I hate all the lies and subterfuge, but I won't give him up.'

'Have you tried telling your father? I mean, he might be able to put your mind at rest.'

'I wouldn't dare. He'd be absolutely furious that I'd been seeing Jack in the first place, and he'd be sure to deny that he'd had an affair with your grandmother. He's so used to wriggling out of difficult situations that I think he's forgotten how to tell the truth.' Isabel opened her handbag and took out a compact, flipping it open and examining her face in the tiny mirror. 'I love my father, and he's a brilliant surgeon, but he's got a terrible weakness for a pretty face. Raif and I realised that a long time ago. I don't know how Mummy puts up with him.' She brushed an almost invisible smut off her nose and closed the compact with a snap, dropping it back into her bag.

'She must love him a lot,' Miranda said slowly. 'I don't think I could put up with a husband like that.'

'I've never been certain how Mummy feels about anything, but I think it's convenient for her to be married to someone who's at the top of his profession. They don't spend much time together. She's going to Hollywood at the end of November when her play finishes.'

'And Raif?' Miranda simply had to ask.

'I haven't seen much of him. I do worry about him though.'

'Has he got anyone special?'

'Not that I know of.' Isabel sat back in her chair as the waitress arrived with a tray of tea and dumped it unceremoniously on the table.

'Sandwiches coming up in a mo.' She stomped off to take an order from the next table.

'Service with a smile,' Isabel said, chuckling.

Miranda picked up the teapot. 'Shall I be mother, or will you?' She hesitated, gazing at Isabel whose face had suddenly crumpled like a baby that was about to cry. 'What's the matter?'

Isabel delved into her handbag once again but this time she brought out a hanky and mopped her eyes. 'I've been trying to ignore the signs,' she murmured. 'But I'm afraid I'm...' She shook her head. 'I can't even say it.'

Miranda had overhead snippets of conversations that started this way in the mess at the priory. She put the teapot down. 'Are you pregnant, Izzie?'

A blush suffused Isabel's face and she glanced

round nervously. 'Keep your voice down. Someone might hear.'

'But are you?'

'I think so, but I'm not absolutely sure. I keep hoping it's a false alarm.'

'Have you seen a doctor?'

'I daren't. Our doctor is a family friend. He'd tell Daddy and then I'd be in even more trouble.'

'I don't see how you could be.' Miranda poured the tea, passing a cup to Isabel. 'I don't know how tea is supposed to help but it's what everyone does in situations like this.'

'It's not funny. My life is ruined.'

'I'm sorry. No, it's not a joke, but you must tell Jack. I'm assuming he's the father.'

'Of course he is,' Isabel said indignantly. 'I've never been with anyone else. We were going to get married before that awful Ivy woman spoilt everything.' Fresh tears poured down her cheeks and she buried her face in her hanky.

'Two cheese sandwiches.' The waitress slapped them down on the table. She glanced at Isabel, raised her eyebrows and walked away.

Miranda stirred her tea thoughtfully. 'You must tell him, Izzie. He'll do the right thing by you.'

'But what is the right thing?'

'I don't think you can decide that on your own. You simply have to talk it over with Jack, and we need to get the truth out of someone.'

'Not my father.'

'Then that leaves my grandmother.'

Isabel took a large bite from her sandwich, chewed and swallowed. 'Will you, Miranda?'

'I think it ought to be Jack who tackles her on

254

the subject, not me.'

'But he isn't here. This is a matter of life and death.'

Miranda stared at her aghast. 'You wouldn't? I mean you really wouldn't, would you?'

'What choice would I have? If I tell Mummy everything she might be able to arrange for me to go into a private clinic in London.'

'Is that what you want, Izzie?'

Isabel's eyes welled with tears. 'No, of course not. If Jack and I had got married as we planned this would have been a happy time.' She took another bite of her sandwich. 'I'm so hungry these days. I'll be fat as a barrel soon and then no one will want me ever again.'

'Stop it.' Miranda leaned towards her, frowning. 'Stop talking like a ninny. You must telephone the aerodrome and see if you can get a message to Jack. Tell him you simply must see him.'

'But it could be days before he gets a pass. I can't leave it much longer, Miranda.'

'Then I'll have a word with Granny. She won't like it, but I'm going to ask her outright.'

Miranda had to wait until after supper when she knew that they would not be disturbed. She found her grandmother in the small sitting room, peering at a knitting pattern. 'May I come in, Granny?'

'Of course.' Maggie tossed the pattern aside. 'Come and sit down. You poor girl, you must be bored stiff being stuck here with nothing to do.'

'Not at all. It's lovely to be here, but I'm afraid my leave will be up soon.'

'Jack will be disappointed to have missed you.'

Miranda pulled up a stool and sat down. 'Granny, there's something I have to ask you and I don't quite know where to start.'

'At the beginning is usually a good place.' Maggie peered at her over the top of her reading glasses. 'What's this all about, Miranda? I sensed that there was something on your mind at supper.'

'It's something that Aunt Ivy said when she'd drunk too much at the party. I need to know if it's true.'

'Ivy's tongue runs away with her when she's had a few gins. What did she say?'

'There's no easy way to put this.' Miranda took a deep breath. 'She said that you'd had an affair with Max Carstairs and that Jack might be his son.'

Maggie stood up, sending knitting needles and wool flying. 'Tittle-tattle. Idle gossip. You should know better than to listen to Ivy. Dreadful woman. I don't know why I've put up with her all these years.' She rounded on Miranda, fixing her with a hard stare. 'Is this about the Carstairs girl and Jack? Did she put you up to this?'

'She's pregnant, Granny. She's expecting a baby and it's Jack's. They were engaged to be married and then Ivy dropped her bombshell. You've got to tell them the truth. If it's lies then they need to know.'

Maggie collapsed onto her chair. 'I can't,' she whispered. 'How could they do this to me?'

'All you've got to do is to deny it. Surely that's not so hard?'

'I suppose it had to come out,' Maggie said

slowly. 'I've been dreading this moment for twenty-five years.'

'But you did have an affair with Max Carstairs.'

Maggie leaned back against the cushions, closing her eyes, and a faint smile curved her lips. 'He was the most exciting man I'd ever met, and I was desperately in love with him.'

'Tell me about it, Granny.'

'It's not easy to talk about something so personal.'

'But this affects others now, especially Jack and Izzie.'

Maggie was silent for a moment and then she nodded her head slowly. 'I suppose it's time to admit the truth, but it happened such a long time ago.'

'I'm listening, and I won't tell anyone unless you tell me I may do so.'

'Well, if I were to start at the very beginning I'd have to say that I met Max briefly when he and your grandfather studied medicine at the Middlesex, but I didn't see him again until years later when we had a posting in Kenya. Max Carstairs walked into the bar of the Nairobi Club one evening and it changed my life forever.'

'Just like that?'

'In a split second, darling. It was like being struck by lightning. George and I were attending some function or other; I can't recall the exact details. All I can remember is being introduced to this intriguing man with a smile that made my toes curl. He wasn't handsome but he was wildly attractive. The first moment our eyes met I was lost.'

'It was love at first sight?'

Maggie's eyes misted with tears. 'Oh, yes. It was the same for both of us. But, of course, there was nothing we could do about it. I was married with two young children. Your father was eight, and Eileen just a baby.'

'So what happened then?'

'We met at social occasions and Max dined at our bungalow several times, but there were always other guests present. It was all terribly proper in those days and he never said he loved me, nor I him, but we both knew. I lived for the moments when we were together, even though we were never completely alone.'

'What about Grandpa? Did he know what was going on?'

Maggie shook her head. 'Your grandfather is a wonderful man, but he is not the most sensitive person in the world. He was ambitious and hard working. He spent long hours at the military hospital and when he came home he was exhausted. But Max and I did nothing wrong. We simply fell in love, and I knew he was attractive to other women. Most of the other army wives would have given their eye teeth to have an affair with the dashing surgeon.'

'What was he doing in Nairobi, Granny? Did he join the army?'

'No, darling. Max spent a few months at the hospital gaining experience in head injuries, which were quite common in those days. The army wasn't mechanised as it is today, and men were regularly thrown from their horses or trampled underfoot. We're going back thirty years or more, and it must be hard for you to imagine.'

'So Max left Kenya after only a short visit.'

'He did and I was absolutely heartbroken. The worst part of it was that I couldn't tell anyone, not even my closest friends. I had to keep up the pretence of being a devoted wife and mother, although of course I was that too. I did love your grandfather and I adored my children, but Max had a special place in my heart. He captured my body and soul, but it simply wasn't meant to be. He went back to London and I remained in Kenya until the outbreak of the Great War when we returned home. Your great-grandfather had died some years previously but your great-grandmother was still alive, although virtually bedridden, and Annie was looking after her. There was no question of our living anywhere else and we moved in here.'

'But you did see Max again.'

Maggie's eyes darkened. 'I didn't expect to. Your grandfather was fighting the war in France and I was left at home with two children and an ailing mother-in-law, but Annie and I coped. I hadn't forgotten Max, and I used to dream about him sometimes, but what I didn't know was that he had bought Thornleigh Court. It wasn't until the accident with poor little Houdini that we met again. I thought at the time it was by chance, but he told me later that he'd found out that I was here on my own. He said he couldn't keep away a moment longer.'

'And he ran over your dog.'

'That was an accident. Max adored animals and we rushed the poor poppet to the vet. Houdini died of old age a few years later.'

'And you fell for Max all over again.'

'We simply couldn't help ourselves, Miranda. Any more than you could help falling for his son.'

'Granny, that's absurd.'

'Is it? I recognised the signs from the start. The Carstairs men have a fatal fascination and it brings nothing but unhappiness.'

'How can you say that when you had such deep feelings for Max?'

'Because Max Carstairs made me love him and then he walked away. I never saw him again.'

'I don't understand.'

Maggie rose to her feet, becoming agitated. She went to the window, staring out into the gathering darkness. 'I'll have to pull the curtains. It's getting dark. I hadn't noticed.'

'Please, Granny. Finish the story. What went so horribly wrong between you and Max? And is Jack his son?'

Chapter Fifteen

Maggie drew the blackout curtains and switched on a table lamp. 'No. Jack isn't his son. One day, completely out of the blue, Max told me that he was about to marry Veronica. He just announced it as if it were the most normal thing in the world. He simply couldn't understand why I was devastated and we had a frightful row. I accused him of all sort of things, but I was beside myself with humiliation and grief. I couldn't believe that he could be so heartless as to make love to me when all the time he was romancing some young actress, almost half my age.' She returned to her chair and sat down. 'It was all such a long time ago, Miranda.'

'How old were you, Granny? If you don't mind my asking.'

'I was thirty-nine, and I thought my child-bearing years were a thing of the past. But then your grandfather came home on leave and that was when I conceived Jack.'

'Why did Aunt Ivy think the worst, then?'

'Ivy and I were school friends. We'd known each other for years and she had found out about my affair with Max. Annie had guessed what was going on but I knew I could trust her to keep quiet about it. I thought I could rely on Ivy too, but I don't think she believed me when I told her that Max wasn't the father. Jack was born eight months after your grandfather returned to the battlefields and I suppose Ivy added two and two and made nine. She always had a spiteful streak and it must have reared its ugly head on the night of the party when she'd had too much to drink. If I'd known what she had said I would have put things straight there and then.'

Miranda mulled this over in her mind but she was still puzzled. 'I can understand why you hate Max, but why does he bear a grudge against this family? Surely he was the one in the wrong.'

'I don't hate him, darling. Oh, I was furious with him at first. I could have killed him with my bare hands, but I've never hated him. I'm afraid it didn't quite end with our parting. Your grandfather found a letter from Max that I'd foolishly kept. I told him that it was over but he was absolutely livid, blaming Max entirely. He insisted on going to London to have it out with him. I learned later that he'd told Veronica about our affair and reported Max's conduct to the hospital governors, which ruined his chances of promotion. Max never forgave him and neither did Veronica.'

'But she went ahead and married him.'

'They were already married, but it must have affected their relationship. I've heard that they live virtually separate lives.'

Miranda could not help noticing the smug tone in her grandmother's voice. 'Are you still in love with him?'

'I'm devoted to your grandfather, darling. I suppose Max still has a teeny-weeny bit of my heart, but perhaps that's just a romantic memory. I couldn't have put up with his affairs, although maybe if we had been together he wouldn't have strayed.' Maggie pulled a face. 'Or maybe that's what I would like to believe.'

Miranda stood up, gazing at her grandmother with a mixture of sympathy and impatience. 'You have to tell Jack that Ivy was mistaken. You and Max have to put things right because what you did years ago is affecting the here and now.'

'I really don't want to rake up the past.' Maggie picked up her knitting. 'I'll tell him in my own good time.'

Miranda snatched the wool from her grandmother's lap and held it out of reach. 'Jack is risking his life every time he takes off in that Spitfire. What if he gets killed without ever knowing the truth? How would you feel if Izzie has an illegal abortion? She's desperate and she might just do something stupid.'

'You're right, of course,' Maggie said slowly. 'I'll speak to Jack when I get a chance. Now please give me the wool.'

Miranda held it out of reach. 'No, Granny. That's not good enough. We'll visit the aerodrome tomorrow, even if we have to walk all the way to Warmwell. You'll tell Jack everything, and if you don't, then I will.'

Next morning, with Annie's help, they persuaded Elzevir to transport them to Warmwell. It was not a comfortable journey perched on the driver's seat of the ancient cart with a load of logs rattling around in the main body of the wagon. They arrived stiff and sore but thankfully in one piece, although Miranda had had her doubts that they would reach their destination when the old horse struggled up the hills and slithered on the downward slopes. Maggie was unusually silent, but Miranda put this down to nerves. She breathed a sigh of relief when they reached the perimeter of the airfield.

Elzevir set them down and drove off to deliver his load with a grudging promise to return later 'That man is a pain in the neck,' Maggie said, frowning. 'He's done nothing but grumble about the trade he's lost by doing us a favour. If I'd had to listen to him for a moment longer, I'd have been tempted to slap him.'

With a growing feeling of misgiving, Miranda eyed the stone-faced airman on guard duty at the gate. 'Never mind old Evil-Eye,' she said in a low voice. 'We've still got to get into the aerodrome and it's not going to be that easy.'

'You're in uniform, my dear, and I'm Jack's mother. I defy anyone to stop me.'

'Oh, well. Here goes nothing.' Miranda approached the young airman with a smile on her lips. 'Good morning. We've come to see Flight Lieutenant Beddoes.'

It took several minutes to persuade him to send a message to Jack, but eventually he disappeared into a hut and they could hear him speaking to someone on the telephone. They waited for a good ten minutes before he reappeared. 'Sorry, ladies,' he said apologetically. 'Flight Lieutenant Beddoes is off duty today. He's billeted in the village. I can give you his address.'

'I knew we should have telephoned first,' Maggie said as they trudged along the narrow lane towards the village. 'He could be anywhere.'

'In the pub most likely, if there...' Miranda leapt aside as someone shot past them on a bicycle. Then with a screech of brakes the bike came to a halt.

'Manda!' Rita leapt off the saddle and propped the machine up against the hedge. She came hurrying towards them, grinning broadly. 'And Mrs B, too. What are you two doing here?'

'We're looking for Jack,' Miranda said before her grandmother had a chance to speak. 'Have you seen him today?'

She shook her head. 'No, but I've got a pretty

good idea where to find him.' She glanced doubtfully at Maggie's court shoes. 'It's quite a long walk, but you can ride my bike if you want to, Mrs B.'

'Thank you, Rita. I'm not in my dotage yet. I can walk. Which way?'

'Straight ahead.'

'Come along then,' Maggie said impatiently. 'Don't loiter, girls. We haven't got all day.' She strode off at a brisk pace.

Rita retrieved her bike and they fell into step behind Maggie. 'The Frampton Arms is where he's most likely to be,' Rita said in a low voice. 'Jack's been hitting the bottle since the party. We've all tried to help him, but he took it really badly when he found out that Max was his dad.'

'Well, we've got good news for him. Jack is a Beddoes through and through.'

Rita let out a whoop. 'Well if that doesn't take the cake.' She quickened her pace. 'I've got to be in on this one, although I'm supposed to be back at the aerodrome. Anyway, I'll say I had a puncture. It's my job to fix it anyway.' She chuckled. 'Yeah. That's it, Miranda. I'm an official bicycle repairer. That's what most of us girls do at Warmwell.' She grinned. 'Apart from keeping up the morale of the glamour-boys, but that's a pleasure, not a duty.'

'What does Tommy think about that?'

Rita shrugged. 'I don't see much of him, and it's none of his business anyway. We're not going steady, Manda. I thought you knew that.'

'I'm sorry. It's just that you've always seemed to get on so well.'

'Toopy's okay, but he's more like a brother. I don't fancy him.' Rita shot her a sideways glance. 'Anyway, what about you? Have you got over your thing with Raif?'

'Rita! Keep your voice down. There's nothing between me and Raif. There never was.'

'I believe you, ducks. Thousands wouldn't.'

Maggie stopped suddenly, turning on them with a look of disapproval. 'Stop nattering, you two, and get a move on.'

'Yes, Granny,' Miranda said meekly.

'We're there anyway.' Rita pointed to the pub. 'I'm pretty certain this is where we'll find Jack.'

'We'll see about that.' Maggie strode the last few yards and stormed into the bar.

'There'll be fireworks now,' Rita said, propping her bicycle up against the outside wall. She was about to follow Maggie when Miranda caught her by the sleeve.

'Wait a moment. There's something else, and I don't know how Jack will take it.'

Rita's eyebrows shot up in surprise. 'What's that?'

'Izzie's pregnant. She's only just found out and she's in quite a state.'

'What's the problem? They were going to get married anyway and now they can. It's that simple.'

'Yes, I hope so for her sake, but Jack might have other ideas.'

'Not Jack. He'll stand by her. I'd bet my life on it. Stop worrying, and let's go inside. I want to see his face when Mrs B tells him the good news.'

They hurried into the lounge bar to find Jack

sitting at a table beside a roaring log fire with a pint glass in his hand, staring up at his mother openmouthed. 'What are you doing here?'

She pulled up a chair and sat down. 'I'm here to sort you out, Jack Beddoes.' She stared pointedly at the half empty glass. 'What do you think you're doing?'

'Having a quiet drink in my local, Mother. I'm sorry, but I'm a big boy now.'

'And you're still acting like a two-year-old.' Maggie snapped her fingers at the astonished barmaid. 'I'll have a pot of tea, please, miss. And whatever the young ladies want.'

'Yes'm.' The barmaid met Miranda's amused gaze with raised eyebrows. 'Tea for three, is it?'

'That's right, love,' Rita said hastily. 'I don't suppose you've got anything on the menu, have you? I'm ravenous.'

'There's only pickled eggs or an arrowroot biscuit. There is a war on you know.'

'What d'you think this is, darling?' Rita pointed at their uniforms. 'Fancy dress?'

'Tea for three then.' The girl flounced out of the bar.

Miranda went to sit at a table in the window and Rita pulled up a chair. 'Let's hope she can sort him out.'

'I do hope so.' Miranda could do nothing other than wait and watch. She could not hear what passed between mother and son, but she could tell by the change in Jack's expression that the truth was beginning to sink into his befuddled brain. By the time the barmaid returned with the tea, Jack was on his feet, hugging his mother until she protested.

'Sit down, Jack. You're making a spectacle of yourself and me.' Maggie straightened her hat. 'Drink your tea, girls. We'd better get back to the aerodrome. I don't want Elzevir to drive off without us, Miranda.'

Jack shot her a reproachful glance. 'Mother, you didn't let that old reprobate drive you all the way from Weymouth?'

'How else were we supposed to get here? And for your information we walked from the aerodrome and my corns are killing me.' Maggie tempered her words with a smile. 'So now I expect you to do the decent thing by that poor girl.'

'I'll have to speak to her father. How would you feel about that, Mother?'

Maggie squared her shoulders. 'After all these years I think it's high time that we all moved on. Anyway, Isabel must be over twenty-one. She doesn't need her parents' permission, and I don't think it would worry her even if they refused to give you their blessing. She might look as fragile as a butterfly, but I would be surprised if there wasn't a core of steel somewhere beneath that fluffy exterior.'

'I'll telephone her tonight, Mother.' Jack took a handful of coins from his pocket and placed them on the bar. 'Have a drink yourself, Edna. You won't be seeing so much of me in the future. I'm going to be married.'

Maggie finished her tea and stood up. 'Come along, Jack. You can accompany us back to the aerodrome.' She glanced over her shoulder at Edna, who was counting the money. 'The tea was awful. I suggest you use fresh leaves next time or you'll lose all your customers, and service with a smile would be an improvement.'

When they arrived back at the aerodrome there was no sign of Elzevir or his horse and cart and it had started to rain.

'Come and wait in the mess,' Jack said, glancing up at the stormy clouds. 'The corporal will let us know if your date turns up, Mother.'

Maggie raised an eyebrow. 'Thank you, Jack. I'm sure that even at my age I could do better than Elzevir Shipway. Besides which he's been like a sulky schoolboy since his supply of raw spirits was cut off. He can't forgive me for stopping your grandfather's chemistry experiments.'

Jack threw back his head and laughed. 'I don't know how Father got away with it for so long, or you come to that, Mother. I heard that you bartered the hooch for extra rations. You and Father really are a pair.'

'Yes,' Maggie said simply. 'We are, and always will be.'

Rita nudged Miranda in the ribs, jerking her head towards the young officer who had just emerged from the watch office. 'Don't look now, but here comes trouble. I'm off, Manda. See you soon, I hope.' She mounted her bicycle and pedalled off towards a row of workshops.

Miranda turned her head to see Raif walking towards them and experienced the familiar undeniable tug of attraction. He walked with a slight swagger and even his worst enemy would have to admit that he looked handsome in his immaculate uniform. Miranda could not help comparing him to Jack who appeared to have thrown his clothes on whilst half asleep, and it was obvious that he had not bothered to shave that morning.

'Mrs Beddoes,' Raif said, tipping his cap. 'Miranda,' he added with a hint of a smile. He glanced at her uniform with a question in his eyes. 'Is this an official visit?'

'No, Flight Lieutenant, it's purely personal,' Maggie said, answering for both of them. 'Miranda is on compassionate leave and I had a family matter to discuss with my son.'

'I'm taking them to the mess,' Jack said hastily. 'They're waiting for a lift home.'

'Better get them inside out of the rain.' Raif inclined his head towards Maggie. 'Good day, ma'am.'

Maggie acknowledged this with a brief nod. She linked her hand through her son's arm. 'Is it far to the mess?'

'No, Mother.' Jack hesitated, casting a wary glance at Raif. 'There's something we need to discuss, Carstairs.'

'Say what you've got to say and be done with it, man.'

Miranda could feel the underlying tensions rising rapidly to the surface, but this was neither the time nor the place to air family matters, especially with her grandmother present, and they were all getting very wet. She laid her hand on Raif's sleeve. 'I'm only here for a short visit. Would it be asking too much for you to show me round the aerodrome? It's quite different from Henlow Priory where I'm stationed at the moment.'

Jack opened his mouth as if to protest but a frown from his mother silenced him. 'Don't be too long, dear,' Maggie said, turning to Miranda. 'We'll leave as soon as Elzevir turns up.' She walked off, leaning on her son's arm.

Raif waited until they were out of earshot. 'Why did you come here today?'

'We had something to tell Jack that changes everything.'

'Does this have anything to do with Izzie?'

She could feel the rain beginning to soak through her uniform. 'Can we go somewhere a bit drier? I'm getting very wet.'

'Of course.' He led the way to a single-storey office block. 'The clerks are at lunch,' he said, opening the door and ushering her inside. 'We won't be disturbed.' He pulled up a chair. 'Take a seat and tell me what's on your mind.'

'Thanks.' She sat down, wondering just how much she ought to tell him. 'Jack really loves Izzie, you know.'

Raif perched on the edge of the desk. 'Yes, I had realised that.'

'I saw her yesterday.'

'How is she?'

His offhand manner grated on her nerves, which were already stretched to breaking point. 'How can you be so calm and detached from what's been going on with your own family? Don't you know that your sister is breaking her heart?'

'Izzie will get over it. She's very young and there'll be other men who are much more suitable than Jack Beddoes. I'm sorry, Miranda, but even if

Jack isn't our half-brother, he's not the sort of chap I'd want my sister to marry.'

'That's the real problem, isn't it? You were against him from the start. You must have been delighted when Ivy spread that malicious rumour about your father and Granny.'

'I've no doubt it was true.'

'Yes, but only in part. I tackled Granny about it yesterday and she admitted having an affair with your father, but she swears that Jack is not his son, and I believe her.'

'Even so, it doesn't make any difference. He's not the man for my sister, so I hope you won't encourage her to think he is.'

She leapt to her feet. 'You have no right to dictate to Izzie. She can make her own mind up.'

'Don't be so dramatic. I'm not doing anything. She's seen Beddoes for what he is – a philandering bastard.'

The urge to slap his smug face was so strong that Miranda had to clench her fists at her sides. She would not stoop so low. 'Your sister is pregnant, so I wouldn't mention bastards in her company if I were you.' She had the satisfaction of seeing him shocked out of his complacency.

'You're lying.' White lines etched the corners of his mouth and his eyes narrowed as he stared at her in disbelief.

'No, I'm not. She told me yesterday and she was so desperate that she was thinking of going to London to get an abortion.'

'That's impossible. Izzie would never do such a thing.'

'She won't now because Jack is going to telephone her the moment she gets back from work. He wants to marry her, Raif. For God's sake leave them alone, and let them work it out together.'

'What a bloody mess.' He stood up and walked to the door. 'This will destroy my family.'

'That's stupid, and so are you if you believe that.'

'Izzie won't be welcome at Thornleigh Court if she marries Jack Beddoes.'

She stared at him aghast. 'I can't believe you said that.'

'My parents' marriage is rocky now. This will finish it completely.'

'And do you think that Izzie being left with an illegitimate baby is going to bring them closer together?'

'It would be better than having to associate with the Beddoes clan. Your grandfather tried to ruin my father's career and very nearly succeeded.'

'What utter rot. From what I've heard my grand-mother wasn't the only woman who fell for Max Carstairs' charms. He's had more affairs than Don Juan.'

'My father is the most eminent man in his field and he's in line for a knighthood. A scandal like this really could ruin him if the press got hold of the story.'

'There won't be any scandal if you all accept the fact that Jack and Izzie are going to be married.' As she met his angry gaze Miranda experienced a sudden wave of revulsion. The glossy image of him that had haunted her dreams suddenly cracked and splintered into shards. 'I always respected you, Raif. I thought you were something special, but now I can see that you're just a shallow, selfish person who cares nothing for his sister or anyone else for that matter.'

He turned his head to look at her and his lips tightened into a thin line. 'I never encouraged your juvenile attentions, Miranda. You can't say I did.'

'Maybe not, but you certainly turned on the charm when we first met. You knew all about the family feud and yet you went out of your way to be nice to me. Why did you do that?'

He shrugged his shoulders. 'I've asked myself that a dozen times. I could see that you were impressed by me, and I suppose I was flattered. I think I was curious about the Beddoes family too. I needed to see the woman whose affair with my father almost cost him everything.'

'And you wanted to get your own back.'

'Nothing so crass.' He turned away to look out of the window. 'It's stopped raining. Perhaps you should go and find your grandmother. I think we're finished here, Miranda.'

She picked up her handbag and gas mask case, pausing at the door to give him a pitying look. 'I feel quite sorry for you, Raif. You've allowed your father's mistakes to blight your life, and that's very sad. Don't ruin Izzie's chances of happiness.' She opened the door and stepped outside, taking a deep breath of the moist air and wrinkling her nose. The rich scent of damp earth was tainted with the smell of high octane petrol and engine oil that still lingered, even though the mighty Spitfires and Hurricanes were idling on the tarmac. She jumped as the frantic ringing of a bell from one of the huts sent aircrews racing towards their machines. Raif emerged from the building and hurried off towards the control tower. She stood for a moment, feeling very small and lost in the roar of the engines and the scramble of the crews to be airborne. It must have been just such a scene as this when Gil took off on his last fatal mission. She realised suddenly that she was crying.

Someone grabbed her by the arm. 'Manda, old Elzevir's turned up. Your gran says you're to come right away.'

She dashed the tears from her cheeks with the back of her hand. 'Okay, I'm coming.'

'What's up?' Rita demanded as she fell into step at her side. 'What did that bugger say to upset you?'

'Nothing really. I just saw him for what he is and realised what a silly fool I'd been.'

'Don't be so hard on yourself, ducks. He's a bit of all right, but that's just window dressing. He's a cold fish when it comes down to it.'

'How come you're so wise suddenly, Rita Platt?'

'Maybe I've just had a bit more experience of the world than you, love. You need to get out there and meet other blokes. Have a bit of fun. Life's too short to bother about chaps like Raif. Give me Jack any time.'

Miranda stopped for a moment, staring at her in surprise. 'Jack? You fancy my uncle?'

'It was just a manner of speaking, Manda. Jack's top notch, but he's not for the likes of me.'

'Don't say things like that. You're as good as any of us; better than most.'

'But I'm not posh like Isabel Carstairs.' Rita

hooked her arm around Miranda's shoulders. 'I'm a dandelion to Izzie's delicate rose; she's a lady and I'm a common girl from the East End. It's the way of the world.'

'Then perhaps this war will change all that. Maybe something good will come out of this damned awful mess.'

They had reached the perimeter gates. Miranda could see her grandmother pacing up and down outside while Elzevir sat on the driver's seat with a pipe stuck between his teeth. Jack was talking to the corporal but he broke off when he saw Miranda. 'I hope you told Carstairs where to get off,' he said angrily. 'You shouldn't have had anything to do with him.'

'Leave her alone, Jack.' Rita squared up to him, bristling. 'It's got nothing to do with you.'

'It has everything to do with me if she told him about Izzie.'

'I did tell him, Jack.' Miranda met his angry gaze with a sudden sense of calm. She knew she had done the right thing. 'There's no use you speaking to him. He's never going to change his mind. You'll just have to go ahead and marry Izzie whether her family agree or not.'

Jack nodded to the corporal. 'Open the gate, please. My niece is just leaving.'

'Cheerio, Rita,' Miranda said, giving her a hug. 'See you soon, I hope.'

'You can bet on it.' Rita sent a warning look to Jack. 'She's right and you know it.'

His angry expression melted into a sheepish grin. 'Trust you to keep me on the straight and narrow, young Rita.' He leaned over to kiss

Miranda on the forehead. 'I'm going to get a special licence. If Izzie agrees to marry me we'll tie the knot as soon as possible.'

'Good for you, Jack.' With a last grateful glance in Rita's direction, Miranda hurried through the gate. Elzevir climbed down to help Maggie up onto the seat.

'About time too, Miranda,' Maggie said irritably. 'You shouldn't have gone off with that fellow. He's so different from his father that I can hardly believe he's Max's son.'

Miranda swung herself onto the cart to sit beside her. 'I didn't want them to have a row in public, Granny. It might have turned nasty.'

'They're grown men, my dear. It's not your problem.'

Elzevir encouraged his horse forward with a flick of his whip. 'What shall us do if there's an air raid warning, ladies?'

'Travel on, Elzevir,' Maggie said firmly. 'Our boys have just taken off and they'll sort Jerry out. I want to get home and we'll work on the principle that a moving target is harder to hit than a stationary one.'

Elzevir reached down into the well of the cart and brought out a familiar-looking bottle. He took the pipe from his mouth and uncorking the bottle with his teeth he took a swig.

'I hope that isn't what I think it might be,' Maggie said suspiciously.

'One of the last bottles to be found in Dorset, ma'am.' Elzevir pushed the cork back into the neck of the bottle. 'Got it in part payment for the logs.'

'How did your customer get a bottle of that stuff in the first place?'

'Well, you see, ma'am, it's like this – sometimes I used to do a bit of trading on the side. In this case I think it was for a pound of blue Vinney. I got a real taste for that cheese and he's the only farmer round here still making it, thanks to them bleddy Jerries, pardon my language, ma'am.'

Miranda stifled a giggle. Elzevir's guileless admission came as something of a relief after the tensions of the morning, and her grandmother's face was a picture of outrage.

'I certainly hope that was the last one in circulation,' Maggie said, radiating disapproval. 'You know what the major said about it, Elzevir.'

'Aye, ma'am. I most certainly do – the embrocation is for external use only.' He put his pipe back in his mouth. 'There goes the siren. Shall us make a run for it then?'

'Get us home as quickly as your poor old horse can make it,' Maggie said, holding on to the seat.

They arrived home safely and although the fighter planes were too far away for them to see the dogfights, they could hear the crump of ack-ack guns firing from the ranges along the coast. Maggie allowed Elzevir to help her down from the cart and she opened her handbag, pausing for a moment and meeting his expectant look with a frown. 'I will pay you for your trouble, but if I discover that you've any more bottles hidden away I'll have to tell my husband.'

Elzevir held out his hand. 'Thank you, ma'am.' He closed his fingers over the coins, tipping his cap and winking. 'But I hardly think as how the major would have me up in court over such a matter. Good day to you both.' He clambered back onto the cart and drove off, leaving Maggie staring after him.

'Well, of all the cheek. That sounded suspiciously like blackmail. What do you think, Miranda?'

'He'd never do anything to hurt you or Grandpa. It was Elzevir's heavy-handed idea of a joke, and anyway, Annie would give him hell if he stepped out of line. Let's go indoors. I think it's going to rain again.' Glancing up at the gathering clouds, Miranda found herself thinking once again of Gil's last moments. He had gone up on just such a day as today, just like the young pilots she had seen at Warmwell. How many of them would return, she wondered sadly. When would it all end?

'Come along, Miranda. I'm dying for a cup of tea.'

Miranda followed her grandmother down the garden path to the house. She could hear the telephone ringing even before the front door opened. Maggie hurried to answer it. 'Hello.' She paused, listening. 'I'm sorry, this is a dreadful line. Who did you say was calling?' She turned to Miranda. 'Do you know someone called Janice? She says it's urgent.'

Chapter Sixteen

'Hello, Janice. What's up?'

'I've been trying to get hold of you all day, Miranda. It's good news for a change. Mad Dog did manage to bail out after all. He was picked up by a motor launch that happened to be in the area and taken to hospital in Great Yarmouth.'

Hardly able to believe her ears, Miranda took a deep breath. 'Was he badly injured?' She waited, drumming her fingers on the hall table. She could hear Janice speaking to someone in the background. 'What's going on?'

'Nothing, pet. I was just asking Val if she had any more info. She was the radio operator when the news came through. We thought you'd like to know.'

'Yes, thanks. I'm glad.' It was an understatement but Miranda was in a state of shock. She had given Gil up for lost, but she knew enough about the injuries he might have received to be cautious.

'Anyway, got to go. See you in a few days, love.'

'Goodbye, Janice. Thanks again.' Miranda replaced the ear piece.

'Was it bad news, dear?'

Miranda turned slowly to meet her anxious gaze. 'No, Granny. At least I don't think so. I've just heard that someone I thought was killed when his plane ditched in the sea has survived.'

'Well that's wonderful news, isn't it? Why the long face?'

'He's in hospital.'

'Why haven't you mentioned this young man before? He's obviously more than just a friend.'

'It's complicated, Granny. Do you mind if I don't talk about it now?'

Maggie patted her on the shoulder. 'What you need is a good strong cup of tea.' She took Miranda by the hand and led her unprotesting to the kitchen. 'Annie, put the kettle on. We need sustenance.' She pressed Miranda down on the nearest chair. 'We've had quite a day of it.'

'What's wrong with you?' Annie demanded, peering at Miranda. 'You're white as a sheet.'

'She's had a shock. Now stop being nosey and make us a pot of tea. I'm black and blue from travelling on your brother's wagon. It's not the most comfortable form of transport.'

'It got you there and back, didn't it?' Annie put the kettle on the hob. 'You've got spoiled riding in that posh motor. I remember the days when you were happy to travel in the governess cart that belonged to old Mrs Beddoes.'

'That was a long time ago and I was younger then.' Maggie opened a cupboard and took out a bottle of brandy. 'I think we both need a tot, Miranda. Purely for medicinal purposes, of course. Would you pass me a couple of glasses, please, Annie? You're nearest.'

Annie shot her a reproachful glance but she put three wine glasses on the table. 'You're not leaving me out, I hope. I've been slaving away all day making supper while you two were off gallivanting.'

Miranda could see an argument brewing. She was used to their little spats and she knew that they enjoyed sparring, but she was not in the mood to listen. She stood up and taking the bottle from her grandmother she poured three large measures into the glasses. She passed them round. 'We'll drink to Jack and Izzie,' she said firmly. 'Bung-ho!'

'So it's history repeating itself,' Annie said, putting the glass to her lips and sipping the brandy. 'Only this time, with luck, there'll be a happy ending.'

'Happy endings,' Maggie said, tossing back the drink in one mouthful. 'Now, Miranda, what are we going to do about you and your young man?'

It had been one of those moments in the middle of the night when it was impossible to sleep. Miranda had got out of bed and gone upstairs to Jack's room where she opened the window and went out onto the widow's walk. A silver path of moonlight rippled on the surface of the sea and it was hard to believe that just a few hours previously the sky had been filled with men and machines locked in deadly combat. She wrapped her woollen dressing gown a little tighter around her body and took deep breaths of the cool night air. She had always found it easier to think up here close to the stars and Gil's description of flying as kissing the clouds came forcibly to mind, making her smile. If she closed her eyes she could summon up a vision of him when he was clowning around in the bar. He had been so full of life then, and he had been the first person to understand that it was shyness fuelling her outward show of reserve. He had seemed to know her better than she knew herself, and she simply could not bear to think of him lying helpless in a hospital bed. Even though she had doubted his sincerity at the beginning, she had a sneaking suspicion that they had been on the brink of something momentous. She knew exactly what she was going to do.

It was not difficult to find Maddern and Son, Auctioneers. Miranda had taken the train to Southampton and a taxi from the station which dropped her off outside the auction house. She paid the cabby and stood on the pavement for a moment, getting her bearings. The name of the firm was emblazoned above the doorway in gold lettering on a midnight blue background, and as luck would have it she had arrived on the viewing day before the next sale. She followed an elderly couple inside and found several people intent on examining the items set out in the barn of a room. There was an eclectic mixture of furniture from different decades, paintings, china and silver with a few piles of books giving off their peculiarly musty smell. There were a couple of porters on duty, and Miranda was just about to ask one of them where she might find Mrs Maddern or her daughter when a young woman emerged from the office. She was wearing the uniform of an ARP warden but Miranda was struck by her resemblance to Gil, and she was in no doubt that this must be one of his sisters. She caught up with her as she was about to leave the building and tapped her on the shoulder. 'Excuse me, but are you Miss Maddern?'

'Yes, I'm Felicity Maddern. How can I help you?'

'Could you spare a minute or two?' Miranda said urgently. 'It's rather personal.'

Felicity glanced at her watch. 'Okay. I'm not on duty for another ten minutes. Come into the office.' She retraced her footsteps and showed Miranda into a room furnished with two antique desks, a breakfront bookcase and a pair of Edwardian desk chairs. 'Do take a seat, Miss er...'

'Miranda Beddoes. I'm a friend of Gil's.'

'Really? I don't think he's ever mentioned you.'

'We haven't known each other for long. I'm stationed at Henlow Priory. That's where we met. I found out yesterday that he'd been rescued and that he's in hospital. I simply had to find out how he is.'

'That's right. He was taken to hospital in Yarmouth, but we don't know the exact extent of his injuries.'

'But they're not life threatening?'

'No, thank God, although they're bad enough.' Felicity met Miranda's anxious gaze with a puzzled frown. 'Tell me, were you close to Gil? Forgive me for asking, but I can't understand why he's never mentioned you.'

'We were just getting to know each other.' Miranda stared down at her hands clasped tightly in her lap. This was not going to be easy. 'I'm afraid I wasn't very nice to him when we first met. I was rather foolish and believed everything I heard about him instead of using my own judgement, but for some odd reason he gave me a second chance.' She raised her eyes and was surprised to see that Felicity was smiling.

'That's sounds so like Gil. He's never been one to go by the rules.' She glanced at her watch for a second time. 'Look, I really have to go, but if you could hang around until four we can have a proper chat.'

'I can get a later train home, but I was hoping I might be able to go on to Yarmouth and see Gil.'

'Mother went there as soon as she got the news. She's trying to get him transferred to a local hospital, but I don't think he's in a fit state to see anyone other than close family.'

'I've been so worried about him.'

'We all have, but I really must fly. I don't want to get into trouble with my supervisor. He's a bit sniffy about me doing two jobs anyway, but joining ARP was the only way I could stay here and help run the business.'

'Shall I meet you back here later?' Miranda rose to her feet.

'I don't suppose you know the town well.' Felicity opened her handbag and pulled out a set of keys. 'Why don't you wait for me at our place?' She unhooked one and pressed it into Miranda's hand. 'You can't miss the house. It's called The Gables and it's just round the corner, about a hundred yards down the road. There's an Anderson shelter in the garden should there be an air raid. Just make yourself at home.'

Miranda stared at her in amazement. 'You're very trusting. I could be a burglar.'

'You have an honest face and I'm sure Gil

285

would never forgive me if I left you to wander the streets on your own. Must go now.' She hurried from the office.

Miranda stared at the key lying in the palm of her hand and she smiled, thinking that the impulsive streak must run in the Maddern family. Felicity and Gil obviously lived life with their hearts firmly stitched to their sleeves. They were so alike that, apart from the fact that Gil was the younger by a couple of years, they could have been twins. She picked up her things and left the office to make her way to the Madderns' home, which as Felicity had said was just around the corner in a wide tree-lined avenue of detached houses set in large gardens.

She let herself into the house, which to her surprise was furnished in the ultra modern art deco style. Somehow she had imagined that it would be filled with expensive antiques but the design was simple, verging on stark, with black and cream dominating the colour scheme downstairs. Feeling like an intruder, she went to the kitchen and was greeted by an elderly spaniel. He staggered from his wicker basket to nuzzle her hand and then went back to bed. She looked round and felt reassured by the mess that Felicity had left in her wake that morning. The sink was piled high with dishes and there was evidence of a hurried breakfast. The table was covered in breadcrumbs and a spoon had been left in the marmalade pot. Whatever Felicity had attempted to cook for her supper the previous night had ended up stuck to the bottom of a saucepan and was blackened beyond recognition.

Miranda took off her cap and jacket, rolled up her sleeves and set about clearing up the mess. It took her the best part of an hour to make the kitchen sparkle, and she rewarded herself with a slice of toast. She did not like to take any of the Maddems' butter ration, so she spread it with a little of the marmalade and hoped that no one would mind. The smell of food enticed the dog from his bed and he sat at her feet, looking up at her with adoring eyes until she fed him a bit of the crust. She made herself a cup of tea and when she had tidied everything away she could not resist the temptation to explore the house. She knew it was a frightful cheek, but curiosity had got the better of her and she had to fill in the afternoon somehow.

Upstairs she peeped into the master bedroom, which as she had expected given the fact that Mrs Maddern had been widowed for many years was very feminine, elegant and decorated in pastel colours. There were three other bedrooms, one of which predictably was a chaotic jumble of discarded clothes, shoes and a dressing table littered with makeup. The spare room was chintzy and inviting, and the fourth room, which was the one that most interested her, was obviously a shrine to a much-loved son.

Sporting trophies adorned the mantelpiece and framed photos of school sporting events hung on the walls, but the photograph that caught Miranda's attention was placed on the bedside cabinet. She picked it up and found herself looking at a much younger Gil holding a spaniel puppy in his arms. He looked so proud and happy that it brought tears to her eyes. That teenage boy could have had no idea of what the future held for him and for so many of his generation. She put it back where she had found it, feeling suddenly guilty for intruding into his private space. She stood for a moment gazing round the room, which could not have changed much since his student days, and she noticed a well-worn and obviously much-loved teddy bear sitting on top of the wardrobe. It looked back at her with its one remaining glass eye, the other one having been replaced by a coat button. She smiled in spite of everything and left the room comforted by the fact that she had learned something of Gil's past and a little more about his character. She knew also that she had a lot to make up for.

Felicity arrived soon after four o'clock, bursting into the kitchen like a uniformed whirlwind. She stopped and looked round with obvious delight. 'Miranda, you've worked wonders, but you really shouldn't have.'

Miranda had been sitting at the kitchen table reading a magazine that she had found in the sitting room. She closed it and stood up. 'I had to do something to fill in the time, and I'm afraid I made myself some lunch – just tea and toast – I hope you don't mind.'

'Of course not. I should have told you to help yourself to anything you could find, although there's not much in the larder. I'm a rotten house-keeper, but then I've never had to do much for myself.' She took off her hat and jacket, tossing them on the nearest chair. 'If you don't mind I'll go up and change out of this ghastly outfit and then we'll have a cup of tea and a chat. Won't be long.' She rushed out of the room leaving Miranda to wonder whether Felicity Maddern did anything at less than top speed. She did not have long to wait as her hostess reappeared minutes later dressed more casually in a sweater and slacks. 'I hate that blessed uniform,' she said, holding the door open. 'Come into the other room, Miranda. I've put a match to the fire and we can chat in comfort.'

'I really can't stay long,' Miranda said, following her into the elegant sitting room that was such a contrast to the cluttered but much cosier rooms at Highcliffe. 'I have a train to catch.'

Felicity threw herself down on a cream leather sofa, kicking her shoes off. 'My feet are killing me. Anyway, that's not your problem. Could you stay tonight, Miranda? I'd love the company and I can tell you everything you ever wanted to know about my younger brother. Living with three sisters he was spoiled and bullied. It's a wonder he grew up to be such a love.'

'I suppose I could stay,' Miranda said doubtfully. 'But I'd have to ring home and tell Granny.'

'Feel free.' Felicity waved her hand in the direction of a new style telephone with a handset and a dial, modelled in tasteful cream Bakelite. 'You could wait until Mummy gets home tomorrow. She's going to take the sale so she promised she'd get here first thing. She'll be able to tell us more about Gil's injuries.'

'What exactly are they? Was he badly burned? I know it happens.'

'I don't think so. Apparently he's broken both

289

legs and his right arm, and hurt his back. I'm scared that he might be paralysed; that would be absolutely awful.'

'Do you think he might be?'

'I honestly don't know. Mummy mentioned something about his condition being due to spinal shock, whatever that is. I'm frightfully ignorant about medical matters. I suppose I should speak to my sister Mary, she's married to a doctor, but Mummy said I wasn't to say anything until we know more. She didn't want the others to worry.' Felicity leaned over to throw a log on the fire. 'I'm the one who has to shoulder the burden alone.' She looked up and grinned. 'But now I've got you. We can worry together, and we'll be terribly lazy and have fish and chips for supper, and eat it out of the newspaper with lots of vinegar, salt and pepper. Telephone home, Miranda. We'll have a lovely girly evening, just the two of us. I think there's a bottle of wine in the drinks cabinet. We'll drink to Gil's speedy recovery and thank God that he's survived, and I hope that they ground him for the rest of this beastly war.'

Next morning Miranda awakened with a bit of a headache, and for a moment she could not remember how she came to be in a strange bed, but then she remembered that she had shared a bottle of Chablis with Felicity and they had chatted into the early hours of the morning. The sound of a car stopping outside the house with its engine running made her leap from her bed and run to the window. She drew back the curtain and saw a taxi pulling away from the kerb. A tall, blonde woman carrying a small overnight bag was walking down the garden path towards the house. It could only be Gil's mother returning with news of his condition.

With her heart racing, Miranda put on her clothes, brushed her hair and hurried downstairs. Felicity and her mother were in the kitchen talking in hushed tones. Fearing the worst, Miranda hesitated in the doorway. She cleared her throat to alert them to her presence. 'Good morning.'

Felicity turned to her with a beaming smile. 'Come in, Miranda. I was just telling Mummy about you.'

'I hope you don't mind me being here, Mrs Maddern,' Miranda said, fending off the attentions of the spaniel as he greeted her like a long lost friend.

'Down, Mike.' Daphne Maddern frowned at the dog and he bounced over to her wagging his tail.

'One word from you, Mummy, and he does what he likes.' Felicity dragged the eager animal away by his collar and knelt on the floor to make a fuss of him. 'Tell Miranda what you just told me.'

'Gilbert is as well as can be expected,' Daphne said with a weary smile. 'But he was in remarkably good spirits considering his injuries. I hope to get him transferred to the Royal Victoria hospital so that we can visit him more often.'

'Was he badly hurt?' The words spilled from Miranda's lips before she could stop herself. She could see that Mrs Maddern was exhausted and emotionally drained, but she simply had to know.

'He broke an arm and both legs – there's a possibility that he might be left paralysed from the waist down.' Daphne Maddern spoke slowly, as if each word caused her physical pain. 'He'll have to spend a long time in traction, possibly months, but at least he's alive. For that I'll be eternally grateful.' Her voice broke and she turned away. 'I'm sorry.'

Felicity gave the spaniel a last loving pat. Rising to her feet she guided her mother to a chair. 'Sit down, Mummy. I'll make some tea and you must try to eat something. You look exhausted. I'll take the sale today. You really should rest.'

Daphne shook her head. 'No, Fliss. Thank you anyway, but I'll take the sale as planned. I snatched a few hours' sleep at the Charing Cross hotel last night, and then I caught the six o'clock train from Waterloo, so I'll be fine.'

'Perhaps I could make the tea, if that would help,' Miranda said, wishing there was something she could say or do to ease the family's pain. For her own part she was so relieved that Gil had survived that she could have danced a jig.

'Thank you, girls, but I'll be fine when I've had a cup of tea and a nice hot bath. I seem to have been travelling almost non-stop for two days.' She pushed the dog away as he attempted to climb onto her lap. 'Fliss, darling. Take him out into the garden and let him wear off some of his high spirits.'

'Yes, of course. When he's excited he forgets that he's an old man.' Felicity went to the back door and opened it. 'Walkies, Mike.' The old dog ambled obediently into the garden and she closed the door. 'I'll take him for a proper walk later, but right now I'll go and run the bath for you, Mummy. Miranda will make the tea.' She hurried from the room.

Daphne sat back in her chair watching Miranda as she filled the kettle and put it on the gas stove. 'Gilbert mentioned your name. He was anxious that you should know he'd survived, but obviously he need not have worried on that score.'

'One of my friends at Henlow telephoned with the good news.'

'And you travelled all this way to find us. You must be quite fond of him.'

'I like him a lot. We were just getting to know each other.'

'But you're not in love with him.'

'I think that's my business, Mrs Maddern. I don't want to be rude, but as I said, Gil and I were just getting better acquainted.' Miranda took what was left of the loaf from the bread bin. 'Toast?'

'Yes, that would be nice.' Daphne sat in silence for a moment while Miranda sliced the bread and put it under the grill. 'I'm sorry. I didn't mean to pry. It's just that Gil seems to have fallen for you and I don't want him to get hurt.'

'What are you saying?'

'Just this, Miranda. I think you're a very pretty and perfectly nice young woman, but in the circumstances it might be better all round if you stayed away from my son.'

'But why? He's my friend, and I care about him.'

Daphne rose to her feet. 'It's possible that Gil

293

might spend the rest of his life in a wheelchair. Whatever happens he's going to have a long convalescence and you'll be stationed miles away. I know it's not your fault, but you won't be around to give him the support and encouragement he needs.'

'I'll stand by Gil. I won't let him down.'

'You're very young, Miranda. You might meet someone else and fall madly in love. What would that do to Gil?'

'No one knows what the future holds, but I can't abandon him now.'

Daphne shook her head. 'I'm being realistic, my dear. You barely know my son, and he's going to need someone who'll be there for him no matter what. Could you promise me that that person would be you?'

'No, of course not, but I'd always be his friend.'

'That wouldn't be kind, and it wouldn't work. This may sound cruel, but I want you to keep away from Gil.'

'I can't do that. It wouldn't be right.'

'I'm not asking you. I'm telling you that this is how it must be. I want you to promise that you won't try to contact him in any way. No phone calls, no letters and certainly no visits. I won't let you break his heart.'

'I'm not making any such promises. You can't tell me what to do.'

'That's where you're wrong. I'm doing this to protect my son.'

'He's a man, Mrs Maddern. You're treating him like a child.'

Daphne gave her a calculating look. 'You don't

understand. I've devoted my whole life to my children. After their father died I had to bring them up alone and run a successful business in what is virtually a man's world. I've had to be tough at times and make difficult decisions, but it was always with my family's wellbeing in mind. I'd do anything to protect my only son from heartbreak – absolutely anything.'

'I do understand, but I think you ought to let Gil be the judge of what is right for him.'

'I'm not going to waste time arguing with you, Miss Beddoes. I've made my position clear.' Daphne moved to the door and opened it. 'I think you'd better leave now and don't even think of getting in touch with Fliss. I'll tell her that you came to the decision by yourself, and if you have any genuine feelings for Gil you'll respect my wishes. Get your things and go before she comes downstairs.'

Chapter Seventeen

Miranda arrived home to find her grandmother and Annie in a state of near panic. Forgetting her own problems, she stood in the doorway, staring at the chaotic scene in the kitchen. Annie was mumbling to herself as she rolled out pastry, sending clouds of flour into the air and punctuating her grumbles with sneezes, while Maggie scrabbled about in the pantry. 'What's all this?' Miranda asked, dodging a crumpled paper bag that her grandmother tossed over her shoulder.

Shaking flour off her hands, Annie snatched up a tea towel and rushed over to the oven. A waft of heat made her recoil as she reached in to take out a tray of jam tarts that were about to incinerate. 'Damnation,' she muttered, slamming it down on the table.

'Are we having a party, or something?' Miranda peeled off her jacket and hooked it over the back of a chair. 'Can I help?'

Maggie emerged from the pantry, wiping a cobweb from her forehead. 'Oh, it's you, Miranda. You were needed here. You shouldn't have gone gallivanting off after your boyfriend.'

Why? What's going on, Granny?'

'A wedding, that's all.' Maggie slumped down on a chair. 'Jack and Isabel are getting married tomorrow at the register office. He's getting a special licence. It will all end in disaster, especially if Max gets to hear of it.'

Miranda had to stifle the sudden urge to laugh. Her nerves were already stretched after the fraught encounter with Gil's mother. There had been an emotional scene with Felicity who had come downstairs just as Miranda had been about to leave the house. She had been puzzled and then furious. She and her mother had had a stand-up row and Miranda had slipped out of the door unnoticed. Coming home was like walking into a Marx brothers' comedy, and something of a relief. After the pristine elegance of the Madderns' house, Highcliffe's homely shabbiness seemed suddenly warm and welcoming. Miranda rolled up her sleeves. 'What can I do to help?'

For the rest of the day she worked to make the house ready for the wedding reception, dusting, sweeping and polishing until everything gleamed. She tried to avoid the kitchen where her grandmother and Annie were constantly reminiscing about the good old days when food was plentiful and wedding breakfasts were sumptuous affairs. They grumbled about the evils of rationing and the indecent haste with which Jack and Isabel were getting married, but they put the blame for everything squarely on Hitler. It was entirely his fault and they would tell him so if he dared to invade England. Miranda left them squabbling over what filling to put in the sandwiches next day and escaped into the garden where, armed with a trug and a pair of scissors, she picked the few remaining chrysanthemums that had not succumbed to the frost and swags of evergreen from the shrubbery. She filled every vase she could find and arranged them strategically around the drawing room and in the entrance hall. She had just finished when her grandfather arrived home from court. He gave her a whiskery kiss on the cheek. 'So you're home, Miranda. We missed you last night. How is the young pilot?'

Miranda bit her lip. She had been trying not to think about Gil or to brood about the way his mother had sent her packing, but now it all came back to her in a rush. 'I'm not allowed to see him, Grandpa.'

He stared at her, frowning. 'We'll have a glass of sherry and you can tell me all about it.'

Miranda followed him to his study and settled

herself in a chair by the fireplace while he poured the drinks. He passed one to her. 'Sip this slowly. You look as though you've had a hard day. Do you want to tell me about it?' He took a seat, waiting patiently while she gathered her thoughts.

She twirled the glass between her fingertips, staring into the amber liquid. 'I don't know where to start, Grandpa.'

'The beginning is always a good place,' he said, smiling. 'Take your time, my dear. At least it's nice and peaceful in here and we're out of the firing line, so to speak.'

She began to relax. It had always been easier to talk to her grandfather than anyone else. He never interrupted and would sit and listen intently until she had poured out all her troubles; then he would think about it for a while before giving his opinion. He was never judgemental and his advice, if asked for, was always sound. She started slowly, gathering confidence as she told him how she had met Gil and ended by telling him what had happened at the Madderns' home that morning.

'Mrs Maddern sounds quite an indomitable lady,' he said slowly. 'But you can see her point of view, I'm sure.'

'I can, I suppose, but she's wrong. How would Gil feel if I simply abandoned him?'

'It might be better for him in the long run. If you aren't sure of your feelings towards this young man, you'd better think long and hard before you go rushing in only to dash his hopes later on.'

'I thought you would be on my side, Grandpa.'

'I am, and I know you'll do the right thing. Give yourself time to think about it, Miranda. Nothing is as it should be in wartime. I've been through it myself.' He laid his hand on hers. 'I think you know what I mean.'

'You're talking about Granny and Max Carstairs.'

'When war turns everything upside down people behave differently. They do things they would never dream of doing in peacetime. Take your mother, for instance. She's given up everything she holds dear to go abroad, risking her life for her country.'

'I know, Grandpa. I miss her terribly, but I try not to think about what she's doing. It's too scary.'

'You have to put your trust in her, Miranda. She's a brave woman.' He patted her hand. 'Don't dwell on what might be, my dear. We have to get on with life to the best of our ability, just like Jack and Isabel. They're getting married tomorrow despite the rift between our families, and I for one wish them every happiness.'

She put her glass on the desk and stood up to give him a hug. 'You're a wonder, Grandpa. You always make me feel better.'

'You'll work it out, Miranda.' He glanced at his watch. 'Do you suppose there's any chance of us getting a meal tonight? I thought I smelled burnt pastry when I came in.'

Jack arrived early next morning looking uncharacteristically nervous and had to be revived with a tot of brandy before the family set off in the Bentley, there being just enough petrol left in the tank to get them to the register office and back again. They were unusually silent during the short journey, and the atmosphere was tense as they waited for Isabel to arrive.

Maggie and Annie sat on hard wooden chairs in the vestibule, clutching their handbags, while George paced up and down on the pavement outside. Standing beside Jack, Miranda noticed that he was perspiring freely although it was cold and draughty in the waiting area. She slipped her hand into his, giving it a reassuring squeeze. 'You'll be fine. I expect Isabel is much more nervous than you are.'

He twisted his lips into a semblance of a smile. 'I'd rather take a Spit up any day. This is terrifying.' He lowered his voice. 'I'm just hoping that old man Carstairs doesn't turn up and do the Barretts of Wimpole Street thing on us. I've seen the film with Norma Shearer and Fredric March. The old man gave them hell.'

The sound of her grandfather's booming voice heralded Isabel's arrival and Miranda breathed a sigh of relief when she saw her enter the building accompanied by Mrs Beasley with Grandpa acting as rearguard.

'Don't stand there like a tailor's dummy,' Miranda said, nudging Jack in the ribs. 'Go and give her a big kiss.'

Moving like a sleepwalker, he went to meet his bride. 'Izzie, you look absolutely beautiful, darling.'

Clutching a posy of white camellias, Isabel smiled up at him.

Just as they were about to go into the room where the ceremony was to take place there was a flurry of activity; Ivy rushed into the vestibule accompanied by the woman who had made Miranda's life a misery when she worked on the haberdashery counter at Morris and Mawson's shop. She could not think why Aunt Ivy had chosen Mrs Dowsett to accompany her and she was tempted to say something, but Granny had spotted them and had already gone in on the attack. 'What are you two doing here? I don't remember inviting either of you.'

Ivy enveloped her in a warm embrace. 'Darling, I wouldn't miss this for anything. I think I might have put my tiny foot in it at your soiree, so I'm here to apologise and wish the young couple well. Dolly loves a wedding and she had the morning off. You love a wedding, don't you, dear?'

Mrs Dowsett smiled and nodded. 'Isabel is a sweet girl, and Miranda was such an asset to us on the haberdashery counter. I miss her terribly.'

'I'll bet she doesn't,' Miranda muttered, glancing at Isabel who was clutching Jack's arm as if afraid to move a step without him.

'How did you find out about this?' Maggie demanded, wriggling free from Ivy's grasp. 'It's supposed to be a quiet family affair.'

Ivy shrugged her plump shoulders. 'Elzevir delivered a load of logs to the guest house where I'm staying until my poor little home is rebuilt. He might have mentioned it in passing.'

Maggie turned on Annie. 'You told him.'

'I never did,' Annie said indignantly.

'Actually, I did, Mother. It was meant to be a

surprise, but Izzie and I will be leaving in style, the old-fashioned way.' Jack tucked Isabel's hand in the crook of his arm. 'You'll see later. Now let's go in. You can come too, Aunt Ivy, and bring your friend. The more the merrier.'

'Not in my book,' Maggie muttered, casting an angry glance at Ivy. 'Don't think you're coming back to the house afterwards, because you're not.'

'Now, now, Maggie,' George said, taking her arm. 'This is supposed to be a happy occasion. Let's put the past behind us. Come along, ladies. We mustn't keep the registrar waiting.'

The ceremony was brief as there were other couples waiting to be married. Miranda thought it all seemed a bit hurried, but Ivy, Dolly Dowsett and Mrs Beasley sniffled into their handkerchiefs. Maggie glowered at them throughout, but Izzie looked radiant and Jack appeared to be happy but relieved when it was all over. As they stepped outside, as if to order, the sun burst through the clouds. Miranda put her hand in her pocket and pulled out a small paper bag which she had filled with confetti hastily made that morning using the paper punch from her grandfather's study. She emptied it over the bride and groom, wishing that they had had time to hire a photographer, but to her surprise Ivy had produced a box Brownie from her capacious handbag and was taking photos with the assurance of a professional.

Laughing and shaking confetti from their clothes and hair, Isabel and Jack descended the steps to where Elzevir's cart was waiting. 'This is my surprise, darling,' Jack said, indicating the wagon, which was decorated with branches of laurel and white bows.

'I supplied the ribbon,' Mrs Dowsett said smugly. 'Using my staff discount.'

'I'll be sending the bill to you, ma'am,' Elzevir said, addressing Maggie as he climbed stiffly from the driver's seat.

Maggie opened her mouth as if to protest but George raised his finger to his lips. 'Not now, my dear. Let's just enjoy the day.'

She subsided, casting a withering look at Elzevir but saying nothing. Miranda crossed her fingers behind her back, hoping that nothing else would happen to ruffle her grandmother's feathers. At least Jack and Izzie were now legally married and even if Max turned up there was nothing he could do about it. Jack helped his new bride onto the driver's seat and was about to climb up beside her when the frantic ringing of a bicycle bell made everyone turn to see who was making such a din.

Rita skidded to a halt at the kerbside. 'Damn it,' she said, panting. 'Am I too late?'

Miranda rushed forward to embrace her. 'I'm so glad you came, but did you ride that bone-shaker all the way from Warmwell?'

'Yes, and I'm whacked.' Rita slid off the saddle. 'My legs have turned to jelly and I seem to have missed the bloody wedding.'

Jack took the bike from her and tossed it onto the cart. 'You could have come with me. I got a lift with the Wingco who happened to be going into town.'

Rita pulled a face. 'Yes, I'm sure he would have approved of me going absent without leave for a few hours, Jack. I'm not supposed to be here.'

'Come back to the house and have something to eat,' Miranda said, smiling. 'You might as well enjoy yourself before they slam you in jankers.'

'Try and stop me.' Rita slipped her arm around Miranda's waist. 'Are we walking, or what?'

'You're a dreadful girl,' Maggie said, shaking her head. 'I suppose we can give you a lift, but we're taking Mrs Beasley and Annie, so you'll have to sit on Miranda's lap or else ride in the cart with your bike.' She glared at Ivy and Dolly. 'You're welcome too, I suppose, but you'll have to find your own way. Come along, George. Let's get home before the next shower.'

'I suppose we'll just have to get the bus then, Dolly,' Ivy said, sighing.

Jack beckoned to Elzevir. 'Could you make the ladies comfortable in the wagon, old man? There's a drink in it for you if you can.'

Mumbling, Elzevir shuffled round to the rear of the cart and pulled down the tailgate. 'You can make yourselves comfy on them sacks, ladies.'

Ivy hesitated for a moment, exchanging anxious glances with Mrs Dowsett who looked distinctly put out. 'I don't know if I can climb up there.'

Elzevir advanced on her, leering and revealing a set of stained and broken teeth. 'I'll lift you up, lady.'

'Thank you, but that won't be necessary. I think we'll catch the bus.'

The look on Ivy's face was one of absolute horror and Miranda had to suppress a giggle. She could not help thinking that it served Ivy right for all the trouble she had caused, but while she was waiting for her to come to a decision Mrs Dowsett pushed past Ivy, holding her arms out to Elzevir. 'Come on then, my good man. I'll take advantage of your kind offer.' She gasped as Elzevir put his arms around her and hefted her into the wagon as if she had been a sack of logs. She straightened her hat and beckoned to Ivy. 'What are you waiting for? Or do you want to walk to the bus stop?'

Reluctantly, Ivy faced Elzevir. 'All right, but be very careful where you put your hands.' She uttered a squeak of protest as he grabbed her round her waist and heaved her up beside Mrs Dowsett, allowing his hands to cup her generous bosom before moving away to secure the back of the wagon. 'I likes a nice rounded woman,' he said, licking his lips. 'I'd let that 'un warm me bed any night she fancied a bit of slap and tickle.'

'Behave yourself, Elzevir,' Annie said, tapping him on the wrist. 'We'll have none of your lewd remarks, thanks very much.'

'Don't let him upset you,' Miranda said, trying not to laugh. 'We all know what he's like and I expect Ivy enjoyed it really. She just likes making a fuss.'

Annie shook her head. 'He'll be the death of me, that brother of mine. But at least he can't get drunk on the embrocation. It's all gone and your grandfather's promised he won't make any more.' She sighed. 'Mind you, it was good for rubbing into sore muscles. It smelt awful, but it was a wonderful cure for backache.'

Miranda waited until Elzevir had climbed onto the driver's seat and she uttered a sigh of relief. 'At least it's all passed off without any terrible scenes. We can go home now and enjoy the rest of the day.'

But despite her surge of optimism, she could not help worrying during the drive home. Crushed against the rear door of the Bentley with Rita perched on her lap and Mrs Beasley squashed in the middle of the back seat with Annie on the far side, it was not the most comfortable way in which to travel. Miranda could see very little as her view was obscured by Rita's back, but she heard her grandmother's cry of distress as the car came to a halt outside Highcliffe and it was not hard to guess the cause.

'If that's who I think it is, there's going to be trouble,' Rita said in a low voice.

'Oh, dear. That's torn it.' Mrs Beasley clapped her hand to her mouth. 'I knew I shouldn't have come.'

'Open the door and let me out,' Miranda said urgently.

'I'm trying, but I've got my leg stuck behind the seat.' Rita wriggled round and finally managed to open the door and clamber out of the car. As Miranda extricated herself from the back seat she spotted Raif standing by the garden gate. Anger turned to dismay when she saw the man standing next to him. They were so alike that they had to be father and son. Even if she had not seen the likeness between them she would have known by the expressions on her grandparents' faces that the man with Raif was none other than the notorious Max Carstairs. She had been dreading this moment, and yet she had not really believed that it would happen. She cast an anxious glance at the main road and in the distance she could see Elzevir's wagon. With a sinking feeling in her stomach she knew that there was nothing she could do to prevent the inevitable scene. She moved a little closer to her grandmother.

'You're not welcome here, Max.' Maggie's voice shook with emotion. 'You shouldn't have come.'

'I'll deal with this,' George said, stepping in between them. 'We'll settle this man to man.'

Max shook his head. 'I've got nothing to say to either of you. This is between me and my daughter.'

'You're too late to do anything about it,' Maggie said icily. 'Isabel and my son are married.'

'I think you mean our son.'

'George is Jack's father, not you.'

Max curled his lip. 'I wouldn't bet on it, my dear. And incest is illegal, so the marriage is invalid.'

'Dad, is this really necessary?' Raif said, frowning. 'Do we need to air our dirty linen in public?'

'You've said enough, Carstairs.' George opened the garden gate. 'If you've got any feeling for your daughter you'll come into the house and talk this matter over in private.'

'That's rich, coming from a man who attempted to sabotage my career out of spite. If you'd managed to satisfy your wife she wouldn't have fallen into my arms.'

Maggie caught hold of George's arm as he took a menacing step towards Max. 'Don't, darling.

That's just what he wants.' She glared at Max. 'Come indoors and behave like a civilised human being, or leave now and let your daughter enjoy her wedding day.'

'It's a farce.' Max fisted his hands. 'I came here to settle an old score with your husband, Maggie. Keep out of this.'

'I won't,' she cried, flying at him and pushing him so that he cannoned into his son. 'You almost wrecked my marriage and I won't let you do the same to Jack and Isabel.'

Raif grabbed his father by the arm. 'I think this has gone far enough, Dad.'

Miranda held her breath. She had never felt so helpless in her whole life, and she could see that matters were going to escalate as Elzevir drew the cart to a standstill behind the Bentley. Jack leapt to the ground barely giving the vehicle time to stop, and Isabel's face crumpled with obvious distress as she climbed down more slowly. Mrs Beasley rushed to her side to put a comforting arm around her shoulders, defying her employer with a stubborn tilt of her chin. Only Ivy and Dolly Dowsett seemed to be enjoying the spectacle as they craned their necks to get a better view.

Jack hurried towards them. 'What's going on?' He glared at Raif. 'I suppose this is your doing. You couldn't bear to let Izzie have her day, could you?'

'I wanted to stop her making the mistake of her life,' Raif said coldly. 'But it seems that we're too late.'

Max pushed him aside, squaring up to Jack

308

with a pugnacious outthrust of his jaw. 'I'll get this marriage annulled. I'm calling my solicitor as soon as I get home.'

'There's nothing you can do about it, Mr Carstairs. Izzie and I are legally married and I'm afraid you'll just have to get used to the idea.'

Miranda moved to Isabel's side. 'Don't get involved, Izzie. Your father can't do anything about it now.'

She shook off Mrs Beasley's restraining hand. 'Thanks, Miranda, but I know my father. He's like a dog with a bone when he gets an idea in his head.' She ran to Jack and wrapped her arms around him. 'We're married, Father. I'd hoped you'd relent when you saw how happy I am and how much I love my husband.'

'Would you feel the same if you discovered that he's my son, Isabel?'

She seized Jack's hand and held it to her cheek. 'I know all about your affair with his mother, and I've found out the real reason why you hate the family. It has to do with your beastly pride, and it's become twisted into a vendetta that's affecting all of us.'

'That's right,' Jack said, giving her a reassuring smile. 'We have no secrets from each other, sir. I was hoping that you might be able to accept the fact that we love each other and we want to spend the rest of our lives together.'

'Never.' Max took a step closer to Jack, glaring at him with narrowed eyes. 'Hell will freeze over before I acknowledge you as my daughter's husband.'

'Leave them alone.' Miranda could see that

Isabel was close to tears. She turned to Raif. 'Can't you do something to stop this? I know you care for Izzie.'

'I think this has gone far enough,' George said firmly. 'Jack, take your wife into the house. It's not good for her to get upset.'

Max rounded on him. 'What the hell do you mean by that?'

'She's pregnant, you idiot,' Maggie said in a low voice. 'You're going to be a grandfather, Max.' She turned her back on him. 'Come along, George. This is a wedding and we should be celebrating.' They linked arms and made their way towards the house.

'Mother's right.' Jack took Isabel by the hand. 'This is our day and I'm not going to let anyone spoil it.'

Isobel hesitated, sending a mute plea to her father, but he turned his head away. With a barely perceptible shrug of her shoulders she allowed Jack to lead her towards the house. Miranda could only imagine what it must have cost Isabel to break the habit of a lifetime and stand up to her father. She would have liked to applaud her bold gesture, but she decided that it would be inappropriate and she did not want to antagonise Max any further. She beckoned to Rita. 'This might be a good time to take the guests indoors,' she said in a low voice.

'Cor blimey, what a show,' Rita whispered, grinning. 'Come with me, ladies. I could do with a drink, I don't know about you.' She held the gate while they filed into the garden.

'You're sacked, Beasley,' Max roared as she

310

scuttled past him.

'No, Father.' Raif faced him angrily. 'This has gone far enough. I'm going to join the party and wish Izzie all the happiness in the world. What's more I'm going tell Mrs Beasley that she's still got her job. We'd be lost without her and Mother would be livid if she knew you'd sacked our housekeeper in a fit of temper.'

Rita strolled up to Max, looking him in the eyes. 'I don't know what Mrs B ever saw in you, mister.' She gave Raif a sideways glance. 'Good for you, Flight Lieutenant Carstairs. I didn't think you had it in you. And before you open your big gob – yes, I'm absent without leave. You can report me if you want to, but it was worth it to see Mrs B face up to your old man.' She hurried after the others, leaving Miranda and Elzevir alone with Raif and his father.

Miranda held her hand out to Raif. 'You've gone up in my estimation today.' She flicked her gaze to his father. 'And you were never my favourite person, even though I hadn't met you. Now I can understand why your children have turned out the way they have.'

Max flushed crimson and the veins in his neck stood out as he spluttered with rage. 'You little bitch. Who do you think you are, talking to me like that?'

'I'm Izzie's friend and actually she's now my aunt, which feels rather odd, but you'd better get used to the idea that she's married to Jack.' She turned to Elzevir as she heard him clearing his throat. 'Yes? What is it?'

He shuffled his feet, glancing at Max beneath his

shaggy eyebrows. 'Someone mentioned a drink, miss.'

'Yes, of course. Follow the others.' She stood aside to let him pass. 'You're still welcome to come in, Mr Carstairs. But if you upset the happy couple, I'll have to get Elzevir to throw you out.'

'I'll come in for a drink,' Raif said, relaxing visibly. 'But I can't stay long. I've got to get back to the aerodrome.'

Max glowered at them both. 'I'm damned if I'll ever set foot in that house again. You can tell Jack Beddoes that he hasn't heard the last of this.' He stormed off towards his car.

'I'm sorry about the old man,' Raif said with a reluctant smile.

'But you brought him here. You must have told him that Izzie was getting married today.'

'Believe it or not, I thought he might mellow a bit if he saw that she was happy. I don't pretend to like Jack and I probably never will, but I love my sister and I genuinely want the best for her.' He proffered his arm. 'Life's too short to bear grudges, Miranda. Can we at least be friends?'

She laid her hand on his sleeve. 'I hope so, Raif.' She chuckled. 'I suppose we're related now in some odd way. If Izzie is my aunt then you must be my uncle-in-law, if there is such a thing.'

'It's high time the family feud ended, although I don't think Father will ever let it go.'

'What about your mother? What will she say when she finds out?'

He shrugged his shoulders. 'Mother is in Los Angeles making a movie. I think the only thing that will upset her is the fact that she's going to be a grandmother. I can imagine she'll want to keep very quiet on that particular subject.'

'How sad for both of them,' Miranda said with feeling. 'I'm afraid it's their loss. Anyway, let's go and join the party.

They found the guests assembled in the drawing room and the atmosphere had lightened considerably now that Max had gone. Ivy and Dolly were already well away, having found the gin bottle, and Elzevir had taken his beer out onto the veranda and was huddled on one of the steamer chairs drinking steadily.

Miranda was relieved to see that her grandparents appeared to have recovered sufficiently to enjoy the party after their encounter with Max, and Jack and Izzie were oblivious to everything other than their own happiness. Miranda circulated amongst the guests, making sure that everyone had a drink and that no one was left out. Rita was chatting to Mrs Beasley and Annie, while Raif did his best to entertain Ivy and Dolly.

No one seemed to mind that the wedding breakfast consisted of Spam sandwiches, slightly burnt jam tarts and rock cakes that were a dental hazard, or that the wedding cake was a simple sponge filled with the last of the homemade strawberry jam. Everyone seemed to have recovered from the unfortunate scene with Max, and the crate of champagne that George had managed to procure had helped to put everyone in a happy mood.

When the last toast was drunk and the speeches had been made, Miranda slipped away from the party and went to retrieve her handbag from the kitchen. She had put worries about Gil to the back of her mind during the day, but now that the stress of the wedding was over she had time to think. She knew that she would not sleep a wink that night if she left it another day. She took out her diary and flipped through the pages to where she had made a note of the Madderns' telephone number. She left the comparative warmth of the drawing room to perch on the elephant table in the cold hallway and pick up the receiver. She dialled and waited, hoping against hope that it would be Fliss on the other end of the line. The ringing tone went on and on and she was just beginning to think that there was no one at home when someone answered the call.

Chapter Eighteen

'Hello.' The soft female voice sounded wary.

'Felicity, it's Miranda Beddoes. Please don't hang up.'

There was a brief pause. 'I'm sorry, but I'm not supposed to talk to you.'

'I understand how your mother feels but I thought that you and I were friends.'

'It's not as simple as that. I do like you, Miranda, but I can't go against Mummy's wishes.'

'I'm not asking you to do anything wrong. I just want to know how Gil is getting on. Surely that's not too much to ask?'

'Mummy phoned the hospital in Yarmouth this morning and they said that Gil was comfortable, whatever that means.'

'But he's no worse.' Miranda uttered a long drawn out sigh of sheer relief. 'I've been so worried about him.'

'The doctors said something about transferring him to the Royal Victoria near here, but not yet. I really can't tell you any more, Miranda.'

'My leave is up in two days and I'll be returning to Henlow. Would it be asking too much for you to drop me a line to let me know how he's getting on?'

'I can't talk now. Please don't phone again.' The line went dead.

Miranda sat for a long moment after she had replaced the telephone on the elephant table. She did not blame Felicity or her mother for their attitude towards her, but she could not abandon Gil without a word, especially when his whole future hung in the balance. At the very least he had been a friend, and she could not bear to think of him lying in a hospital bed thinking that she did not care if he lived or died. She walked slowly to the drawing room, where the furniture had been moved and the carpet folded back so that couples could dance. A Joe Loss record was playing on the gramophone, and to Miranda's surprise Raif was partnering Rita. Although they were not dancing cheek to cheek he was holding her rather closer than was strictly necessary and Rita was smiling up at him. Jack and Izzie were in each other's arms, moving dreamily to 'Crying My Heart Out for You'. In complete contrast

Dolly and Ivy were attempting to waltz although they could not seem to decide who was leading. Looking on with some amusement, Annie and Mrs Beasley sat side by side on the sofa, sipping port and lemon, while Elzevir was still on the veranda, huddled on a steamer chair with a bottle of stout clutched in his hand.

Miranda waited until the music ended and her grandparents came towards her, hand in hand like a young married couple. She felt almost envious of their obvious devotion to one another, and she could not help wondering if she would ever experience something as lasting and wonderful. If Max Carstairs could see them now and feel the warmth and affection that filled the room, he would see how wrong he had been. She met them with outstretched arms and gave them a hug. 'I love you both,' she said, swallowing hard as her eyes misted with tears.

'Now, now,' Maggie said briskly. 'Don't get maudlin, my girl.'

Miranda drew away with an affectionate smile. 'I'm not, Granny. I just wanted to say thank you for everything, and I'll be leaving early tomorrow morning.'

'I thought you had another two days.'

'I have, but I'm going to Great Yarmouth before I go back to the priory. I need to see Gil no matter what his mother thinks or says.'

Miranda had lied to the sister on duty, telling her that she was Gil's fiancée, as only close family members were allowed to visit. It was a white lie, she told herself as she entered the side ward where Gil lay with both his legs in traction and one arm in plaster. She had not known what to expect but she was surprised to find him fully conscious and staring up at the ceiling. He raised his head a little as he heard her footsteps on the bare linoleum and a slow smile spread across his face. 'Miranda.'

She hurried to his bedside and drew up a chair. 'How are you?' She pulled a face. 'I'm sorry, that's a silly question.'

He grinned. 'I know I look like an Egyptian mummy, but to be honest I don't feel much at all. They pump me full of morphine if the pain gets too bad. You might be a drug induced delusion for all I know.'

She took his good hand in hers and gave it a gentle squeeze. 'I'm no illusion, Gil. I came as quickly as I could.'

'How did you get past Sister Cerberus?'

'Wasn't Cerberus the dog that guarded the gates of Hades?'

'I rest my case. But seriously, how did you get in? I was on the main ward for a while and I heard the chaps complaining because she was so strict about visitors.'

'I said I was your fiancée. I hope you don't mind.'

'I'm flattered. But even if it were true I wouldn't hold you to it now.'

She was silent for a moment, feeling his inner pain as if it were her own. 'That's definitely the morphine talking,' she said briskly. 'You just need time for the injuries to heal and you'll be the old Mad Dog. You'll be back in your Spit, doing what you do best.'

He looked away. 'I might be paralysed from the waist down. It could be permanent and I'd spend the rest of my life a cripple.'

'You don't know that, Gil.'

'I overheard the nurses talking and I'm not a fool. I might be flying high on drugs but it doesn't mean I don't know what's happening to me.' He tightened his grasp on her hand. 'But thanks for coming, Miranda. It's meant a lot to me.'

'That sounds like goodbye.'

'It has to be. I don't need your pity.'

Anger and frustration bubbled up inside her and she drew her hand away. 'Stop wallowing, Gil. I'm sorry you were injured but I'm here because you mean a lot to me. I care very much what happens to you.'

He raised his eyes to her face. 'Do you?'

'Of course I do.' She dropped her gaze, staring down at their entwined fingers. 'But I broke my word to come here today. Your mother loves you very much, and I understand why she did it, but she made me promise that I wouldn't try to see you or contact you in any way.'

'Why in hell's name would she do that?'

'She was just trying to protect you.'

'She told me that you'd been to The Gables, but that was all.' Gil closed his eyes. 'Sorry, I'm starting to drift off again.'

'I've booked into a guest house near the hospital and I'll come again this evening, if they let me.' She was not sure if he had heard her, but she leaned over and kissed his cheek before rising from her seat. She stood for a moment, gazing down at him. He looked very young and vulnerable and her heart went out to him, but she was painfully aware how easy it would be to mistake pity for a stronger emotion. She was about to leave when the door opened and a young nurse bustled in carrying a kidney basin covered with a spotless white cloth.

'I was just going to ask you to leave, miss. It's time for Flight Lieutenant Maddern's medication.'

'I'll come again this evening,' Miranda said firmly. 'Is there a set visiting time?'

'His mother asked me the same thing on the phone just now. She'll be coming too. It'll be a nice family reunion, but Sister says you can't stay long and only one visitor at a time.'

Miranda went back to the boarding house and sat in her room for an hour, wondering whether she ought to face Mrs Maddern and admit that she had broken her promise, or whether to stay away and risk upsetting Gil. She could not help thinking that perhaps his mother had been right, and that she had done him more harm than good by indulging her need to see him and clear her conscience. She was even more confused as to her feelings for Gil, and she realised that she had handled a difficult situation badly.

In the end she could not bear to be shut up in the dreary little room for a moment longer. The cracked pink linoleum with the sickly flower pattern and the mismatched furniture that had seen better days were beginning to get on her nerves. The flock-filled mattress on the bed promised a sleepless night to come and she needed to get out into the fresh air. She put on her cap, picked up her handbag and gas mask case and left the room, descending three flights of stairs to the ground floor where she was greeted by the noxious smell of boiled cabbage and Jeyes Fluid.

After walking to the sea front and filling her lungs with the bracing east coast air, she found a small café and enjoyed a meal of fish and chips, washed down with several cups of strong, sweet tea. Feeling better but unable to face going back to the guest house, she went to the cinema and watched *That Hamilton Woman* with Vivien Leigh and Laurence Olivier. The story of the doomed love affair between Nelson and Lady Hamilton was tragic, but Miranda was finding it difficult to concentrate as her thoughts kept returning to Gil lying helpless in his hospital bed. She knew that Mrs Maddern would find out about her visit and she could not blame her if she was angry, but Gil's mother ought to understand – that they both had his best interests at heart. She rose from her seat before the film ended and hurried from the cinema.

Dusk was swallowing up the town and soon it would be too dark to see where she was going in the unfamiliar streets. Having made enquiries in a tobacconist's shop she found the nearest bus stop and after a short wait caught a bus to the hospital. She had no intention of going in and challenging Gil's mother at his bedside, but she hoped to catch her as she left when visiting time ended. It was dark now, but the moon shone from a cloudless sky giving just enough light to see the world in monochrome, like a black and white film. It was bitterly cold and already frost was glittering on the paving stones. After the relatively mild climate on the south coast Miranda was feeling the change in temperature and wishing she had worn her overcoat. She paced up and down for half an hour and was beginning to think she had missed her when she spotted Mrs Maddern amongst a group of visitors who had emerged from the hospital.

Miranda hurried up to her. 'I know I broke my promise, but I couldn't allow Gil to think I'd deserted him.'

'Were you thinking of yourself or of him, Miss Beddoes?'

'He told you that I'd been to see him?'

'Yes. He was delighted. I hope that salves your conscience. Now you can go away and get on with your life knowing that you've given my son false hope. He really believes that you'll stand by him.'

Daphne Maddern's bitter tone etched into Miranda's consciousness like acid. She was hurt but also very angry. 'That's not fair. I can't be at his bedside as much as I'd wish because I have to return to Henlow in the morning, but I'll write to him every day, and I'll visit him as soon as I can.'

'That's all very fine and I'm sure you will, but we've had this conversation before. I think you have the best of intentions but what happens if you meet someone else? How will you tell my son that you won't be seeing him any more?'

'Stop it,' Miranda cried angrily. 'We can only take things one day at a time. All I can say is that

I care deeply for Gil. I can't foretell the future and neither can you. If he wants me to keep in touch then I don't care what you or anyone else says, but I won't let him down now or ever.'

'Fine words indeed, but I've had considerably more experience of life than you have, and I've told the hospital staff that you aren't allowed to see him again.' Daphne raised her hand to attract the attention of a cab driver who had pulled up at the kerb. She turned her head as she was about to climb inside. 'I'll be here for another two days, arranging transport to take my son back to Hampshire, so don't even think of trying to see Gil or contacting him in any way. I'll make your excuses to him.' She took her seat and slammed the door. The taxi drove off, disappearing into the darkness.

Miranda started walking towards the bus stop but the sound of the air raid siren sent people scurrying towards a public shelter and she found herself caught up in their midst. She spent the next few hours wedged between an elderly man with a bronchitic cough and a fat woman who had just been visiting her sick husband in the hospital. By the time the all clear sounded Miranda had been subjected to the woman's life history, including the many operations she had undergone and the treatment she was having for her current ailments. Having exhausted her medical woes she went on to complain about her husband, who worked on the railway, and her five children all of whom were too young to be in the forces except her eldest son, Norman, who was in the army serving somewhere abroad. 'Our Norman is delicate,' she said, sighing. 'He had whooping cough when he was six months old, then he got measles when he was three, chickenpox when he was three and a half, mumps when he was five and scarlatina when he was just six. It's a wonder he's still with us, but I just hope the army are taking care of him proper. You never know what he might catch in them foreign parts.'

By the time the all clear sounded Miranda was cramped and exhausted both physically and emotionally. She had also missed the last bus which would have taken her back to the guest house and she had no choice other than to set off on foot. The buildings on the skyline were silhouetted against a background of raging fires and plumes of smoke rising from bomb-damaged houses. The acrid smell of burning filled her nostrils and the air was filled with clouds of dust, making it necessary to cover her nose and mouth with her scarf in order to breathe. The quiet of the night had been shattered and people were wandering about in their nightclothes, shocked and crying or scrabbling amongst the rubble searching for loved ones or lost possessions.

She could not simply turn her back on such a disaster and she found herself helping an elderly woman whom she found sitting on what was left of a brick wall outside the ruin of her house. She took her to a Red Cross first aid station and having made sure that she was being cared for Miranda returned to the streets to see if there was anything else she could do. The clanging of fire engine bells echoed off the buildings that remained intact and the rumble of falling masonry was accompanied by shouts of warning from the ARP wardens and the police who were attempting to restore order out of chaos. Miranda spent the rest of the night taking survivors to the warmth and safety of the emergency shelter.

As dawn broke the true devastation caused by the air raid became even more apparent, but only those beyond help were left beneath the bomb-ravaged buildings. Tired, dirty and traumatised Miranda made her way back to the guest house. She hoped and prayed that the hospital had not been one of the casualties of the bombing raid. She arrived at the guest house to find the land-lady outside sweeping the path as if nothing had happened, and perhaps in her world nothing had changed since the previous day as the houses in this particular street remained unscathed.

She gave Miranda what Annie would have called a very old-fashioned look. 'You're a bit of a dirty stop-out, miss, if you don't mind me saying so.' She removed the cigarette end from her lips and tossed it onto the bare soil in a flowerbed.

Miranda was too tired to argue. 'At least your house was spared,' she said dully. 'Think yourself lucky, Mrs Doughty.'

'No need to take that tone with me, miss. I was just passing the time of day.'

'I'm sorry, but I'm tired and I'm dirty. I've been helping the bomb victims all night and I'd really like a bath and perhaps something to eat before I leave.'

'Mr Doughty's about to have his weekly bath, so there's no hot water and I don't light the boiler until tea time. There's some cold fishcakes in the pantry and some bread in the crock, but don't use all the marg because that's the last of our ration for this week.'

'Fine. Thank you.' Miranda acknowledged her with a vague wave of her hand. The thought of eating cold fishcakes was enough to turn anyone's stomach. With the prospect of washing in cold water and nothing but dry bread for breakfast, she went to her room.

She did her best to spruce up her uniform and even a cold wash was better than nothing, but her thoughts were with Gil lying helpless in his hospital bed. She had not thought to bring any writing paper with her and she tore a page from her diary, penning a brief note, explaining that she had to leave for Henlow Priory that morning, but she said nothing about her meeting with his mother. She promised to write often and to visit him on her next leave, whenever that might be. She had filled the page and she signed it, adding a kiss for good measure.

She went downstairs to the kitchen, hoping to get a cup of tea before she paid her landlady and left Alma Villa with no intention of ever returning. She found Mr Doughty sitting at the kitchen table smoking a cigarette and looking very grubby, but at least he greeted her with a smile. 'Hello, ducks. Want a cuppa? There's some left in the pot.'

'Thank you.' She put her case down and took a seat at the table, eyeing a slice of toast which was propped up against a jam jar with just a scraping of what might be some kind of berry jam in the bottom.

'It's yours if you want it, love,' Mr Doughty said, stubbing the dog end out in an overflowing ashtray. 'I had something at the station before I came off night duty, so I ain't that hungry. She gets on at me if I waste food, so you eat it and welcome.'

Miranda realised suddenly that she was very hungry. The toast was cold and the jam was thick and did not taste of anything in particular, but it was sweet and just what she needed to revive her flagging spirits. She poured tea for herself and sipped from the cracked cup, taking care to avoid the sharp edge.

'You going back to the aerodrome today, ducks?' Mr Doughty seemed in the mood to chat, despite the fact that he had dark circles beneath his eyes and he looked as though he needed his bed. 'We was lucky to escape the bombing last night.'

'It was terrible. I saw dreadful things.'

'Got caught up in it, did you?' He shook his head. 'Bad do. Bloody Jerries.'

'I don't suppose you know if the hospital was hit, do you?'

'Not that I heard of. One of the day-shift blokes come that way and he never mentioned it when he relieved me. They missed the railway lines too. The bastards! I'd give 'em what for.'

Miranda could have hugged him with sheer relief, but he was covered with dirt and engine oil and anyway he did not look the huggable sort of person. She smiled and nodded. 'I'm sure you would.'

He stood up, sending a shower of what looked like rust onto the linoleum. 'Got to have me bath now. Bloody five inches of water. Who do they think they are that expect a working man to get hisself clean in a bloody puddle?'

'You wouldn't have an envelope and a postage stamp I could buy, would you, Mr Doughty?'

He put his head on one side, grinning. 'Want to send a love letter to your boyfriend, do you, ducks?'

'Something like that.'

He went to the mantelpiece above the coke boiler and tweaked an envelope from a letter rack filled with what looked like utility bills. 'Haven't got any stamps, but you've got to pass the post office on your way to the station.'

Miranda took it from him with a grateful smile. 'How much do I owe you?'

'No charge. Her outside says you never slept in your bed so consider it a bit of a rebate. She'll charge you full whack despite the fact that she don't have to wash the sheets.' He ambled from the room whistling tunelessly.

It was early evening when Miranda arrived at Henlow Priory. She had had to wait several hours for the train and then the journey was slow, stopping at all stations. She had waited for what seemed like an eternity for the bus which took her to the village and had walked the last couple of miles, arriving tired, muddy and extremely hungry.

Hut five seemed warm and welcoming and almost like coming home after her experience in Alma Villa and her meeting with Mrs Maddern. Corporal Fox was almost effusive in her greeting and Val was positively ecstatic.

'It's good to have you back, Beddoes,' Corporal Fox said, adjusting her cap and making for the outer door. 'I've rostered you to start on Monday morning. Thought I'd give you a chance to settle in.'

'Thanks,' Miranda said with a weary smile. 'I appreciate that, Corp.'

Val waited until the corporal had left the hut before slumping down on Miranda's bed. 'That was a welcome from old Frosty Fox. She must like you.'

Miranda glanced round at the rows of empty beds. 'Where is everyone?'

'The ones who aren't on the night shift are in the ablutions tarting themselves up for a night out. The others are on duty. Nothing's changed.'

At that moment Angela breezed in carrying her towel and wash bag. Her face lit up when she saw Miranda and after an emotional greeting she sat beside Val, curling her long legs around her. 'So tell all, darling. How did it go at home?' She gave a start as Val nudged her in the ribs. 'Don't look at me like that. I was only asking.'

Miranda shrugged off her jacket and hung it in her locker. 'I'll tell you everything, but would you mind if I went and had a shower first? I was up all night helping the Red Cross workers during an air raid and I haven't had a proper wash for two days.'

'Go!' Laughing, Angela pointed to the door. 'Come back when you're fit for human company and not before.'

The girls were all sympathetic and supportive when they heard about Miranda's difficulties with Mrs Maddern. Janice volunteered to take the lady on and tell her that she would be lucky to have someone as nice and caring as Miranda who was willing to put up with a cripple, but this idea was firmly vetoed by everyone, including Miranda.

Despite the fact that she was among friends, Miranda was finding it difficult to settle down again after her home leave. The emotional turmoil of those closest to her had left its mark and Mrs Maddern's intransigent attitude had made her even more determined to keep in touch with Gil. She wrote to him every day, addressing the envelopes to the hospital in Yarmouth for a week, and then more in hope than certainty she posted them to the Royal Victoria hospital at Southampton. She also wrote to Felicity, begging her to send her news of Gil's progress, but none of her letters were answered.

Miranda waited eagerly for some response, but when none came she became increasingly frustrated and desperate. Christmas came and went with a few parties in the mess, but no more home leave and no word from Gil or Fliss. The New Year celebrations were muted and January was a bleak month.

'You ought to stop moping around here, darling,' Angela said to her one Saturday evening when they were both off duty. 'Let's go to the pub for a quiet drink.'

'We're going dancing,' Janice said, leaping off her bed to perform a quick demonstration. 'Come with us to the palais de dance, village hall style.'

Miranda chuckled at her antics but she shook her head. 'Thanks, but I might pass on that one,

329

Jan.' She turned to Angela with a sigh. 'Maybe a quick one at the pub, although I'm not really in the mood.'

'That's one of my favourites,' Janice said, humming the tune. 'And I just love "Blues in the Night" too. Are you sure you won't join us, love?'

'You've told us that a dozen times, Janice,' Angela said lazily. 'Stop pestering Miranda. You're a frightful bore when you keep on at people.'

'Pardon me for breathing.' Janice stuck her tongue out and waltzed out of the hut swinging her wash bag.

'What I didn't mention in front of big ears,' Angela said in a conspiratorial whisper, 'is that the glamour-boys are sure to be there this evening.'

'I'm not interested in meeting other chaps, Angie.'

'So your heart belongs to Mad Dog, does it?'

Miranda felt the blood rush to her cheeks. 'I – I don't know. It just feels wrong.'

'I'd say you'd fallen for him, hook line and sinker.' Angela put her arm around Miranda's shoulders. 'Don't look so tragic, darling. It happens to the best of us at one time or another. Actually I've got a bit of a pash for a certain squadron leader, so I completely understand.'

'No. You're wrong.' Miranda twisted away. 'I'm just sorry for Gil, and I feel responsible in some way. Maybe if I'd been nicer to him and not so suspicious things might have been different.'

'That's crazy logic, darling. You didn't shoot his plane out of the sky, and you didn't give him a mother who's a Gorgon. But whether you like it

330

or not, he's in love with you.' Angela smiled and nodded. 'And you are halfway to being in love with him, unless I'm very much mistaken.'

'That's ridiculous.' Miranda moved away to her locker and searched for something other than her uniform. 'All right, I'll go to the pub with you.'

Angela flicked her long hair back from her face with a smug smile. 'And there might just be some of Gil's friends popping in for a pint or two. It might be a good move to get one of them to send your letters on to Gil. I don't suppose that Mother Maddern would dream of opening something that came from a chap, would she?'

The pub was crowded as usual and noisy with the sound of male voices and bursts of laughter. Angela led the way to the bar, acknowledging several of the men in uniform with smiles and nods, responding cheerfully to their banter. Miranda followed on, feeling ill at ease as she remembered her last meeting here with Gil. They had been happy on that occasion with no thought of what might lie ahead. Lives were lost or blighted in the blink of an eye, and she felt suddenly sad and wished that she had not come, but Angela was chatting to an officer at the bar and she was beckoning to her. Reluctantly, she went to join them.

'Have you met Lionel Castle, Miranda? He's Gil's squadron leader and best friend.'

Lionel slid off the bar stool and held out his hand. 'How do you do, Miranda? Gil was always talking about you. It's a pleasure to meet you at last.'

Angela gave her a gentle push towards him. 'Here's your chance, darling. Don't get in a funk now.'

Chapter Nineteen

'How do you do?' Miranda shook hands.

Angela slipped her arm around Lionel's shoulders. 'I think Miranda wants to ask you something, don't you, darling?'

'It seems an awful cheek when we've only just met,' Miranda murmured, wishing the floor would open up and swallow her. She gave him a sideways glance and was surprised to see that he was regarding her with a sympathetic smile.

'It's all right, Miranda. Angela's filled me in on the background and I'd be only too pleased to help.'

'You would? I mean, that's very good of you.'

His eyes crinkled at the corners and Miranda could see what had attracted Angela to him. He was not the best-looking man in the bar but he had kind eyes and a generous mouth. He gave the impression of being someone you could trust utterly and completely. She found herself launching into a detailed account of her visit to The Gables and her confrontation with Mrs Maddern outside the hospital. 'I know she's only trying to protect her son, but I wouldn't abandon Gil. Even if he spent the rest of his life in a wheelchair I'd always be there for him.'

332

Lionel nodded. 'I'm sure you would, and these things have a way of working themselves out. We don't know for certain that Gil won't walk again. He hasn't been invalided out of the RAF so the powers that be are obviously working on the assumption that he'll be fit enough to return to duty at some time in the future.'

'Do you really think so?' Miranda fumbled in her handbag and brought out the hanky that Gil had given her in what seemed now like another lifetime. It had been laundered again and again, but she kept it with her as if it were a talisman against ill fortune. She blew her nose, making a pretence of having a cold.

'We all have to keep positive,' Lionel said firmly. 'You in particular mustn't give up on him, Miranda. He never stopped talking about you from the day you met. If ever a chap was smitten it was Gil. I'll forward your letters with pleasure.'

Angela beamed at him. 'You're an absolute poppet, Lionel. But what happens if Mummy Maddern finds out?'

'Gil's a big boy and he's quite able to make his own decisions. He doesn't need his mother to take over his life, even if she has the best of intentions.' Lionel pushed his pint glass across the counter, raising his hand to catch the barman's eye. 'Another pint, please, squire, and whatever the ladies want.'

'I'll have a G and T, please, darling,' Angela said with a hearty sigh. 'I need a pick-me-up after listening to Miranda's tussle with her future mother-in-law.'

'Hold on,' Miranda protested. 'You're going too

fast, Angela. I haven't said anything about marriage.'

'Call me a romantic, but I can see it happening,' Angela said, slanting a mischievous look in Lionel's direction.

He smiled indulgently. 'Is that a hint?'

'It might be, or it might not.' Angela covered his hand with hers. 'But life is too short to be cautious, darling. Maybe we ought to give it serious consideration.'

The barman gave them a superior look as he served Angela's drink. He turned his attention to Miranda. 'What's yours, miss?'

'A glass of cider, please.'

'Wait a moment, squire.' Lionel slipped his hand into his breast pocket and produced a small jeweller's box. 'I wasn't going to do this here, but this seems like a good moment, although I'm not going down on my knees.' He flipped the lid open to reveal a diamond ring, holding it out to Angela with a tentative smile. 'You've all but done the job for me, my love. Will you?'

With a squeal of delight, Angela flung her arms around his neck. 'Of course I will, Lionel. I thought you'd never ask.' She released him, holding out her left hand. 'Make it official, darling.'

He slipped the ring on her fourth finger, receiving a round of applause, whistles and shouts of encouragement from everyone in the bar.

'Treat her to champagne, you skinflint.' The shout from the ingle nook made everyone laugh and Lionel bowed to his audience. 'I'd buy drinks all round but I'm afraid that my squadron leader's pay won't run to it.' He turned back to the barman amidst catcalls and boos. 'But if you've got a bottle of champers, that would be super.'

Angela and Lionel were married three weeks later in the village church. Her parents could not attend as they were in India where her father was employed in the colonial service, and her only brother was captain of a destroyer on convoy duty in the Atlantic. The girls from hut five were her wartime family and all those who were not on duty attended the ceremony, including their section leader and Corporal Fox. It was a quiet affair with a wedding breakfast in the pub followed by a one night honeymoon in a country hotel not far from the aerodrome, but Angela could not have looked happier had she been married in Westminster Abbey with a celebration at the Ritz and the prospect of a honeymoon in the Bahamas.

When she returned to hut five after the wedding Miranda had her first opportunity to read the letter that Lionel had given her just before the ceremony. She sat on her bed and her fingers trembled as she opened the envelope and unfolded the single sheet of paper. The writing was spidery and the message was short, but it was from Gil and he told her how happy he was that she had taken the trouble to write to him. He explained that it was difficult to hold a pen with his right arm still in plaster, but it seemed that he had only received one or two of the letters that she had sent before Lionel had agreed to forward them. She clenched her fists and pummelled the hard flock mattress in a fit of impotent rage.

'Bloody war,' she muttered. 'Bloody, bloody war.'

She was on duty that night, having volunteered so that at least one other girl could stay and enjoy the party. Audrey and a shy new recruit called Mabel had also said they would do the graveyard shift, and after a quick wash and tidying her hair into a bun at the nape of her neck Miranda went to the ops room to take over from Janice, who wanted to hear all the details of the wedding before she went off duty.

It was a busy night and Miranda had little time to think about anything but the task in hand. She was relieved at eight o'clock next morning and a pale yellow sun was forcing its way through the clouds as she crossed the forecourt heading for hut five. She heard her name being called and stopped, turning her head to see her section leader beckoning her from the steps of the priory. She went to her office expecting the worst. No one was summoned to the inner sanctum unless it was bad news.

'I'm so sorry, Beddoes. We had a similar conversation not so long ago, and now I'm afraid I have to give you more sad news. Please sit down.'

Miranda thought immediately of Gil and she sat down rather more suddenly than she intended. 'Yes, ma'am?'

'I have to inform you that your aunt, Mrs Isabel Beddoes, was at work in the torpedo factory when it took a direct hit last night. Your grandmother telephoned me early this morning. There were several fatalities and your aunt, sadly, was one of them. I am truly sorry, Miranda.'

'Izzie's dead?' Miranda stared at the officer,

hardly able to believe her ears. 'She can't be. There must be some mistake.'

'I'm afraid not. Your grandmother was absolutely certain of the facts.'

'But she was pregnant,' Miranda murmured, shaking her head. 'I can't believe that both she and her baby are dead.' She covered her eyes with her hands, trying to banish the vision of Izzie's happy face on her wedding day. She took a deep breath, struggling to retain her self-control as the section leader maintained a tactful silence. She dropped her hands to her lap, shaking her head. 'Poor Jack. He'll be devastated.'

'Would you like to talk to the padre? Perhaps he could help you through this.'

'No, but thank you.' She rose unsteadily to her feet. 'There's one thing you could do for me, ma'am.'

'If it's within my power, then yes, of course I will.'

'I was thinking about it before this terrible thing happened, but I'd like a transfer to another station. If possible I'd like to be nearer home. I know that's what everyone would want, but my...' She hesitated, finding it difficult to put her relationship with Gil into words. 'My close friend, Flight Lieutenant Maddern, is in Southampton hospital and I've only been able to visit him once. My grandparents are elderly and they need me. If it's at all possible please could you work something out?'

'In the normal course of things I'd have to say no, but yours is a rather special case. I can't promise anything but I'll see what I can do. If it were simply up to me I wouldn't hesitate, but I have to go through official channels.'

Miranda nodded dully. 'I understand.'

'You'll be excused duties this evening. Now try to get some rest.'

'May I have permission to phone home, ma'am?'

She rose to her feet. 'Of course. Use the telephone in the outer office.'

What strings the section leader had pulled Miranda was never to know, but by the end of the week her transfer had come through, and she could hardly believe her luck when she discovered that she was being sent to RAF Warmwell. On her last night the girls threw a party in hut five which went on long after lights out, courtesy of Corporal Fox, who in a sudden spurt of generosity had donated a bottle of gin to the proceedings.

Miranda could never have imagined how sad she would be feeling on saying goodbye to the friends she had made at Henlow Priory. When she left next morning there were tears all round and promises to keep in touch, even though Miranda knew that most of these, although well intentioned, would soon be broken. Perhaps she would hear from Angela from time to time, but she doubted if Val or Audrey would sit down and put pen to paper. Janice was soon to marry Cyril Shakeshaft, her boyfriend with the safe job at the gas board, and Gloria was being transferred and taking her twenty a day habit to the plotting room at RAF Filton. The old team was splitting up and Miranda could not help feeling some regret as she climbed into the truck which happened to be going into town to collect supplies from the depot. She leaned out of the window, waving to Val and Janice who had just come off night duty and were strolling across the gravel drive towards the mess.

The driver dropped her off at the station, and wished her good luck as he climbed back into the cab. He drove off and she knew that this was her final goodbye to Henlow Priory, but she was going home, or as near home as was possible in wartime. She would at least be able to offer some comfort to Jack, but she could only imagine how he must be feeling at this moment. She had lost her father, it was true, but Jack had lost his elder brother and now his wife and unborn child had been taken from him. In any other circumstances Miranda would have been overjoyed to be returning home, but it would hardly be a happy homecoming. She tried to keep her thoughts positive during the long journey involving several changes of train, and by the time she reached Weymouth station she was tired, hungry and looking forward to sleeping in her own bed, if only for one night. Tomorrow she was to report to Warmwell, and then she would have to face Raif who must also be racked with grief. It was not going to be easy.

As she stepped out of the station she was surprised once again to see Tommy standing by an army staff car, smoking a cigarette. Taking a last drag he tossed it on the ground and strode towards her, grinning. 'Give us your case, Miranda.'

She handed it to him. 'Have you come especially to meet me?'

He opened the passenger door and tossed her suitcase onto the back seat. 'Rita told me you were coming and I had to bring the colonel into town. He said I could pick you up and take you home. Hop in.'

Miranda needed no second bidding. She slumped down onto the padded leather with a sigh of relief. 'I thought I might have to walk.'

Tommy slipped into the driver's seat. 'I'll have you back at Highcliffe in two ticks.' He started the engine. 'Sorry to hear about young Mrs Beddoes. I only met her the once, but it's still very sad.'

'Yes, thanks, Tommy.'

He shot her a sideways glance as he pulled out of the station forecourt. 'I know someone who'll be very pleased to see you.'

'Rita?'

'Yes, of course. She's organised a billet for you at the castle, sharing a room with her.'

'The castle? Is it a pub?'

Tommy chuckled. 'No, it's a joke. Some of the officers are billeted at Woodsford Castle, but Rita and a couple of the other girls are living in a tumbledown farmhouse on the edge of the village. They call it their castle.'

'I can't wait to see it.'

They lapsed into silence for the rest of the short ride to Highcliffe and Tommy left her at the gate, driving back into town to collect his colonel. Miranda walked slowly down the path towards the house. For the first time she was afraid of what she was going to face when she entered the house of sadness. She wondered how her grandparents and Jack were coping with the second tragedy to befall the family in such a short space of time. She had been thinking about it during the long train journey, and she had realised with a sense of shock that she had not yet come to terms with the loss of her father. He might have been a rather distant figure while she was growing up, but she remembered how much she had looked forward to seeing him when he came home on leave, and how sad she had felt when he went away again. But he was gone forever now, and so were Izzie and her baby.

She hesitated for a moment before raising the doorknocker and letting it fall so that its sound echoed around the entrance hall like the toll of a monastery bell. She braced herself to meet her grandmother with a cheerful face but it was Annie who opened the door, greeting her with a genuine smile of welcome. 'Thank goodness you've come, Miranda. It's a pity they didn't send you home in time for the funeral, but you're here now and that's all that matters.'

She stepped over the threshold. 'How are they taking it, Annie?'

'I've never seen Mrs B so down, but it'll do her the world of good to have you at home.'

'I'm only here until tomorrow. I've got to report to my new posting in the morning.'

'Well, that's better than nothing. It'll buck her up to know that you're going to be close and she'll see you more often. The major has tried to cheer her up, but he's more upset than he lets on. I don't think he's quite got over all that hoo-ha with Max Carstairs.'

'Max has lost his only daughter and his grandchild. You'd think it would bring the two families closer together.' Miranda dropped her case onto the tiled floor and taking off her cap she tossed it onto the hallstand. She felt a little more relaxed now that she was home, despite the sad circumstances that had brought her here. The old house seemed to live in a time warp where nothing changed. The smell of Mansion polish and Brasso still lingered in the air, but the elephant table needed dusting and the stair carpet was threadbare in places. The grandfather clock had stopped at half past six and no one had bothered to adjust the weights and get it started again.

Annie picked up Miranda's case. 'You'll find Mrs B in her sitting room. She's done nothing but sit and stare out of the window since we got the news about Mrs Jack.'

'That's not like Granny. She's always bounced back in the past. This must have hit her harder than I imagined. I didn't know she was so fond of Izzie.'

'A person can only take so much and I think she'd reached her limit. She hasn't eaten enough to keep a fly alive. Maybe she'll pick up now you're here.'

'I'll go and see her now, and then perhaps we could both have something to eat. I had a sandwich at Waterloo but it was awful.'

'Look on the bright side,' Annie said with a grim smile. 'At least you won't have to pretend to enjoy your granny's rock cakes today. The poor soul hasn't felt like baking, and we can't barter for extras from Farmer Drake now we've run out of the embrocation. Mind you, Elzevir's been much better for being sober.' She headed for the stairs. 'I'll put your things in your room and then I'll see what I can find in the pantry, but don't expect anything fancy.'

Miranda went to the small sitting room and found her grandmother, as Annie had predicted, sitting in her chair staring out over the garden to the sea with Dickens curled up asleep on her lap. 'Granny.'

Maggie turned her head and Miranda was shocked by the gauntness of her face and the dark shadows underlining her eyes. Granny had always looked younger than her years but suddenly she looked her age and more. Miranda rushed over to put her arms around her. 'I'm here now. I came as soon as I could.' Dickens leapt to the floor, waving his tail in affront, and went to sit on the windowsill where he proceeded to wash himself.

'There's no need to strangle me, dear,' Maggie said, sounding a little more like her old self. She returned the hug and then pushed Miranda gently away. 'Sit down and let me look at you.'

Miranda pulled up the stool and sat down. 'How is Jack taking it, Granny?'

'Badly, I'm afraid. He's got a couple of days' compassionate leave left, but I'm afraid he's in no fit state to fly a plane. He stays in his room, pacing the floor or standing on the widow's walk staring into nothing. He won't eat and I doubt if he sleeps much either. I've never seen him like this, Miranda. It frightens me.'

'I've never known you to be scared of anything, Granny. If you give up then who do we turn to? Maybe Jack needs you to give him a proverbial kick up the arse.'

Maggie recoiled visibly. 'Miranda. I never thought I'd hear such vulgar words coming from your lips. You're obviously mixing with the wrong sort of people.'

'I've been out in the real world, Granny. I'm not the prissy young snob that I was when the war started. They used to call me Goody Two-Shoes when I first arrived at Henlow, but I've lived that nickname down now.'

'I'm not sure I approve.'

'But at least I've got you talking. Annie's very worried about you.'

'She's an old woman and she fusses.'

'And you are the one who keeps this family together. Please go upstairs and talk to Jack. He'll listen to you.'

Maggie stared at her for a moment, and then she rose to her feet. 'You're right, Miranda. I've been thinking too much about my own feelings and not enough about poor Jack. I've neglected your grandfather too.' She twisted her lips into a wry smile. 'Perhaps I needed a kick up the arse too.'

Miranda was sitting at the kitchen table finishing off her boiled egg and soldiers. Eating a nursery meal in such familiar surroundings was both nostalgic and comforting, even if Annie seemed to think that she was still a child. She looked up expectantly as the door opened and her grandmother walked in and slumped down at the table opposite her.

'How is Jack? Is he all right?'

Maggie nodded dully. 'He will be, in time. I think I've persuaded him to come down later but perhaps you'd go up and see him, Miranda. He might be able to speak more freely to you than to me.'

'The hens are laying well,' Annie said, standing arms akimbo. 'You can have yours boiled, poached or scrambled, Mrs B.'

Miranda left the table and hurried from the kitchen, leaving them to argue about how her grandmother wanted her egg cooked. The sound of their raised voices was an encouraging sign and she hoped that perhaps things would slowly return to as near normal as was possible after such a terrible loss. If her grandmother and Annie ever stopped their verbal sparring, life at Highcliffe House would never be the same again. She headed for the stairs with a feeling of relief mixed with trepidation. She must face Jack but she felt suddenly at a loss for words.

He was outside on the widow's walk and he had his back to her. She glanced round the room and her heart contracted as she saw Isabel's things scattered about on the bed and the small nursing chair in the far corner. The dressing table was littered with makeup, hair brushes and combs and a framed photograph of Jack and Isabel on their wedding day. A suitcase, half packed, lay open on the floor. They must have been planning to move into a place of their own before the fatal air raid. Miranda swallowed hard and braced herself to face Jack. She went to the window and threw up the sash, bending down in order to step outside into the sunshine.

'I thought that Mother would send you up next,' Jack said, without looking at her. 'She told me that you were here.'

Miranda stood beside him. 'You must miss her terribly. I know it's stating the obvious, but I don't know what else to say.'

'I still can't believe that she's gone.' Jack clutched the parapet. 'Sometimes I think I'll chuck myself off the cliff into the sea and end it all.'

'I can understand that.'

He turned his head to stare at her in surprise. His eyes were swollen and red-rimmed and he had two days' growth of stubble on his chin. 'What am I going to do, Miranda?'

She had never seen him like this before and it was a shock, but she made an effort to hide her feelings and she managed a smile as she rested her hand on his. 'Try having a wash and a shave as a first step. I'm not being horrible, Jack, but you don't smell too good.'

His dark eyes filled with tears and he twisted his lips into a rictus grin. 'Trust you to be practical, kid.'

'That's me, Jack.' She stepped back into the bedroom and waited until he was safely inside the room before closing the window. 'I don't want to interfere, but might I clear away some of Izzie's things while you're in the bathroom? Just to tidy them up, Jack. You know she wouldn't want to see you living in such a mess.'

He hesitated for a moment, staring at the open suitcase. 'She was such a tidy girl. She'd started packing because she'd found a flat in town. She telephoned me at the aerodrome to tell me about it and she was so excited...' His voice broke on a sob. 'Sorry. I still can't bear to talk about it.'

'She was happy. You made her happy and that's what you've got to hold on to.'

'But she's gone and I'll never see her again. I'll never know if our child was a boy or a girl. I don't think I can carry on without her.'

Miranda took a step towards him but she realised that this was not the time for overt sympathy. She wanted to give him a cuddle and tell him that everything was going to be all right, but she knew that it was untrue. Jack had loved Isabel deeply and the pain of losing her and their child might fade in time, but would never quite go away. She laid her hand on his arm. 'She wouldn't want you to give up, Jack. You've got to keep up the fight. You can't let a tyrant win.'

'When did you grow up, Miranda? Just yesterday you were a little girl.'

'War does that to people, and I'm on your side, Jack. I've been transferred to Warmwell, starting tomorrow. We'll face this together.'

His lips twisted into a travesty of a smile as he moved to the door and opened it. 'I suppose I'd better tidy myself up before I go downstairs.'

'Good for you.' Following him onto the landing, she heard Annie's voice calling her name with a degree of urgency. Miranda leaned over the banisters. 'What is it?'

'There's a young lady to see you. Says her name's Fliss or it could have been Phyllis, my hearing isn't what it used to be.'

Miranda was already halfway down the first flight of stairs before Annie had finished speaking.

Chapter Twenty

Felicity Maddern was standing in the hallway, looking distinctly uncomfortable.

'Fliss,' Miranda said breathlessly. 'Has something happened to Gil? He hasn't taken a turn for the worse, has he?'

'No. It's nothing like that.' Felicity stood awkwardly, clutching her handbag with gloved hands. 'I tried to contact you at Henlow but they told me you'd come home on compassionate leave.'

Miranda's heartbeats had slowed from racing madly to almost normal. She took a deep breath, forcing herself to be patient with Felicity who obviously had something to say but was having difficulty in finding the words. 'Come into the drawing room and you can tell me what's on your mind.' Without waiting for an answer she led the way, opening the door and ushering Felicity into the room. 'Make yourself comfortable and I'll get Annie to make us some tea.'

Felicity slumped down on the nearest chair. 'No, please don't bother. I'd rather get this off my chest first.'

'Okay.' Miranda took a seat close to her. 'Fire away.'

'Gil thinks that you've forgotten him. He told me he wrote to you but you didn't reply.'

'But I've written to him every day. Didn't he tell you that?'

Felicity averted her gaze. 'Mummy found out that someone was forwarding your letters to Gil and she intercepted them. I wanted to tell him but he's going through a bad patch, and I didn't know how he'd take it.'

'But you said he wasn't any worse.'

'It's not his physical condition. In fact he's improving daily and the doctors are quite optimistic, but of course they won't commit themselves to anything. It's Gil's mental state that's worrying me. He's terribly depressed and I'm certain it's because he thinks you've given up on him.'

Miranda leapt to her feet. 'That's awful and it's absolutely untrue. I asked for a transfer to an aerodrome nearer home so that I could visit him in hospital.'

'Really?' Felicity relaxed visibly. 'I'm so glad, Miranda. I think my mother was wrong to keep you from seeing Gil. He's crazy about you and if anyone can cheer him up, it's you.'

Miranda stared at her, frowning. 'I've got to start at Warmwell tomorrow but I could come with you today, if you think you can get me into the hospital without some dragon stopping me. I can imagine that your mother has had sentries posted at all the doors.'

'That's not so far from the truth.' Felicity rose to her feet. 'Could we leave right away?'

'Yes, of course, but we'll have to hurry if we're to get the midday train.'

'No need. I've been saving my petrol ration and I drove here in the hope that you'd come to the hospital with me. I can't wait to see Gil's face when he sets eyes on you.'

His wheelchair had been placed beneath an oak tree in the hospital grounds. The early spring sunshine sent a dappled shade through the branches where tight bronze leaf buds were beginning to unfurl. He was well wrapped up against the blustery wind, and an open book lay on his lap, but he was staring into space, apparently lost in thought.

Miranda approached him slowly, and was suddenly nervous. It had seemed so right when she agreed to accompany Felicity to the hospital, but now she was having second thoughts and wondering if she had done the right thing by coming to see Gil. Giving him hope might prove to be a cruel deception, particularly when she was still unsure of her own feelings. Maybe she ought to have listened to his mother's warnings. Miranda was tempted to turn and run in the opposite direction, but although she could not see his face she could sense his helplessness and feel something of the desperation that must accompany such a disability in a previously strong and active young man. She drew nearer. 'Gil.' She had spoken in a whisper but he turned his head and a smile suffused his face.

'Miranda. You came.'

'I would have been here sooner but things were difficult.'

He gulped and swallowed, shaking his head. 'You'll have to forgive me for being such a fool, but I get emotional over such little things these days. It must be my second childhood or something.'

She knelt on the damp grass beside him, taking

his good hand in hers. 'You've been incredibly brave, and you're looking heaps better than when I last saw you.'

'It's the nurses' obsession with fresh air that's done it. I'm wheeled about the grounds like an infant in a pram.' He shook his head. 'Sorry. That sounds pathetic.'

She squeezed his fingers. 'No, it doesn't. You've been to hell and back and I wish I'd been able to help.'

'You are helping. Just seeing you has made me feel better.' He withdrew his hand gently, his smile fading. 'How are things with you?'

His tone was suddenly polite but impersonal and he seemed to have retreated into himself. She shivered even though it was not a cold day, and she rose to her feet. 'I'm not the important one, Gil. It's how you are that matters.'

He shrugged his shoulders. 'I'll live. I might not walk again but I'll survive.'

The bitterness of his voice shocked her. 'Stop it. Don't talk as if you've given up. That's not the Mad Dog I know.'

'Mad Dog died when he ditched his kite in the sea.'

'That's rubbish. Stop feeling sorry for yourself. You can't give up now. I won't let you.'

He shot her a sideways glance, squinting into the sunlight. 'Do you really care, Miranda? I mean it's nice of you to visit the halt and the lame, but you can return to your normal life. I can't.'

'I do care. I care terribly and I've written to you every day even though you only replied to one of them.' She was angry now; too angry to bother to

351

conceal his mother's attempts to keep them apart. 'But it seems that my letters never reached you.'

He stared at her, unblinking. 'What?'

'Your mother decided that I would be a bad influence. She thought that I might lead you on and then abandon you, or something like that. I asked your friend Lionel to forward my letters to you so that Mrs Maddern wouldn't recognise my handwriting.' She dug her fingernails into her palms in an attempt to stop herself crying with frustration. This was supposed to have been a happy reunion which would jolt Gil out of his depression, but things were not going well. 'Perhaps I'd better go. I seem to be making matters worse.' She was about to walk away when he reached out and grasped her hand.

'Don't go. Stay and talk to me if you can put up with a self-pitying idiot who ought to know better.'

She raised his hand to her cheek. 'I do care about you, Gil. I'm really sorry you thought I'd abandoned you.'

'You're here now and that's all that matters, but I'll have a few words to say to my mother when I next see her.'

'Don't fall out with her on my account. I'm sure she thought she was doing her best for you, and it's Fliss we have to thank for bringing me here today.' Miranda glanced over her shoulder to where Felicity was sitting on a bench chatting to a man in army uniform. 'She's a great girl. I'm so glad we're friends again.'

Gil followed her gaze and smiled. 'She needs to watch out for old Forbes. He's quite a ladies' man.'

'I was told much the same thing about you,' Miranda said, chuckling. 'It almost ruined our friendship.'

'We are friends, aren't we, Miranda?'

'Of course, and I'm going to visit you at every possible opportunity until they discharge you from hospital.'

'That would be wonderful, but where are you stationed now?'

'Warmwell in Dorset. I start tomorrow.'

'I'll be happier to know that you're not so far away.'

'And I feel much better now I've seen you again.' She forced her lips into a smile. 'Who knows? This time next year you might be back in the air, kissing the clouds as you used to say.'

'Maybe, but I doubt it.'

'You mustn't say things like that. You've got to concentrate on getting better, Gil. You asked me out that last evening in the pub, if you remember.'

'Of course I do.'

'And I'm holding you to it. You won't get out of buying me dinner so easily.'

He glanced down at the plaster casts on both legs, pulling a face. 'I doubt if I'll ever be asking you to dance.'

'That's defeatist talk, but I won't let you give up. I can be a very stubborn person when I set my mind to it.'

He was about to answer when a nurse came bustling across the grass. 'Flight Lieutenant Maddern, it's time for your physiotherapy.'

Miranda could see that he was about to argue

and she laid her hand on his shoulder. 'I should be going anyway, Gil. I've got a train to catch.'

'It's too soon. You've only just got here.'

The nurse shook her head. 'Visiting time is over. We have to keep to our routine or we won't get better, will we?'

'Can't we bend the rules just this once, Nurse Brown?' Gil gave her his most charming smile.

She shook her head. 'You won't get round me that way.'

'I'll come again as soon as I get a day off,' Miranda said hastily. 'I won't have too far to travel now.'

Gil patted her hand as it rested on his shoulder. 'All right, I'll go to physio and do my exercises like a good boy. I've got even more incentive to beat this thing now.'

Nurse Brown took charge of his wheelchair. 'That's the spirit.'

Gil turned his head and waved as he was wheeled away. 'Keep on writing to me, darling.'

The term of endearment had slipped off his tongue so easily that Miranda wondered if she had imagined it. She stood for a few moments, watching until he was out of sight. Her feelings for Gil had always balanced on a knife edge. From the start there had been an undeniable tug of attraction to the wild boy of the squadron, but that had changed subtly when she had begun to know him better, although now she was uncertain whether it was love or pity she felt for him. She knew that she must not confuse the two emotions, but it was not going to be easy. She walked slowly towards Felicity who was still deep in conversation with the young army officer, whose injuries at first appeared to be superficial, but as Miranda drew closer she could see an empty sleeve pinned to his chest, and one side of his face was badly scarred.

'Are you ready to leave, Fliss?' she asked, glancing at her watch. 'I'd be in time to catch the four o'clock train if we left now.'

'Yes, of course.' Felicity rose to her feet. 'Goodbye, Captain Forbes. It was so nice meeting you.'

He stood up, bowing gallantly over her hand. 'Goodbye, Miss Maddern. Perhaps we'll have the opportunity to chat, when you next visit your brother.'

'I'd like that.'

Miranda gave him a vague smile as she walked away, but her thoughts were with Gil and the long road he would have to travel to make a full recovery. Felicity fell into step beside her. 'War is absolutely beastly,' she said when they were out of earshot. 'These poor men make you want to cry.'

'Yes,' Miranda said, thinking of Gil. 'It's awful to see such brave chaps struck down in their prime.'

'Well, I'm going to do something about it. I'll be twenty-one next month and Mummy won't have a say in it. I want to do something more than just being an ARP warden, and so I've decided that I'm going to train as a nurse. I'll be doing something really useful then.'

'Good for you, Fliss. I think you'll make a jolly good nurse.'

'And you'll keep on seeing Gil, won't you?

Mummy will do her best to keep you apart, but you won't let him down, I know it.'

'Of course not,' Miranda said firmly. 'I won't be far away and I'll visit him as often as possible.'

'You do love him, don't you, Miranda?'

Her naïve belief in romance and her absolute trust went straight to Miranda's heart. Looking into Felicity's eyes she could not have lied if she had wanted to, but she had to be absolutely honest. 'I care very deeply for him, Fliss. I don't know if that's love.'

'I hope so for both your sakes. I mean, I'm sure that Gil will make a full recovery. He's very determined when he makes up his mind to something, and now he knows that you're back in the picture I'm certain he'll make an even bigger effort.'

'I'll do my best to help him. That's a promise.'

Feeling like a new girl at school, Miranda was even more nervous on her first day at Warmwell than she had been at Henlow. Arriving in style in her grandfather's Bentley with Jack at her side, Miranda was pounced upon by her new section leader who bristled with efficiency and was totally lacking in a sense of humour. She dismissed Miranda's experience in the plotting room with a curt laugh. 'You'll have to get yourself transferred to Filton if you want to join the la-di-dah girlies in the ops room,' she said, curling her lip. 'You'll be given clerical duties, Beddoes, starting right away. Think yourself lucky that you haven't been sent to the repair shops maintaining bicycles, or to wait on tables in the mess.' She narrowed her eyes. 'But that could all change, so you'd better show me what you can do.'

Miranda spent the rest of the morning doing menial jobs in the office, but at midday Rita burst into the room and greeted her with a cheery smile. 'I won't hug you, love,' she said, holding out her arms to demonstrate her oil-streaked and mud-strained overalls. 'I've come to take you to the mess for din-dins.' She angled her head, frowning. 'What's up?'

'Nothing,' Miranda said, hoping she sounded more cheerful than she was feeling. 'I expect I'm just hungry.'

'Well that's easily settled. Let's go.' She opened the door. 'The good news is that you're billeted in the castle with me and the girls.'

'That sounds lovely.'

Miranda's first impression of the castle, as the girls jokingly called the near derelict farmhouse, was one of shock and then amusement followed by disbelief. 'You're pulling my leg,' she said as she propped her bicycle against a rickety wooden fence. 'This place is a ruin.' She stared in horror at the thatched roof which was bald in places with clumps of moss in great green patches. The chimney stack looked as though it might collapse at any moment, and panes of glass were missing from the upstairs windows.

Rita wheeled her bike through the muddy yard and leaned it against the cob wall. 'It's not Buckingham Palace that's for certain, but we've done a good job inside.' She unlocked the front door and heaved it with her shoulder so that it juddered, creaked and lurched open. 'Come in and see.'

Miranda followed her inside and stood blinking as her eyes grew accustomed to the gloom. There were two small lattice windows on either side of the door and another at the far side of the room. The ground floor seemed to consist of one large open area with blackened oak beams supporting a low ceiling, and an ancient cast-iron range taking up most of one wall. She could feel the chill rising from the flagstone floor and a draught wafted down a wooden flight of steps that led to the upper storey. The only furniture was a pine dresser, a large deal table and several ill-assorted kitchen chairs, but Miranda noticed that someone had made patchwork cushions for the seats in an attempt to make the place a little more homely, and there was a jam jar filled with primroses in the middle of the table.

'Home sweet hovel,' Rita said proudly. 'It's nice and cosy when we get the fire going at night. Come upstairs and I'll show you where you'll sleep.' She headed towards the stairs. 'Mind your head on the beam at the top, and watch out for the top step, it's a bit worn.'

Miranda followed her up the crudely made staircase to the upper floor, which again seemed to consist of one large room. Four camp beds were set beneath the sloping ceiling and Miranda was disturbed to see daylight filtering through gaps in the thatch. She could hear scrabbling sounds in the rafters, which was even more worrying. 'What's living up there? I hope it isn't rats.'

'Dunno,' Rita said airily. 'I haven't seen any livestock, and if they don't bother me, I won't bother them.' She shot Miranda a mischievous look. 'Don't worry, ducks. It could be bats or mice.' She pointed to a camp bed on the far side of the room. 'That's yours, and I'm in the one opposite. You'll meet the other girls tonight at supper. It's my turn to cook so it's pot luck, but it'll probably be Spam fritters because that's my entire repertoire. I'm probably about as good a cook as Mrs B, or even slightly worse.'

'I'll look forward to it,' Miranda said drily. She laid her suitcase on the bed. 'Where's the bathroom?'

Rita shook her head. 'I was waiting for you to ask that. The lav is outside and we take turns on latrine duty.'

'And the ablutions?'

'My God you are spoilt,' Rita said, chuckling. 'We've got a tin bath we fill with hot water once a week and take it in turns. The water comes from a pump in the yard, so if you want a wash you either do it outside or if it's cold and rainy fetch a bucketful and wash in the kitchen. You'll soon get used to it.'

'I'm sure I will,' Miranda said, doubtfully. 'Is there any chance of using the ablutions at the camp?'

'It's not worth the bother. Trust me, I've tried every trick in the book. Come downstairs and I'll show you where the lav is, although don't expect much and you won't be disappointed.'

That evening Miranda met her new roommates, Vivienne and Joan. Vivienne waited on tables in the mess and helped in the cookhouse and Joan worked in the bicycle repair shed with Rita. They sat round the table eating Rita's Spam fritters with baked potatoes, followed by a generous helping of plum duff that Joan said was surplus to needs in the officers' mess.

'As it's your first night we'll do the washing up,' Vivienne said magnanimously. 'But tomorrow you're on kitchen duties, new girl.'

'And it's bath night tomorrow,' Joan added, grinning. 'It'll be your turn to fetch the water and fill the tub.'

'Fine by me,' Miranda said, refusing to be drawn into an argument on her first evening. She could sense that she was being tested, but she had learned to stand up for herself at Henlow.

'Go easy on her,' Rita said, frowning. 'This is my best mate, Miranda. She's one of us.'

'Keep your hair on, old girl,' Vivienne said, taking a packet of Gold Flake cigarettes from her handbag and offering them round. 'Smoke, anyone?'

Joan took one but Rita shook her head. 'Trying to give up, love.'

'What about you, Miranda?'

'No, thanks, Vivienne. I gave up some time ago.' Miranda pushed back her chair and stood up. The heat from the range was intense and the fumes from the paraffin lamp were making her feel slightly queasy as they mingled with the smell of hot fat and cigarette smoke. 'I think I'll get a breath of air, if you don't mind, girls.'

Rita smiled and nodded. 'That's right. Get your bearings. It'll all seem a bit strange at first but you'll get used to the old place. It's not too bad unless it's raining and then it's hell.'

Miranda went outside, taking deep breaths of cool evening air. The lengthening shadows softened the harsh outlines of the disused and crumbling outhouses, making them look hazy and romantic. The bustling life of the aerodrome seemed like another world, and in this idyllic landscape the only wings in the sky were those of birds coming home to roost for the night. It was a scene of peace and tranquillity but suddenly the silence was broken by the crunch of bicycle tyres on the rough road surface and Raif pedalled into the yard. He dismounted and left the bike at the gate. 'Jack told me where to find you,' he said before she had a chance to speak.

'I'm so sorry about Izzie,' she said softly. 'I don't know what to say.'

He took both her hands in his, looking deeply into her eyes before dropping his gaze. 'I know. I can't believe that I'm still here and she's gone forever.'

'I couldn't get home for the funeral, Raif.'

'It was very quiet. Your grandparents were there and Jack, of course, but apart from that there was just Father and me. My mother couldn't get back from America and its probably just as well. It was awful seeing Izzie's coffin and knowing that I'd been so against her marrying Jack. Then there was all that business with my father and your grandparents, and I ask myself what was it all about? In the grand scheme of things nothing matters when you're faced with the death of someone you love; two people if you count Izzie's baby. The whole thing was desperately sad and

I'm glad you didn't have to go through it. I know you loved Izzie and she loved you.'

Miranda slid her arms around his neck and they stood motionless in the twilight for a long moment until they moved apart. Miranda rested her hands on his shoulders. 'Is there anything I can do, Raif?'

'Thanks, but no. There's nothing anyone can do now. I'd give anything to be able to turn the clock back and do things differently, but I can't and I'll just have to live with it for the rest of my life.'

She let her hands fall to her sides, feeling helpless in the face of such guilt-ridden grief. 'Izzie wouldn't want you to be unhappy.'

'She was worth ten of me. I should have bought it, not her.' He raised his head to look her in the eye. 'I'm sorry. I didn't mean to burden you with all this. I just wanted to see you, and make things right with you, while I've got the chance. It could be my turn next.'

She felt a chill run down her spine. 'Don't talk like that. I'm your friend and always will be.'

'Thanks. That means a lot to me.' He turned on his heel and strode away to retrieve his bicycle.

She hurried after him. 'Raif, don't go like this. Stay and talk to me. I can't very well invite you inside as it's a bit crowded, but we could go for a walk. You really shouldn't be on your own.'

'I'm on duty. I shouldn't have come, but I had to see you. Call it unfinished business, but you mean a lot to me, Miranda.' He mounted the bicycle and rode off before she had a chance to stop him. She ran into the lane but he had already been swallowed up by the encroaching night.

It was some time before she felt calm enough to join the others.

She found it hard to sleep and when she eventually drifted off she dreamed that Izzie was standing by her bedside and she was weeping. Tears trickled down her pale cheeks and fell on Miranda's face. She brushed them away but they kept falling. She wanted to wake up but Izzie would not go away. She was shaking her and calling her name.

'Miranda, wake up.'

She opened her eyes and saw Rita silhouetted against the gaping hole in the thatch. 'What's the matter?'

'It's pouring with rain, you idiot. You're soaked to the skin. Get up and we'll move your bed.'

Joan raised herself on her elbow. 'What's going on?'

'Nothing, go back to sleep,' Rita said, dragging Miranda to her feet. She hesitated, cocking her head on one side. 'That's all we need – a bloody air raid warning. Get up girls. We'd better go down to the cellar.'

Joan groaned and turned over. 'I'd rather die in my bed than be buried alive.'

Vivienne struggled to her feet. 'I need a pee now. Blast the bleeding Luftwaffe.'

'Wrap this round you, Miranda,' Rita said, pulling the blanket off her bed. 'Go downstairs and I'll put the kettle on. I'm not a fan of the cellar either, and they'll be trying to bomb the airfield, not us.'

'They'll be scrambled,' Miranda said through chattering teeth.

'Of course they will.' Rita steered her towards the stairs. 'The glamour-boys will sort out the Jerries. Now go downstairs while I move your bed. Go and sit by the range and dry out or you'll catch double pneumonia.'

Miranda stumbled down the rough wooden steps with Raif's last words ringing in her ears. *Call it unfinished business.* She knew then what he meant, and what Izzie had been trying to tell her in the dream. Raif was intent on revenge and nothing and no one would be able to stop him. He had taken his Spitfire into the air with one thing in mind: to kill or be killed.

Chapter Twenty-One

'I've got to stop him.' Miranda came to a halt in the middle of the kitchen. The nightmare was receding but the resounding thuds of ack-ack fire shook the old building, and the drone of aircraft engines overhead brought the combat terrifyingly close to home. She shrugged off the blanket. 'I must get dressed and go to the aerodrome.'

'What the hell are you doing?' Rita demanded, catching her by the wrist.

'I've got to stop him taking off. Let me go, Rita. I have to do this.'

'Calm down and stop talking like a mad woman.'

'Raif told me that he had unfinished business. I

364

know that he's going to get himself killed. He's on a suicide mission and I've got to stop him.' Tears flowed freely down her cheeks as she struggled to free herself, but a slap across the face made her gasp with shock. 'Why did you do that?'

'You had a nightmare. Come and sit by the fire. I'll soon get it going again and you can have a nice hot cup of tea.' Rita guided her towards the range and pulled up a chair, pressing her down on the seat. She retrieved the blanket and wrapped it around Miranda's shoulders. 'You'll be all right. It was just a bad dream.' She waited for a moment and when Miranda did not respond she turned her attention to the range, riddling the ashes and pulling out the damper.

A gust of wind and rain blew into the kitchen as Vivienne rushed in and slammed the door. 'God, what an awful night. I'd give anything for an indoor lavvy.' Shaking the rainwater from her hair, she stopped to stare at Miranda. 'What's up with her?'

'Get some logs from the store,' Rita said, frowning. 'Miranda's bed got soaked. We must do something about that bloody roof.'

Vivienne hesitated, staring at Miranda. 'There's no need to get in a state about it, love. If having a bad dream and getting soaked is the worst thing that's happened to you since the war started, all I can say is that you've had it easy.'

'Shut up, Viv, and get the logs.' Rita flicked a cinder at her. 'D'you want tea or cocoa?'

'Cocoa. If I don't drown on my way to the log store.' Vivienne opened the door and went outside to brave the storm for the second time.

Miranda rose to her feet. 'I'm okay now, Rita. Please don't slap me again, but I've got to go to the aerodrome. If there's the slightest chance that I can stop Raif taking off then I've got to do it.'

'Don't talk rubbish, Manda. They'll have been scrambled before the siren went off and there's nothing you can do about it.' Rising to her feet, Rita took a small bottle from its hiding place behind the clock on the mantelshelf. 'Rum,' she said, pulling out the cork. 'A slug of this in your tea will make you feel a different woman.' She put the bottle to her lips and sipped. 'Blimey, that warms the cockles of your heart.' She passed it to Miranda. 'Take a swig now and we'll share the rest with Viv and Joan. Us girls look after each other – all for one, et cetera et cetera.'

Miranda's worst fears were realised when she arrived at the aerodrome next morning and discovered that not all the fighter planes had returned from last night's sortie. Jack had managed to limp back to the airfield on one engine, and two Spitfires were confirmed as lost, but there was no information as to the fate of Raif's Spitfire. Miranda received the news with little surprise, having already convinced herself that he had carried out his death wish. When Jack came to see her in the office later that day he seemed relieved that she was taking it so well. 'I always thought you had a bit of a crush on him, Miranda.'

She shuffled the papers on the desk in front of her and laid them tidily in the filing basket. 'I did, but that was a long time ago now. I was such a little idiot when all this started but I've had to grow up.'

He perched on the edge of the desk. 'It ought to have been me who bought it last night. God alone knows how I managed to bring my kite home. I thought about ditching in the sea, but for some reason I couldn't do it.'

Jolted out of her apathetic state, Miranda stared at him in dismay. 'You mustn't think like that, Jack. Izzie wouldn't want you to do anything stupid. She loved you and she wouldn't want you to waste your life.'

He shook his head. 'I can't imagine a future without her. I really don't care what happens to me now.'

Miranda was about to protest when Rita stuck her head round the door. 'Ready for off, Manda?' Her smile faded when she saw Jack and she entered the room, closing the door behind her. She put her arms around him. 'You were nearly a goner, you daft bugger. Don't scare us like that again.'

Jack's grim expression softened into a smile. 'You really know how to make a chap feel good, Rita.'

She loosened her hold, staring at him with concern in her eyes. 'If you think I'm going to let you wallow in misery, you've got another think coming, young man.'

Miranda held her breath. She would not have spoken to Jack in such a way, but to her astonishment he did not seem to mind. If anything he appeared to relax a little, and he held Rita at arm's length, studying her grubby overalls with a

367

wry expression. 'You look a mess and you've got lubricating oil in your hair.'

'Ta, ever so. It's nice to know I'm appreciated.' Rita pulled away from him, grinning. 'I'm going to have a shower and then you can buy me and Manda a drink in the pub, since we're not allowed in the mess with the snobby officers.'

'I'm not really in the mood,' Jack said wearily. 'I've only had a couple of hours' sleep.'

'All the more reason to have a couple of drinks and a meal and you'll drop off as soon as your head hits the pillow and sleep like a baby. I'm not taking no for an answer, Flight Lieutenant Beddoes.' She shot a meaningful look in Miranda's direction. 'Keep an eye on this bloke. Don't let him out of your sight. He's in the chair and you're coming with us. I'm not having you moping about Raif Carstairs. If he's bought it, he's no great loss. That's my opinion and I'm sticking to it.' She winked and with a mock salute left the room.

'She's like a whirlwind when she gets going.' Jack sighed and rubbed his hand across his eyes. 'I'm not good company these days, and to be honest I'd much rather get my head down for a few hours.'

Miranda rose from her seat and snatched her cap from the coat stand. She put it on, checking her appearance in a mirror placed strategically on top of the filing cabinet. 'I understand how you feel, but I wouldn't refuse if I were you. She's quite capable of turning up at your digs and dragging you out of bed.'

'I don't think I'd have done if she hadn't taken

368

me in hand. She seems to sense when I'm feeling low and she pops up like the genie from Aladdin's lamp. I think I'd have slit my throat after Izzie died if it hadn't been for Rita.'

'She's got your best interests at heart. She might be an unlikely guardian angel, but you can rely on her to be there when you need a shoulder to cry on.'

His lips curved in a smile. 'She's certainly changed a lot since you first brought her to Highcliffe. You'd never think she was the same skinny little thing that Mother took in because old Mrs Proffitt was in hospital.'

'Practically the first thing she told me was that she wanted to be a pin-up girl and have her photos in glossy magazines. Now she's mending bicycles and wearing greasy overalls. She's still a stunner, only now she doesn't think about it.'

'Yes,' he said slowly. 'I suppose she is. It's funny but I've never really thought about Rita as anything but a kid and a bit of a pest.'

'Let's go wait for her in the pub. We can raise a glass to Raif. There's still a chance he might turn up, isn't there?' Her voice broke and Jack slipped his arm around her shoulders.

'We'll just have to hope he managed to bail out, even though there weren't any reports of parachute sightings over the Channel.'

'He might have managed to land somewhere. I'm not going to give up on him yet.'

'That's the ticket.' Jack kissed her on the cheek and went to open the door. 'Come on then. Let's go to the pub.'

Miranda took her cap from its peg. 'I miss

being in the plotting room, Jack. At least we were in the thick of it and knew what was happening. Except that I wasn't on duty when Gil was shot down, and I had the news second-hand. I'm not sure how I would have handled it if I'd been listening to his Mayday over the tannoy.' She shot a sideways glance at Jack but he seemed lost in his own thoughts.

'I can't say I liked Raif, and we never saw eye to eye.' He raised his head to look her in the eyes. 'But we both loved Izzie.'

It was obvious that he had not heard a word she had said, but she knew that he was thinking of Izzie and she gave him an encouraging smile. 'We'll drink to them both, unless Rita's got her own ideas about that as well as everything else.'

'I've never met such a stubborn, hard-headed woman in my whole life, except perhaps my own mother.' He ushered Miranda out of the office.

'I don't think either of them would be flattered by the comparison,' she said, chuckling.

After several months when there was no news as to Raif's fate everyone, except Miranda, seemed to have accepted the fact that he had been killed in action and that his Spitfire was at the bottom of the English Channel. It was yet another tragic loss but life at the aerodrome went on as usual. Casualties and deaths occurred with virtually every sortie, and the Luftwaffe was relentless in its attempts to bomb the RAF into submission and destroy the military airfields.

When she was not working Miranda kept herself busy cleaning the castle and attempting to make it more homely, or attempting to cook on the antiquated range and make tasty meals out of their sparse rations. She visited Gil as often as possible, although her days off were few and far between. His progress was slow, but eventually his plasters were removed and replaced by bandages and splints. He was determined to walk again and his hero was Douglas Bader. He had a photograph of him pinned on the wall in his room, together with one of his mother and Felicity. He hastened to reassure Miranda that he had her photo tucked away in his wallet.

'It's not that I don't want Mother to know that we're seeing more of each other,' he explained during one of Miranda's visits. 'But I don't want her to start interfering when you and I are just getting to know each other.' He reached out to hold Miranda's hand. 'We'll tell her when it suits both of us. I can stand up to her, but I'd rather do it when I'm on my feet than laid up in hospital. When Mother gets a bee in her bonnet she's hard to convince otherwise.'

'I know someone else like that,' Miranda said, smiling. 'I think your mother and my grandmother would make a good pair.'

Gil gazed down at their entwined fingers. 'I don't want to scare you off, Miranda. Seeing you has been the one thing that's kept me from giving up entirely, but you don't owe me anything. I wouldn't want to tie you to a cripple, and I'm not made of glass. I won't splinter into shards if you tell me you've had enough.'

'Shut up, Gil.' She leaned over to brush his lips with a kiss. 'I come because I want to see you and

I don't care who knows it.'

'Just so long as you realise that I won't hold you to anything.' He released her hand with a guilty start as a nurse entered the room. 'Don't tell me it's that time already.'

'It is indeed, Flight Lieutenant Maddern.'

Miranda rose to her feet. 'I'd better go, but I'll be back, Gil, and that's a promise.'

With the approach of autumn and the prospect of harsh winter weather looming ahead, Viv and Joan decided one day that the roof repairs could wait no longer. As there was nobody they could call upon to help, they opted to try their hand at thatching. Joan said that she had a good head for heights and she had been brought up on a farm in East Anglia where she had seen thatchers at work. She was confident that she could do just as well, but when she slipped off the ladder and tumbled several feet to the ground there was a moment of panic. She lay groaning in agony, with her right arm bent beneath her and a large bruise on her forehead.

'You silly cow,' Viv said crossly. 'I told you it was dangerous.'

'My arm,' Joan murmured, closing her eyes. 'I think it's broken.'

'We ought to get her indoors,' Rita said, frowning. 'It's going to rain any minute.'

Miranda shook her head. 'We mustn't move her. She might have hurt her back. You'll have to cycle to the aerodrome, Rita. She needs an ambulance.'

'If only we had a telephone.' Viv stared anxiously

at Joan. 'They'd have a phone at the railway station, wouldn't they?'

'Yes, but the aerodrome would be our best bet. I'll be as quick as I can.' Rita rushed off to the lean-to where they kept their bicycles and without stopping to get a coat or hat she leapt on the saddle and pedalled off.

Viv clutched her hand to her mouth. 'I feel sick.'

'Don't think about it,' Miranda said hastily. 'Go indoors and get a blanket. She should be kept warm or she might go into shock.'

Joan moaned even louder and Viv raced off, disappearing around the corner of the building. Miranda knelt down on the concrete path. 'You'll be okay. Hang on, Joan.'

It seemed like an eternity as they waited for the ambulance to arrive but they made Joan as comfortable as possible, and Viv insisted on making a pot of tea. Miranda said that Joan ought not to have anything to drink in case she had to be anaesthetised when she reached the hospital. On hearing this Joan started to sob, but Miranda managed to calm her down and Viv drank the tea.

Eventually Rita came clattering round the side of the house, flushed and breathless but obviously very pleased about something. 'Guess who's driving the ambulance, Manda?'

'I haven't the faintest idea. Is it here?'

'They're just getting the stretcher out. It's old Toopy. He's a medic now. Would you believe that?'

Miranda could not have cared less if the devil himself was driving the vehicle if it would bring relief to Joan, who was looking alarmingly pale

and, even more frightening, had stopped complaining.

Tommy was calm and professional as he
examined her. He chatted cheerfully as if it were
the most natural thing in the world to be dealing
with a young woman who had fallen off a roof,
and he gave her something to ease the pain before
he and his colleague lifted her onto the stretcher.

'Well done, Tommy,' Miranda said as she followed them round to where the ambulance was
parked in the lane. 'But why did they send you?
You're stationed at Bovington, aren't you? I was
expecting the local ambulance to come.'

'We were the nearest and the best.' He grinned
down at her. 'Anyway, the others were all out on
emergencies and we happened to be available.'

'I'm so glad you were. Poor Joan took a terrible
tumble.'

'She'll be okay.'

'You've surprised me, Tommy. I didn't think
you had it in you.'

He puffed out his chest. 'I've found my calling.
When the war's over I'm going to be a civilian
ambulance driver.' He leaned over to pat Joan on
the shoulder. 'All right, love. We'll get you fixed
up in no time. Hold tight.'

Miranda stood back as they manoeuvred the
stretcher into the vehicle. She looked round to
see if Viv or Rita wanted to go with Joan but they
were nowhere in sight. 'I'll come with you, if
that's all right, Tommy.'

'That's okay. Hop in.'

Joan had fractured her arm and would be out of

action for several weeks until her broken bones knitted together, and this left them short-handed in the repair shop. Miranda found herself promoted or demoted, whichever way she chose to look at it, to take over Joan's work. It had been Rita's idea, of course. Rita was always at the forefront when it came to organising the people around her. She knew that Miranda hated clerical work with a passion, and she had somehow manipulated their section leader into thinking that to move Miranda to the repair shop had been her decision. Miranda for her part did not argue. Anything, she thought, would be better than filing and filling out requisitions all day, and she did not mind getting her hands dirty. It was all a means to an end, and even when Joan was fit to return to duty after Christmas, Miranda opted to stay where she was and Joan was given clerical duties.

Whenever she had some free time Miranda cycled to Highcliffe. Dickens seemed to sense her imminent arrival and he would amble somewhat arthritically along the garden path to greet her, arching his back and purring loudly as he nuzzled her hand when she bent down to stroke him. She felt a sense of calm descending upon her as she gazed up at the old house. It was as ugly as ever and its paint might be peeling and its brickwork needed pointing, but it was still standing alone and defiant on the cliff top as if offering a challenge to the enemy.

She had the comfort of knowing that despite the traumas of war, nothing much would have changed at home. Her grandparents, with characteristic stoicism, were still doing their bit for the war effort. Her grandfather was still heavily involved in the Home Guard, and despite his advancing years he was a fine figure of a man. Miranda thought how distinguished he looked in uniform, and when he enveloped her in a great bear hug she felt like a child again, safe and secure. The clean spicy scent of him lingered long after they parted and she knew that this was how she would always remember him, even when she was an old woman, if she survived that long. She tried not to think too far into the future and took comfort from her time spent with her grandmother, timing her visits so that she caught her in between shifts at the WVS canteen.

On one such visit they had been sitting on the veranda enjoying the spring sunshine when the sky clouded over and a cool breeze tugged at their clothes and hair. Maggie shivered. 'Let's go indoors.' She stood up, displacing Dickens who had been snoozing on her lap. He gave her a baleful look and leapt back on the seat, curling his tail around himself and closing his eyes. 'Stubborn animal,' Maggie said fondly. She opened the French windows. 'Come inside, Miranda. We'll have tea before you go back to your wretched hovel.'

Miranda followed her indoors. 'Is Dickens all right out there, Granny? I mean he's getting old now.'

'Aren't we all?' Maggie moved to an armchair and sat down. 'We'll have some cake if there's any left. I've been entertaining some of the young American soldiers who are stationed close to town. They're good company, but they eat us out of house and home.'

'There are Americans at Warmwell too.'

'They're charming boys and so far from their homeland. I feel the least I can do is invite some of them to Sunday lunch every week.'

'That's very kind of you, Granny.'

'They don't seem to mind what they eat, even if it's only meat loaf or Woolton pie. Or perhaps they're simply too polite to complain. Annie grumbles, of course, but they sweet-talk her and she absolutely loves it. I'll really miss them when they eventually return home.' She glanced at the clock on the mantelpiece. 'Will you go and see what's keeping Annie? She should have brought the tea tray by now. I'm afraid she's getting quite slow these days, but then we're all getting older.'

Miranda leaned over the chair and kissed her grandmother's lined cheek. 'You'll never be old, Granny. You'll live to be a hundred and still be beautiful.'

'Flatterer.' Maggie shooed her away, but she was smiling.

Miranda found Annie sitting at the kitchen table. She gave a guilty start as the door opened, covering whatever it was she had been munching with her hands. She relaxed visibly when she saw Miranda. 'I thought it was Mrs B,' she said, lifting her hand to reveal a Hershey bar. 'The American GIs give them to me, only your gran doesn't approve. She says I shouldn't take things from them when it's their rations.'

'I wouldn't worry about that, Annie. I'm sure they can spare a bar of chocolate or two. Anyway, if you refused it might offend them.'

'Quite right.' Annie stuffed the last piece of chocolate into her mouth, chewed and swallowed. 'I have to eat them here because Elzevir has a sweet tooth. If I took them home that would be the last I ever saw of my candy.' She licked her lips, smiling. 'That's what the Yankees call it. They don't say sweets like we do.'

'Granny sent me to remind you about tea.'

'They're such polite young men, Miranda. They thank me very nicely and call me ma'am. One of them gave me some nylon stockings as well as the chocolate. Not that I wear such things; lisle is quite good enough for me. I gave them to my young niece.'

'And I'm sure she was very pleased,' Miranda said patiently. 'Shall I put the kettle on, or will you?'

Annie inclined her head graciously. 'I'll do it. You're a guest, Miranda. Go and chat to Mrs B and think yourself lucky that there aren't any of her rocks to eat. What with rationing and feeding the whole of the American army, we don't get a chance to eat cake ourselves.'

'But you have your Hershey bars,' Miranda said, chuckling. 'Don't worry. I won't tell Granny.' She left Annie to make the tea and made her way back to the drawing room.

'What are you grinning at?' Maggie demanded. 'Where's my tea?'

'It's coming. Annie was just waiting for the kettle to boil.' Avoiding her grandmother's suspicious gaze, Miranda resumed her seat.

'She's up to something, Miranda. That woman

will be the death of me.'

'You don't mean that, Granny. You'd be lost without her.'

'Hmm.' Maggie tossed her head. 'I doubt that. Anyway, tell me about that young man of yours. Mad Bull, or whatever he's called.'

'His call sign was Mad Dog, and his name is Gilbert Maddern – Gil for short.'

'Well, dear, no one's perfect. Anyway, how is he? Is his mother still playing up? I could always have a word with her.'

'I think she's rather given up, Granny. I visit Gil in the hospital whenever I can, and we write to each other almost every day. He's doing very well now and the doctors say he'll walk again.'

'I like the sound of him much better than Raif Carstairs.'

'He's still missing and I don't think there's much hope of ever finding out what happened to him.' Miranda stared down at her tightly clasped hands.

'It's just as well, Miranda. Raif was too much like his father. Max Carstairs nearly wrecked my life and I wouldn't want to see history repeating itself.'

'It won't, Granny.'

'I should hope not. It's bad enough knowing that your mother is risking hers by spying on the Germans without you falling for someone who would break your heart.'

'I haven't heard anything from Maman,' Miranda said, biting her lip. 'I try not to think about the awful risks she's taking in France. I wish I could talk to someone in authority and find out if she's safe.'

Maggie took a hanky from her pocket and handed it to her. 'Don't start blubbing, Miranda. You'll start me off.'

Miranda dabbed her eyes. 'Sorry.'

'And don't apologise. Actually there is some news of her. Your grandfather has been in touch with an old army chum in the War Office.'

'What did he say?' Miranda leapt to her feet. 'Why didn't you tell me sooner?'

'I didn't want to raise your hopes in case it all went terribly wrong. Apparently she's been in Paris all this time, but now there's talk about bringing her home.'

'But that's wonderful.'

Maggie shook her head, frowning. 'It is, of course, but she isn't out of danger yet. Your grandfather didn't want me to tell you until we were absolutely certain, and now I wish I'd kept my mouth shut.'

'I'm not a little girl now, Granny. I'm very glad you told me. I was beginning to think I'd never see her again, but you've given me fresh hope.' Miranda glanced over her shoulder as the door was pushed open and Annie marched in carrying a tray of tea. 'Have you heard the news, Annie? My mother is coming home.'

'That's nice.' Annie placed the tray on the table near Maggie's chair. 'I found some biscuits at the bottom of the tin.'

Maggie glared at her. 'You've been eating chocolate. It's all round your mouth.'

'So what?' Annie demanded, wiping her hand across her lips. 'It was given to me by that nice young private, Joe Wysocki. At least someone appreciates me.' She tossed her head and flounced out of the room, slamming the door behind her.

'One day she'll go too far,' Maggie said, reaching for a biscuit. 'She knows I like chocolate.'

Miranda smiled to herself as she sat down to pour the tea. Nothing ever changed at Highcliffe.

An hour later she rode back to Warmwell feeling much happier than she had for a long time. It was dark when she arrived at the castle and there was an army ambulance parked in the yard. She did not think anything of it as she stowed her bicycle in the lean-to as Tommy had taken to visiting on a regular basis. She had thought at first that he had renewed his interest in Rita, but then she realised that it was Joan who had caught his eye, and that the feeling was mutual. Viv and Rita teased them mercilessly but Tommy parried their comments with his usual good humour, and Joan simply shrugged and told them to mind their own business.

Miranda hurried inside, shutting the door to keep to the strict blackout regulations that applied even in such an isolated spot. She had been about to tell them her good news but everyone had stopped talking. 'What's the matter?' she demanded. 'Why are you all staring at me?'

Rita stood up hastily and pulled out her chair. 'We've been waiting for you to come home. I think you'd better sit down.'

Chapter Twenty-Two

Miranda found that her legs had turned to jelly and she slumped onto the hard wooden seat. 'What's happened? For heaven's sake tell me.'

'Don't panic,' Rita said, patting her on the shoulder. 'It's good news.'

Miranda waited for someone to elaborate but there was a sudden silence. She looked from Joan to Viv and back to Tommy. 'What?'

'Stop shilly-shallying about, Rita,' Joan said impatiently. 'It's quite simple. Raif Carstairs ditched in the Channel and was picked up by the Germans. He's been a prisoner of war all this time, but the news has only just filtered through to us here.'

Miranda frowned as she struggled to come to terms with the fact that Raif had survived. 'I suppose his father must have known. How typical that he didn't choose to share it with Jack and me. That man is unbelievable.' She glanced round at their anxious faces. 'Was there any more information?'

'We don't know what sort of shape he's in,' Rita said cautiously. 'But he's alive and that's the main thing.'

'Well, it is good news.' Miranda managed a smile. 'But you frightened the life out of me. I don't think I could stand many more shocks today.'

'What's happened?' Rita demanded. 'Mad Dog hasn't had a sudden relapse, has he?'

Miranda took a deep breath, hoping that she was not going to let herself down and burst into tears of happiness. 'My mother might be coming home soon. I only found out this afternoon.'

A cheer went round the table and Tommy reached across Joan to grasp Miranda's hand. 'That's good news.'

'She's gone a bit pale,' Viv said, eyeing Miranda warily. 'Is there any booze left in the bottle? She looks as though she could do with something to buck her up.'

Rita went to the mantelpiece. 'Some blighter's drunk the last little drop. Who's the guilty party?'

Miranda started to laugh and found that she could not stop.

'She's hysterical.' Viv leapt to her feet. 'Shall I slap her?'

'Put the kettle on,' Tommy said hastily.

She glared at him. 'What good will that do?'

'It'll stop you from slapping her for a start.' Tommy put her arm around Joan's shoulders. 'Are you all right, love? You're very quiet.'

Joan shook her head. 'I'm fine, but Miranda's in a state of shock. That's your department, Tommy. You're the medic.'

Miranda took several deep breaths. 'I'm okay now. I'm sorry, but it was one thing coming on top of another. I suppose we've all got used to expecting the worst and now the end of the war's in sight it seems almost too good to be true.'

'Tell you what,' Rita said, taking her coat from its peg. 'Let's all go to the pub. Jack said he'd meet us there if Miranda got back in time. I'm sure we all need something stronger than tea.'

Everyone was chatting over drinks at the bar, but Jack drew Miranda aside. 'How do you feel about Raif? I know it's none of my business, but you're my niece and I'm very fond of you. I wouldn't want to see you hurt.'

She swallowed a mouthful of cider, almost choking on her drink. 'I might have fancied him once, but not now.'

He nodded but his expression was serious. 'I'm glad to hear it. He might be Izzie's brother but he's too much like Max for his own good.'

'I think you're being a bit hard on him. It's not fair to put Raif in the same category as his father.'

'Maybe not, but I'm glad that you've escaped the fatal Carstairs charm. It almost wrecked my parents' marriage and very nearly stopped Izzie from marrying me. I wouldn't want the same thing to happen to you.'

'I love you, Uncle Jack,' Miranda said, smiling and stressing the word uncle. 'So don't take it the wrong way if I tell you to mind your own business.'

'I suppose I deserved that, but you know I'm only thinking of your own good.'

She drained the last drop of cider from her glass and held it out to him. 'Buy me the other half and we'll forget all about it.'

Although the story of Raif's survival was the main topic of conversation in the workshop next day, Miranda was aware that the girls were deliberately avoiding the subject in her presence. She was at first puzzled and then resentful. When she overheard a scrap of conversation between Viv and Rita during their tea break and his name was mentioned, she had simply had enough. 'What's the matter with you all?' she demanded angrily. 'Don't stop talking about him just because I'm here.'

'It's not like that.' Viv's cheeks flushed scarlet and she glanced helplessly at Rita.

'We were just saying that he had a lucky escape,' Rita said defensively.

'So why stop when you saw me coming? Everyone's talking about him in whispers.'

Rita thumped her enamel mug down on the workbench. 'Because we all knew you had a thing for him, Miranda. Don't deny it. I was there when you first met. Remember?'

'But that was years ago. It was a crush, that's all.'

'One you never quite got over.'

'That's nonsense. You all know that I've been seeing Gil.'

Viv backed away. 'I'll leave you two to fight it out. It's got nothing to do with me.'

Miranda caught her by the sleeve. 'No, you don't, Viv. Let's sort this out once and for all. I am not interested in Raif Carstairs romantically or in any other way. I might have been once, but not now. I'm in love with Gil.' She recoiled, clapping her hand to her mouth. 'I don't believe I just said that.'

A slow smile curved Rita's lips. 'At last.' She turned to Viv, nodding her head. 'Isn't that what

we were saying before Miranda started eaves-
dropping?'

Viv nodded energetically. 'Yes. That's right.'

'And you've finally admitted your feelings for
Gil,' Rita said smugly.

'It just came out.' Miranda felt her cheeks
burning. 'I didn't mean it.'

'You're seeing him next week on your day off,
aren't you?' Rita said slyly. 'That should be in-
teresting.' She nudged Viv. 'I'd love to be a fly on
the wall then, wouldn't you?'

Miranda caught an earlier train than she had
intended to and when she reached Southampton
she took a taxi to the sale rooms. She had spent
several sleepless nights thinking things through
and had decided that she could not go on playing
a cat and mouse game with Gil's mother. Fliss
might be on her side, but she was now living in
the nurses' home and her time was taken up with
work and study. Miranda also suspected that Fliss
had more than a professional interest in Captain
Forbes, and although she was sympathetic, her
mind was on other things.

After much soul searching, Miranda had decided that it would be best to turn up unannounced. She had telephoned the office the
previous day in order to check that Mrs Maddern
would be taking the sale, and so far everything was
going to plan. She paid the cabby and braced
herself for her encounter with the woman who had
the power to spoil everything. She was under no
illusion as to Gil's feelings for his mother, and the
last thing she wanted was to put him in a position

386

where he was forced to choose between them. Bracing her shoulders, she went inside.

The office door was ajar and she could see Daphne Maddern sitting behind her desk with her immaculately coiffed head bent over what looked like a sale catalogue. Miranda was suddenly nervous. Everything depended on the outcome of her confrontation with the most important woman in Gil's life. Taking a deep breath, she tapped on the door and entered without waiting for a response.

Daphne raised her head and her expression hardened. 'What can I do for you, Miss Beddoes?' Her tone was icy.

Miranda took a seat in a buttoned leather chair. She chose to sit rather than stand so that their heads were more or less on a level and she could look Mrs Maddern in the eye. 'I think it's time we had a talk.'

Daphne closed the catalogue with a decisive snap. 'I don't think there's anything I have to say to you.'

'Maybe not, but I have a great deal to say to you.'

'I'd prefer it if you left now.'

'I'm sure you can spare me a few minutes when it's your son's future in the balance.'

Daphne threw back her head and laughed. 'Oh, please. Don't be so dramatic. Gil is doing very well without you.'

'And have you asked yourself why that is?'

'He's receiving the best treatment available and he's determined to conquer his disabilities. Gil is a very special person.'

387

'I couldn't agree more. I've got to know him really well while he's been in hospital. We've corresponded regularly and I've visited him as often as possible.'

'He didn't tell me that.'

'Gil loves you and that will never change, so don't make him choose between us.'

'I don't know what you're talking about. Gil would never go behind my back.'

'Ask Fliss if you don't believe me.' Miranda rose to her feet. 'I love your son and I believe that he loves me.'

'You mean you've come here to boast about a relationship that exists only in your imagination?'

'No. Gil was too honourable to tell me he loved me when he thought that he'd be confined to a wheelchair for the rest of his life, but even if that were the case it wouldn't make the slightest bit of difference to me.'

'The doctors say that he'll walk again,' Daphne said slowly. 'His rehabilitation will take time and even then he'll never be fit enough to fly. Are you telling me that you would be happy to spend your life with a disabled husband?'

'I've been a long time admitting it to myself, but I love him for the wonderful person he is. Nothing else matters.'

Daphne leaned back in her chair, staring at Miranda. It was hard to imagine what she was thinking but Miranda gave her look for look. She would not be the first to turn away. The silence between them stretched into infinity but was broken by one of the porters who stuck his head round the door, clearing his throat. 'Excuse me,

Mrs Maddern, but the sale is due to start in ten minutes.'

'I'll be there.' Daphne dismissed him with an imperious wave of her hand. She waited until the door was closed before rising from her chair. She walked round the desk, coming to a halt in front of Miranda. Her expression softened. 'Do you know, I think I believe you? You've certainly got sticking power and you've got a nerve coming here to face me.'

Miranda inclined her head. 'I won't disagree with that, but this is too important to me to do anything by halves. I don't want to sneak about as if I were doing something wrong.'

'That hasn't stopped you before.' A glimmer of humour lit Daphne's steel-blue eyes.

'No, but that was different. I'm a different person now – I've lost people I loved because of the war, including my father. I haven't seen my mother since she was sent to France to work under cover, and my uncle's young wife and unborn child were killed by a German bomb. All that's happened has made me think very hard about what's important. I've also come to realise that however much Gil cares for me, it would ruin our chances of making a future for ourselves if it made you unhappy.'

Daphne stared at her, frowning. 'I can't make out if you're sincere or merely trying to manipulate me for your own ends.'

'Do you really think I'd have come here today if I wasn't in earnest? I want everything you want for Gil. I'd do anything for him.'

'I think I might have misjudged you, Miranda.'

Daphne's eyes were bright with tears, but she held up her hands as Miranda made a tentative move towards her. 'I don't hug. Anyway, you'd crease my costume and I'll be going outside in a few minutes to take the sale.'

'And you don't mind if I continue to see Gil? Nothing is settled between us. He might have changed his mind for all I know.'

'I won't stand in your way.' Daphne moved to the door and opened it. 'Actually, I think I'd be quite disappointed now if it didn't work out between you. You've got courage and you know your own mind. Perhaps he needs someone like you.'

'Thank you.'

'And now I've really got to do my job.'

Miranda followed her out of the office and had to push past a queue of people waiting to take their seats for the auction. It was not until she was outside standing on the pavement that she realised she was shaking from head to foot. She leaned against the fascia until she had regained control of her limbs. Even then, as she waited for a bus to take her to the hospital, she could hardly believe that she had managed to win Daphne Maddern's trust. It had been a battle hard fought, but now she had won she would have to face Gil. He had tried to explain his feelings to her on numerous occasions but she had always managed to change the subject. It was not going to be easy to find a way to tell him that she had been a blind fool. It would be even harder to admit that a small part of her had been in love with Raif all along, and that news of his survival had somehow released her. If she could not understand the workings of her own emotions, how could she explain them to him?

She arrived at the hospital with butterflies in her stomach, feeling like a child waking up on Christmas morning expecting to find that Santa Claus had left a pile of presents on the end of the bed. It was something of a shock to find Gil's bed empty and neatly made up. There was no sign of him and for a moment she imagined that he had been stricken with a terrible affliction and had died in the night. Then commonsense reasserted itself and she realised that she was panicking for nothing. There must be some innocent explanation and allowing herself to fall apart was not going to help. She sat down, waiting for her pulses to stop racing, but almost immediately the door opened and she leapt to her feet again as Fliss helped Gil into the room. To Miranda's surprise and delight he was walking with the aid of crutches.

'Look at me, Miranda,' he said, grinning. 'I bet you never thought to see me on my feet again. I'd almost given up hope myself.'

'Isn't it marvellous?' Fliss guided him to the chair that Miranda had just vacated. 'He's surprised everyone by his rapid progress. However, it's very early days.' She took his crutches and leaned them against the wall. 'You mustn't overdo things, Gil.'

Miranda licked her dry lips and swallowed hard. 'I don't know what to say. It's absolutely fantastic.'

'I'll be flying my Hurricane again before you know it.' Gil reached out to hold her hand and his smile faded. 'What's the matter, Miranda? Aren't you pleased for me?'

The thought of Gil returning to active duty almost paralysed her with fear, but she could not tell him so. 'Of course I am,' she said, making an effort to sound enthusiastic. 'But the war's got to end soon, and they won't need fighter pilots.'

'I wouldn't bet on it. But whatever happens now I'm on the mend, and I'm going to get away from this place soon, even if I have to tunnel my way out.'

'You'll have to tie him to the bed if he doesn't do as he's told,' Miranda said, turning to Fliss with an anxious smile.

Gil chuckled. 'That has different connotations now, girls.'

'Don't be naughty, Gil.' Fliss frowned at him, but her lips twitched. 'Anyway, I'll leave you two to have a chat. I've got other patients to look after and some of them are really sick, not malingering like you, brother dear.' She bustled out of the room.

'She's all starch and bossy as hell,' Gil said fondly. 'I never thought my big sister would become an angel of mercy.'

Miranda withdrew her hand gently. 'Actually, I came to tell you something, Gil.' She pulled up a chair and sat down beside him.

'That sounds ominous.'

'I've been wrong about so many things, Gil. I don't quite know where to start.'

'I told you once you'd make a rotten poker player.' His smile faded. 'I can tell by your face that it's something important.'

392

'It's me. I've been a complete idiot.' She took a deep breath. 'You remember I told you that Raif had been killed?'

He eyed her warily. 'Yes, of course.'

'Well, he's not dead. He's been a prisoner of war all this time. When I heard about it something seemed to click in my brain. Everything's different now, Gil. I don't know how to put this but...'

He held up his hand. 'It's all right, Miranda. You told me on our first date that you'd had a thing for Raif Carstairs since you first met him.'

'That was then, Gil. Things are quite different now.'

'Yes,' he said gently. 'They are and I won't hold you to anything. You've been absolutely marvellous, and I don't think I could have kept going if you hadn't written those wonderfully funny and charming letters. I've lived for your visits, but we've got to be realistic.'

She shuddered, chilled to the bone by his words. 'No, you really don't understand.'

He took her hand in his and squeezed it. 'You don't have to break it gently. I'd be a complete ass if I thought that things would work out between us now.'

'I don't know what you mean.' Miranda felt that she was sinking in quicksand and the more she tried to explain her feelings the deeper she sank. If she could not make him understand, she would drown.

'Let's be practical. I've still got a long way to go before I'm back to something close to normal, if ever. What I said about flying again was balderdash. I'm held together with nuts and bolts and

393

bits of wire.'

'That doesn't matter to me, Gil.'

'I wouldn't want to tie you to a semi-invalid. You deserve better, my darling.'

'But I love you, Gil.'

He was silent for a moment, looking deeply into her eyes, and then he shook his head. 'Don't mistake pity for love, Miranda. If you'd said that to me before all this happened I'd have been the happiest man in the world, but I wouldn't want you to stay because you were sorry for me, especially when I know there's someone else in the background.'

She snatched her hand away. 'How can you be so stupid? I don't want Raif, I want you. How can I make you believe me?'

'What's going on?' Fliss erupted into the room. 'I could hear you from down the corridor.'

'He won't listen to me.' Miranda leapt to her feet. 'Your brother is a stubborn idiot.'

'You should go,' Fliss said, frowning. 'You need to calm down; you're upsetting him.'

Miranda dashed her hand across her eyes. 'I am calm. It's Gil who's being difficult.'

He had paled alarmingly and as he made an unsuccessful attempt to stand Fliss abandoned Miranda and hurried to his side. 'I don't know what's gone on between you two but this isn't doing him any good. Please leave now, Miranda.'

She hesitated in the doorway. 'Gil?'

He leaned back in the chair, closing his eyes. 'Do as Fliss says, please.'

'All right, but I'll come again as soon as I get another day off.'

'Better not,' he said softly. 'Don't feel bad about it. I do understand.'

Fliss gazed down at her fob watch as she took his pulse. 'I'd better get Sister to take a look at you, Gil.' She turned a stony face to Miranda. 'I have no idea what this is all about but his pulse is racing.'

'I've simply been trying to tell him that I love him and I want to be with him.'

Fliss took her by the shoulders and ejected her from the room. 'Give him some time to get himself together, Miranda,' she said, moderating her tone. 'I'm not unsympathetic but I must put his needs first. He's still got a long way to go and he's being sent to a rehabilitation centre next week.'

'But I can't just leave things as they are.'

'I can't talk now. I'll let you know his new address and you can write to him.' Fliss hurried off, leaving Miranda staring after her. She wanted desperately to make things right with Gil but she could not risk upsetting him again, and, with the greatest reluctance, she left the hospital.

She had plenty of time to think during the journey home and she went over their conversation again and again in her mind, blaming herself entirely for her failure to convince Gil that she meant every word she had said. She had told him that she loved him but he had chosen to believe that she still harboured feelings for Raif. If only she had left those few lines out of her last letter to him. The words kept repeating in her head to the rhythm of the iron wheels going over the points, until she wanted to put her hands over her ears and scream. She had won the battle with his mother only to lose Gil over a stupid misunderstanding.

She stumbled off the train at the end of the line barely conscious of her movements. The only taxi had already been taken and she was forced to walk to the seafront to wait for a bus to take her back to Highcliffe. She was only dimly aware of the activity in the bay, which was packed with military vessels. The town was heaving with soldiers, both British and American, but she was oblivious to it all. She arrived home to find the front door wide open and she hurried inside. She hesitated, looking round and half expecting to see the doctor with his black Gladstone bag coming down the stairs, or a police officer manhandling a burglar, but all was quiet. She took off her hat and hung it on the hallstand but in the process she knocked over the umbrella stand. The sound echoed through the house, and as she picked it up she heard her grandmother's voice calling her name. 'If that's you, Miranda, we're in the drawing room. Come in here, darling. I've got a surprise for you.'

The sight that met her eyes as she entered the room completely took her breath away. She came to a sudden halt. 'Maman!'

Jeanne Beddoes crossed the floor to fling her arms around her daughter. 'Ma chère Miranda. I've missed you so much.'

'It really is you, Maman.' Miranda held her at arm's length, taking in her mother's changed appearance. She was thinner than before and lines of fatigue were etched on her fine features, but her dark eyes were bright with emotion and she was smiling.

'It's me all right,' Jeanne said, gazing at her fondly. 'But you've changed, Miranda. You were just a girl when I left and now you're a beautiful young woman.'

Miranda threw her arms around her mother, holding her as though she would never let her go. 'I thought I'd never see you again. I couldn't believe it when Granny told me you might be coming home.'

Jeanne stroked Miranda's hair back from her forehead. 'There were times when I thought I wouldn't make it, but I'm here now, chérie. I'll never leave you again, I promise.' She pulled a hanky from her pocket and dabbed her eyes.

'Don't get weepy,' Maggie said, rising from the sofa. 'You'll start us all off if you do, and this is a day for celebrations.' She turned to her husband who had been sitting quietly in his usual chair. 'George, surely we've got a bottle of something hidden away somewhere. We must celebrate.'

'I might have a tot of brandy in my study,' he said, rising from his seat by the open window. 'I'll have a look.'

'You could always ask Annie,' Maggie said with a wry smile. 'I'm sure she's got some cooking sherry tucked away in the pantry.'

'I'll see what I can do.' George said, making for the doorway. 'Perhaps I should get Annie in to share the moment.'

Maggie nodded emphatically. 'Of course.' She turned to Miranda. 'And how did it go with your young man?'

'What's all this about?' Jeanne asked, smiling. 'I've missed so much. You must tell me everything.'

'He sent me away. I couldn't make him understand.' The iron self-control that Miranda had been exerting since she left the hospital suddenly deserted her. Tears flooded down her cheeks and she sobbed against her mother's shoulder. 'First Dad and now Gil; they're both gone.'

'I'd better leave you to it, Jeanne.' Maggie headed for the doorway, almost colliding with her husband. She shooed him out of the room. 'Not now, George. Let's give them a bit of privacy. Time for celebrations later.'

Gradually and in between hiccuping sobs, Miranda managed to tell her mother everything. Jeanne held her hand, exerting a gentle pressure when needed and passing a clean hanky when Miranda's was too wet to absorb any more salty tears.

'I'm sorry,' Miranda said, wiping her eyes. 'I shouldn't be burdening you with my troubles when you've just arrived. God knows what you went through in France, and you must miss Dad terribly.'

'Of course I do, Miranda. He was the love of my life and I don't expect to find that again, but you mustn't apologise, chérie. I'm just glad to be here now and my story will wait. Anyway, tomorrow I've got to go up to London for a debriefing at the War Office, although it's just a formality.'

'And I've got to go back to the aerodrome.' Miranda moved to the mantelpiece and took down the photograph of her father. She held it out to her mother. 'I kept this safe for you.'

Jeanne's dark eyes filled with tears as she took the photo frame and she held it to her lips. 'Mon cher Ronnie, you will always be in my heart.'

Miranda cleared her throat. 'What will you do after the debriefing? Will you come back here?'

Jeanne shook her head. 'I've talked it through with your grandmother, Miranda. I need to stay in London for a while and find out what help we can get to rebuild the house, if that's at all possible. I'll stay with friends until everything is sorted and then I'll decide what to do.'

'I hadn't thought how people would manage after the war,' Miranda said thoughtfully. 'Although it's not over yet.'

'The Allies have liberated Rome, and judging by the number of ships and landing craft in the bay I think it's safe to say that something momentous is about to happen.'

'I know. The town was heaving with soldiers and the streets are lined with tanks, but I didn't give it much thought.'

'The end is in sight, chérie, and I think you should take the first opportunity to go and see your young man again. You need to put him straight on a few matters.' Jean subsided gracefully onto the sofa, still clutching the photograph of her late husband. 'He is the one, isn't he, Miranda? You aren't still harbouring feelings for Raif Carstairs?' She smiled ruefully. 'Your grandmother told me what's been going on in my absence. I can understand your dilemma.'

'I know my own mind. Why won't anyone believe me?' Miranda went to stand by the French windows, staring out at the incredible scene in the bay.

'You have to believe it yourself, ma chère. You're the only one who knows exactly how you feel, and you can't blame Gil for being worried when a man like Raif Carstairs is his rival.'

'You don't know Raif, Maman.'

'No, but I met his father once at a cocktail party in London. Now I know the full story I can understand how he managed to sweep Maggie off her feet, and if his son is anything like him, then I can see why you were so smitten. Sometimes it's hard to get over one's first love.'

'It was just a crush.'

'It's yourself you need to convince, chérie.'

Chapter Twenty-Three

Jeanne left for London next day and Miranda returned to Warmwell to find the aerodrome on full alert with all leave cancelled. No one knew exactly what was planned, but it was obviously going to be a major push to liberate France.

That night the incessant drone of planes filled the skies and next morning the airfield was deserted. The girls crowded round the wireless in the mess later that day to hear the news that the Allies had landed in France and beaten the Germans back, but the war was far from over.

Once again Miranda had to force herself to

settle into a daily routine, putting her personal problems aside. She had written to Gil in the hope of making him believe that she had been sincere in her feelings for him. She sent the letter to the address that Fliss had given her, but she had so far not received a reply. Rita was sympathetic but advised her to wait and be patient. 'Give him time to recuperate,' she said one night when she discovered Miranda downstairs in the kitchen in the early hours of the morning, drinking tea. She sat down at the table and poured a cup for herself. 'Give him a chance to get back on his feet, Manda.' She lit a cigarette in the flame of the paraffin lamp, inhaling deeply and blowing smoke rings into the beamed ceiling. 'How would you feel if you were a bloke and hardly able to totter around on your pins, and you thought that your girl was stuck on a handsome flyboy who was still in a POW camp? You'd be pretty sick about it, if you ask me.'

'I can barely remember what Raif looks like.'

'But Gil doesn't know that. He's like all men, he wants to sweep you off your feet and feel he's the only one in the world for you.' She flicked ash into the dying embers of the range. 'I know, because I've waited long enough for Jack to see me as a woman. Of course he'll never forget Izzie, but life goes on.'

Miranda stared at her in amazement. 'I always knew you liked him, but I didn't think it was anything serious.'

'Well, there you are,' Rita said triumphantly. 'You can't see what's beneath your nose.'

'So are you and Jack a couple now?'

Rita stubbed her cigarette out in the ashtray. 'Filthy habit. I've promised Jack that if he manages to stay alive, I'll give up smoking, and then we'll see.'

'You mean he's asked you to marry him?'

'You don't think it's too soon after Izzie's death, do you?'

Miranda leapt up to give her a hug. 'No, of course not. She adored Jack and she wouldn't have wanted him to mourn forever.'

'I was hoping you'd say that.'

'I've been so wrapped up in myself that I've been blind. I think it's wonderful and you're just what he needs. Have you set a date?'

Rita shook her head. 'Not yet. We'll have to join the queue. It'll be Tommy and Joan who tie the knot first, then me and Jack. It's up to you what happens next.'

Tommy and Joan were married in August 1944 with Viv, Rita and Miranda as bridesmaids. The reception for just a few close friends was held in the Frampton Arms. Rita was showing off a large diamond and sapphire engagement ring, and Viv had a burly army sergeant in tow. Miranda was very conscious that she was the only one without a partner, but she was determined not to allow her personal feelings to spoil Joan's big day.

She had continued to write to Gil but he had not replied to any of her letters, and although Fliss wrote occasionally her scribbled notes were brief and contained very little information other than the fact that she was engaged to Robert Forbes. She said that Gil was progressing quite well and

Miranda had to be content with that. She had thought about visiting him at the convalescent home, but it was not simply pride that held her back. She was afraid he might have met someone else during their long months of separation. After all, Captain Forbes had fallen in love with Fliss, and Gil would have been surrounded by attractive young women who tended to his every need. Miranda had never felt so helpless or so completely alone.

Jack and Rita were married in the local church at the beginning of May and once again Miranda and Viv were bridesmaids. Joan was heavily pregnant and had declined Rita's invitation to act as matron of honour, saying with a wry smile that it would take a mile of parachute silk to make a dress that would fit her and she would still look like a Zeppelin. She attended the service but stole the limelight at the reception in the church hall by going into labour. Tommy had to rush her to hospital, where she gave birth to twin boys.

Rita and Jack spent their one night honeymoon in a hotel on Weymouth seafront, and Rita returned to work the next day. She found Miranda in the workshop mending a puncture. 'Fancy having to come back to this dump,' she said, pulling a face. 'Especially when I'm supposed to be the blushing bride.'

Miranda cast a sideways glance in her direction. 'You've never blushed in your life, Rita Platt, I mean Mrs Beddoes.'

'Doesn't that sound lovely?' Rita gazed into a fly-blown mirror above the workbench. 'We'll

403

have a proper honeymoon when it's all over,' she said, grinning broadly. 'It's not as if it was our first time.'

Miranda held up her hand. 'I really didn't need to know that, thanks.'

'It's about time you stopped being a vestal virgin, Manda. Have you done anything about seeing Gil? He must be well and truly on the mend by now, or have you given up?'

'No, I haven't given up as you put it. I had a letter from Fliss yesterday as it happens. She told me that Gil expects to be allowed home quite soon. He's going to work for the family firm as soon as he gets his discharge from the RAF.'

'So what are you going to do about it?'

Miranda shrugged her shoulders. 'I don't know. It's been a long time since I last saw him and he hasn't bothered to answer my letters. Maybe he was trying to tell me that his feelings had changed, but didn't know how to break it to me.'

'And you're an idiot if you believe that.'

'Shut up, Auntie Rita.'

'Oo-er,' Rita said, chuckling. 'I hadn't thought about being your aunt, but as I am you'd better pay attention to me, my girl.'

Miranda stuck her tongue out and walked over to the bicycle with the tyre slung over her shoulder.

'Oh, very adult,' Rita called after her. 'I'll have to report you to your uncle.'

Miranda came to a halt as Viv raced into the workshop. 'It's over, girls. The bloody war's over. I just heard it on the wireless in the mess.'

The news took some assimilating at first. After

404

more than five years it seemed almost impossible that the conflict in Europe was at an end. Miranda, Viv and Rita were demobbed relatively quickly as their services were no longer needed, and Joan was already a full-time housewife and mother. Tommy had found them a cottage in one of the outlying villages and he was just waiting for his papers so that he could apply for a job as an ambulance man. Jack and Rita had moved into Highcliffe until they could find a more permanent home, although Jack had to travel daily to the aerodrome while he waited for his demob to come through.

Miranda was under pressure to move back to London and live with her mother, who had rented a small flat in Chelsea until the rebuilding of their house in Woodford was completed. Jeanne had returned to the War Office with promotion and a considerably higher salary. She suggested that Miranda might apply for the job of copy typist in her department, but Miranda could not see herself settling down to work in an office. She was no longer the carefree young girl who had left London at the beginning of the war. She had changed and nothing was the same. There was no going back for her, but she could not see the way forward. She left the castle and all its memories, closing the door on that part of her life, and returned to Highcliffe.

Her grandparents were delighted to welcome her home, but they were busy all day and Rita spent most of her time house hunting, which left Miranda alone with Annie and Dickens, neither of whom had much in the way of conversation.

Annie's main topics were rationing and Elzevir, who was always doing something to upset her. Miranda knew she ought to be looking for work, but she could not settle down to anything. She spent her days helping about the house and in the garden.

She was busy weeding the vegetable bed one morning in preparation for planting lettuce seed when she heard a footstep on the gravel path. She looked up and saw Jack coming towards her. 'Hello. Why aren't you at work?'

'You haven't heard, have you?'

'What haven't I heard?'

'He's home. Raif arrived back at Thornleigh Court yesterday.'

Miranda scrambled to her feet. 'Are you sure?'

'Absolutely certain. It was in the local paper.'

'Then it must be true.'

'I've got the rest of the day off and I'm going to see him. I feel it's only right that I should tell him about Rita and me before he hears it from someone else. I know he cared a lot for Izzie and I don't want him to think I've betrayed her memory.'

'I suppose that's the right thing to do, but why are you telling me all this?'

'I'd like you to come with me, Miranda. Just for moral support, of course.'

She was going to refuse, but she knew she must face Raif at some point. 'Okay, if you really want me to.'

They drove to Thornleigh in the newly resurrected Chloe. The house had survived, even though the parkland had been ploughed up to

406

grow crops and the American army had requisitioned it as a base for the duration. They had left now, with only the marks of caterpillar tyres scarring the ground to bear witness to their occupation of the old house.

Miranda was suddenly nervous as Mrs Beasley showed them out onto the terrace, but Raif greeted them civilly enough, and Jack did all the talking. She was free to observe Raif closely and she could see a change in him that went deeper than the pallor of his skin and the gauntness of his face. He seemed to have retreated to an inner world where no one and nothing could intrude upon his deepest thoughts. He listened politely to everything Jack said, but his lean fingers drummed incessantly on the wrought-iron table and he seemed ill at ease.

'So you don't mind that I've remarried,' Jack said as he finished his carefully prepared speech. 'You don't think it's too soon?'

Raif shook his head. 'One thing I've learned in all this is that life goes on, if you're lucky. You have to do what is best for you.'

'What about you, Raif?' Miranda said softly. 'Have you any plans for the future?'

He flicked a sideways glance at her but he did not look her directly in the eye. 'It's early days, but I think I might just stay here and manage the estate. Our chap bought it at El Alamein and the place has gone to rack and ruin during the war.'

'I never thought of you as a farmer,' Miranda said, smiling.

'Nothing is the same now.' Raif raised himself from his seat, holding out his hand. 'Thanks for coming to see me, Beddoes. I don't suppose we'll meet very often, but I think we should put the past behind us. My father has retired and he and Mother are going to live in the States.'

Jack stood up and shook his hand. 'You're right. It's time that peace was declared between the Carstairs and the Beddoes clans.'

Raif turned to Miranda, meeting her gaze with a shadow of a smile. 'Goodbye and good luck, Miranda. Grab any chance you get for happiness.' He turned and walked into the house, leaving them staring after him.

She rose to her feet. 'What was all that about?'

'I think it was his way of ending a chapter in his life and yours.'

'Is that why you brought me here today?'

'Blame Rita. It was her idea.'

'I'll have something to say to her when I see her again.'

'Thank you would be good. She's done you a favour, because I don't think there ever was anything serious between you and Raif. It was a bit of a romantic myth – Capulets and Montagues and all that rot. Mother's affair with Max made it all seem inevitable, but it wasn't.'

Miranda smiled as she followed him towards the car, which was parked outside the main entrance. 'You've grown quite wise in your old age, Jack.'

He stopped and waited for her to catch up, linking her hand through his arm. 'And you'll take the first opportunity to go to that convalescent home and knock some sense into your chap's head.'

'I will,' she said meekly. 'I'll be on the first train

tomorrow morning.'

'I've been saving my petrol ration for just such an important occasion. I'll drive you there myself. We'll pick Rita up first and be on our way before you have second thoughts.'

The convalescent home was situated at the edge of a pretty Hampshire village. The house itself was set in well-kept grounds surrounded by trees and manicured lawns. Jack and Rita had dropped Miranda at the gates, intending to find a pub where they could get some lunch, with a promise to return later. The delicate colours of early summer made everything seem vital and alive as she walked between the rows of late flowering cherry trees. Their petals fell like confetti on the gravel drive and the air was filled with birdsong.

Miranda had telephoned and made an appointment to see the matron, but she had asked her not to warn Gil of her coming in case he refused to see her. She rang the doorbell feeling as nervous as a child on her first day at school. She was excited at the thought of seeing Gil, but also scared. The suspense was physically painful.

The door was opened by a young girl wearing a white pinafore and cap. She smiled shyly. 'Can I help you, miss?'

Miranda explained that she had arranged to see the matron and the maid scuttled off to find her, giving Miranda time to observe her surroundings. She had feared that the ambience might prove to be cold and clinical but she felt as though she had just entered someone's much-loved home. The highly polished furniture was elegant but not too formal, and vases filled with white lilac and crimson tulips made bright statements of colour against the dark oak panelling. The appetising aroma of baking wafted from the kitchen, mingling with the heady scent from a bowl of pink hyacinths on the hall table.

The matron duly appeared and led her into a small office off the main hall. She motioned Miranda to take a seat. 'I wanted to speak to you before I let you see him,' she said, smiling. 'Gilbert is one of my favourite clients. We don't call them patients, and as you see we don't wear uniform.' She indicated her smart silk afternoon dress with a wave of her well-manicured hands. 'We try to keep everything as informal as possible. I haven't told him that you were coming, as you requested, but please be aware that he, like so many other brave young men, has come through an extremely traumatic experience. He is fully recovered physically, but he needs to regain confidence in himself. Handle him with kid gloves, Miss Beddoes.'

'Of course. May I see him now?'

'You'll find him in the arbour at the end of the rose garden. It's quite private there.'

Gil was seated, as the matron had said, on a rustic bench beneath an arch festooned with early roses. He was reading a book, but as Miranda trod the gravelled path he looked up, and his face lit with a smile that went straight to her heart. He stood up to greet her and she ran towards him. Forgetting all her good intentions she flung her arms around his neck. Their lips met in a tentative kiss and realising what she had done Miranda drew away. 'Sorry. I didn't mean to do that.'

He took her hands in his. 'Never say sorry to me, Miranda. I've been a stubborn fool, but I didn't know how to make amends for my stupidity. I've been hoping that you'd come, but I was afraid to ask in case you'd changed your mind about us.'

She met his anxious gaze with a tremulous smile. 'That was stupid, but I've been just as bad. I've made a complete mess of things.'

He drew her slowly towards him. 'I've been dreaming about this moment, my darling. But I never really believed that it would happen, and then just now when I saw you walking towards me I knew that everything was going to be all right.'

'What changed your mind? It nearly broke my heart when you didn't answer any of my letters. I just didn't know what to do.'

'I'm so sorry. I must have been crazy, and it was my mother of all people who put me straight. She came to see me last week and she told me about your visit to the auction rooms. She said she'd kept quiet about it until she was certain that I was really on the mend. I just wish I'd listened to you when you came to the hospital all those months ago, and I cringe when I remember what I said to you.'

She laid her finger on his lips, shaking her head. 'Forget all that now. I've had to take a good look at myself since then too. I was a bit confused about everything, but I'm not now. I know what I want and it's you. Say the word and I'll never

411

leave your side. I can look after you. I can get a job and support both of us.'

He silenced her with a kiss. When they finally drew apart he brushed a stray strand of hair back from her forehead, smiling tenderly. 'I'm not crippled, Miranda. I couldn't run a marathon and I'll always have a bit of a limp, but I've been passed fit to leave this place whenever I like. Funnily enough I'm still technically in the RAF, but I don't think I'll ever fly again.'

'When can you leave here?'

'I could have left months ago, but I suppose I was afraid to face the world. It sounds a bit feeble, but they've been marvellous here.'

'Could you come with us today? Jack and Rita brought me here in Chloe. It would be a bit cramped but you could come back to Highcliffe with me now. I want you to meet Granny and Grandpa, and Dickens the cat, and of course Annie, who's the one who keeps everything going, and I'll telephone Maman in London and get her to come down at the weekend...'

He stopped her talking with a kiss that went on for a very long time. 'I can't wait to meet your crazy family,' he said, punctuating his words with kisses. 'I want them to meet my family too.'

'That's not a problem. We can invite your mother and Fliss and her fiancé for Sunday lunch. Annie will grumble, of course, but she'll love to show off what she can do with a few potatoes and a bit of scrag end.'

'It sounds wonderful, but there's something I need to know first.'

'What?'

He was suddenly serious. 'Do you think you could put up with a boring auctioneer with a gammy leg for the rest of your life?'

'Is that a roundabout way of proposing to me?'

'I love you, Miranda. I've loved you since the first moment I saw you, and if that's corny I'm not going to apologise, because it's true. I've been desperate to see you again and I know I'm rushing things and doing this really badly, but please say yes.'

She looked deeply into his eyes and she knew that this was where she had always wanted to be. She smiled as she traced the outline of his jaw with the tip of her finger. 'Yes, a hundred times yes. I love you too, Mad Dog Maddern.'

The publishers hope that this book has given you enjoyable reading. Large Print Books are especially designed to be as easy to see and hold as possible. If you wish a complete list of our books please ask at your local library or write directly to:

Magna Large Print Books
Magna House, Long Preston,
Skipton, North Yorkshire.
BD23 4ND

This Large Print Book for the partially sighted, who cannot read normal print, is published under the auspices of

THE ULVERSCROFT FOUNDATION

Date Due